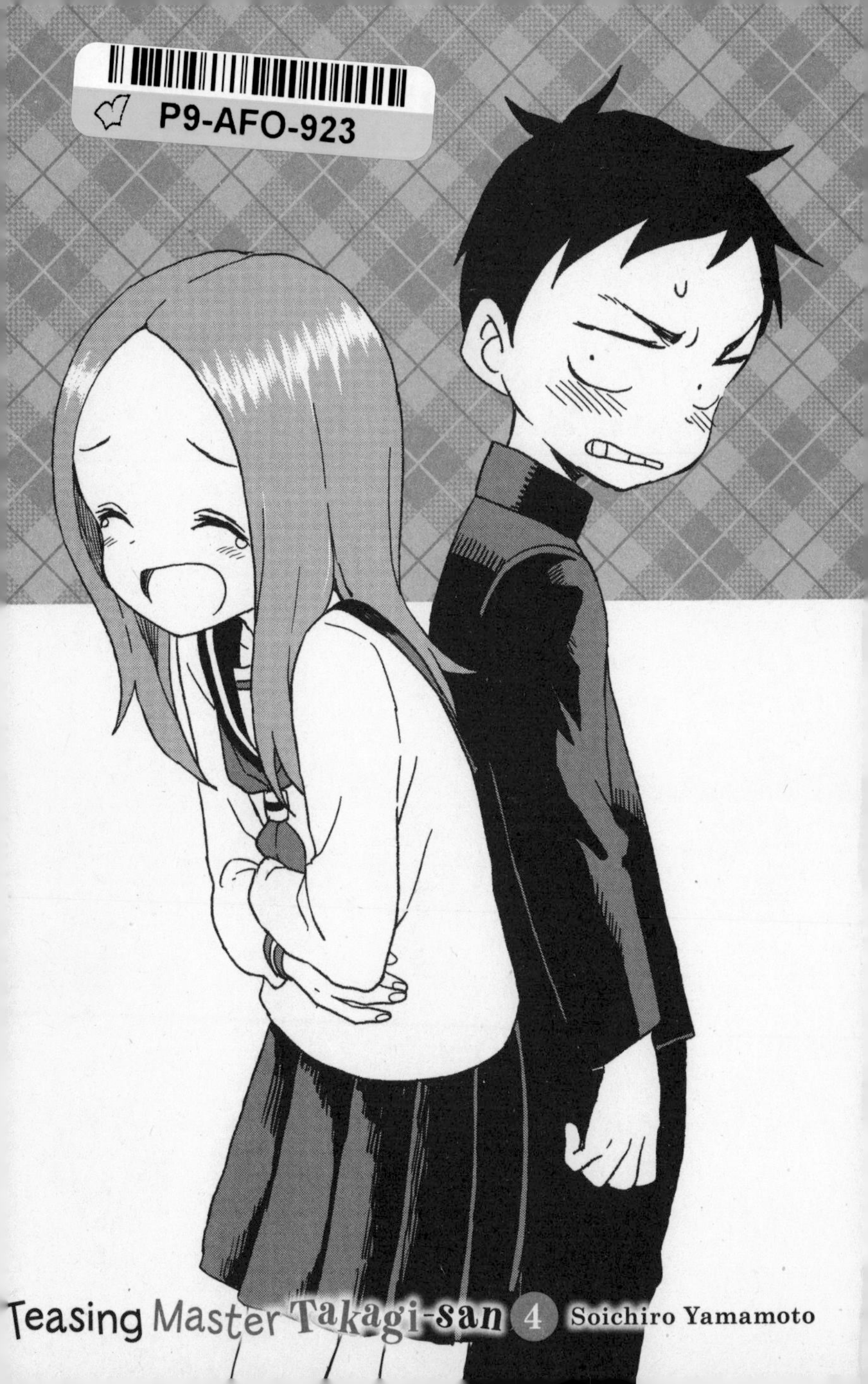

Teasing Master Takagi-san 4

Soichiro Yamamoto

Contents

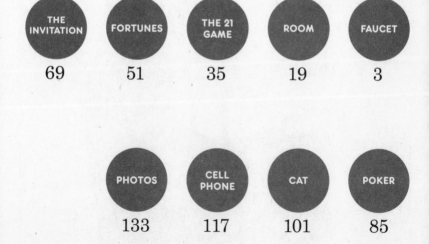

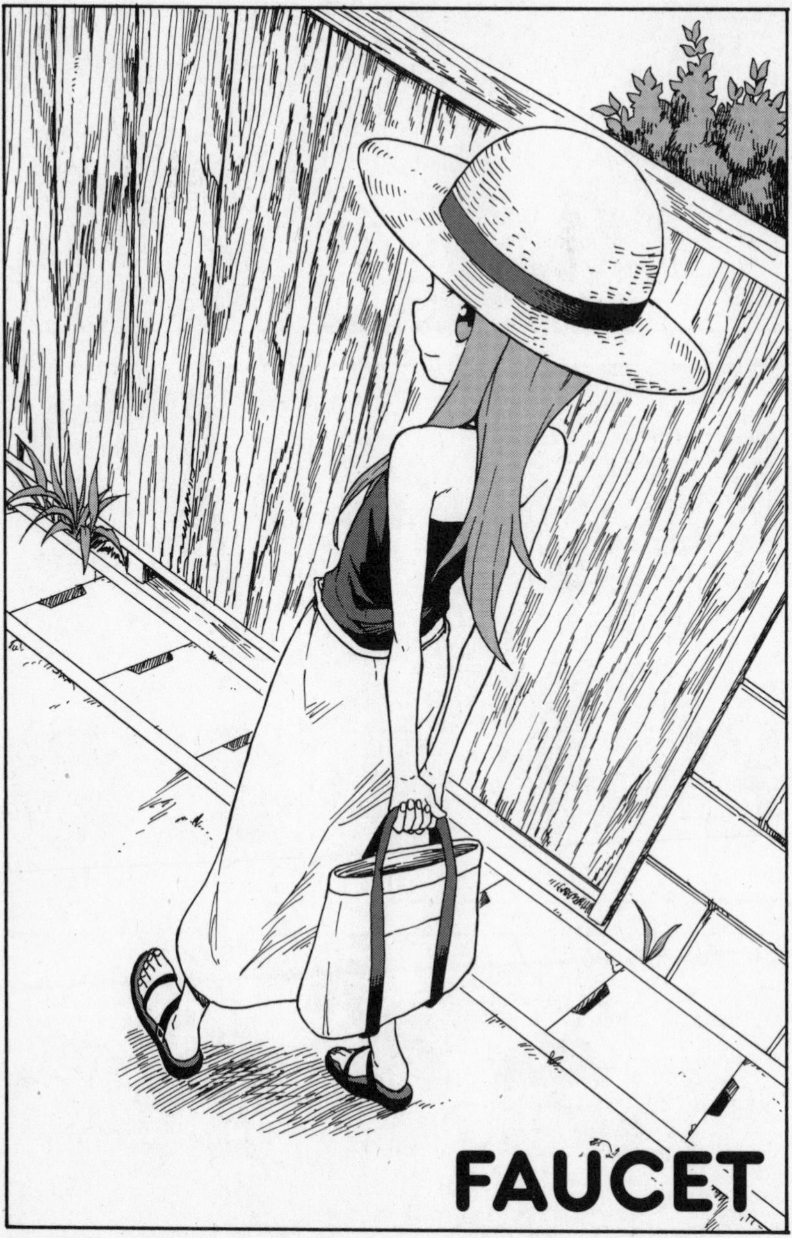
FAUCET

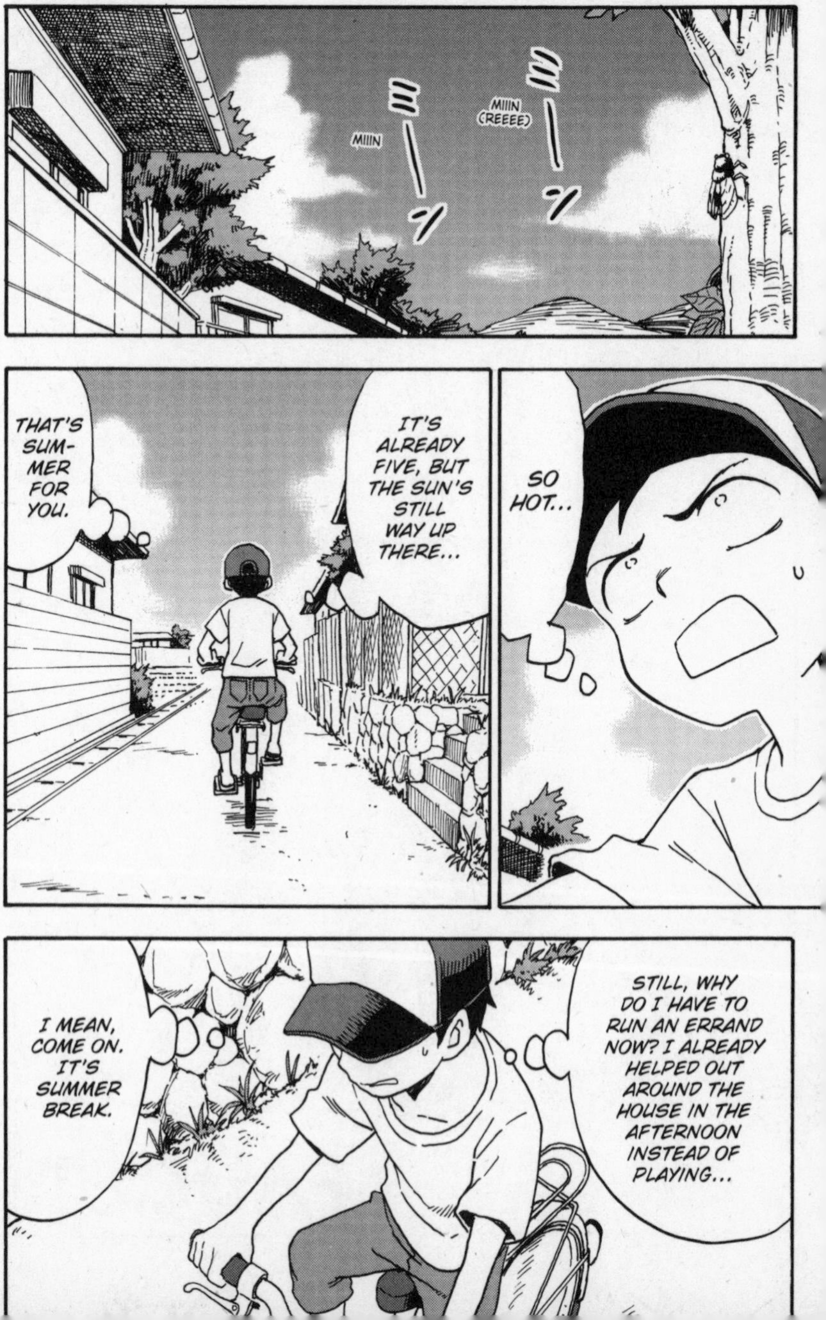
ミーン
MIIN (REEEE)
ミーン
MIIN
SO HOT...
IT'S ALREADY FIVE, BUT THE SUN'S STILL WAY UP THERE...
THAT'S SUMMER FOR YOU.
STILL, WHY DO I HAVE TO RUN AN ERRAND NOW? I ALREADY HELPED OUT AROUND THE HOUSE IN THE AFTERNOON INSTEAD OF PLAYING...
I MEAN, COME ON. IT'S SUMMER BREAK.

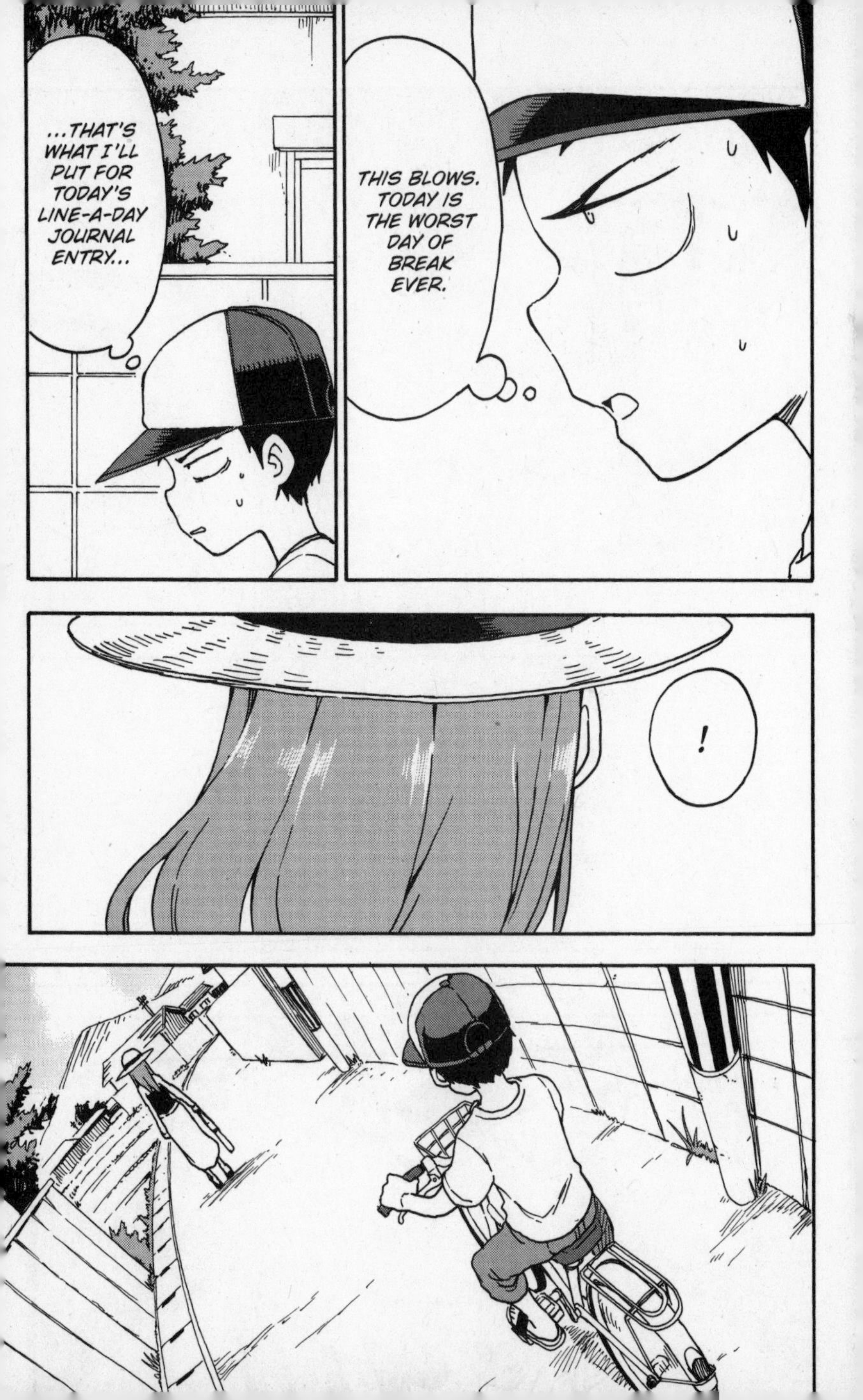
THIS BLOWS. TODAY IS THE WORST DAY OF BREAK EVER.
...THAT'S WHAT I'LL PUT FOR TODAY'S LINE-A-DAY JOURNAL ENTRY...
!

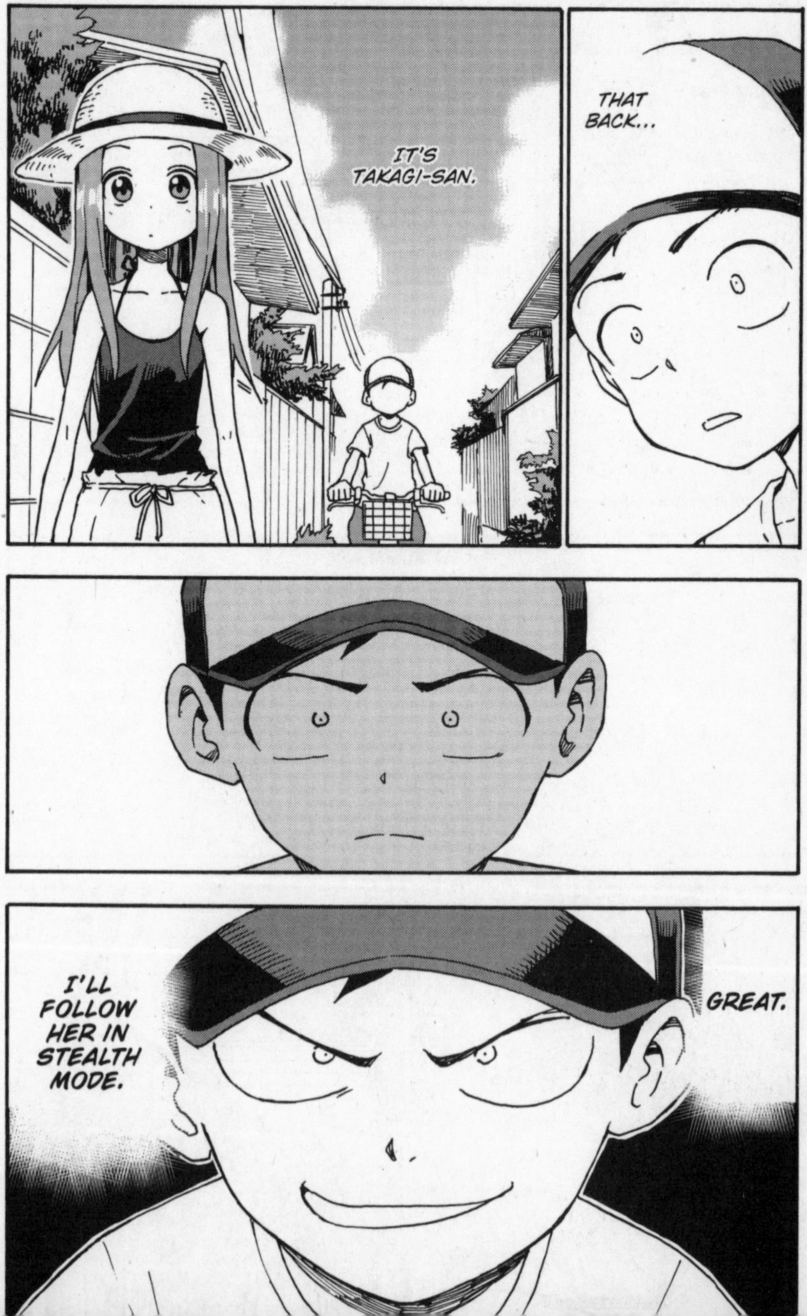
THAT BACK...
IT'S TAKAGI-SAN.
GREAT.
I'LL FOLLOW HER IN STEALTH MODE.

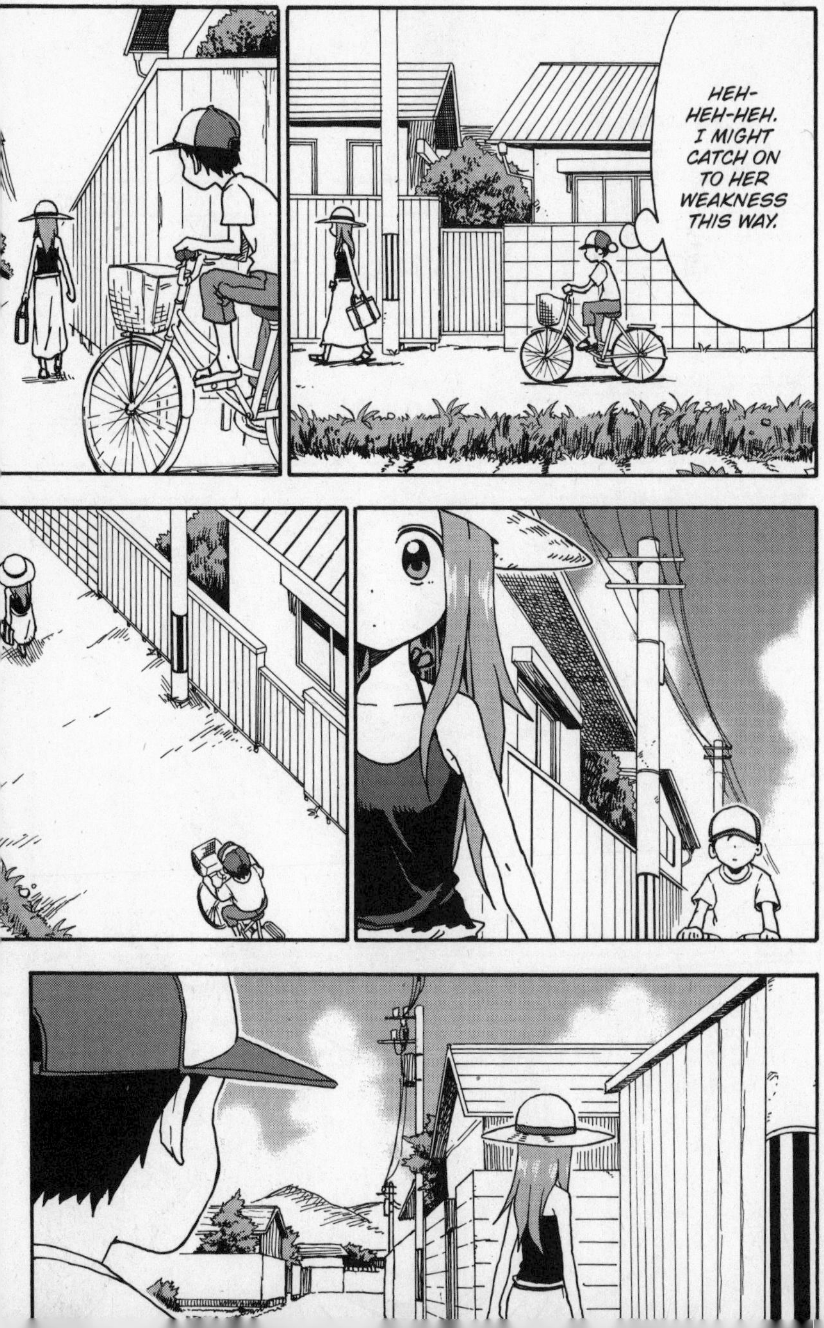
HEH-HEH-HEH. I MIGHT CATCH ON TO HER WEAKNESS THIS WAY.

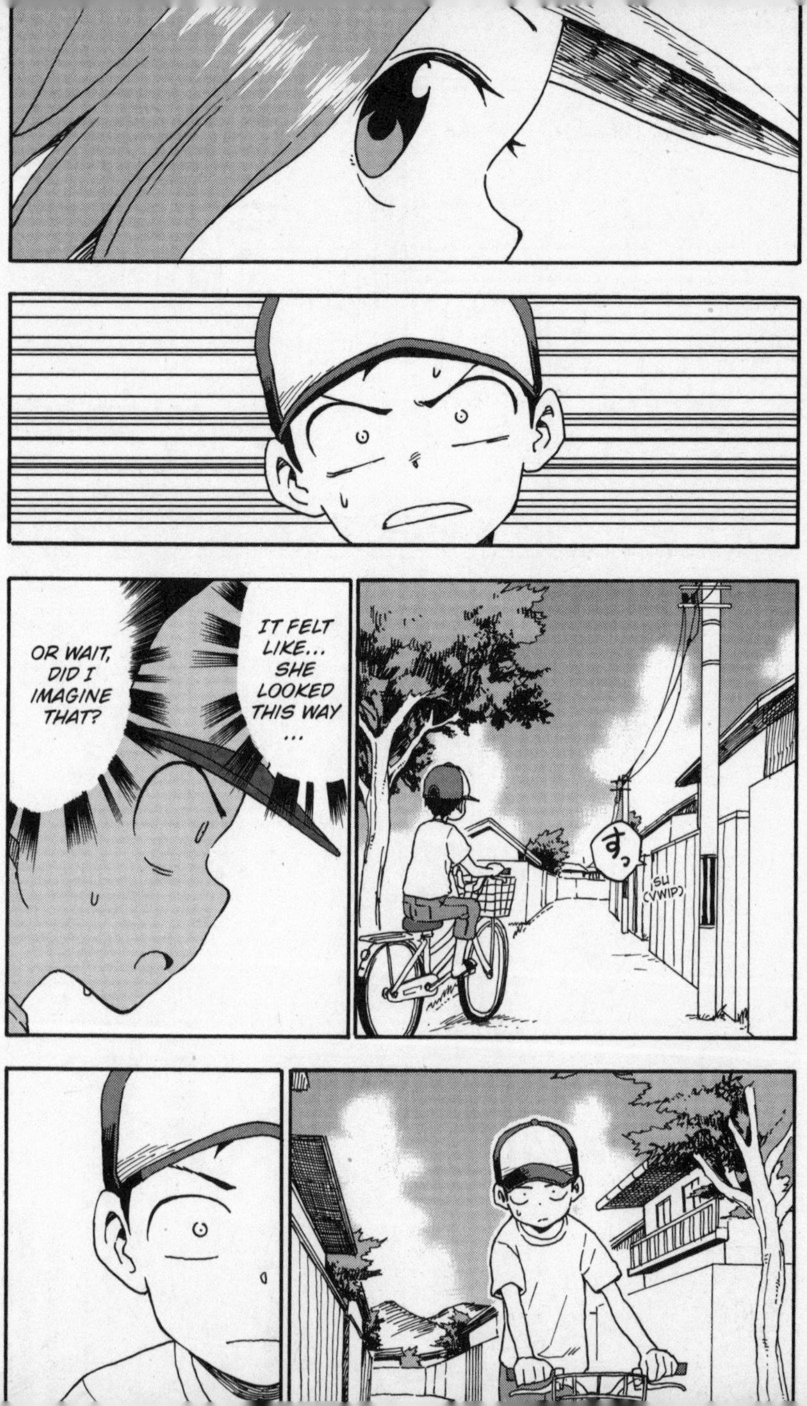
すっ
SU (VWIP)
IT FELT LIKE... SHE LOOKED THIS WAY ...
OR WAIT, DID I IMAGINE THAT?

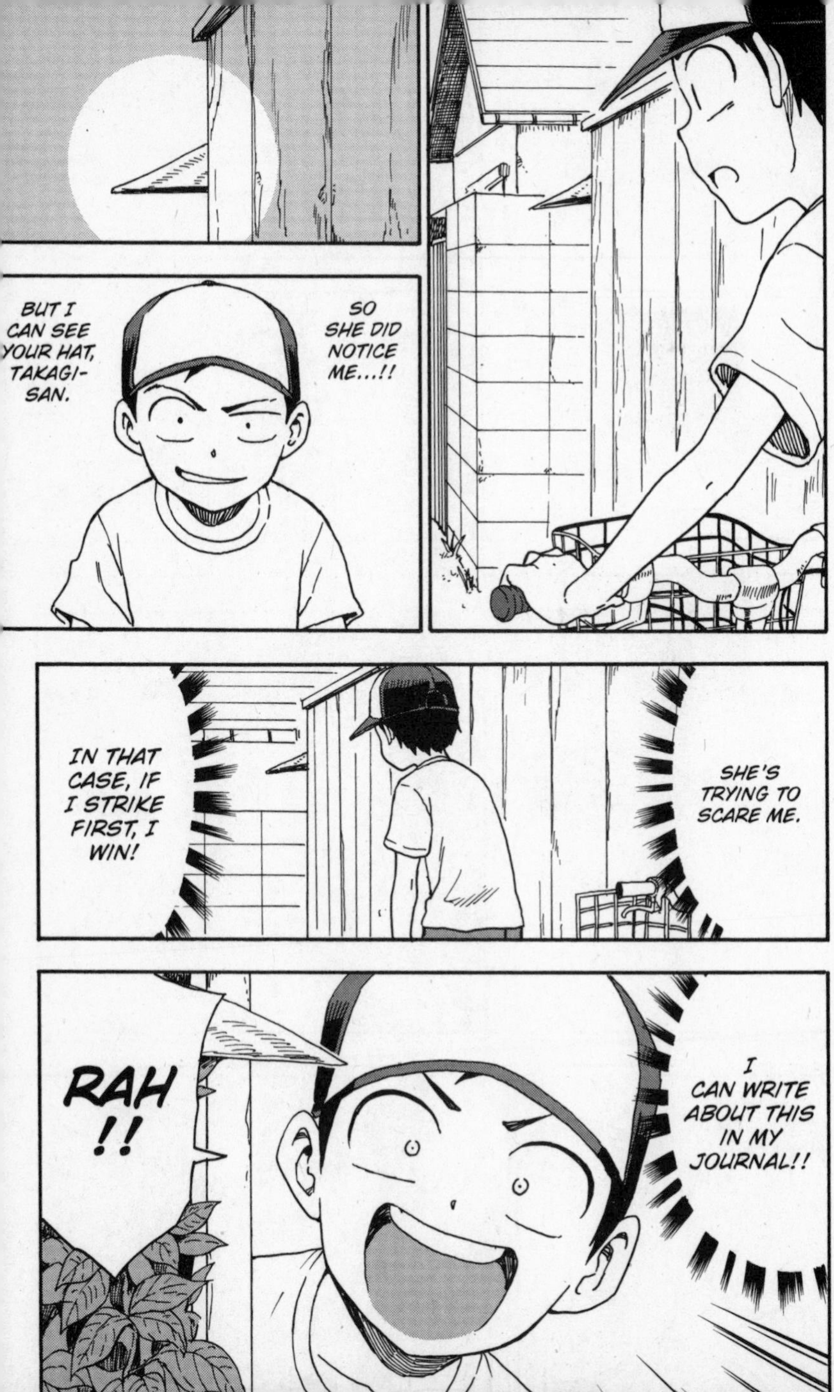
SO SHE DID NOTICE ME...!!
BUT I CAN SEE YOUR HAT, TAKAGI-SAN.
SHE'S TRYING TO SCARE ME.
IN THAT CASE, IF I STRIKE FIRST, I WIN!
I CAN WRITE ABOUT THIS IN MY JOURNAL!!
RAH!!

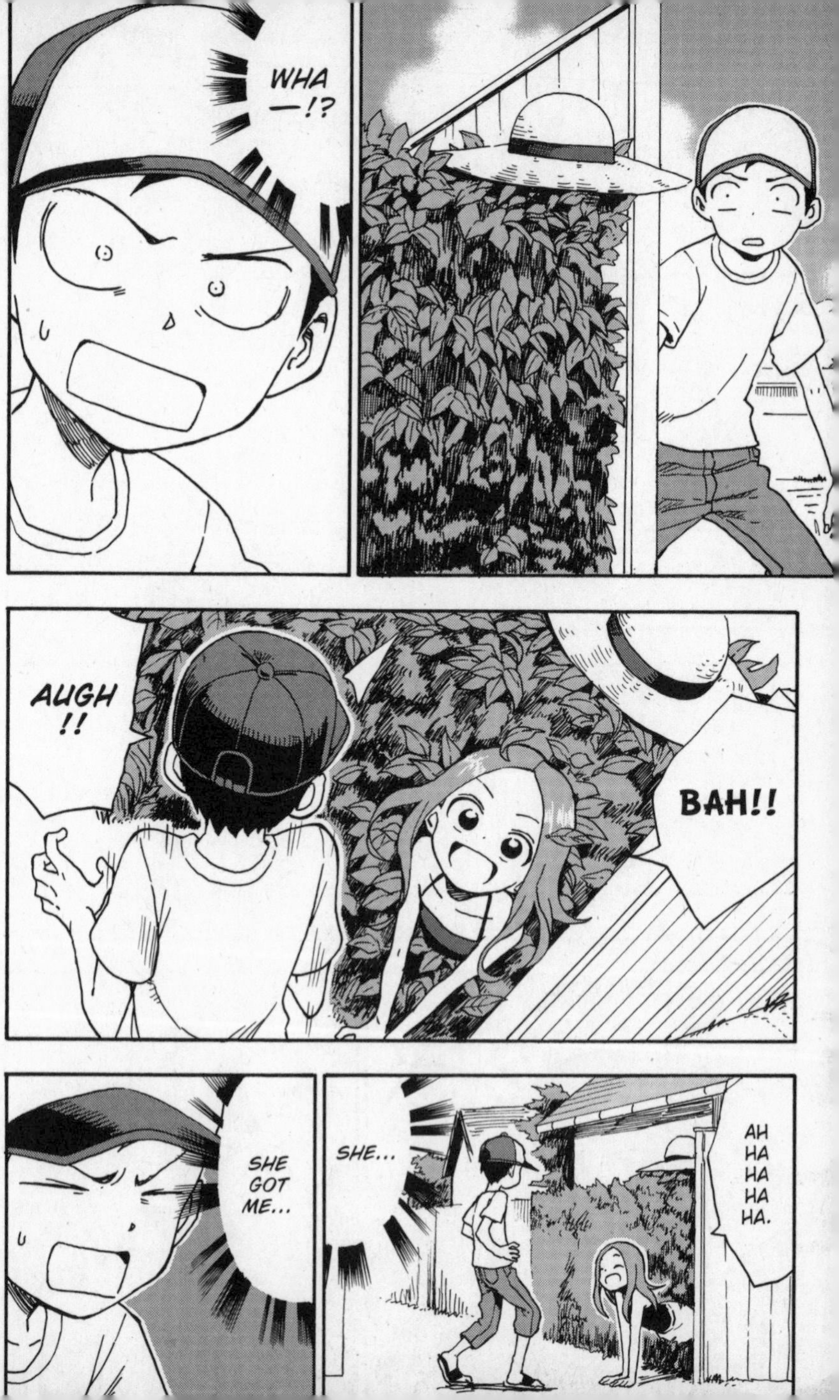

WHA—!?
BAH!!
AUGH!!
AH HA HA HA HA.
SHE...
SHE GOT ME...

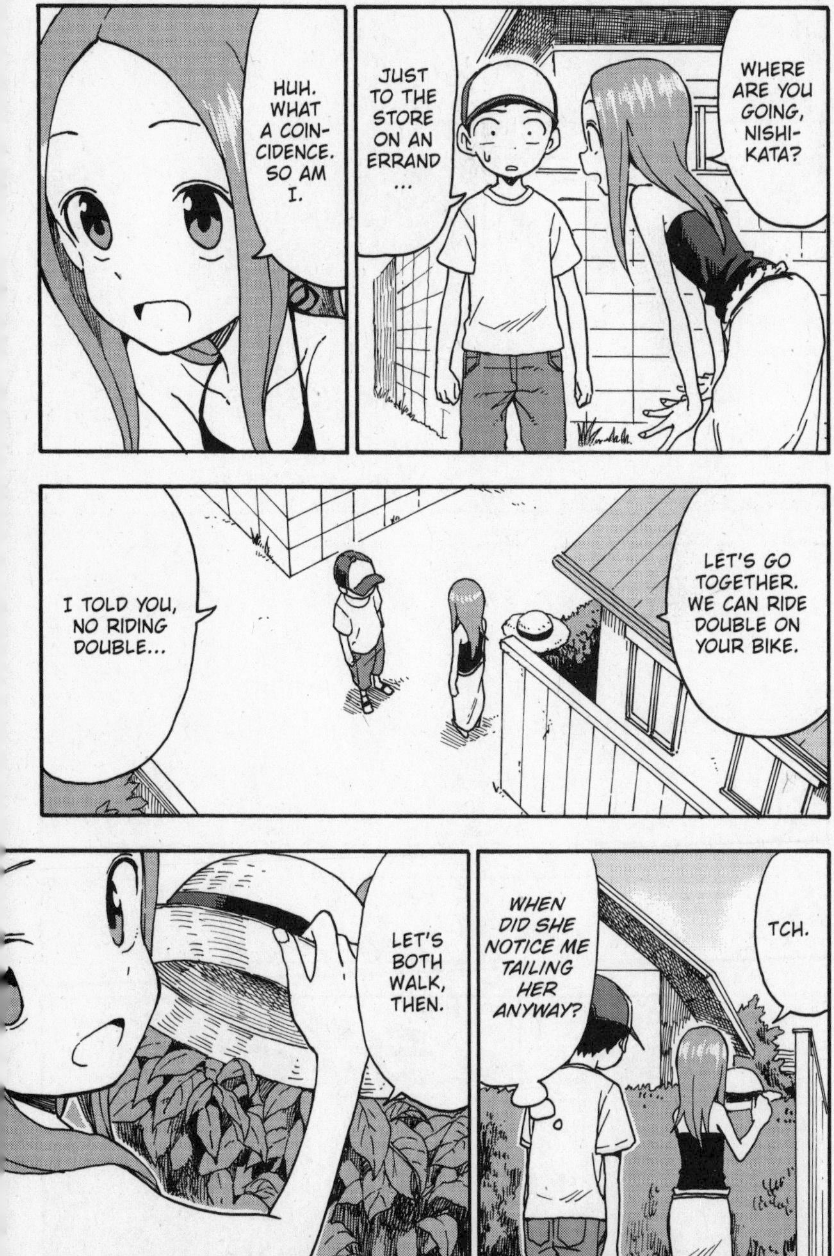

WHERE ARE YOU GOING, NISHI-KATA?
JUST TO THE STORE ON AN ERRAND ...
HUH. WHAT A COIN-CIDENCE. SO AM I.
LET'S GO TOGETHER. WE CAN RIDE DOUBLE ON YOUR BIKE.
I TOLD YOU, NO RIDING DOUBLE...
TCH.
WHEN DID SHE NOTICE ME TAILING HER ANYWAY?
LET'S BOTH WALK, THEN.

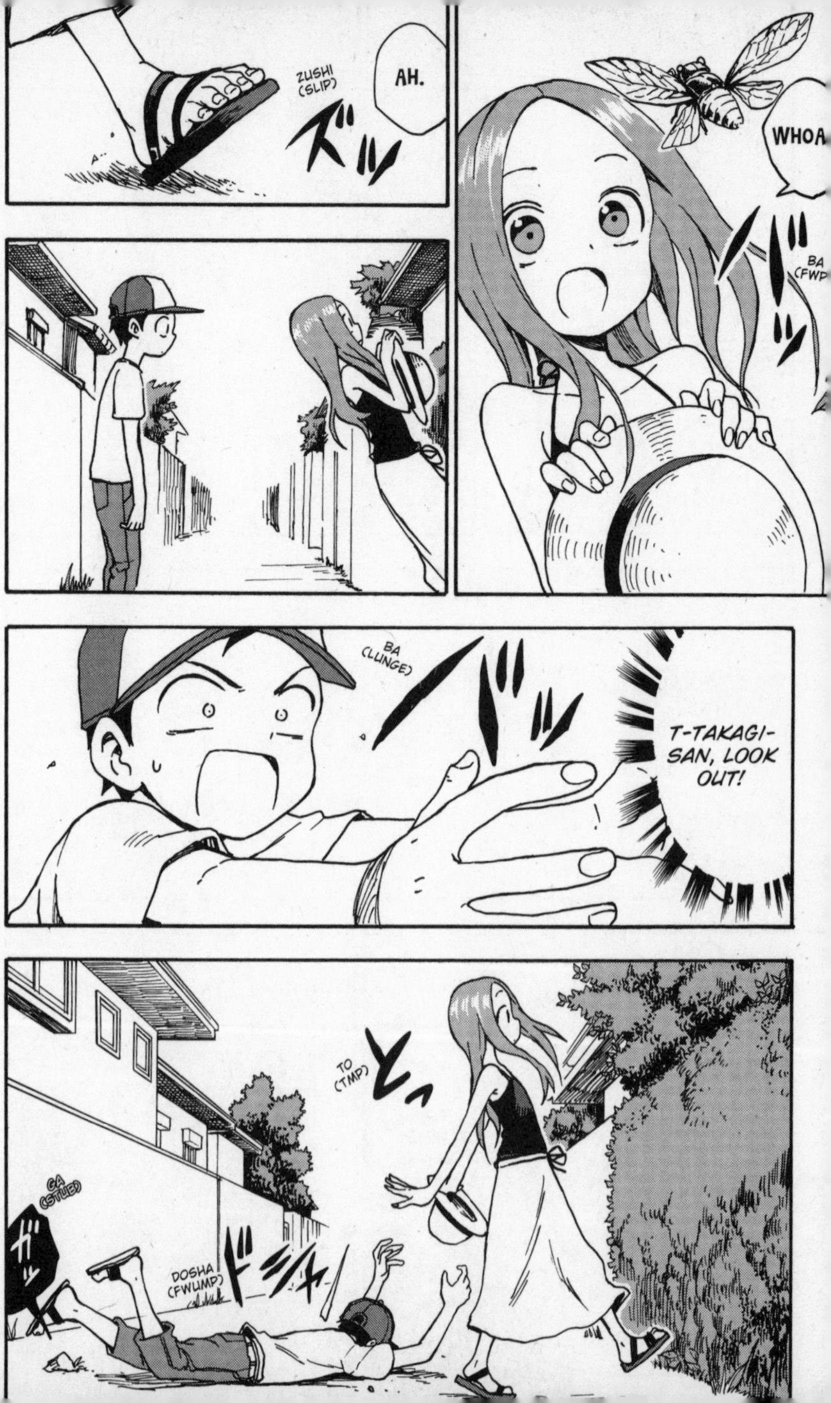
WHOA
BA (FWP
AH.
ZUSHI (SLIP)
A...
BA (LUNGE)
T-TAKAGI-SAN, LOOK OUT!
TO (TMP)
DOSHA (FWUMP)
GA (STUB)

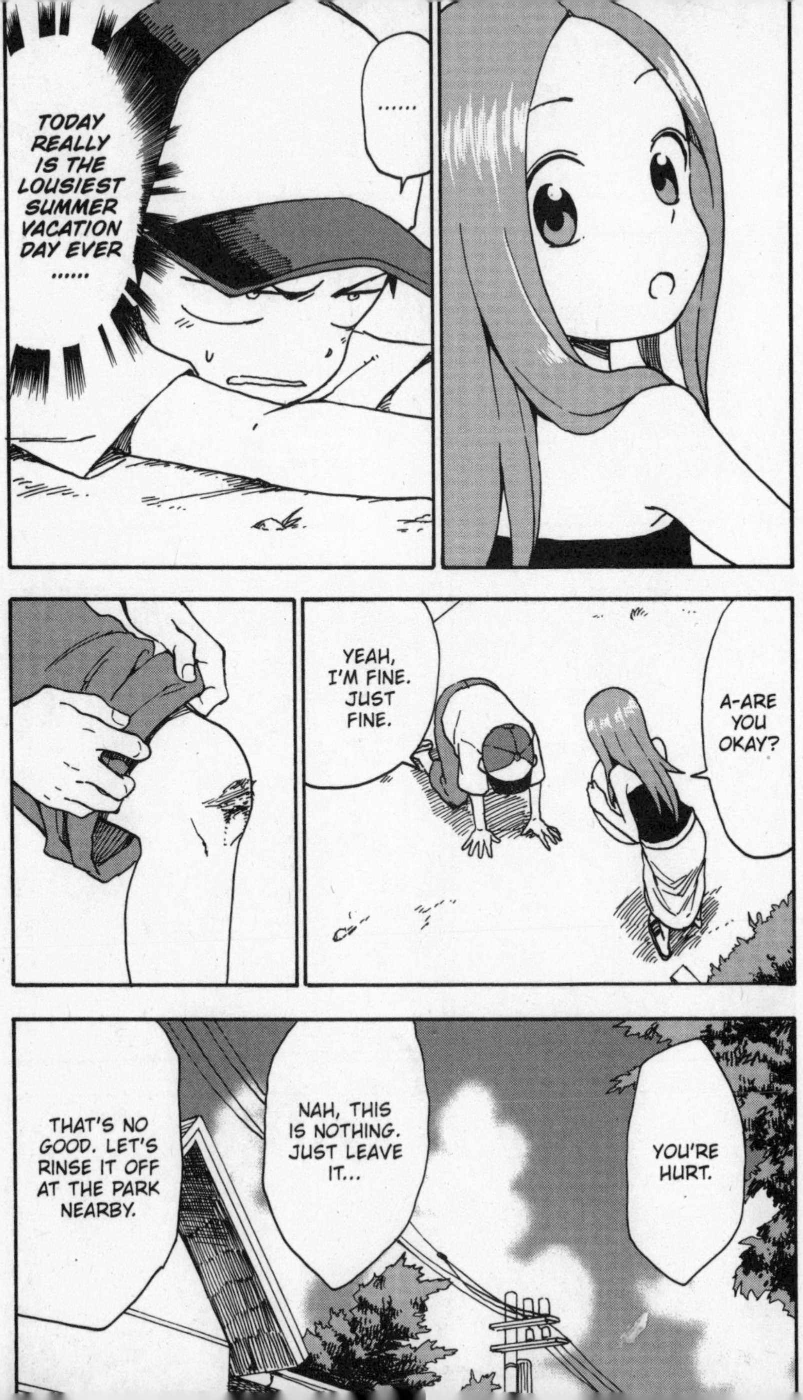
......
TODAY REALLY IS THE LOUSIEST SUMMER VACATION DAY EVER ......
A-ARE YOU OKAY?
YEAH, I'M FINE. JUST FINE.
YOU'RE HURT.
NAH, THIS IS NOTHING. JUST LEAVE IT...
THAT'S NO GOOD. LET'S RINSE IT OFF AT THE PARK NEARBY.

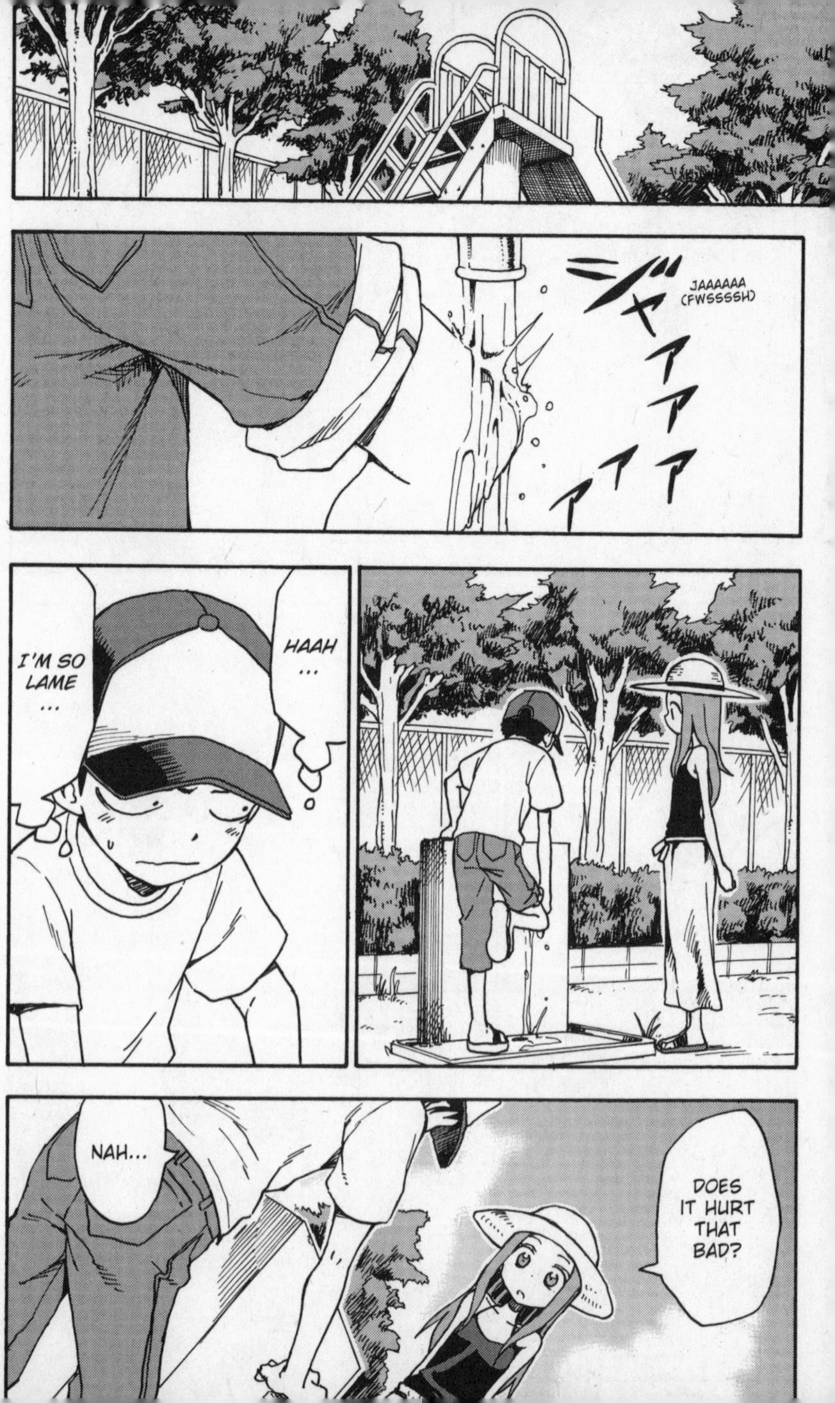
ジャアアアア
JAAAAAA (FWSSSSH)
HAAH...
I'M SO LAME...
DOES IT HURT THAT BAD?
NAH...

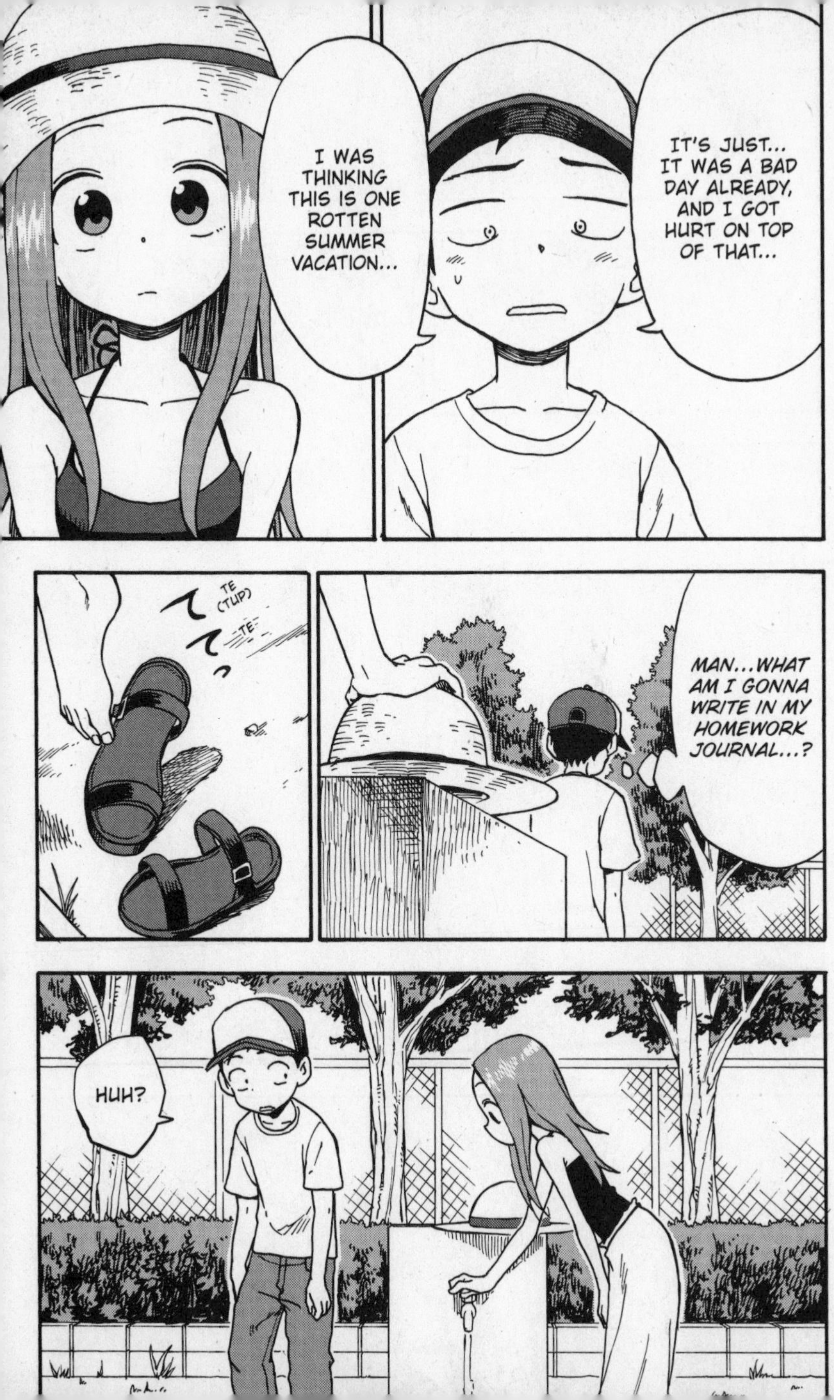
IT'S JUST... IT WAS A BAD DAY ALREADY, AND I GOT HURT ON TOP OF THAT...
I WAS THINKING THIS IS ONE ROTTEN SUMMER VACATION...
MAN...WHAT AM I GONNA WRITE IN MY HOMEWORK JOURNAL...?
TE (TUP)
TE
HUH?

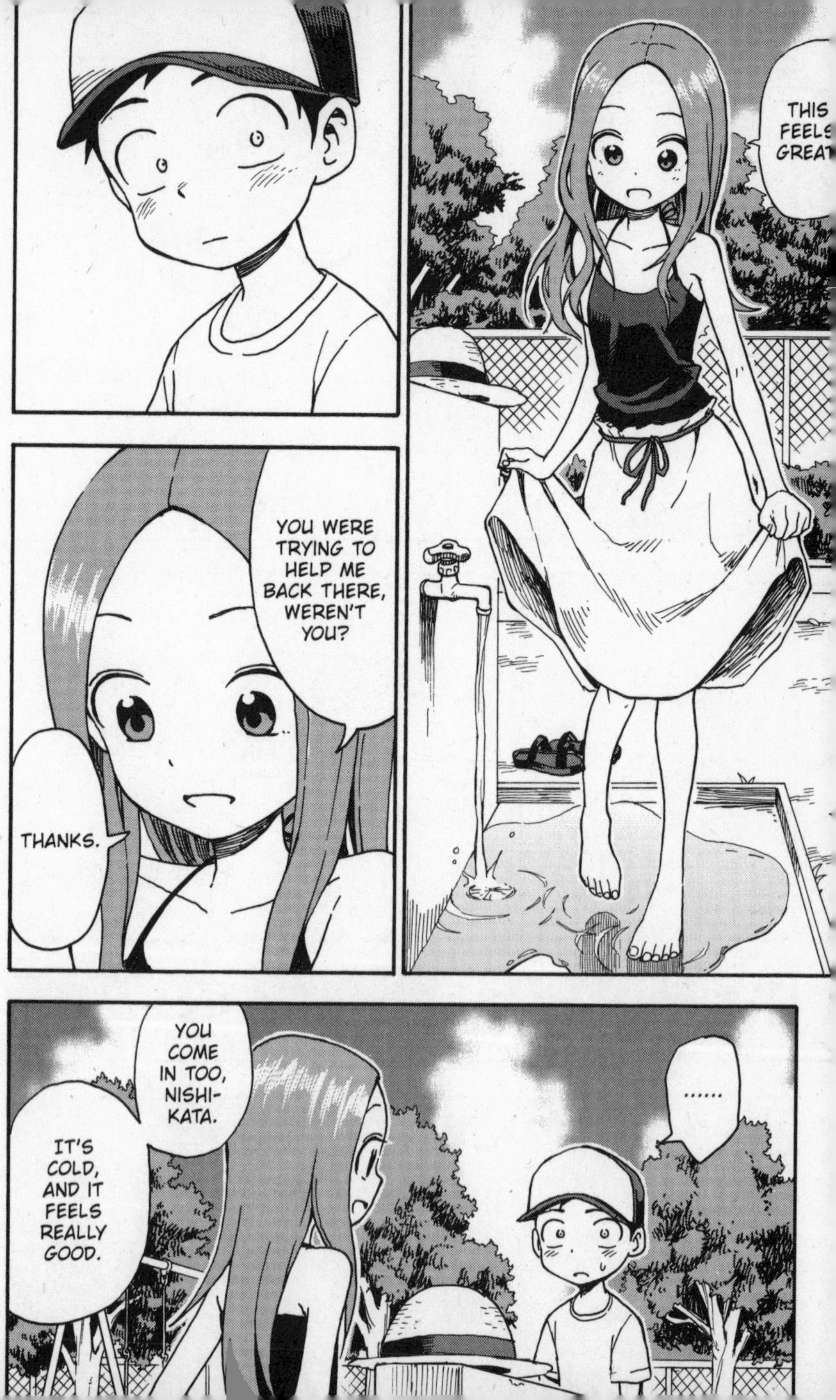
THIS FEELS GREAT
YOU WERE TRYING TO HELP ME BACK THERE, WEREN'T YOU?
THANKS.
......
YOU COME IN TOO, NISHI-KATA.
IT'S COLD, AND IT FEELS REALLY GOOD.

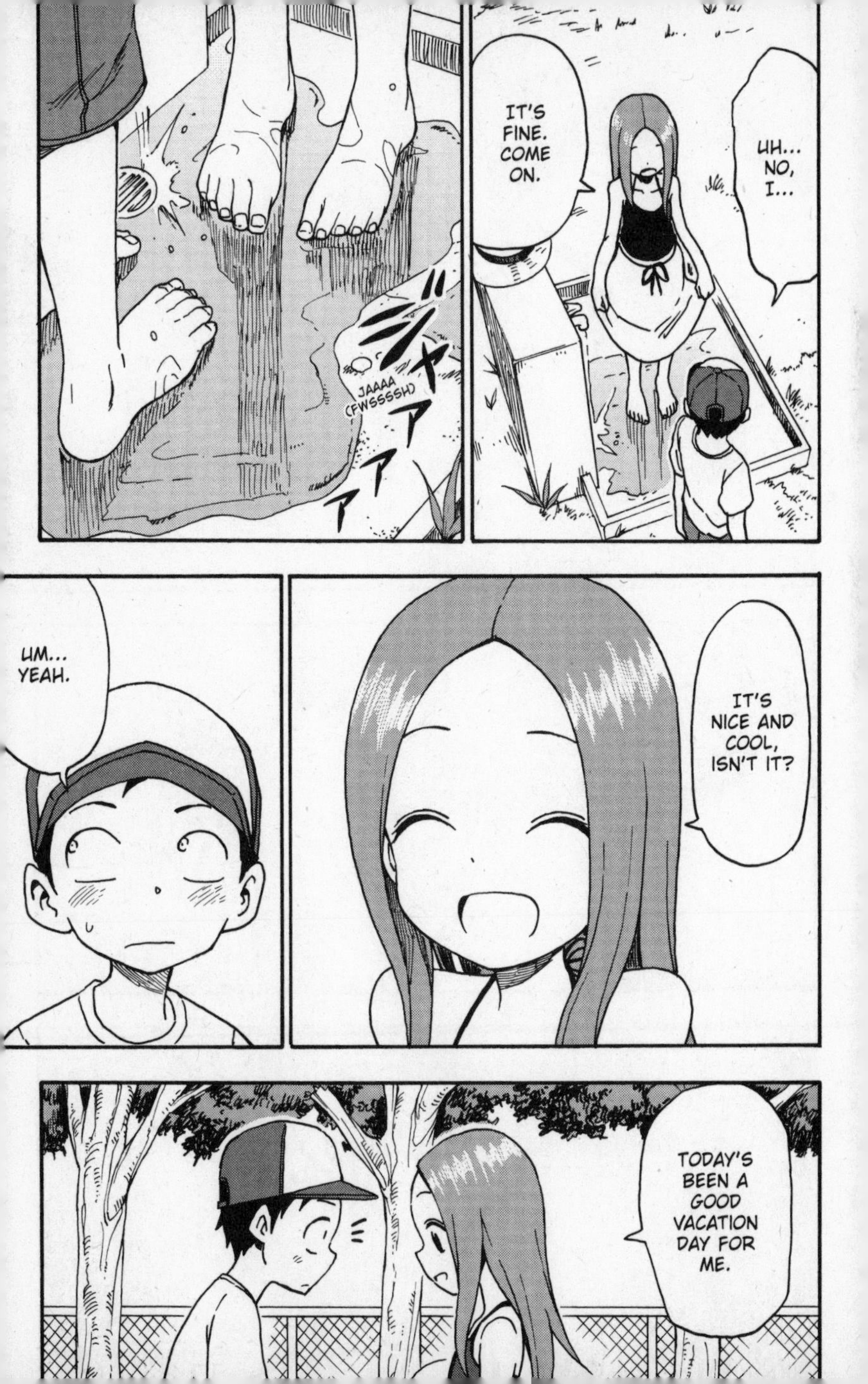
UH... NO, I...
IT'S FINE. COME ON.
JAAAA (FWSSSSH)
IT'S NICE AND COOL, ISN'T IT?
UM... YEAH.
TODAY'S BEEN A GOOD VACATION DAY FOR ME.

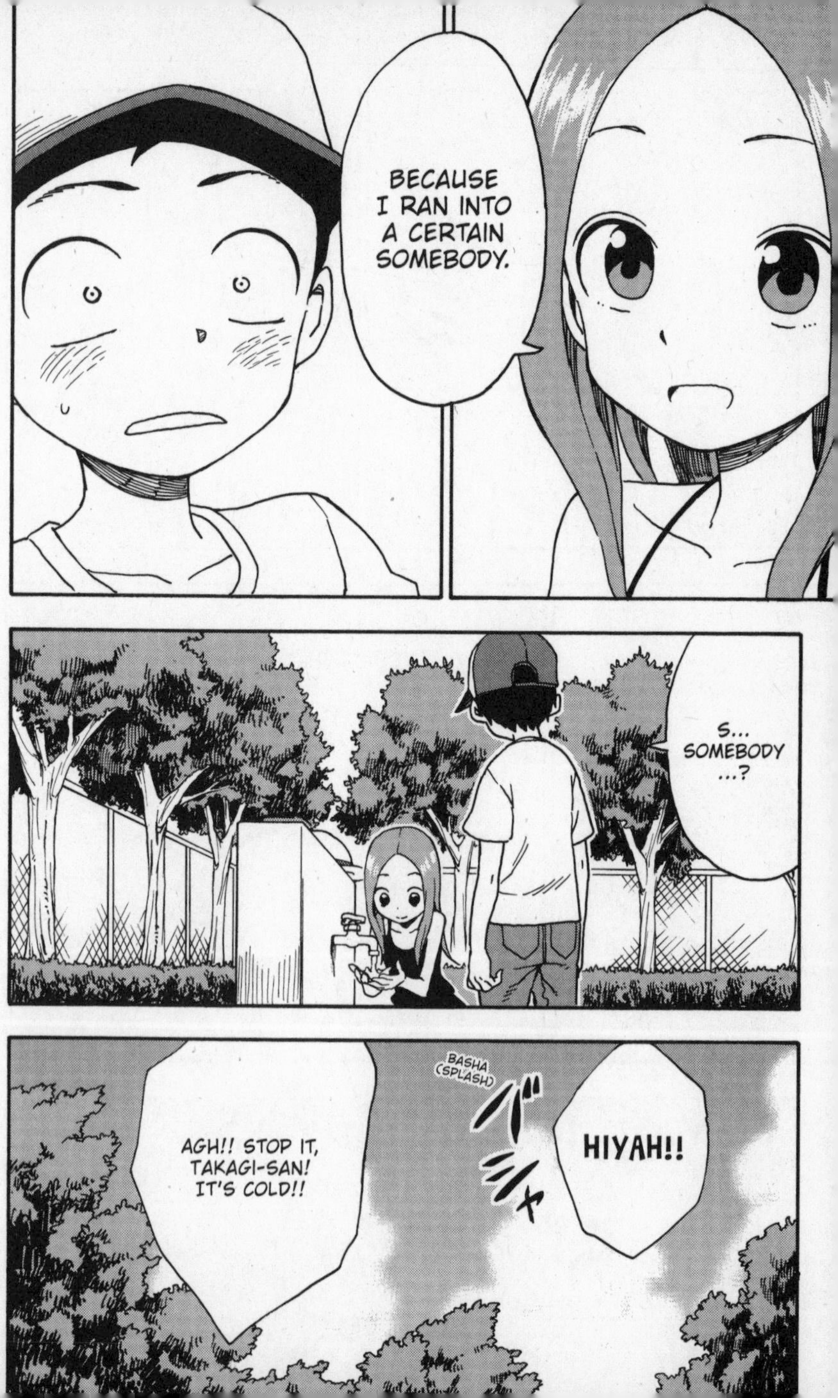
BECAUSE I RAN INTO A CERTAIN SOMEBODY.
S... SOMEBODY ...?
HIYAH!!
BASHA (SPLASH)
AGH!! STOP IT, TAKAGI-SAN! IT'S COLD!!

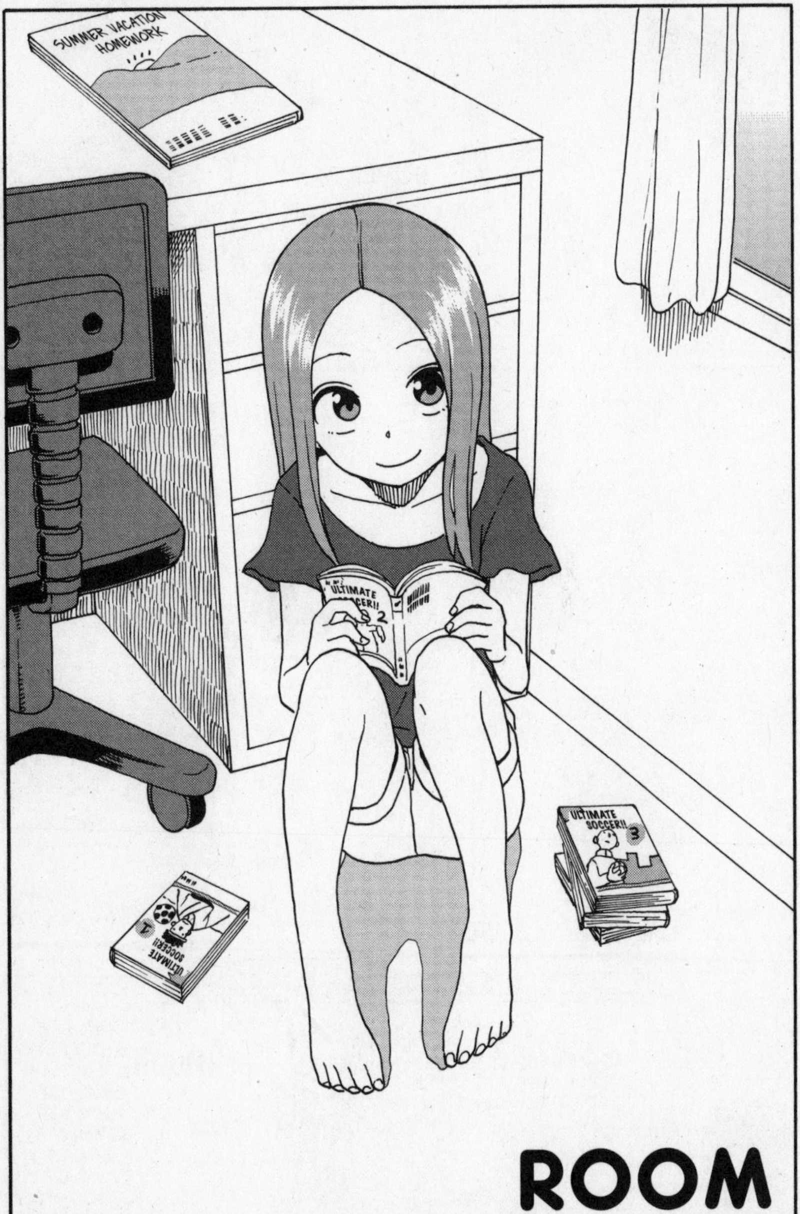
SUMMER VACATION
HOMEWORK
ULTIMATE
SOCCER!!
2
ULTIMATE
SOCCER!!
3
ULTIMATE
SOCCER!!
1
ROOM

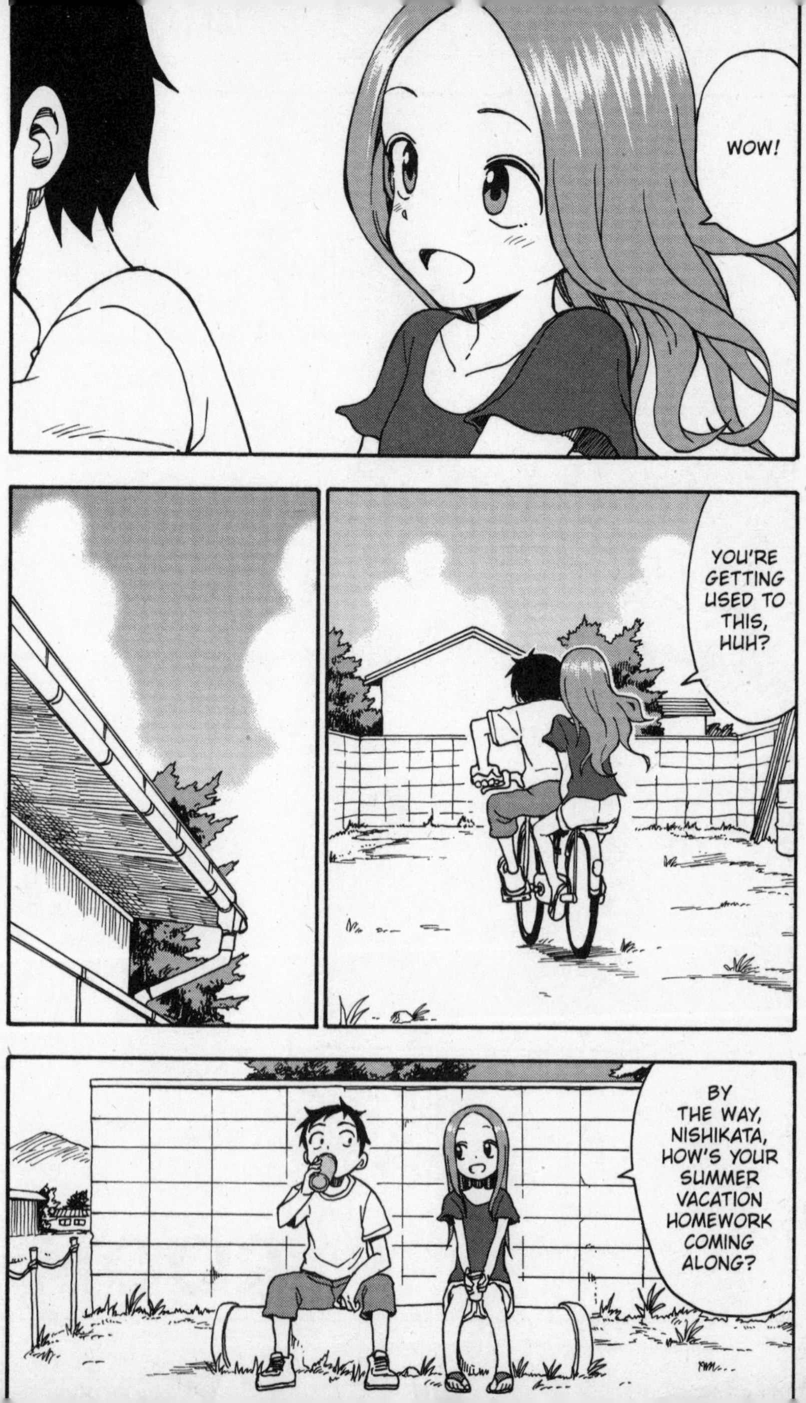
WOW!
YOU'RE GETTING USED TO THIS, HUH?
BY THE WAY, NISHIKATA, HOW'S YOUR SUMMER VACATION HOMEWORK COMING ALONG?

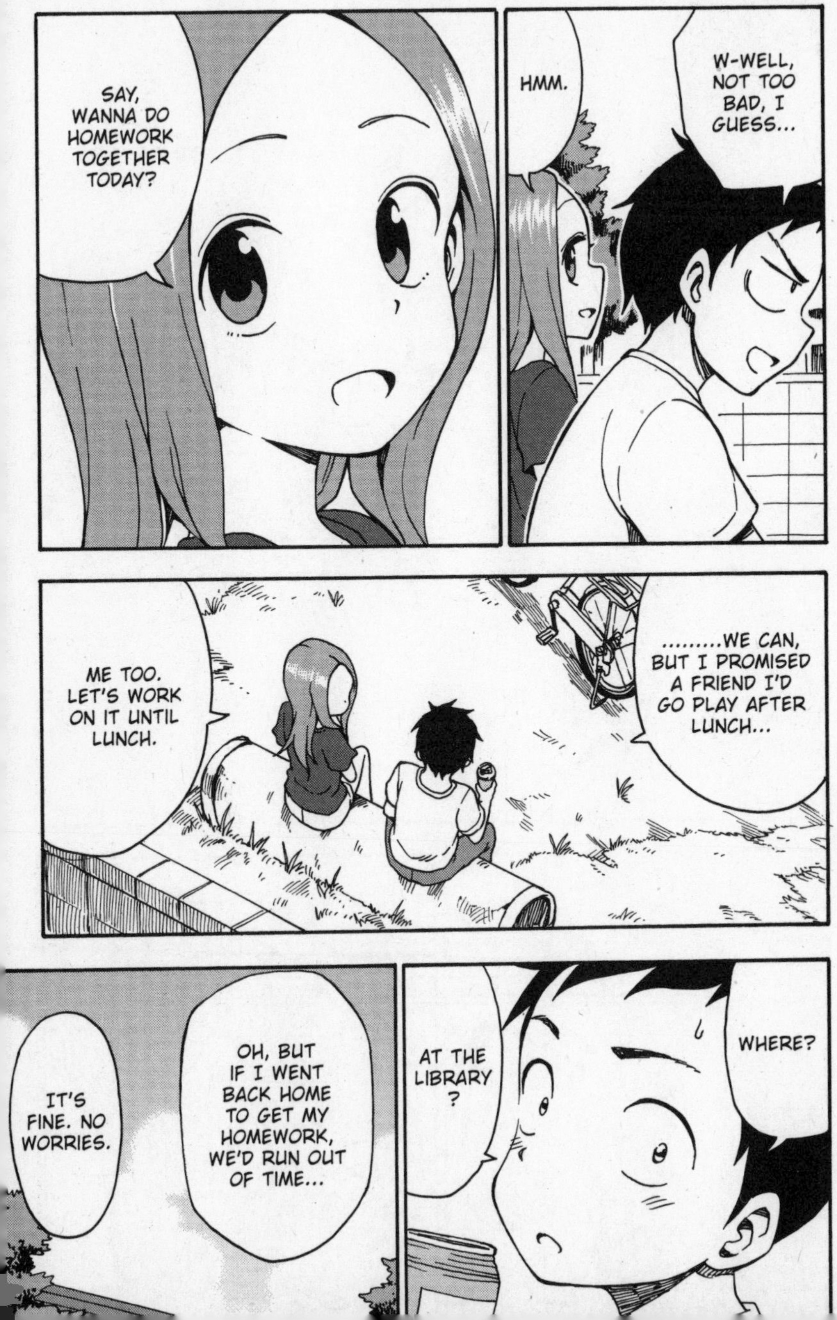
W-WELL, NOT TOO BAD, I GUESS...
HMM.
SAY, WANNA DO HOMEWORK TOGETHER TODAY?
.........WE CAN, BUT I PROMISED A FRIEND I'D GO PLAY AFTER LUNCH...
ME TOO. LET'S WORK ON IT UNTIL LUNCH.
WHERE?
AT THE LIBRARY?
OH, BUT IF I WENT BACK HOME TO GET MY HOMEWORK, WE'D RUN OUT OF TIME...
IT'S FINE. NO WORRIES.

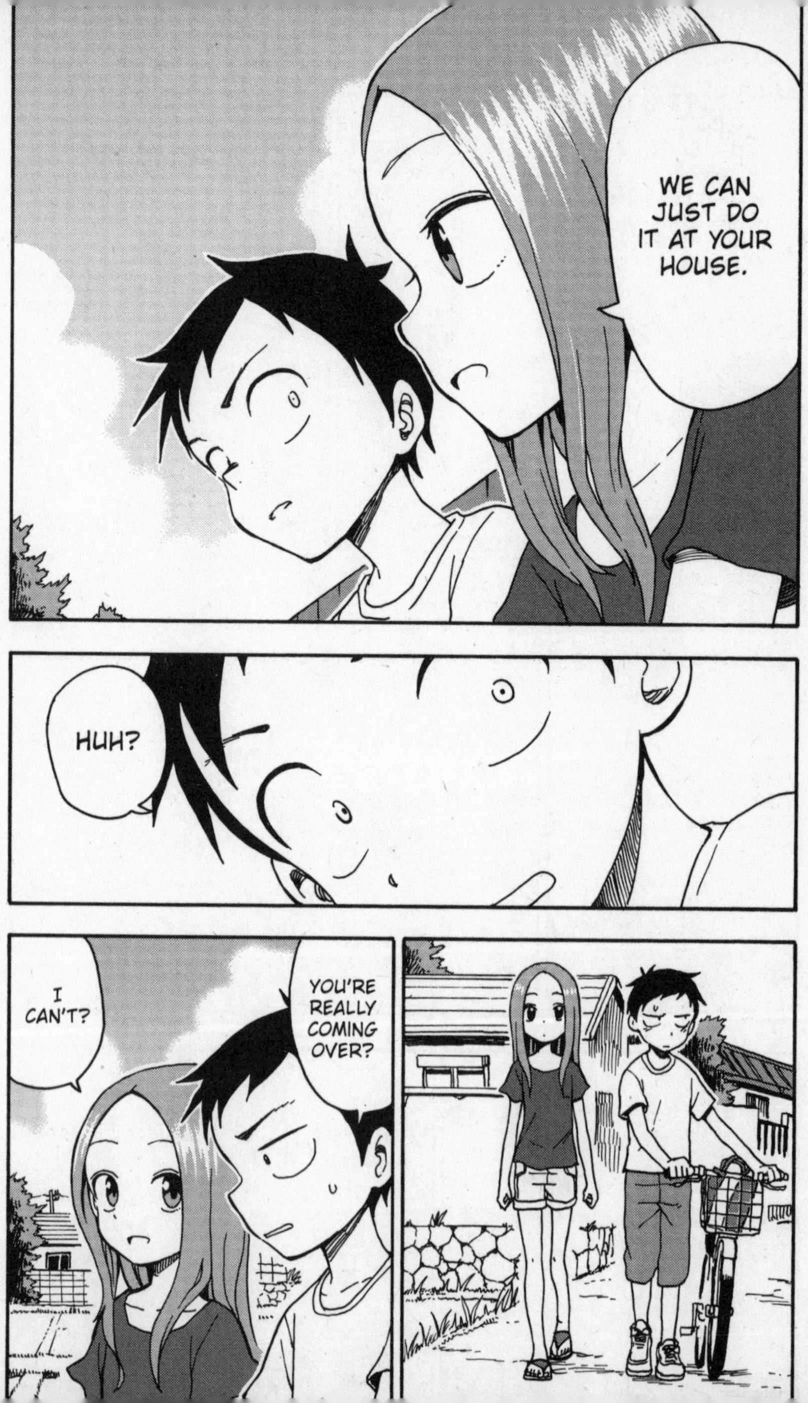
WE CAN JUST DO IT AT YOUR HOUSE.
HUH?
YOU'RE REALLY COMING OVER?
I CAN'T?

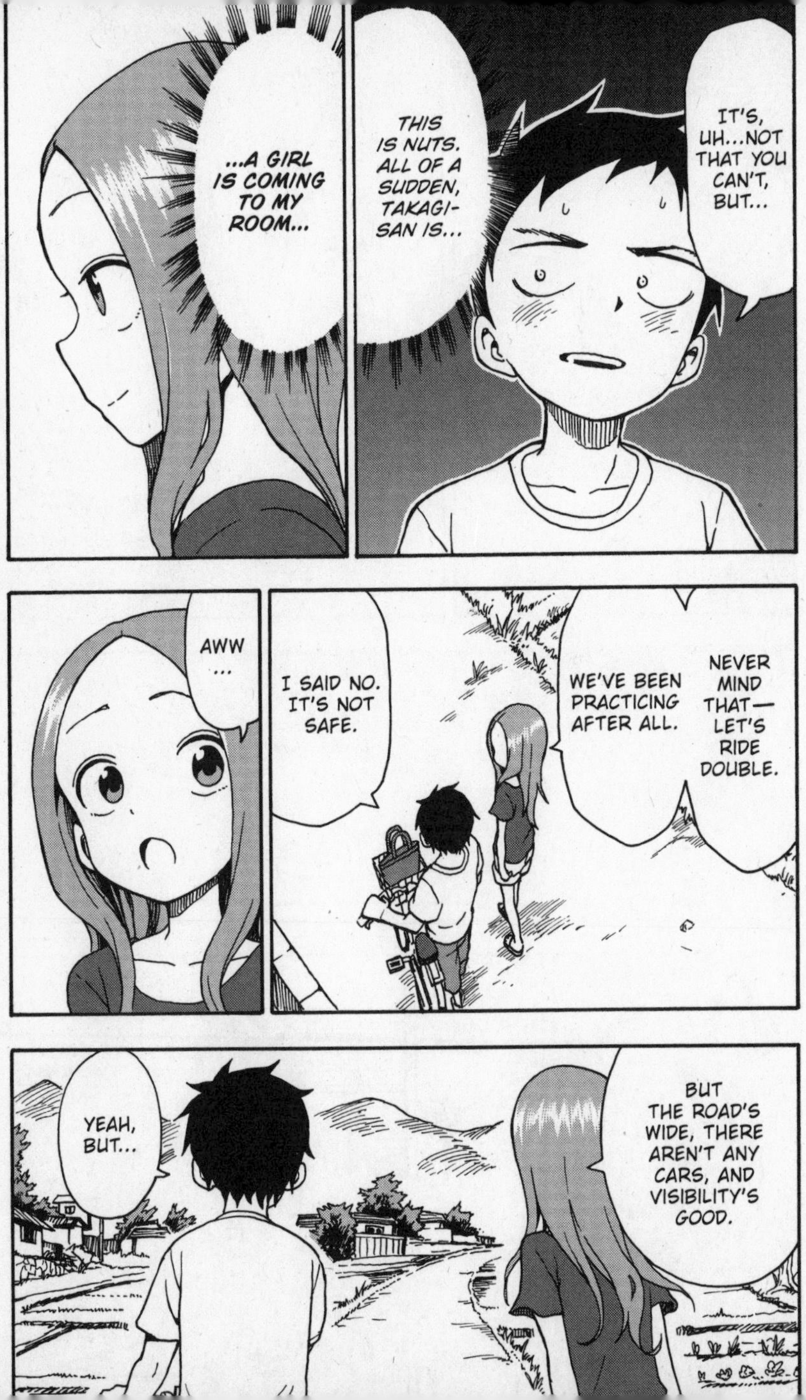
IT'S, UH...NOT THAT YOU CAN'T, BUT...
THIS IS NUTS. ALL OF A SUDDEN, TAKAGI-SAN IS...
...A GIRL IS COMING TO MY ROOM...
NEVER MIND THAT—LET'S RIDE DOUBLE.
WE'VE BEEN PRACTICING AFTER ALL.
I SAID NO. IT'S NOT SAFE.
AWW...
BUT THE ROAD'S WIDE, THERE AREN'T ANY CARS, AND VISIBILITY'S GOOD.
YEAH, BUT...

IF YOU RIDE DOUBLE, I'LL LET YOU COPY THE HOMEWORK I BROUGHT ALONG.

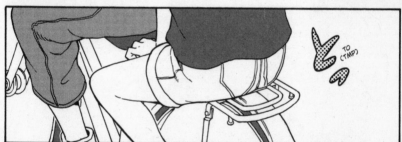

TO (TMP)

GU (PUSH)

MM-HM.

J-JUST THIS ROAD, THOUGH.

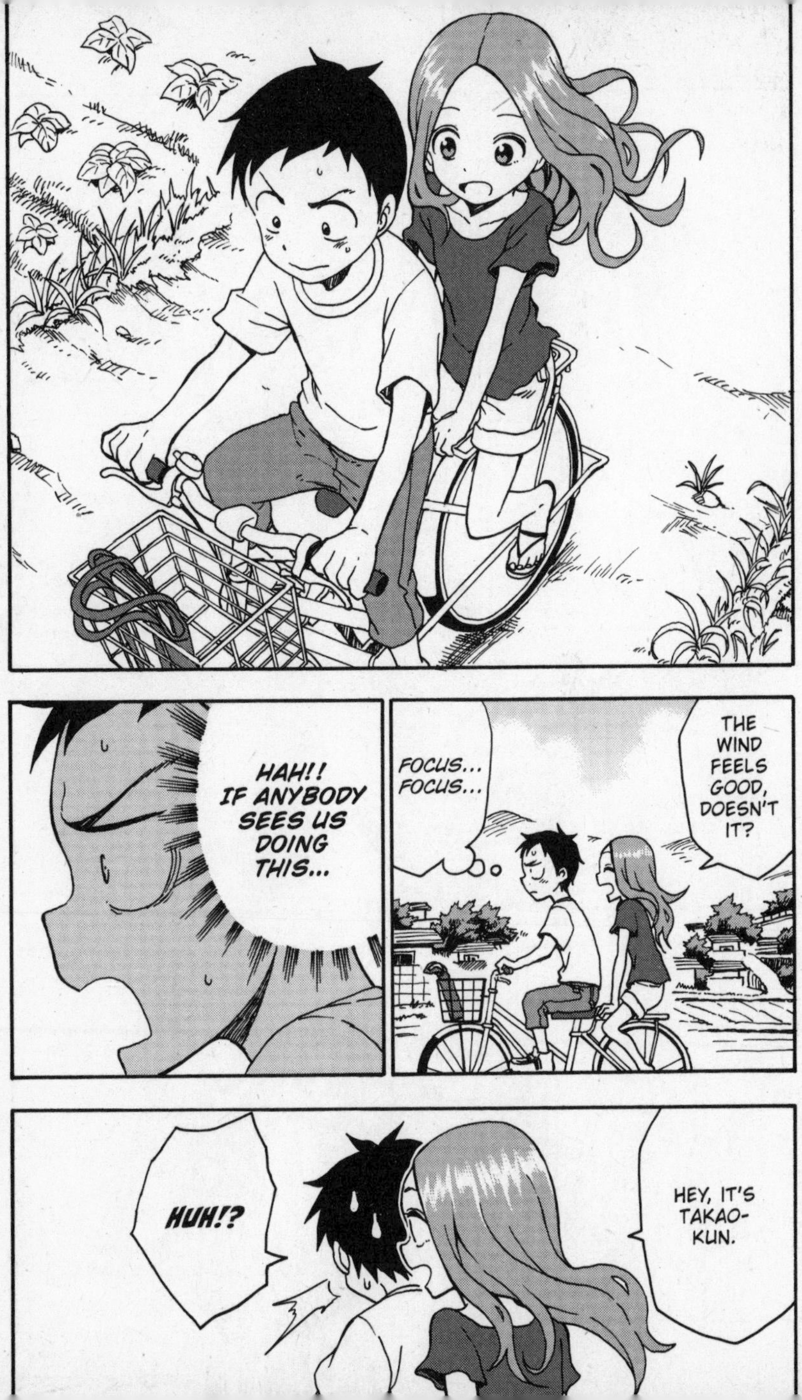
THE WIND FEELS GOOD, DOESN'T IT?
FOCUS... FOCUS...
HAH!! IF ANYBODY SEES US DOING THIS...
HEY, IT'S TAKAO-KUN.
HUH!?

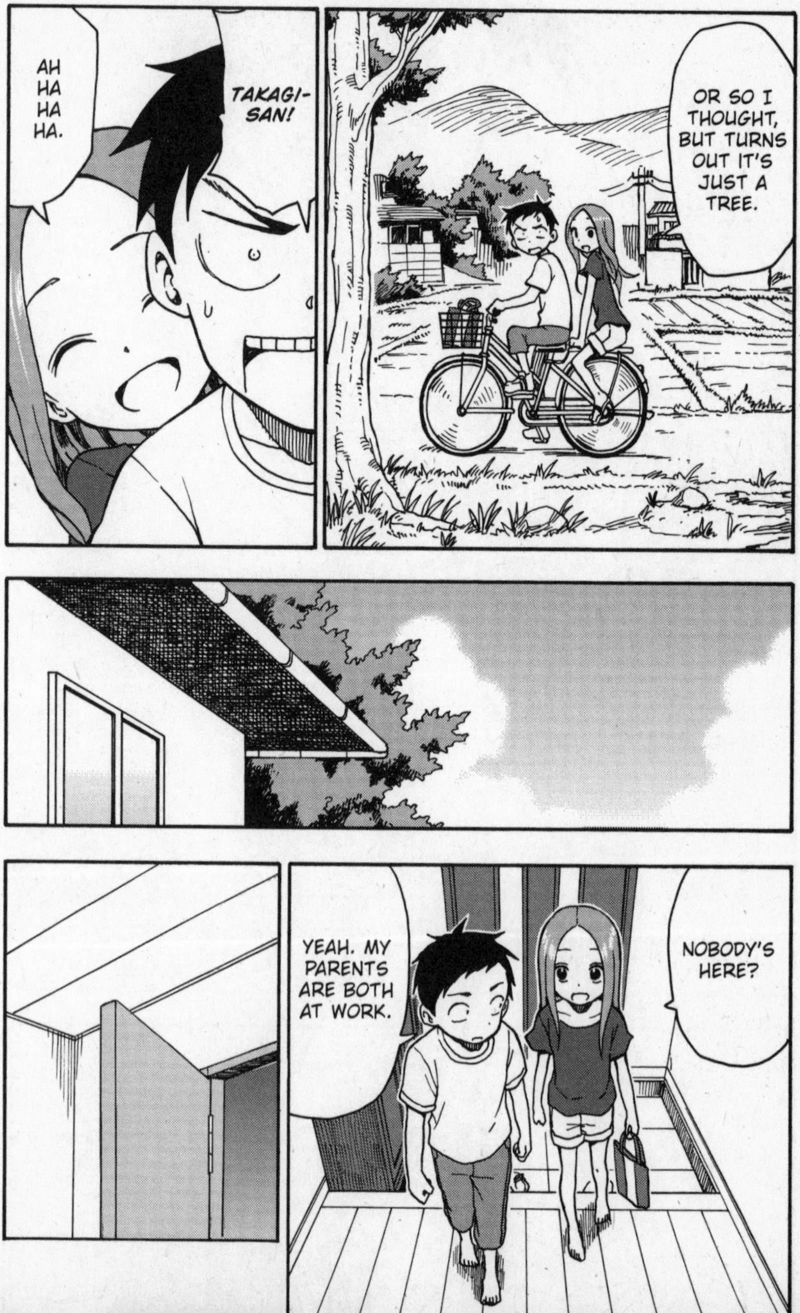
OR SO I THOUGHT, BUT TURNS OUT IT'S JUST A TREE.
TAKAGI-SAN!
AH HA HA HA.
NOBODY'S HERE?
YEAH. MY PARENTS ARE BOTH AT WORK.

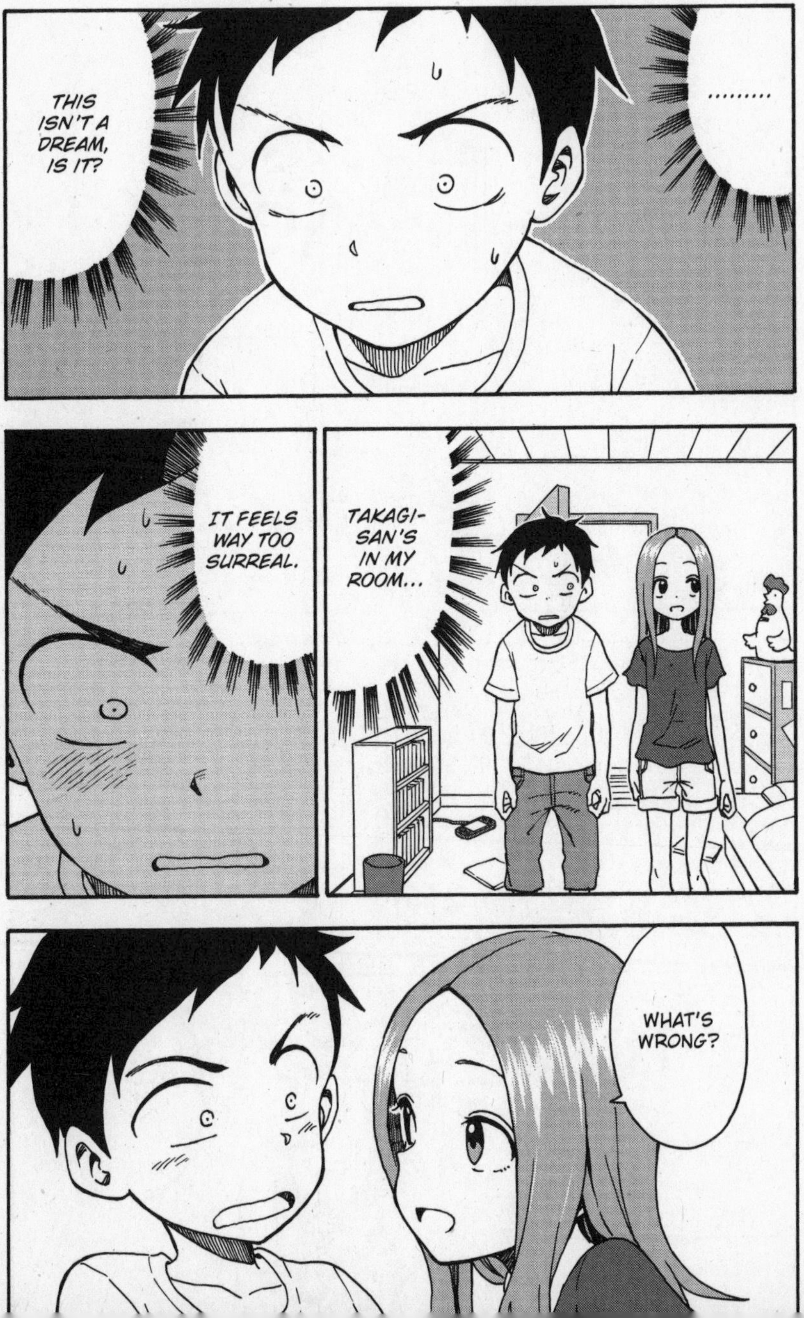
....
THIS ISN'T A DREAM, IS IT?
TAKAGI-SAN'S IN MY ROOM...
IT FEELS WAY TOO SURREAL.
WHAT'S WRONG?

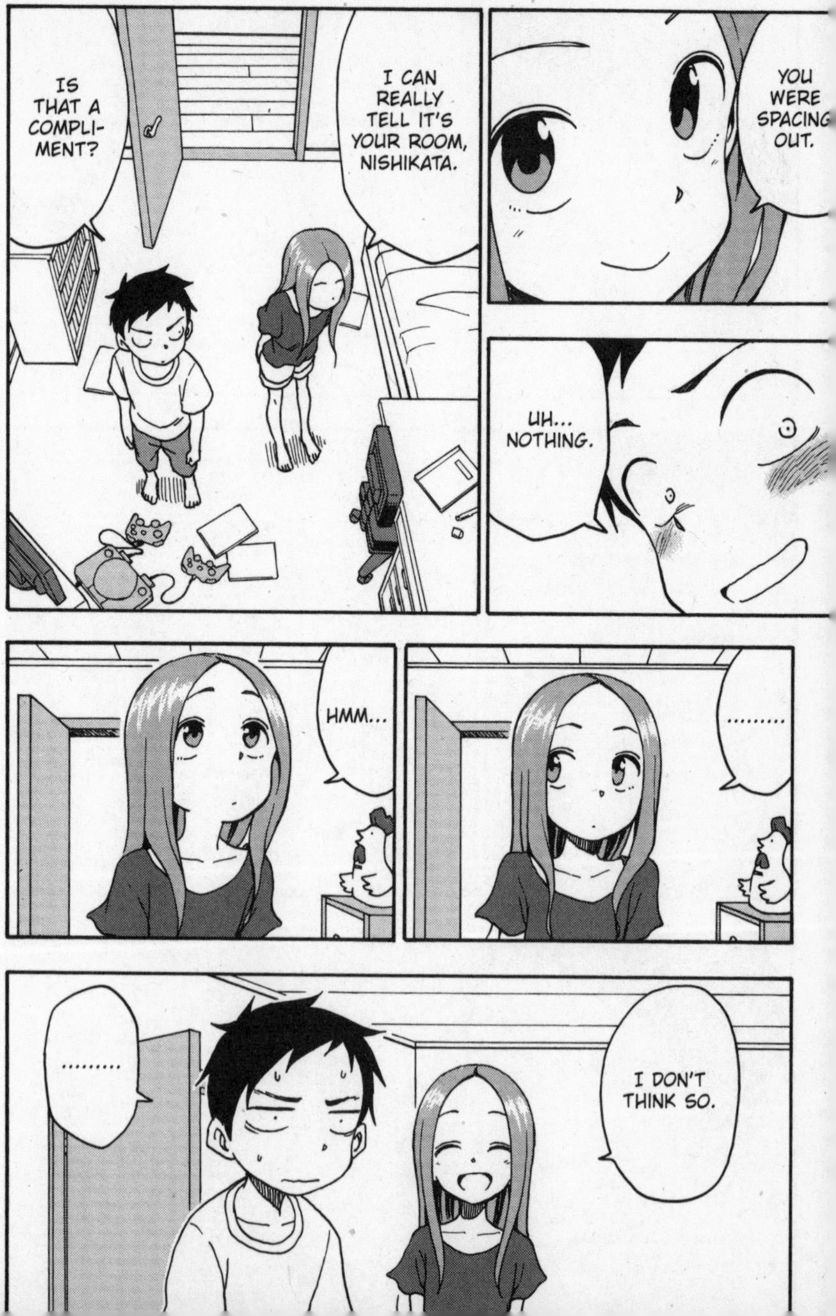
YOU WERE SPACING OUT.
UH... NOTHING.
I CAN REALLY TELL IT'S YOUR ROOM, NISHIKATA.
IS THAT A COMPLIMENT?
....
HMM...
I DON'T THINK SO.
....

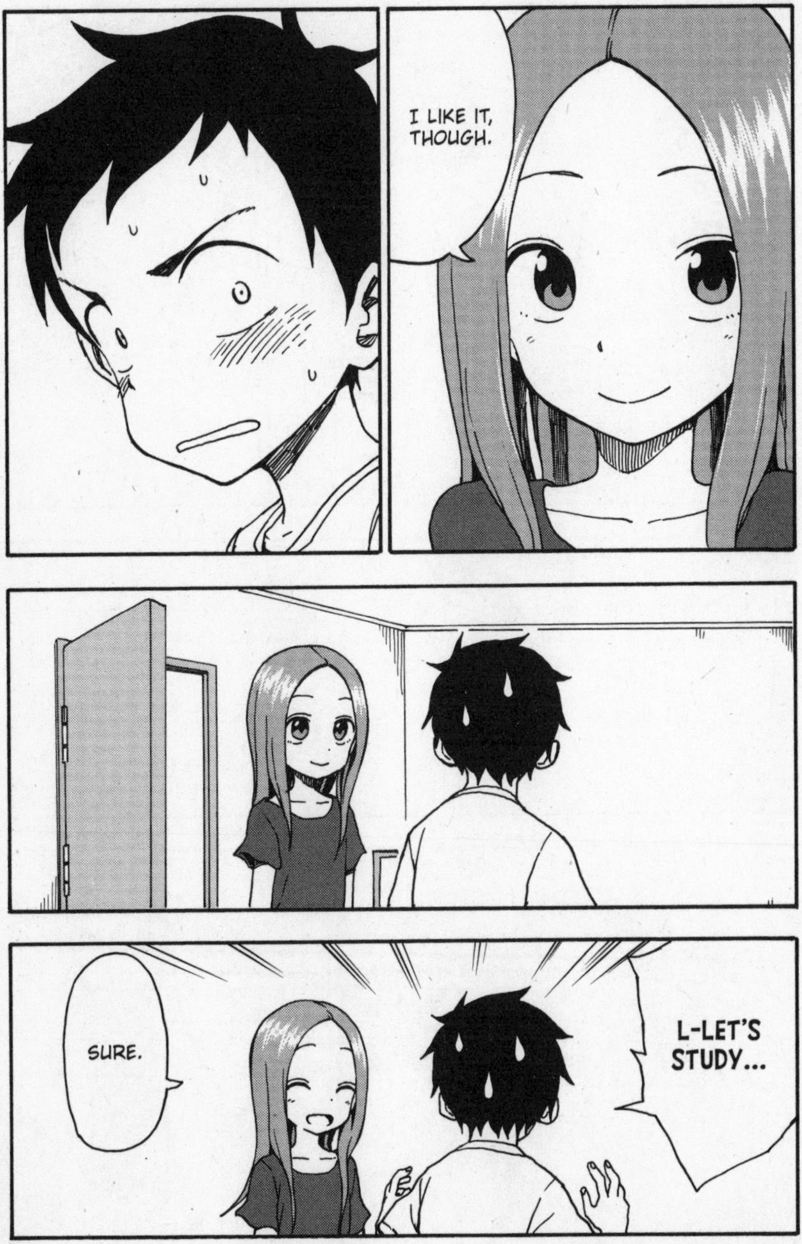
I LIKE IT, THOUGH.
L-LET'S STUDY...
SURE.

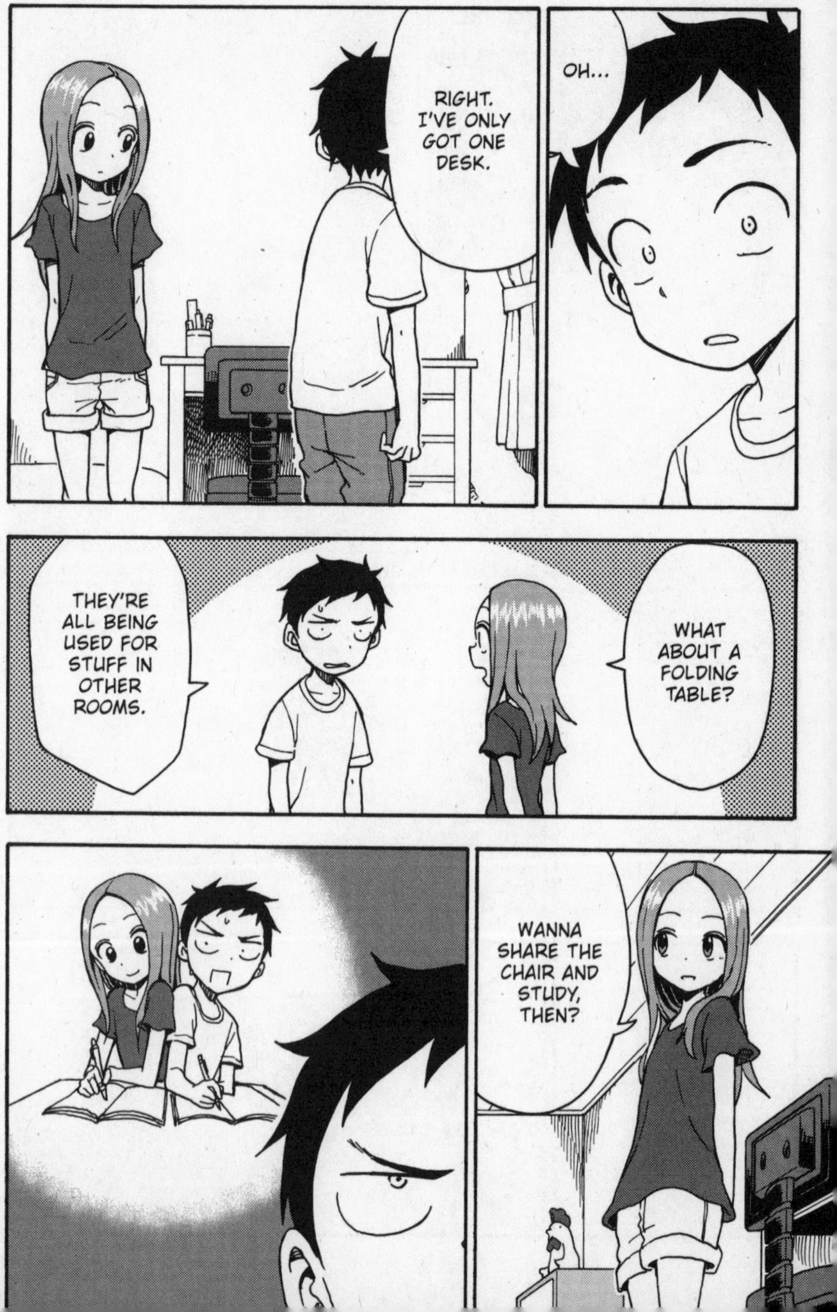
OH...
RIGHT. I'VE ONLY GOT ONE DESK.
WHAT ABOUT A FOLDING TABLE?
THEY'RE ALL BEING USED FOR STUFF IN OTHER ROOMS.
WANNA SHARE THE CHAIR AND STUDY, THEN?

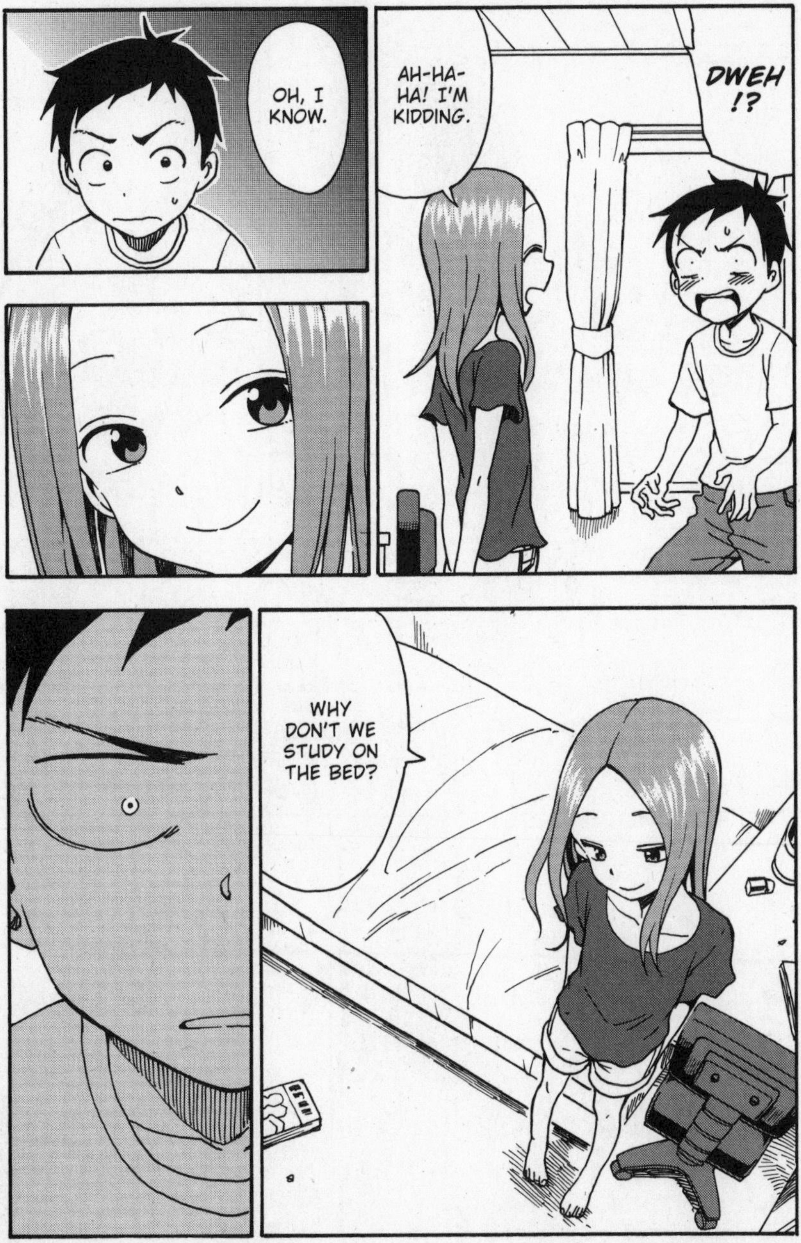
DWEH !?
AH-HA-HA! I'M KIDDING.
OH, I KNOW.
WHY DON'T WE STUDY ON THE BED?

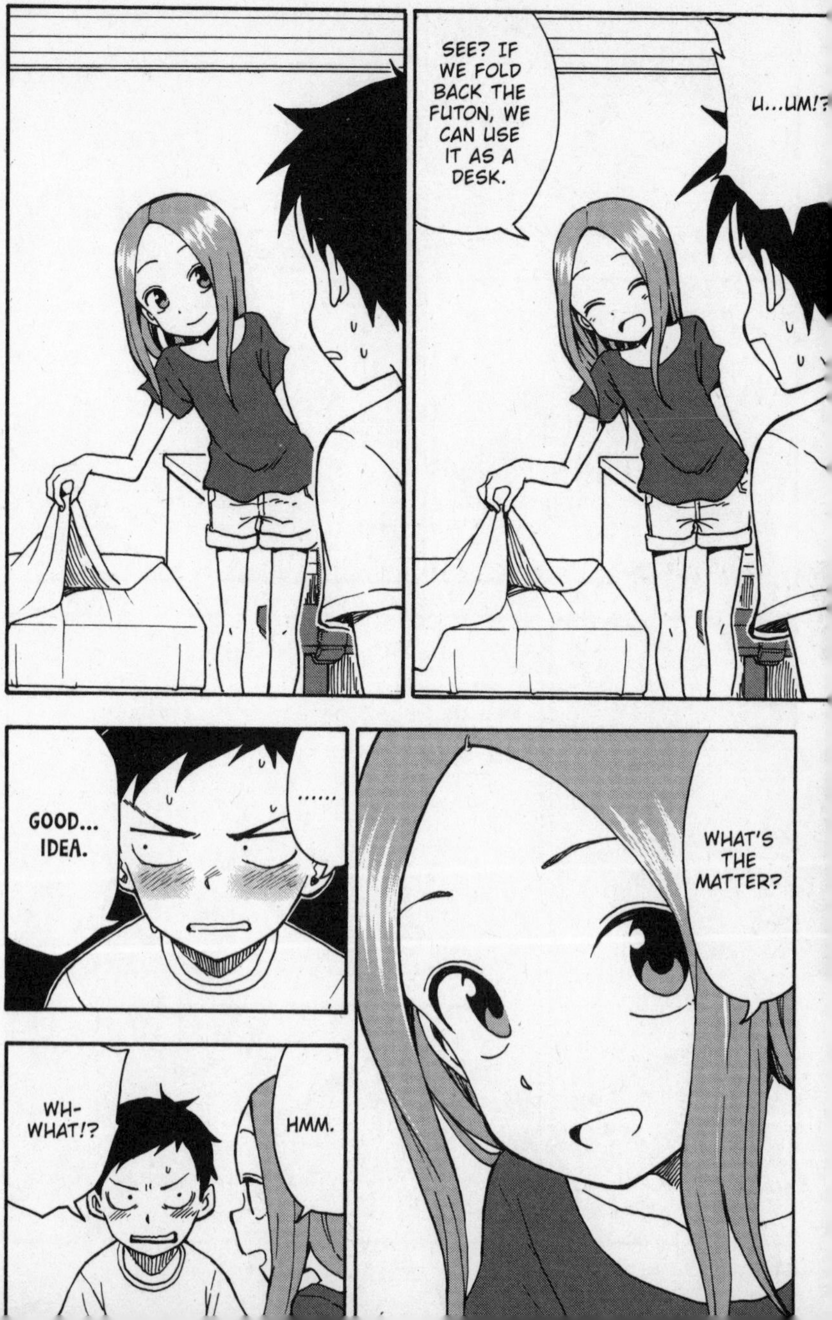
SEE? IF WE FOLD BACK THE FUTON, WE CAN USE IT AS A DESK.
U...UM!?
WHAT'S THE MATTER?
......
GOOD... IDEA.
HMM.
WH-WHAT!?

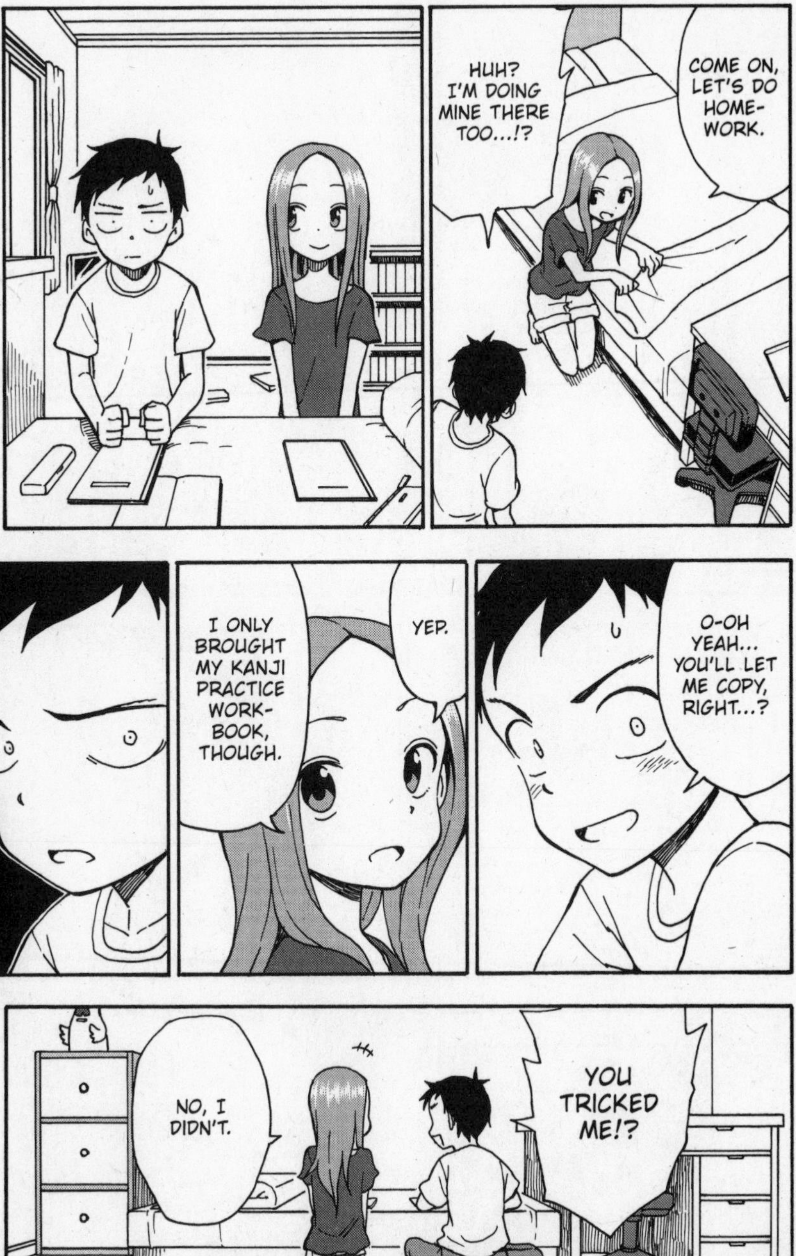
COME ON, LET'S DO HOME-WORK.
HUH? I'M DOING MINE THERE TOO...!?
O-OH YEAH... YOU'LL LET ME COPY, RIGHT...?
YEP.
I ONLY BROUGHT MY KANJI PRACTICE WORK-BOOK, THOUGH.
YOU TRICKED ME!?
NO, I DIDN'T.

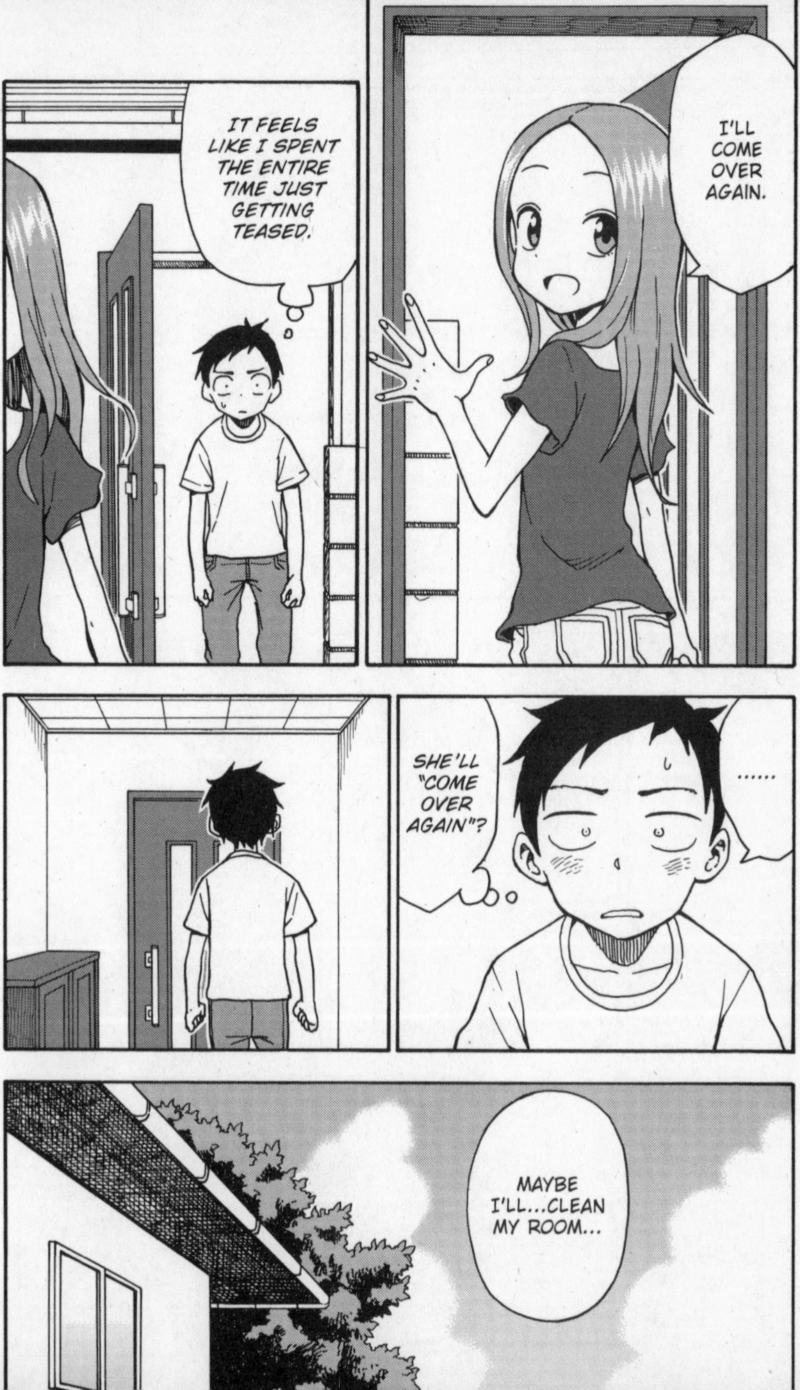
I'LL COME OVER AGAIN.
IT FEELS LIKE I SPENT THE ENTIRE TIME JUST GETTING TEASED.
......
SHE'LL "COME OVER AGAIN"?
MAYBE I'LL...CLEAN MY ROOM...

THE 21 GAME

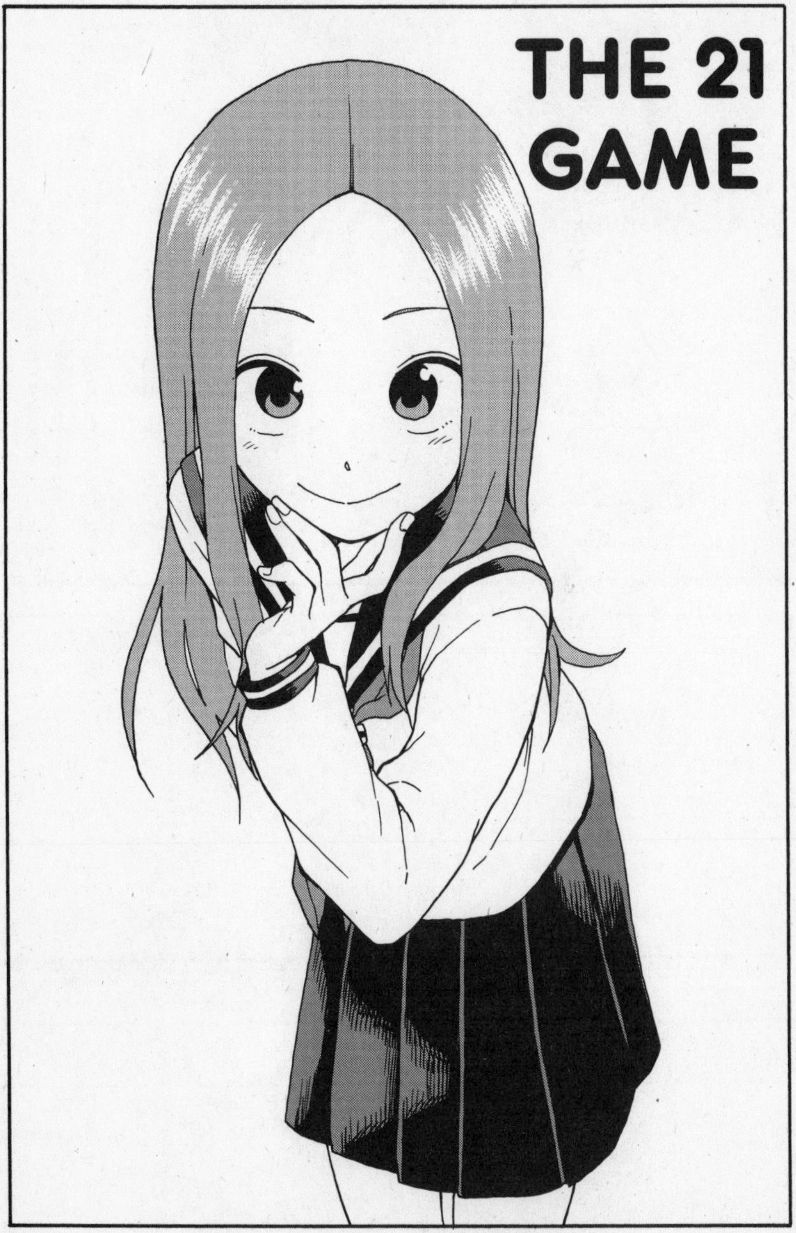

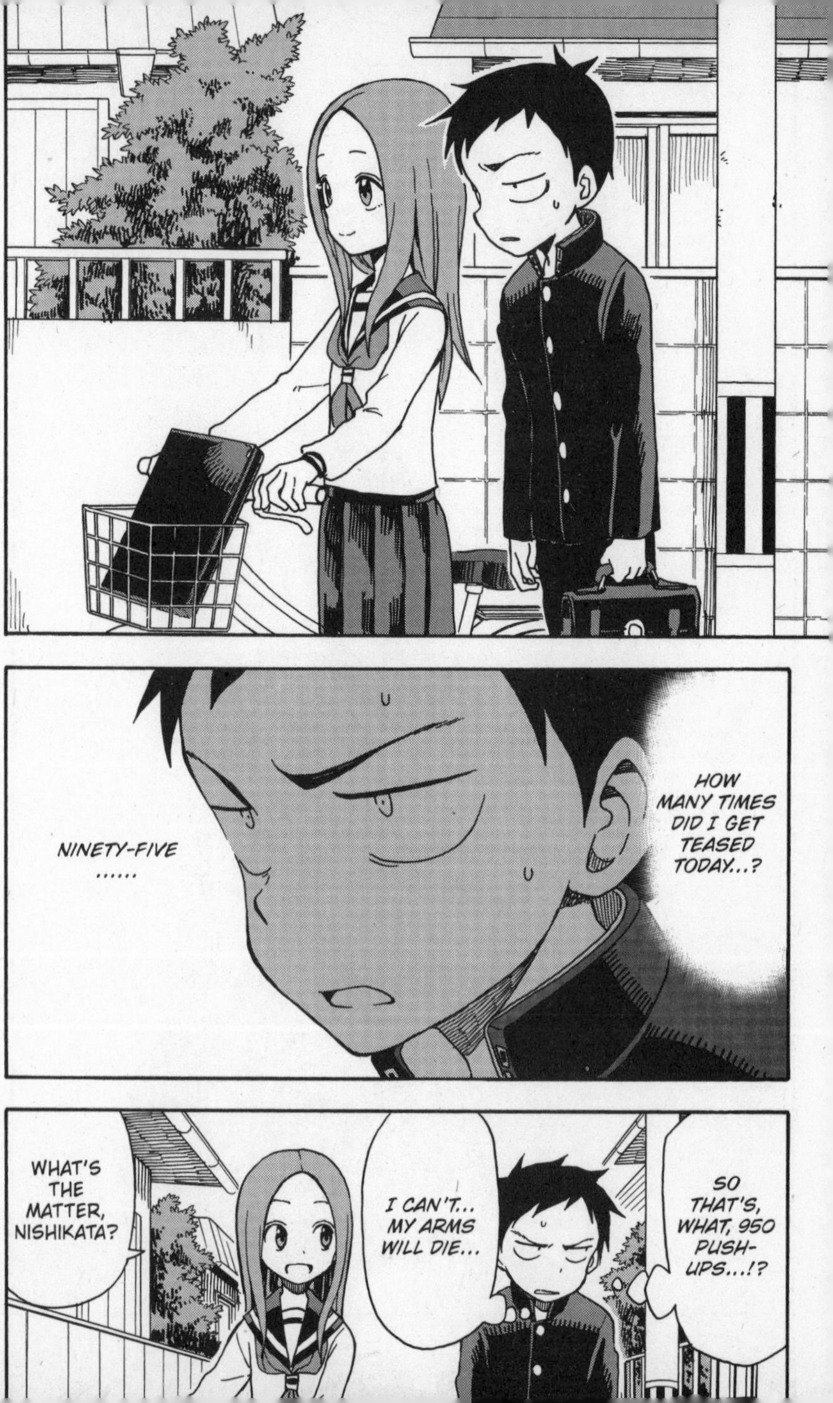
HOW MANY TIMES DID I GET TEASED TODAY...?
NINETY-FIVE ......
SO THAT'S, WHAT, 950 PUSH-UPS...!?
I CAN'T... MY ARMS WILL DIE...
WHAT'S THE MATTER, NISHIKATA?

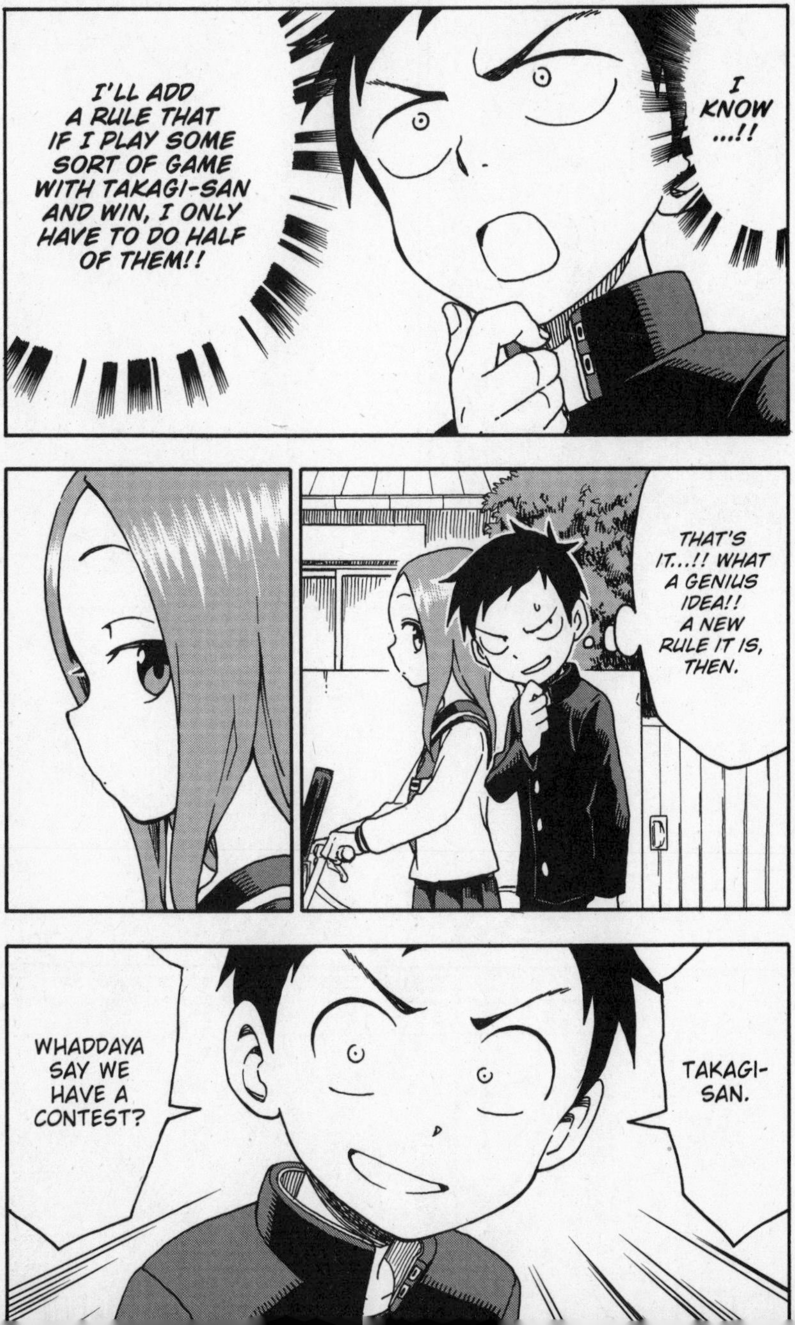
I KNOW ...!!
I'LL ADD A RULE THAT IF I PLAY SOME SORT OF GAME WITH TAKAGI-SAN AND WIN, I ONLY HAVE TO DO HALF OF THEM!!
THAT'S IT...!! WHAT A GENIUS IDEA!! A NEW RULE IT IS, THEN.
TAKAGI-SAN.
WHADDAYA SAY WE HAVE A CONTEST?

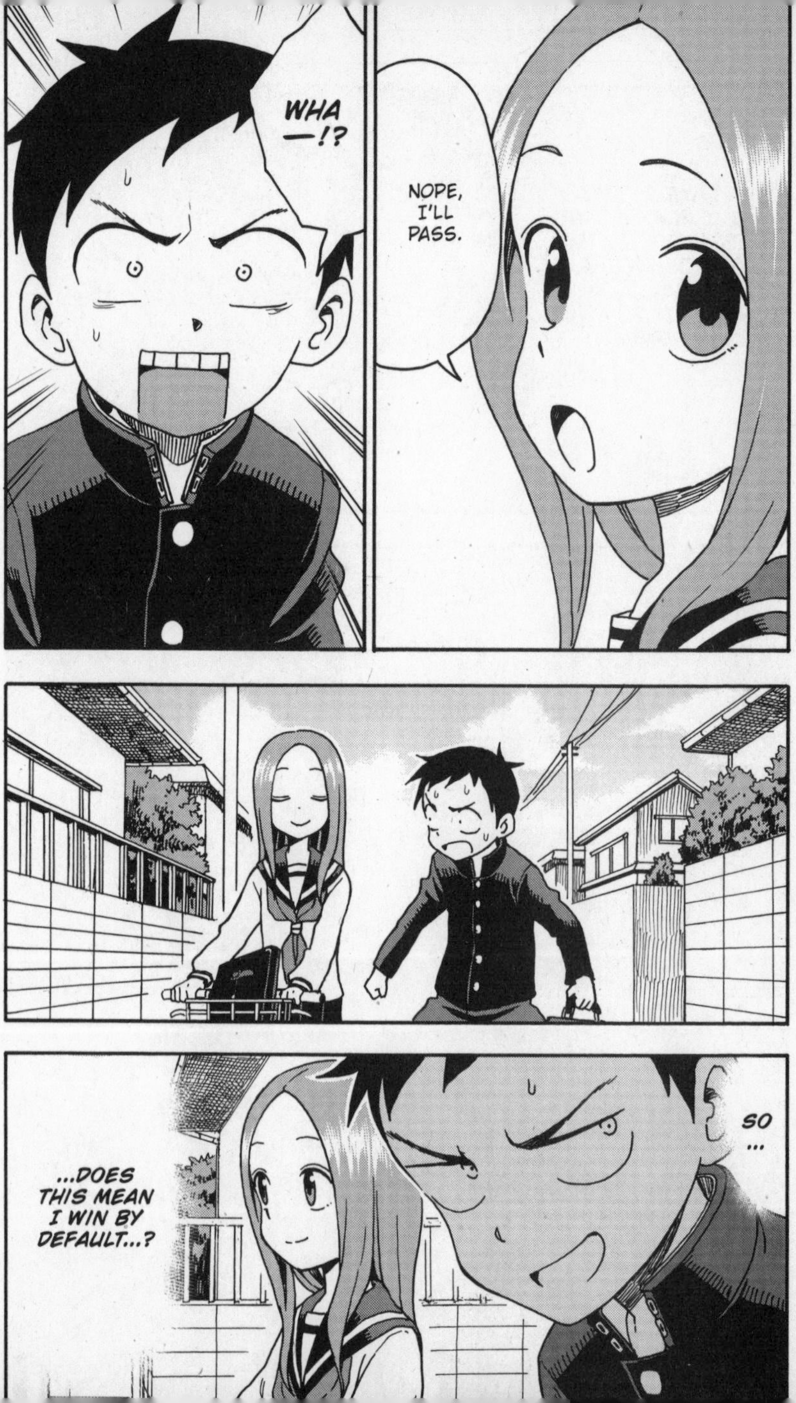
NOPE, I'LL PASS.
WHA —!?
SO ...
...DOES THIS MEAN I WIN BY DEFAULT...?

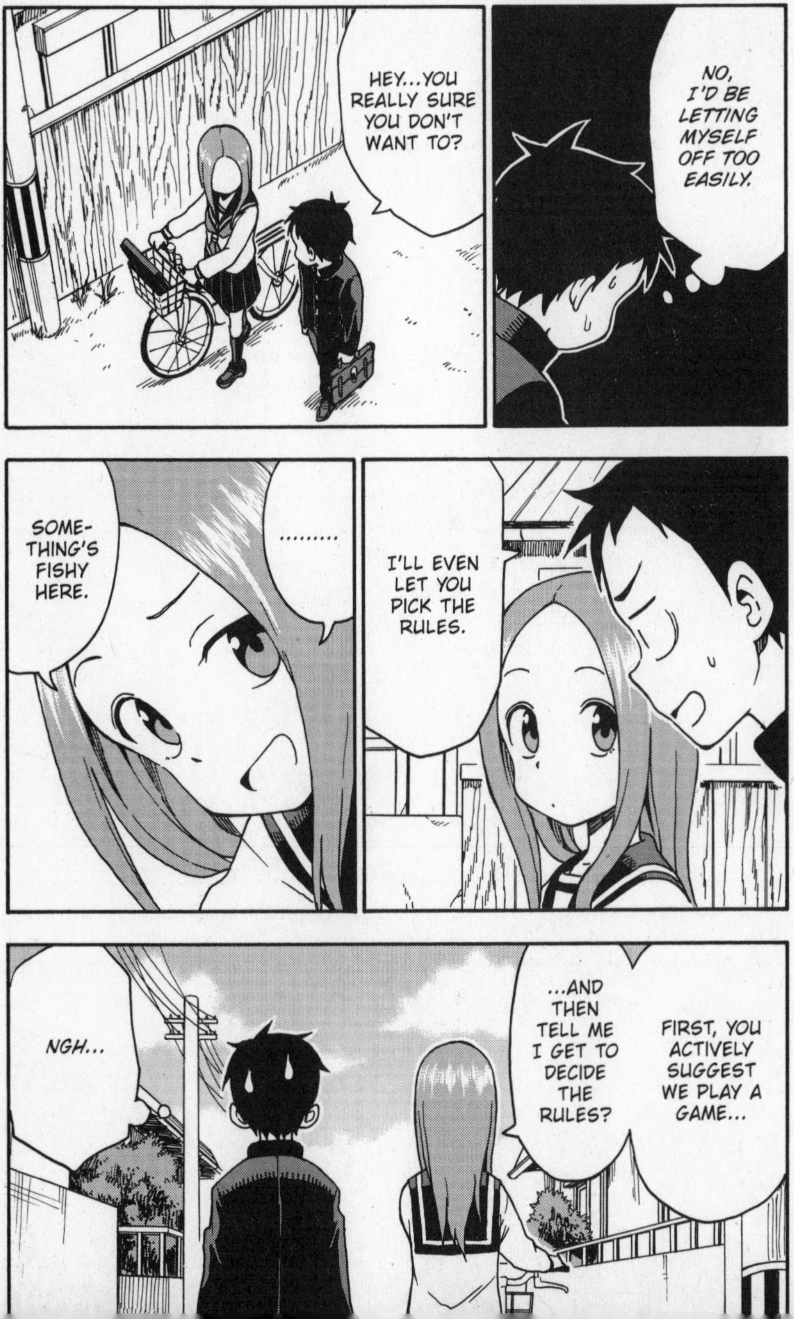
NO, I'D BE LETTING MYSELF OFF TOO EASILY.
HEY...YOU REALLY SURE YOU DON'T WANT TO?
I'LL EVEN LET YOU PICK THE RULES.
....
SOME-THING'S FISHY HERE.
FIRST, YOU ACTIVELY SUGGEST WE PLAY A GAME...
...AND THEN TELL ME I GET TO DECIDE THE RULES?
NGH...

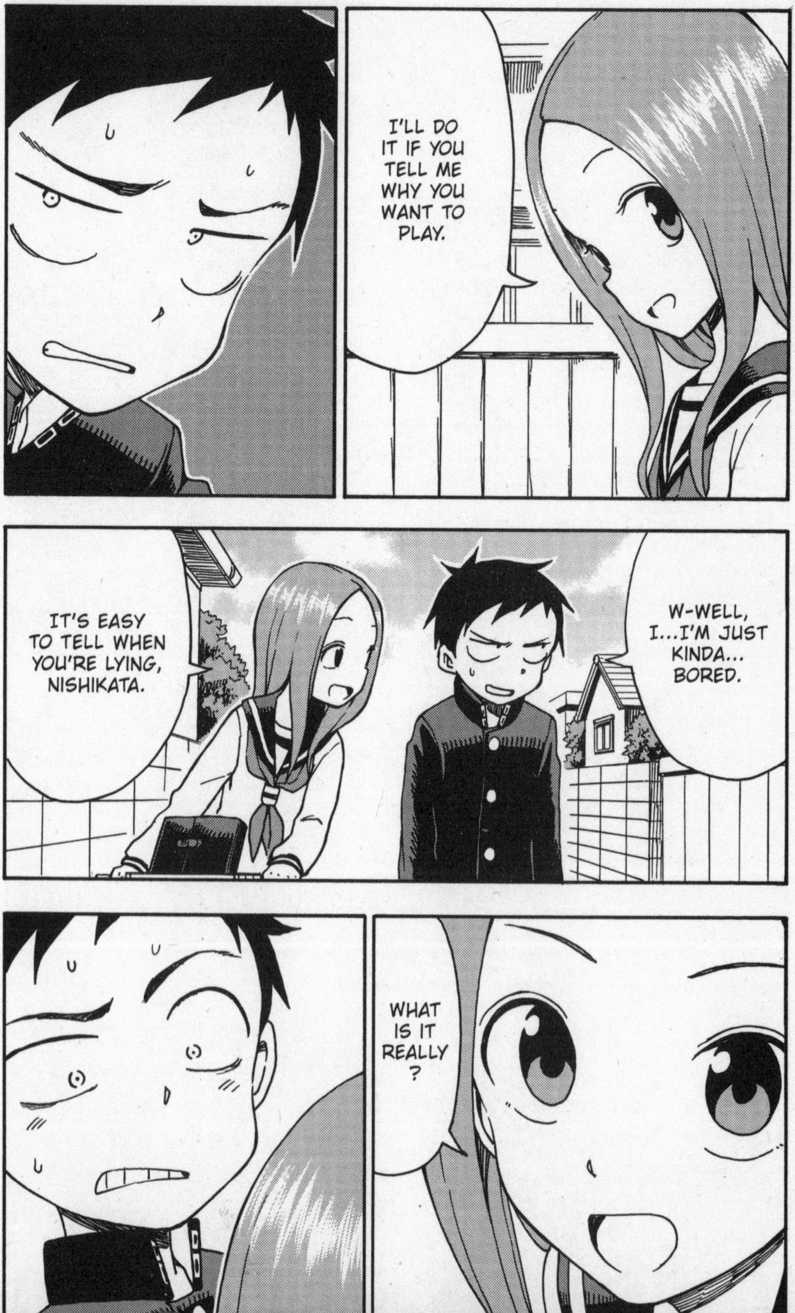
I'LL DO IT IF YOU TELL ME WHY YOU WANT TO PLAY.
W-WELL, I...I'M JUST KINDA... BORED.
IT'S EASY TO TELL WHEN YOU'RE LYING, NISHIKATA.
WHAT IS IT REALLY?

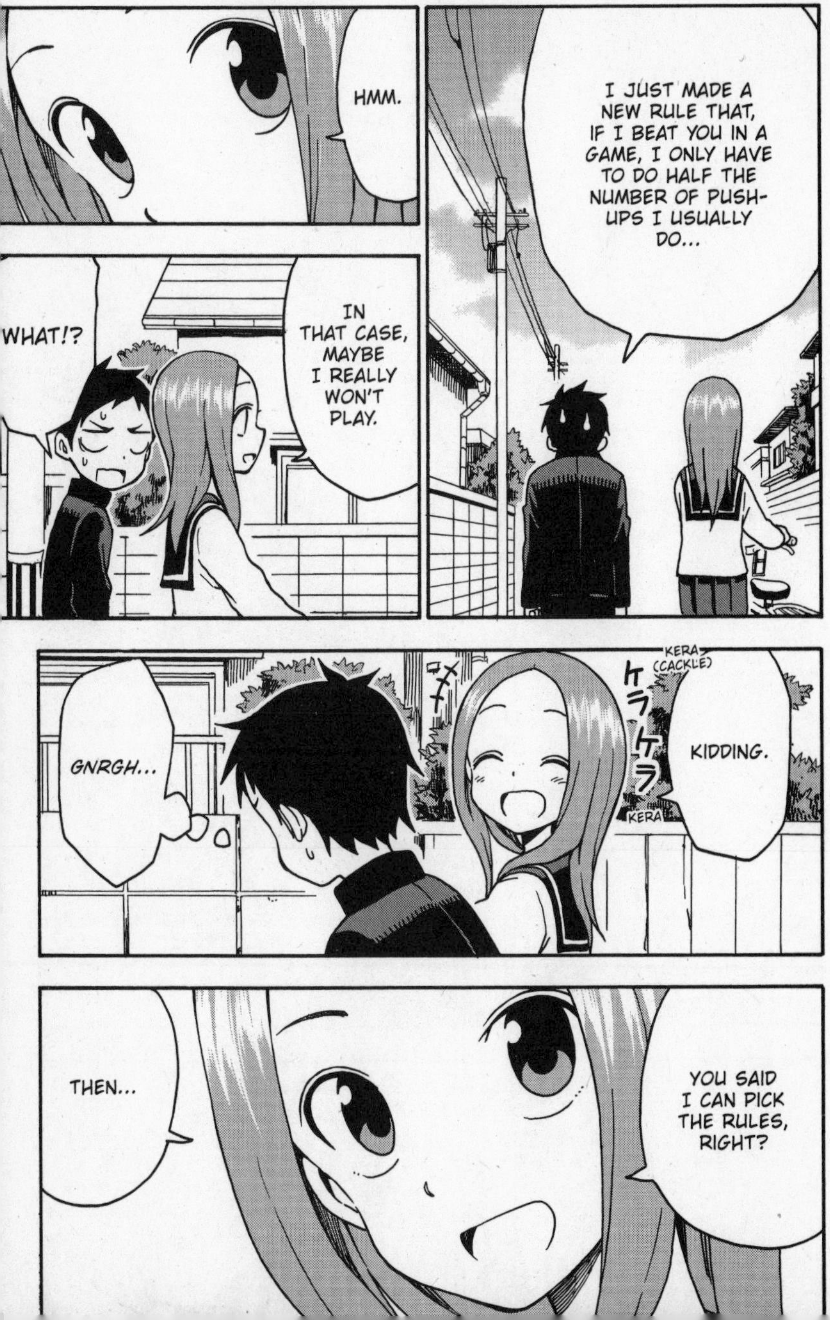
I JUST MADE A NEW RULE THAT, IF I BEAT YOU IN A GAME, I ONLY HAVE TO DO HALF THE NUMBER OF PUSH-UPS I USUALLY DO...
HMM.
IN THAT CASE, MAYBE I REALLY WON'T PLAY.
WHAT!?
KIDDING.
KERA (CACKLE) ケラ
ケラ KERA
GNRGH...
YOU SAID I CAN PICK THE RULES, RIGHT?
THEN...

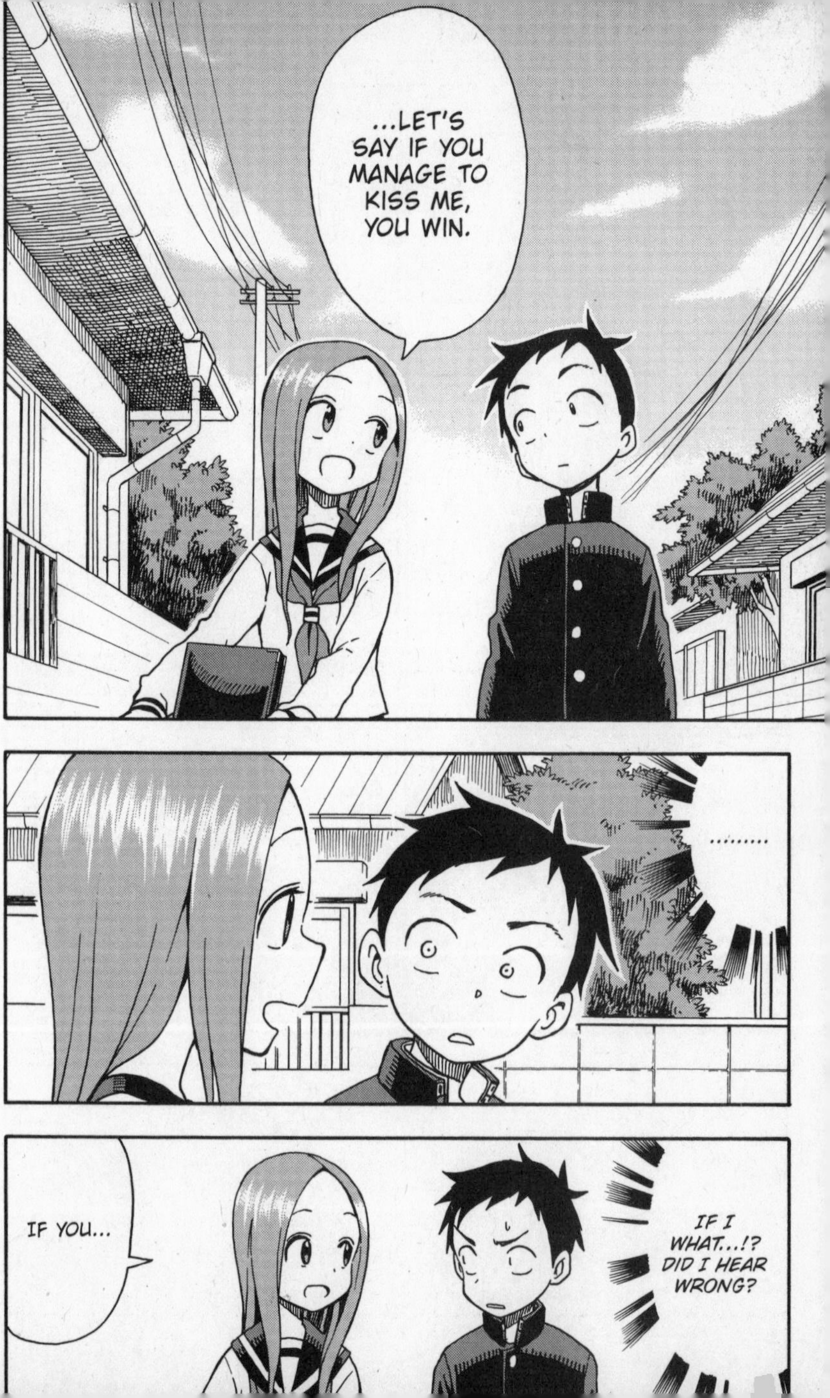
...LET'S SAY IF YOU MANAGE TO KISS ME, YOU WIN.
....
IF I WHAT...!? DID I HEAR WRONG?
IF YOU...

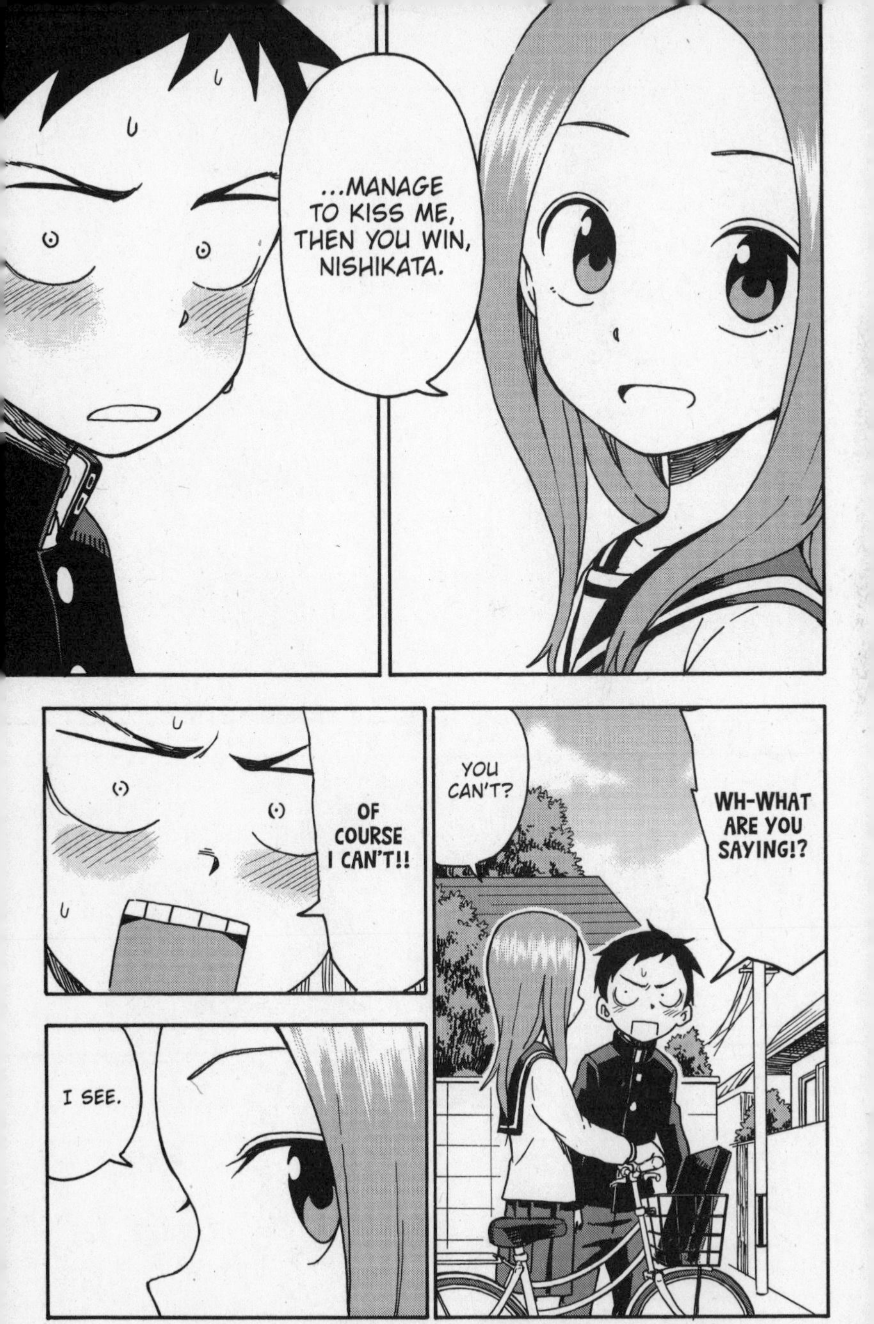
...MANAGE TO KISS ME, THEN YOU WIN, NISHIKATA.
WH-WHAT ARE YOU SAYING!?
YOU CAN'T?
OF COURSE I CAN'T!!
I SEE.

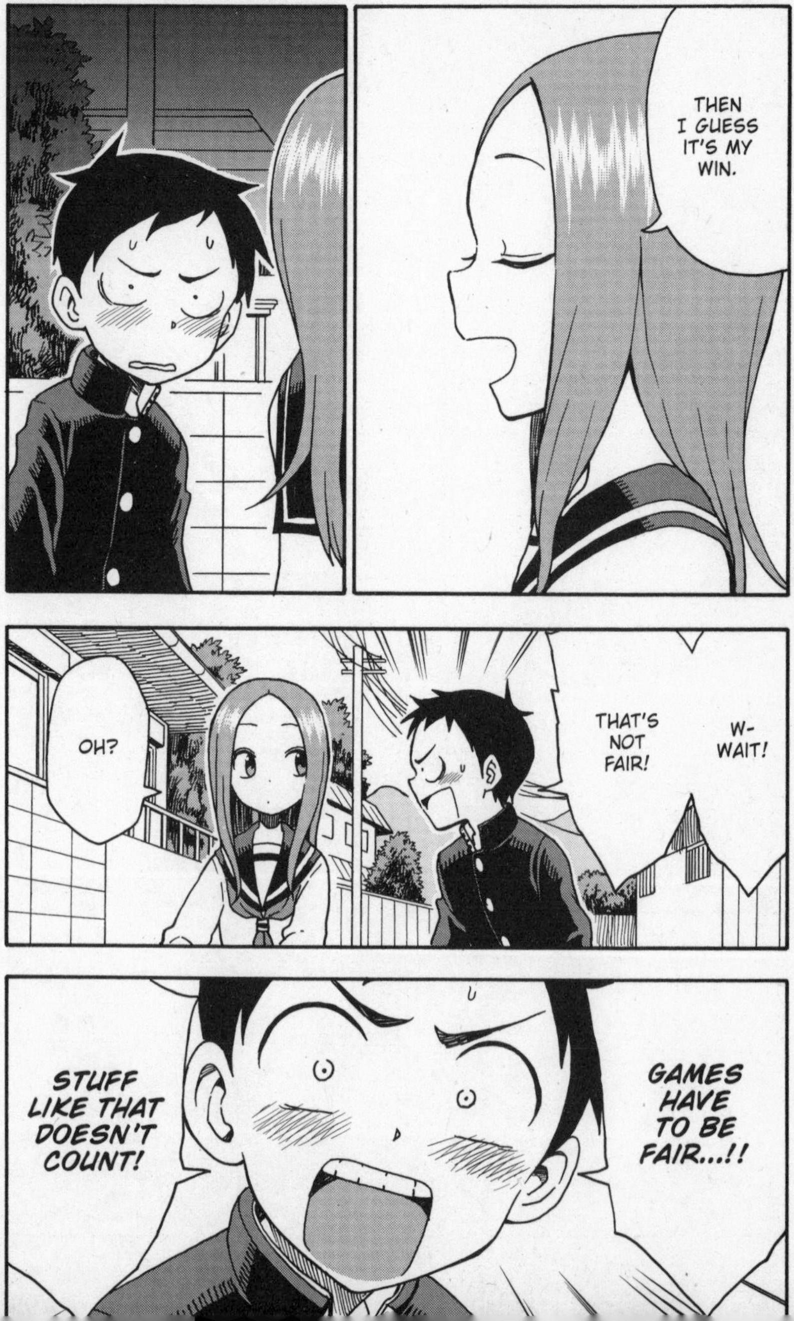
THEN I GUESS IT'S MY WIN.
W- WAIT!
THAT'S NOT FAIR!
OH?
GAMES HAVE TO BE FAIR...!!
STUFF LIKE THAT DOESN'T COUNT!

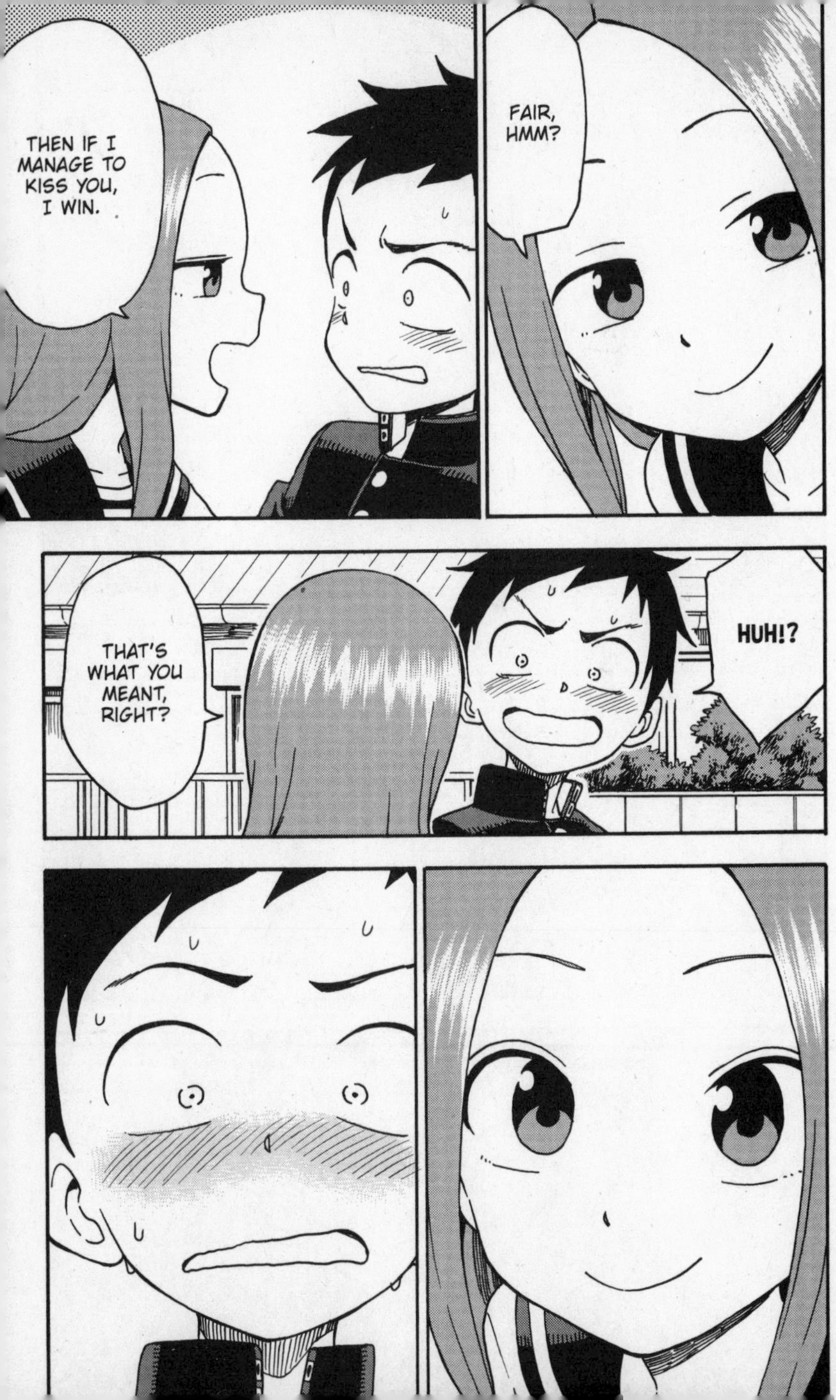
FAIR, HMM?
THEN IF I MANAGE TO KISS YOU, I WIN.
HUH!?
THAT'S WHAT YOU MEANT, RIGHT?

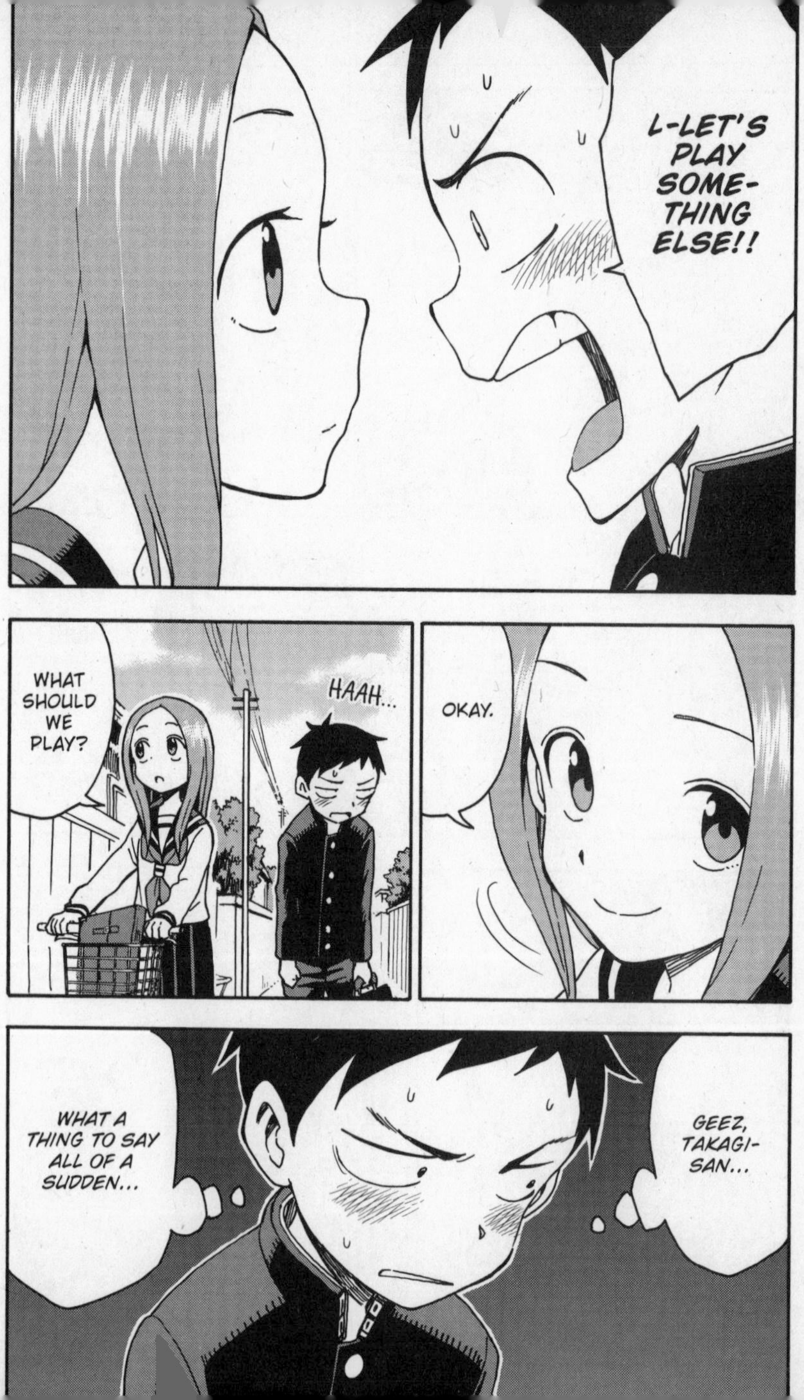
L-LET'S PLAY SOME-THING ELSE!!
OKAY.
HAAH...
WHAT SHOULD WE PLAY?
GEEZ, TAKAGI-SAN...
WHAT A THING TO SAY ALL OF A SUDDEN...

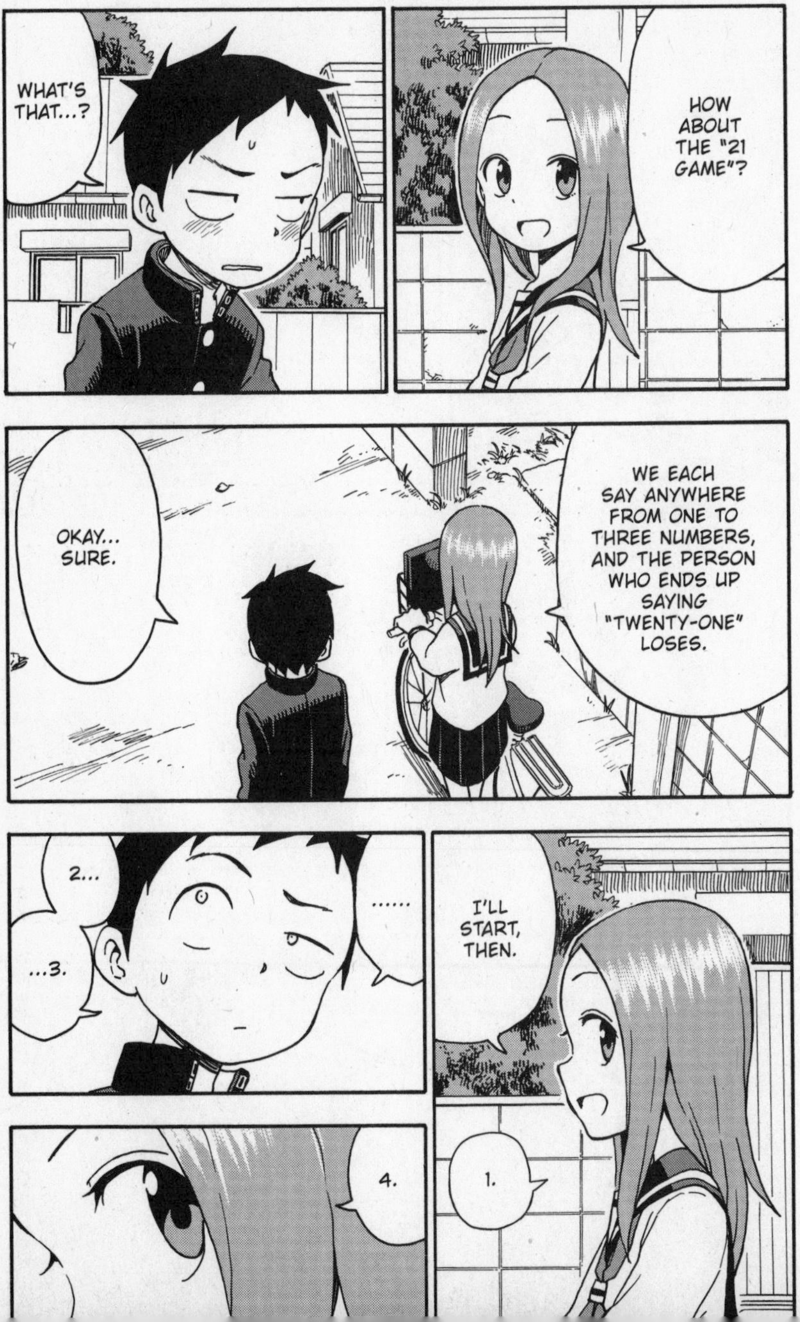
HOW ABOUT THE "21 GAME"?
WHAT'S THAT...?
WE EACH SAY ANYWHERE FROM ONE TO THREE NUMBERS, AND THE PERSON WHO ENDS UP SAYING "TWENTY-ONE" LOSES.
OKAY... SURE.
I'LL START, THEN.
1.
......
2...
...3.
4.

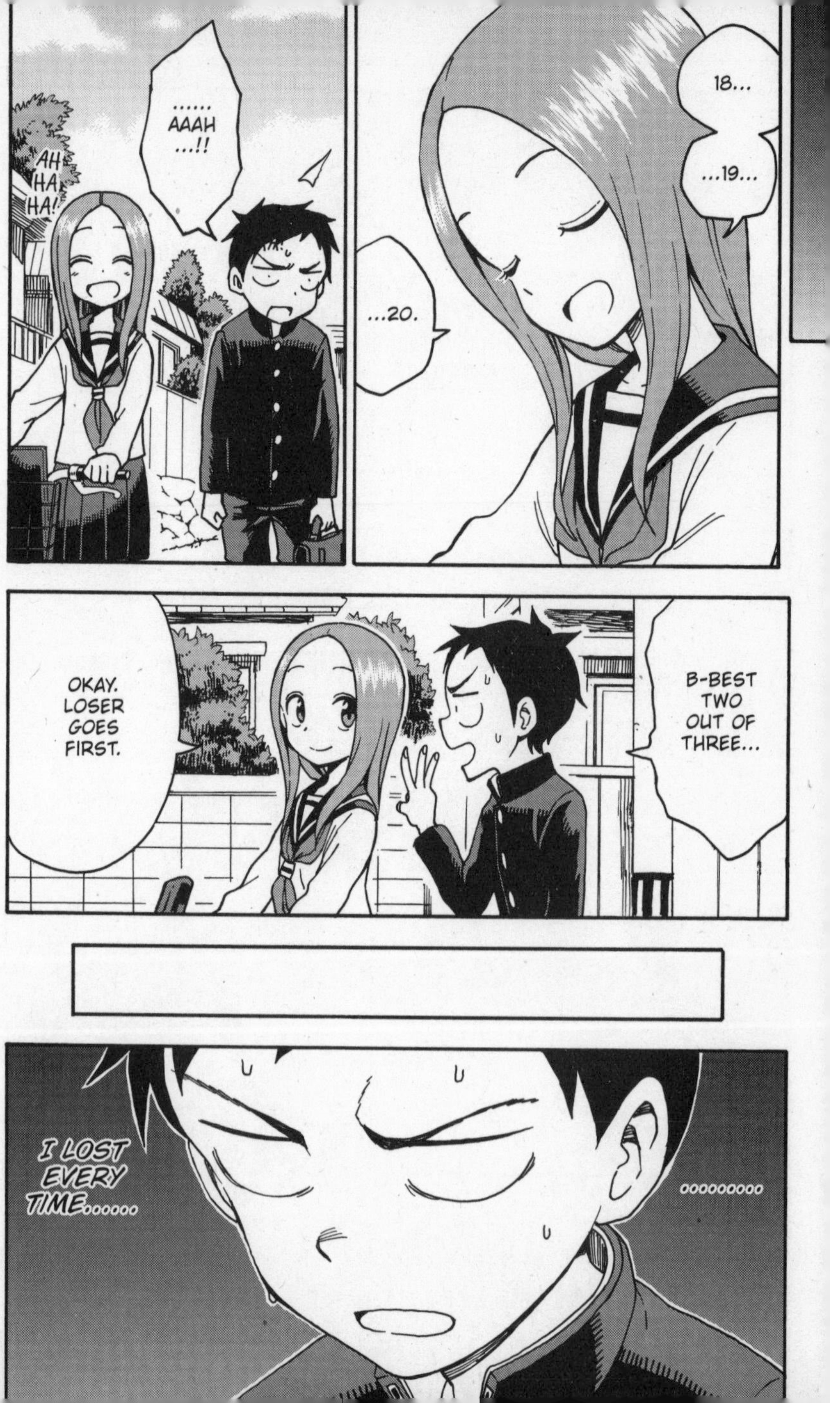
18...
...19...
...20.
......AAAH...!!
AH HA HA!
B-BEST TWO OUT OF THREE...
OKAY. LOSER GOES FIRST.
OOOOOOOOO
I LOST EVERY TIME......

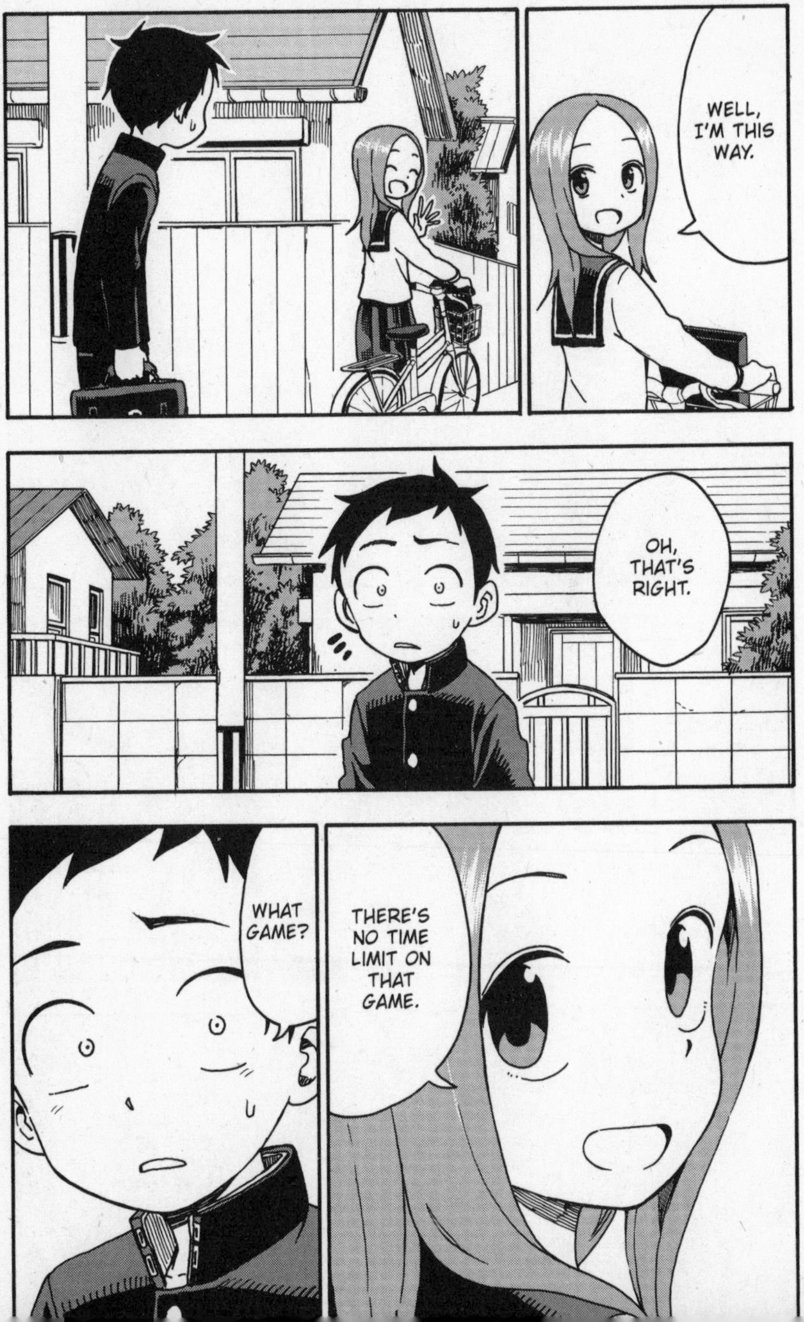
WELL, I'M THIS WAY.
OH, THAT'S RIGHT.
THERE'S NO TIME LIMIT ON THAT GAME.
WHAT GAME?

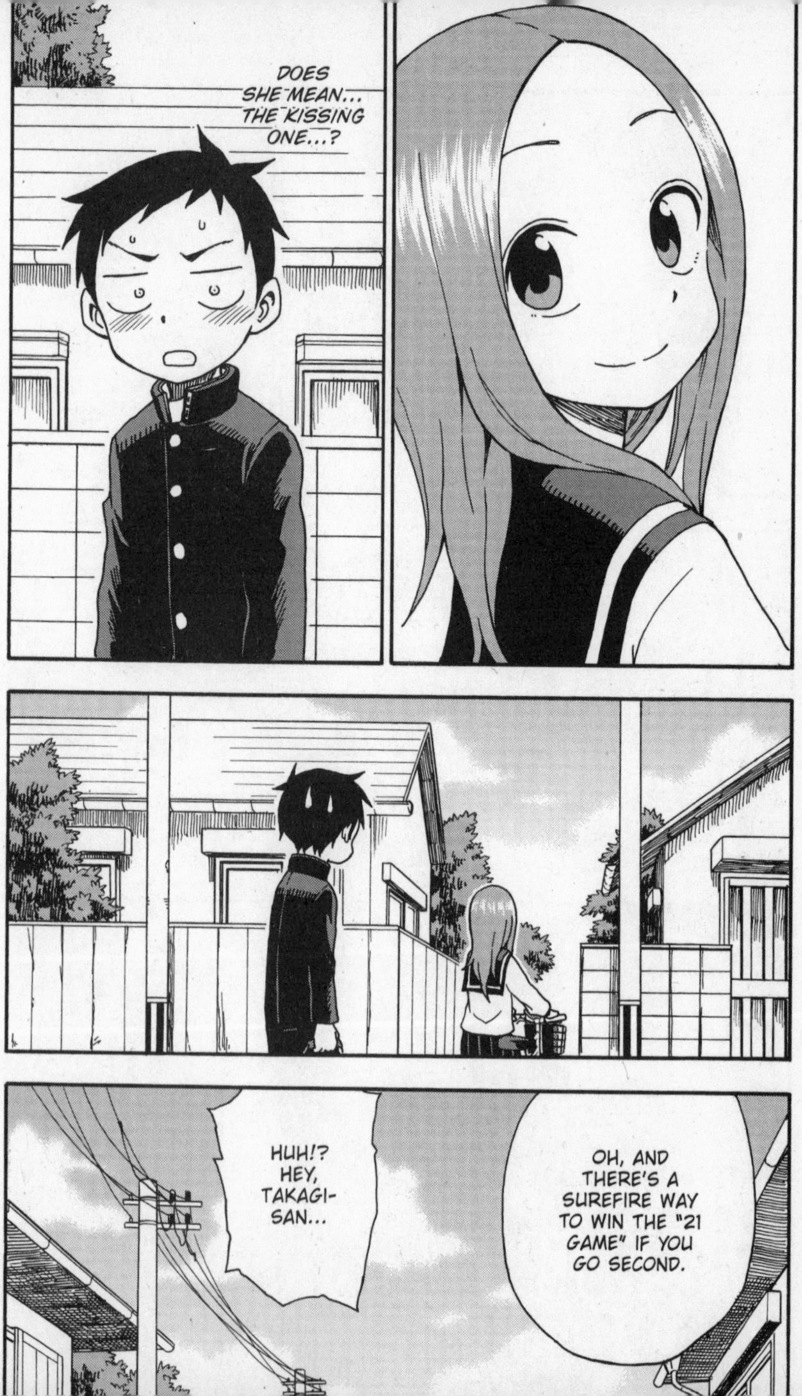
DOES SHE MEAN... THE KISSING ONE...?
OH, AND THERE'S A SUREFIRE WAY TO WIN THE "21 GAME" IF YOU GO SECOND.
HUH!? HEY, TAKAGI-SAN...

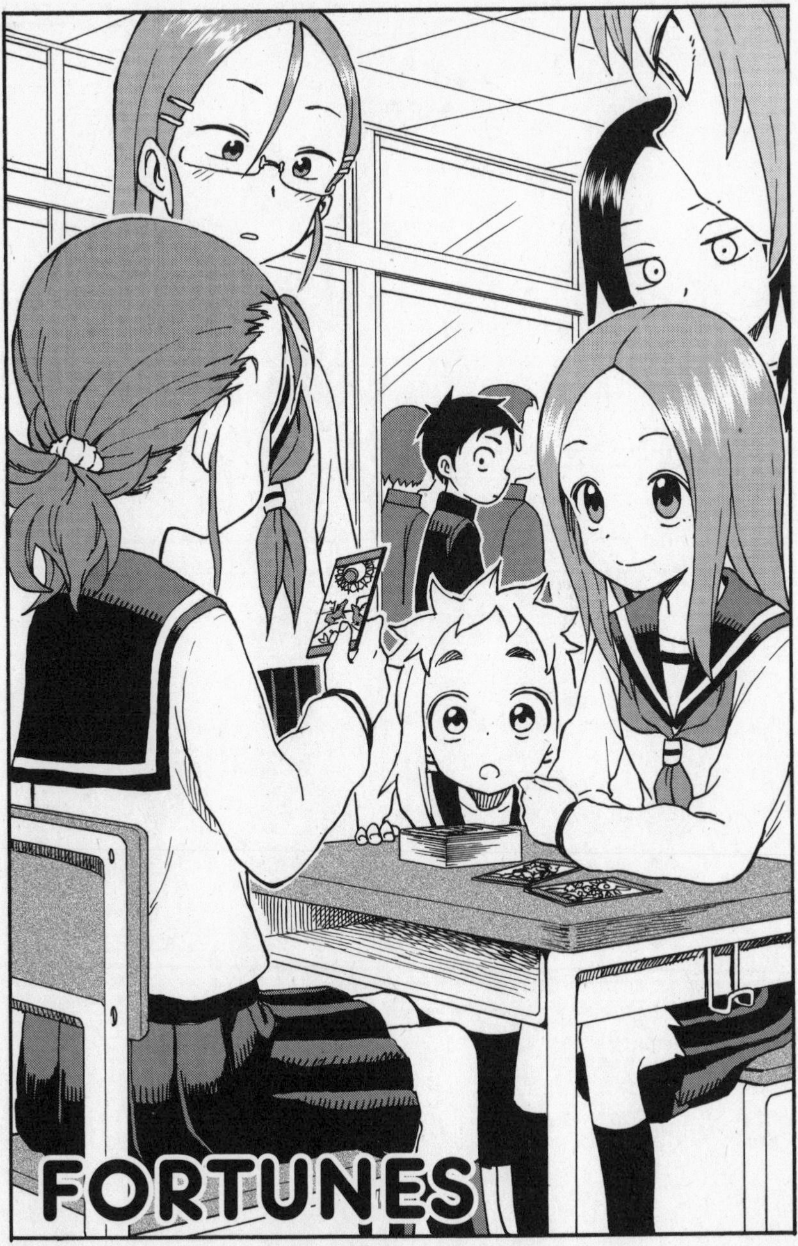
FORTUNES

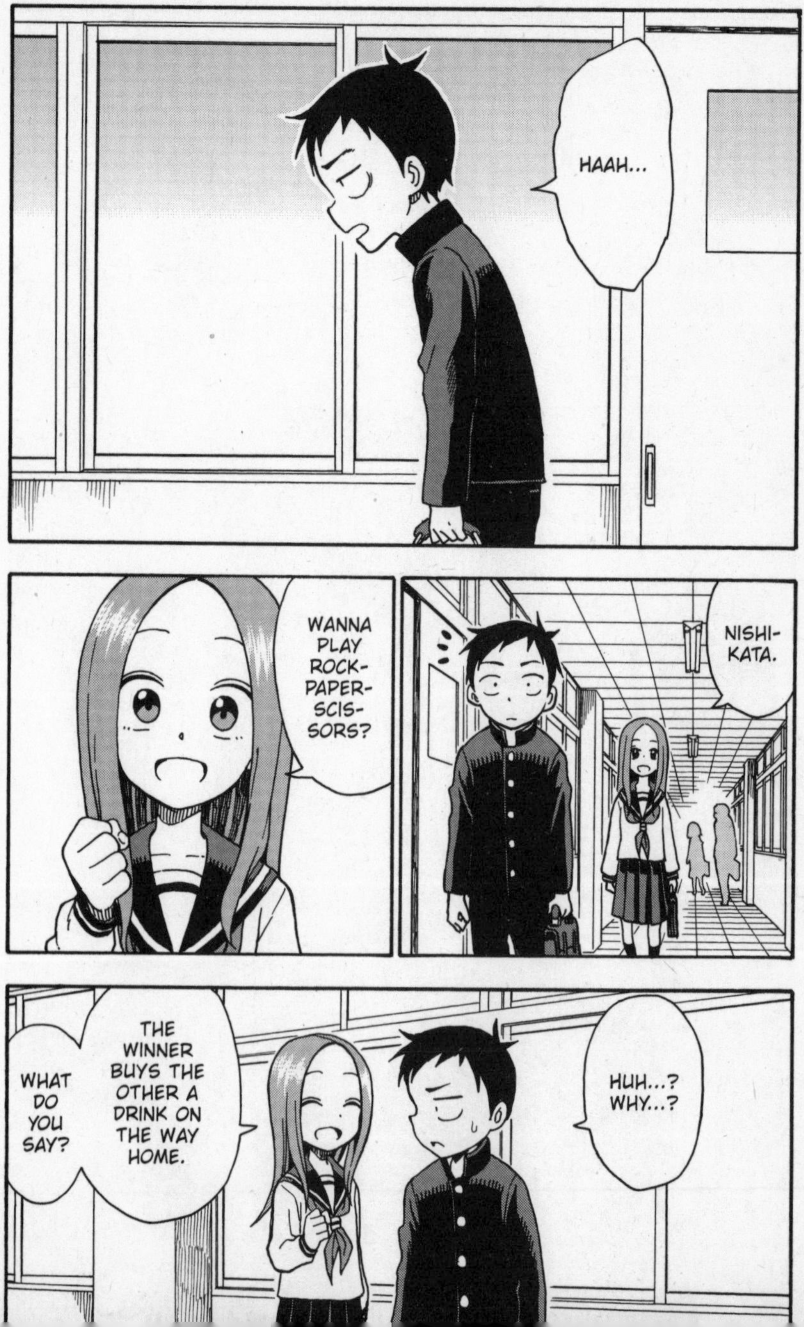
HAAH...
NISHI-KATA.
WANNA PLAY ROCK-PAPER-SCISSORS?
HUH...? WHY...?
THE WINNER BUYS THE OTHER A DRINK ON THE WAY HOME.
WHAT DO YOU SAY?

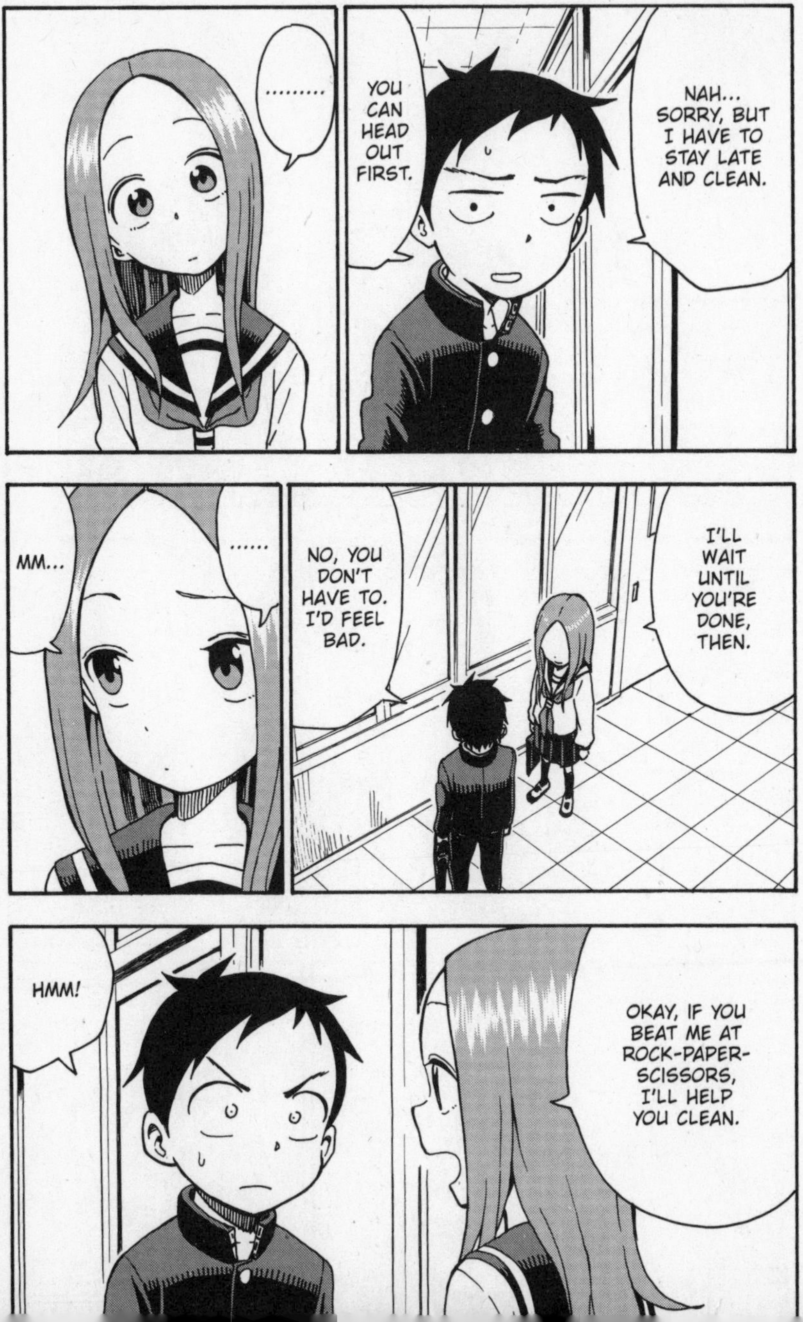
NAH... SORRY, BUT I HAVE TO STAY LATE AND CLEAN.
YOU CAN HEAD OUT FIRST.
....
I'LL WAIT UNTIL YOU'RE DONE, THEN.
NO, YOU DON'T HAVE TO. I'D FEEL BAD.
......
MM...
OKAY, IF YOU BEAT ME AT ROCK-PAPER-SCISSORS, I'LL HELP YOU CLEAN.
HMM!

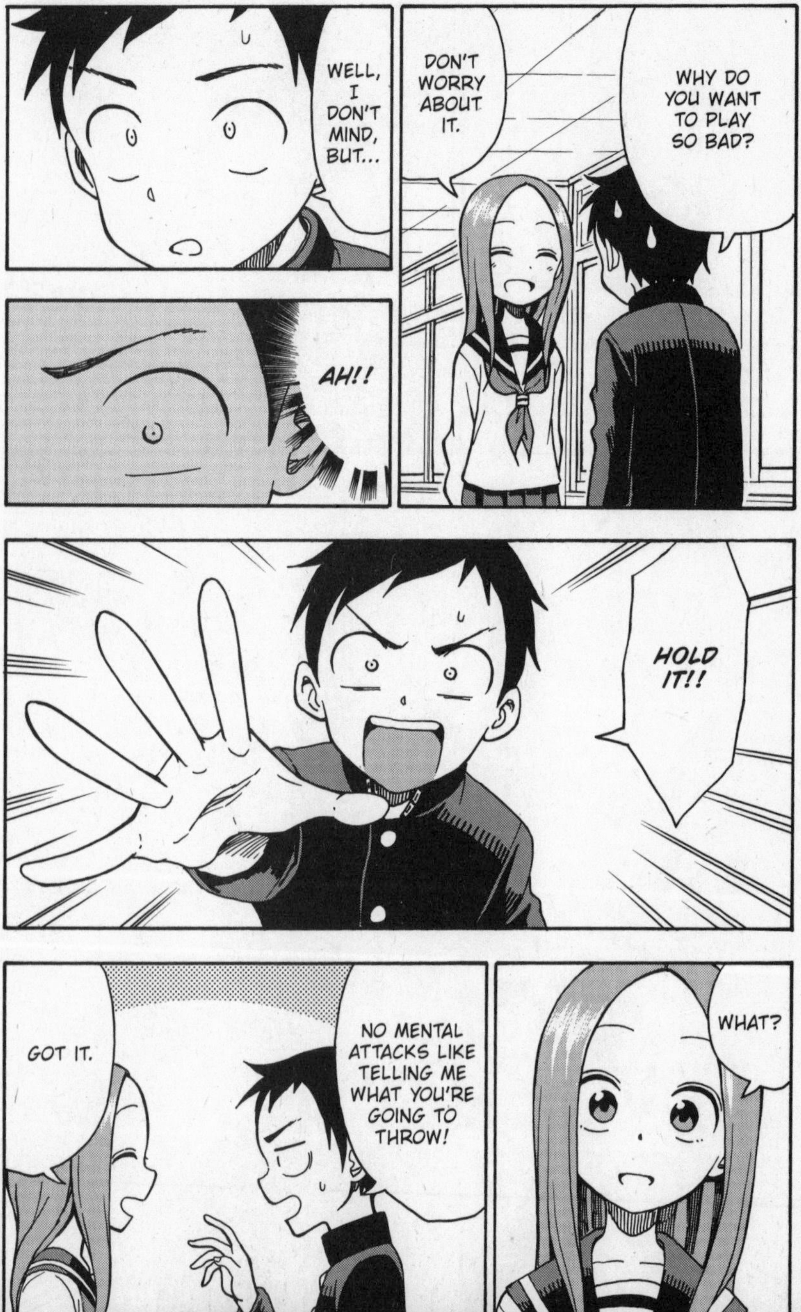
WHY DO YOU WANT TO PLAY SO BAD?
DON'T WORRY ABOUT IT.
WELL, I DON'T MIND, BUT...
AH!!
HOLD IT!!
WHAT?
NO MENTAL ATTACKS LIKE TELLING ME WHAT YOU'RE GOING TO THROW!
GOT IT.

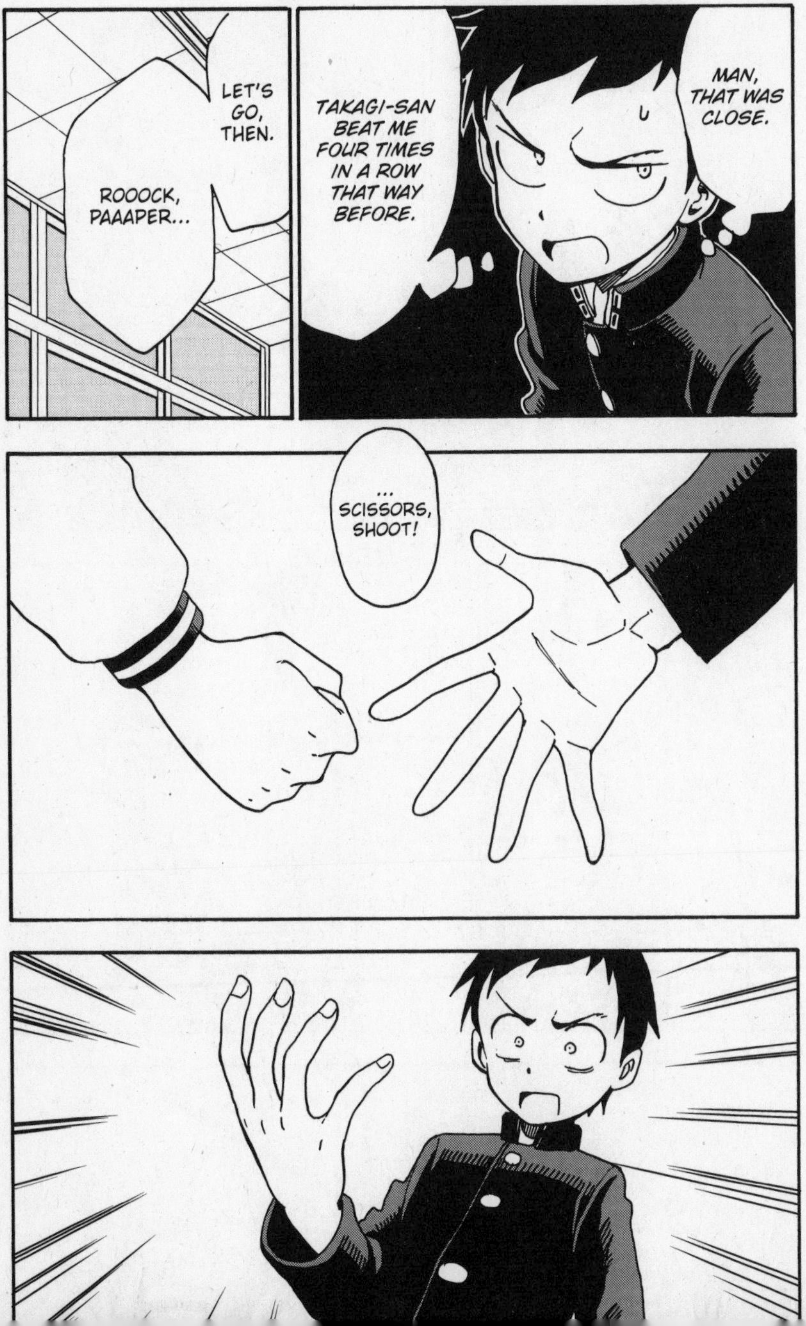
MAN, THAT WAS CLOSE.
TAKAGI-SAN BEAT ME FOUR TIMES IN A ROW THAT WAY BEFORE.
LET'S GO, THEN.
ROOOCK, PAAAPER...
... SCISSORS, SHOOT!

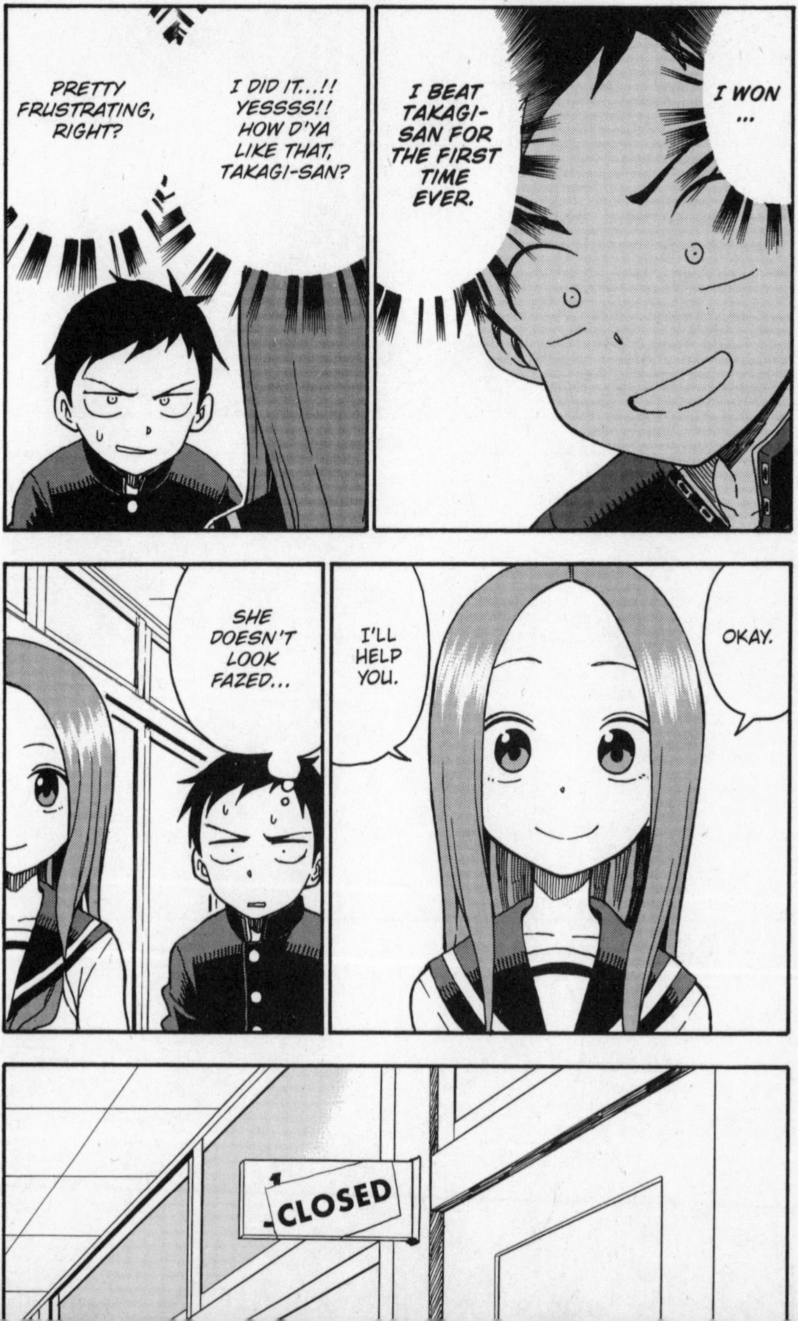
I WON ...
I BEAT TAKAGI-SAN FOR THE FIRST TIME EVER.
I DID IT...!! YESSSS!! HOW D'YA LIKE THAT, TAKAGI-SAN?
PRETTY FRUSTRATING, RIGHT?
OKAY.
I'LL HELP YOU.
SHE DOESN'T LOOK FAZED...
CLOSED

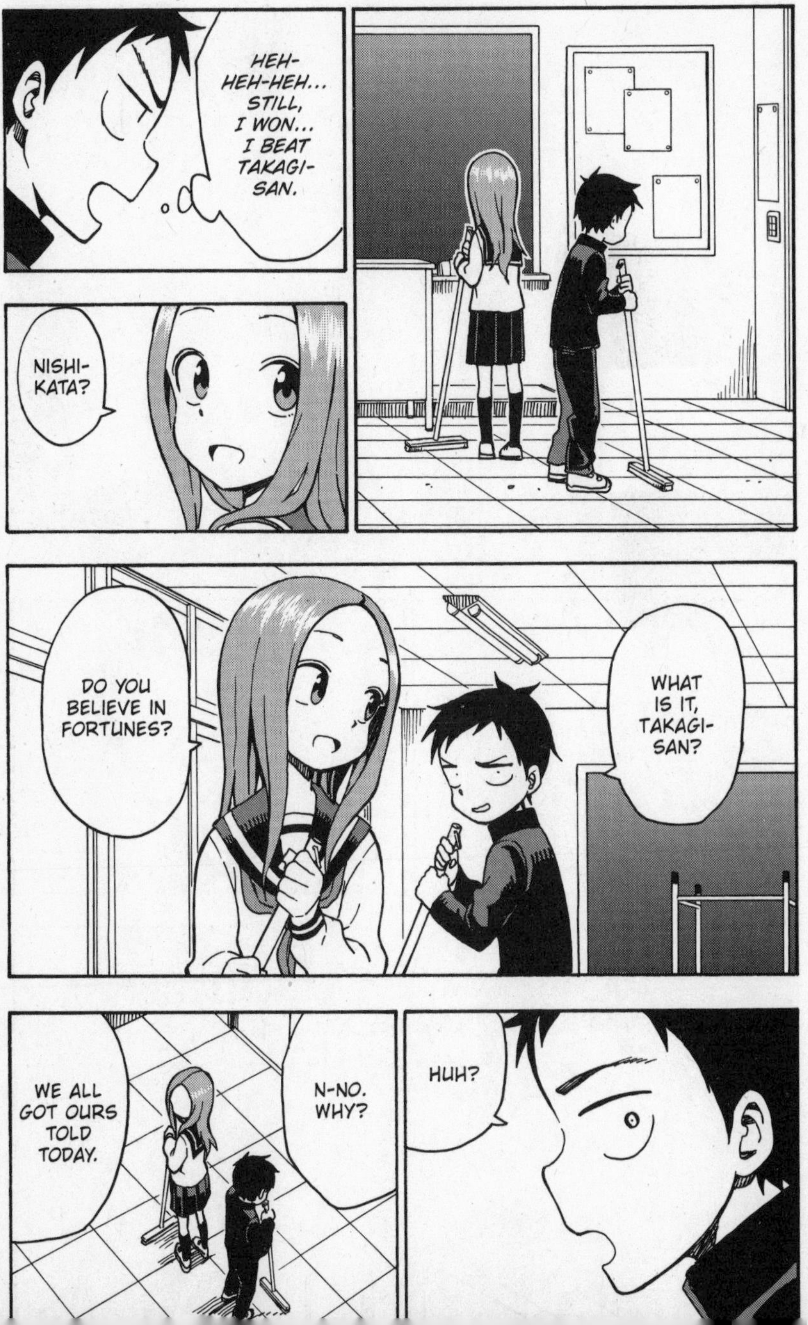
HEH-HEH-HEH... STILL, I WON... I BEAT TAKAGI-SAN.
NISHI-KATA?
WHAT IS IT, TAKAGI-SAN?
DO YOU BELIEVE IN FORTUNES?
HUH?
N-NO. WHY?
WE ALL GOT OURS TOLD TODAY.

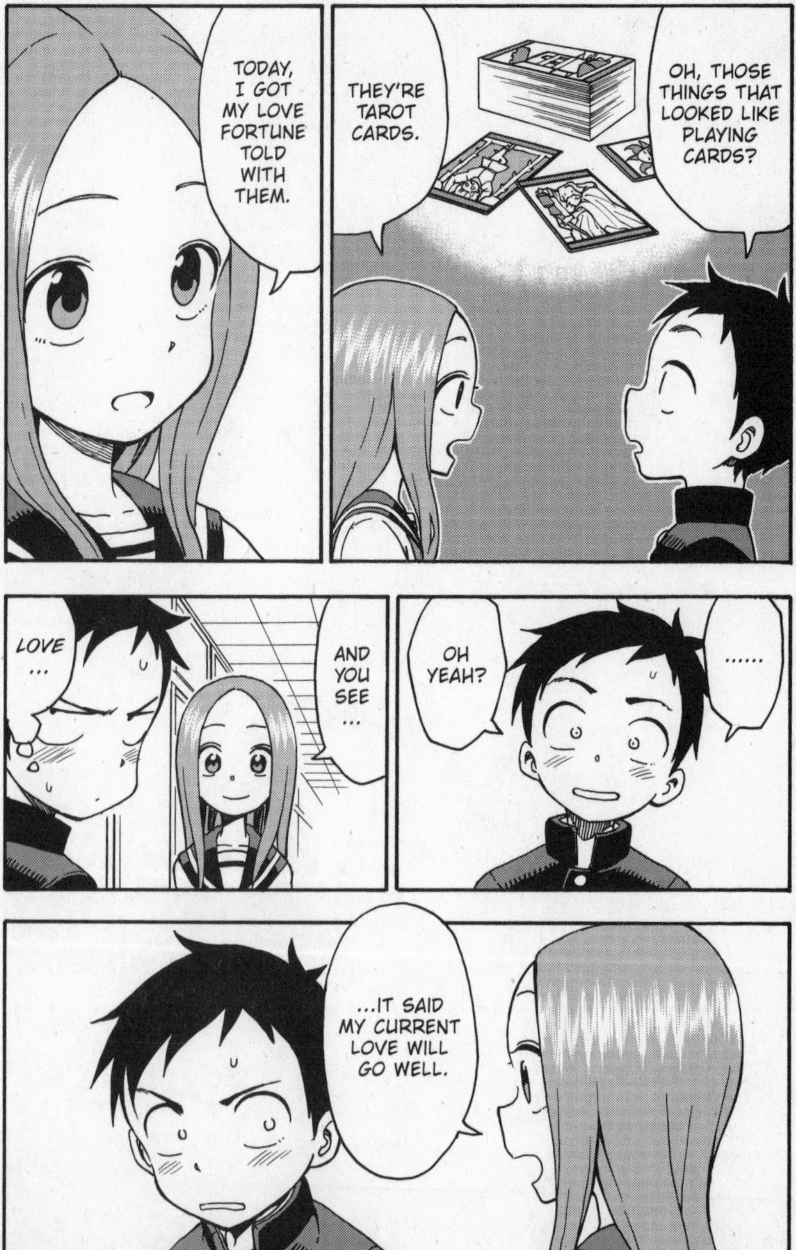
OH, THOSE THINGS THAT LOOKED LIKE PLAYING CARDS?
THEY'RE TAROT CARDS.
TODAY, I GOT MY LOVE FORTUNE TOLD WITH THEM.
......
OH YEAH?
AND YOU SEE ...
LOVE ...
...IT SAID MY CURRENT LOVE WILL GO WELL.

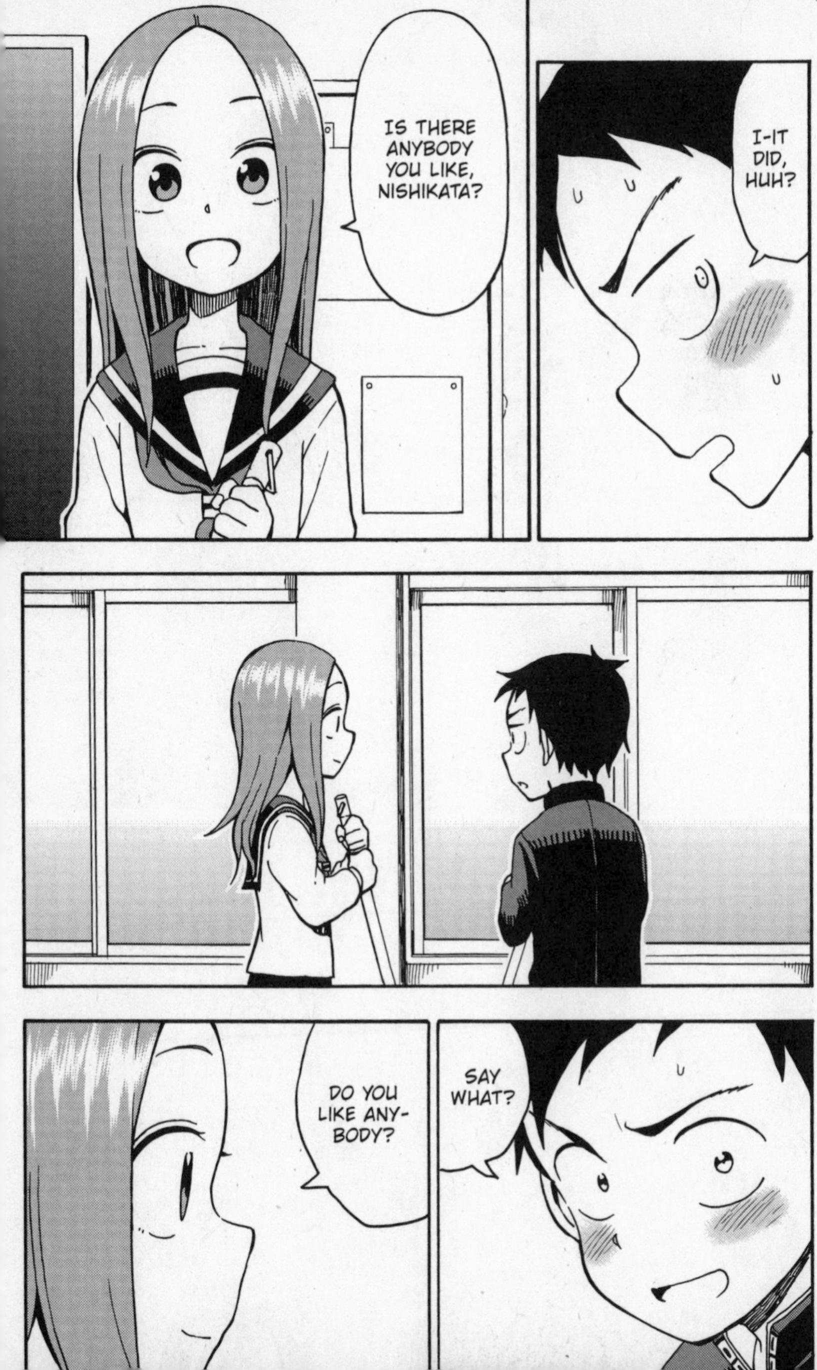
I-IT DID, HUH?
IS THERE ANYBODY YOU LIKE, NISHIKATA?
SAY WHAT?
DO YOU LIKE ANY-BODY?

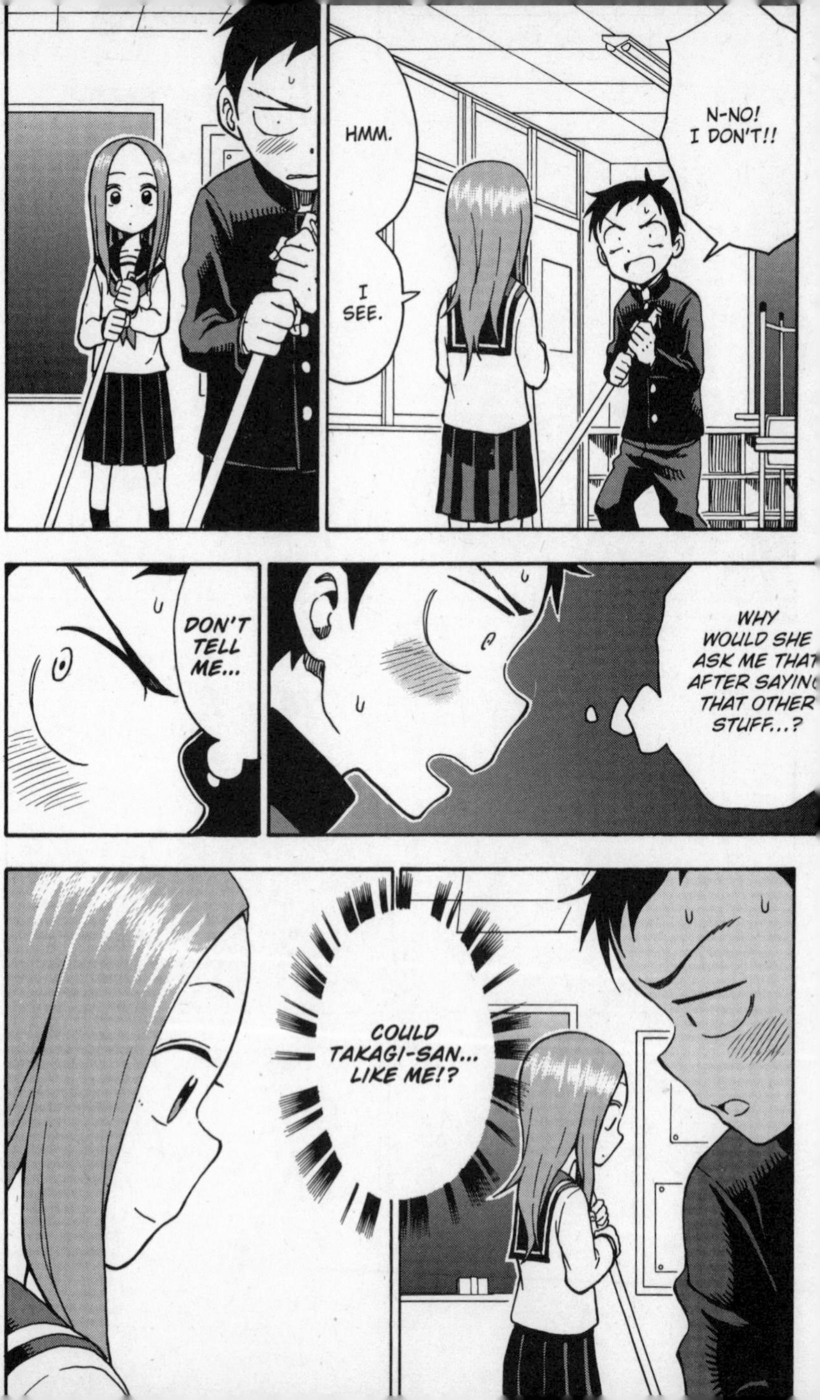
N-NO! I DON'T!!
HMM.
I SEE.
WHY WOULD SHE ASK ME THAT AFTER SAYING THAT OTHER STUFF...?
DON'T TELL ME...
COULD TAKAGI-SAN... LIKE ME!?

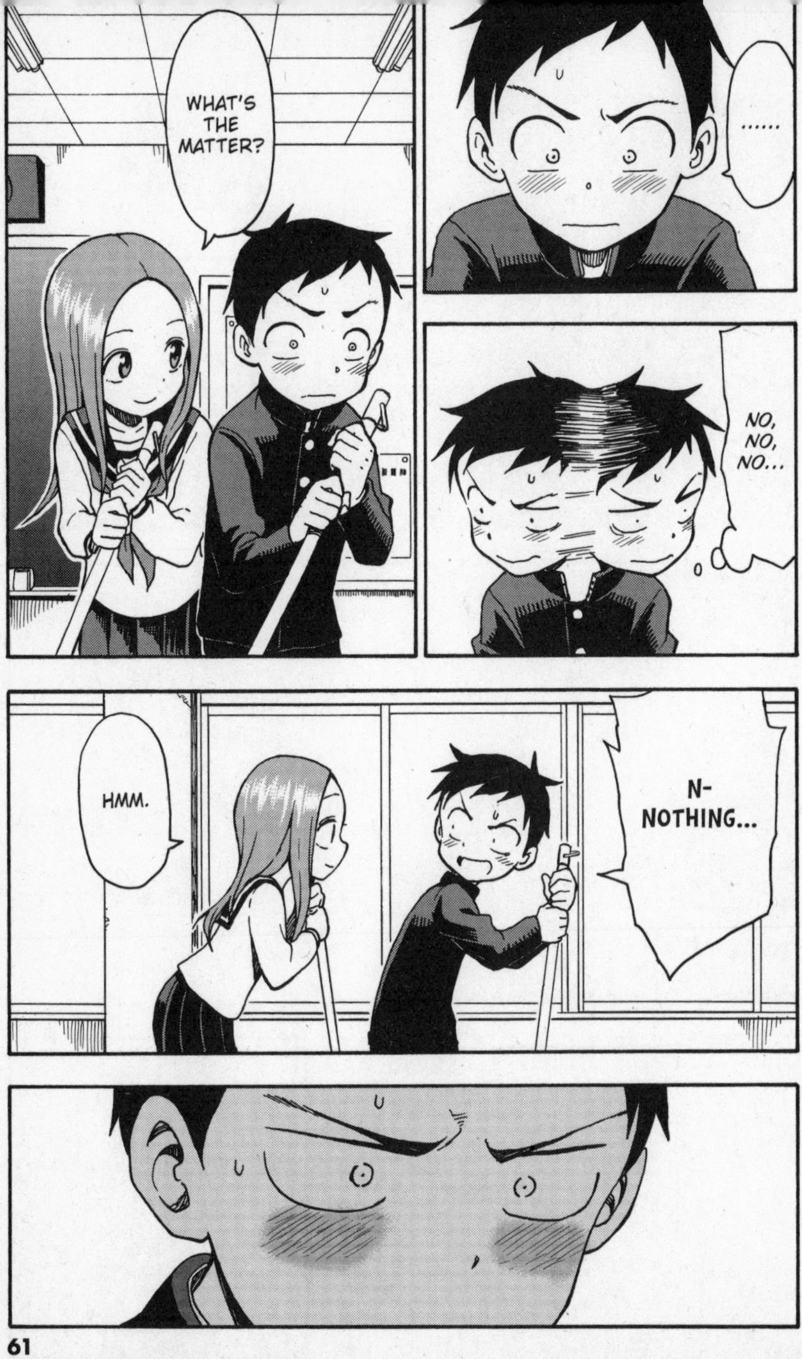
......
NO, NO, NO...
WHAT'S THE MATTER?
N- NOTHING...
HMM.

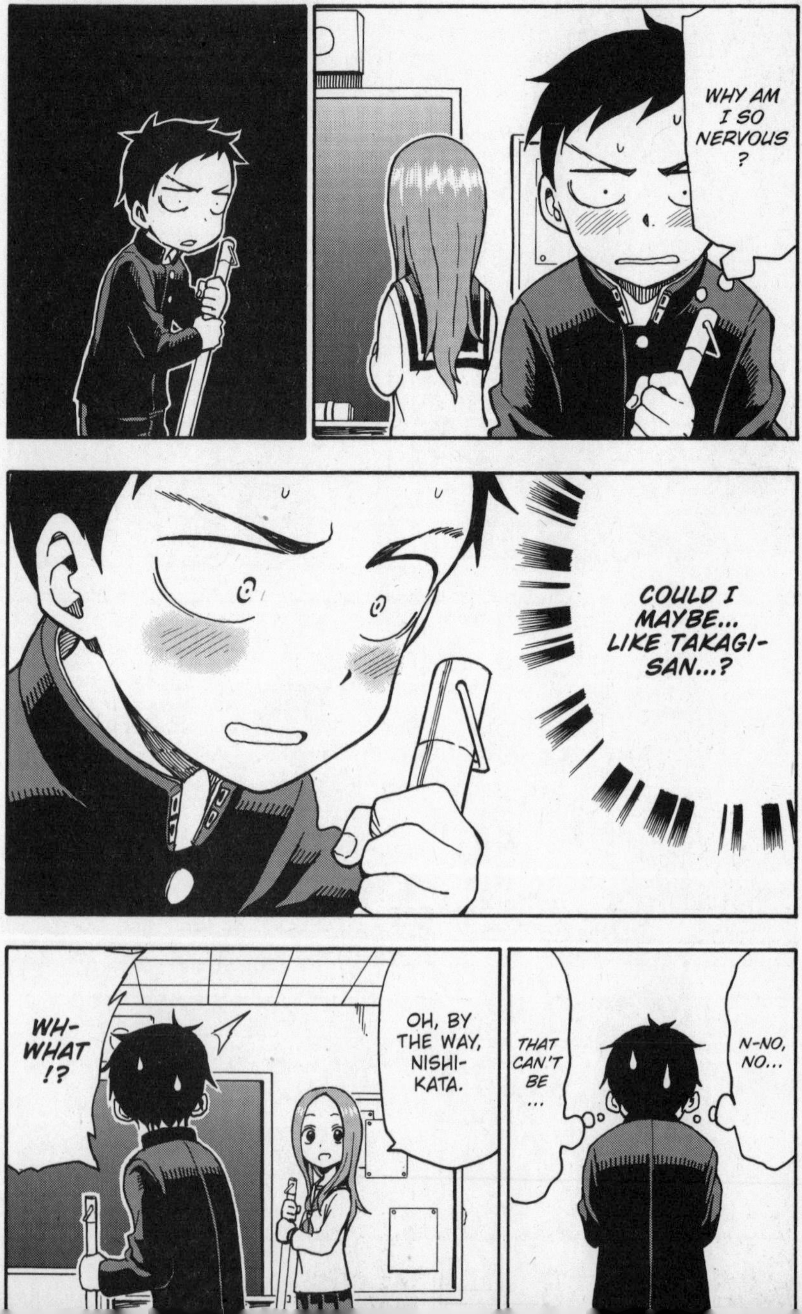
WHY AM I SO NERVOUS?
COULD I MAYBE... LIKE TAKAGI-SAN...?
N-NO, NO...
THAT CAN'T BE ...
OH, BY THE WAY, NISHI-KATA.
WH-WHAT!?

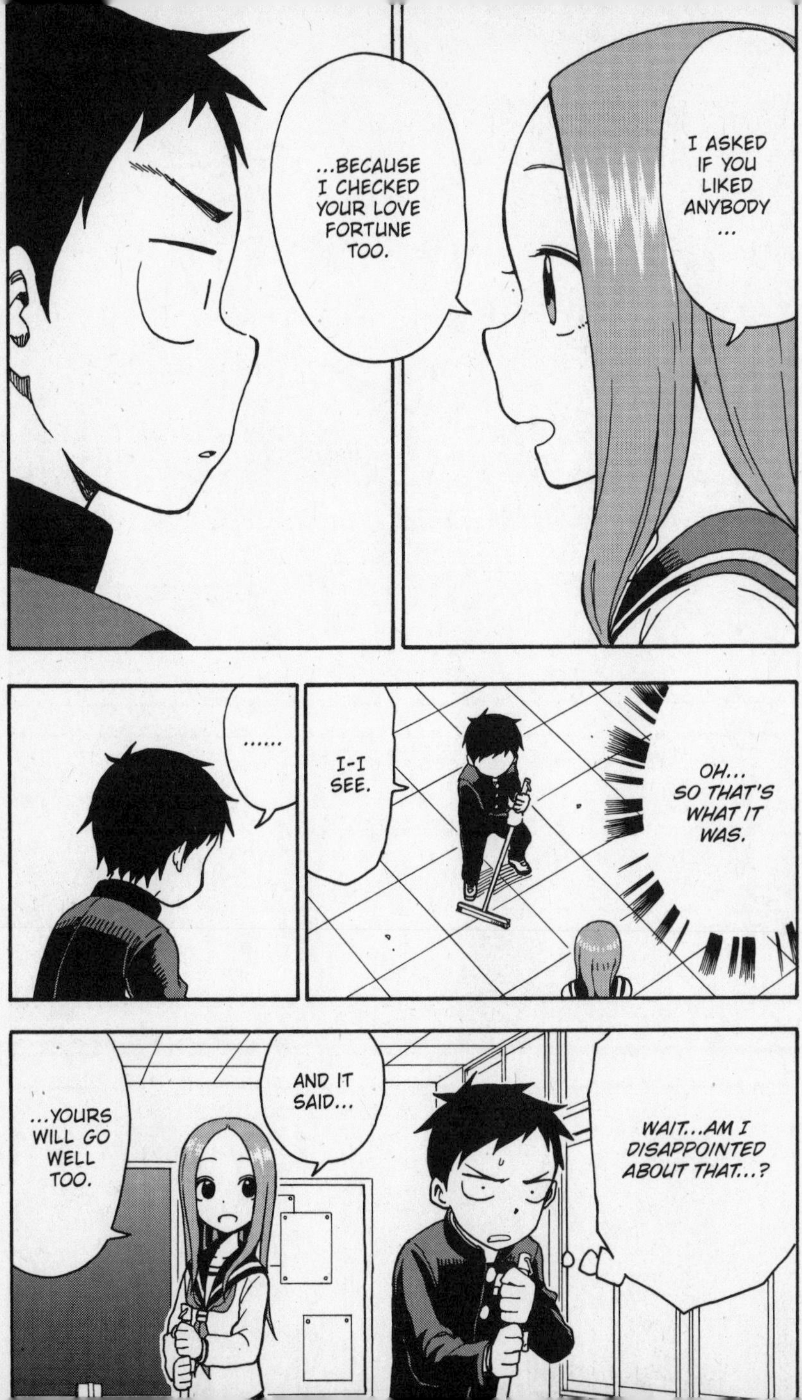
I ASKED IF YOU LIKED ANYBODY ...
...BECAUSE I CHECKED YOUR LOVE FORTUNE TOO.
OH... SO THAT'S WHAT IT WAS.
I-I SEE.
......
WAIT...AM I DISAPPOINTED ABOUT THAT...?
AND IT SAID...
...YOURS WILL GO WELL TOO.

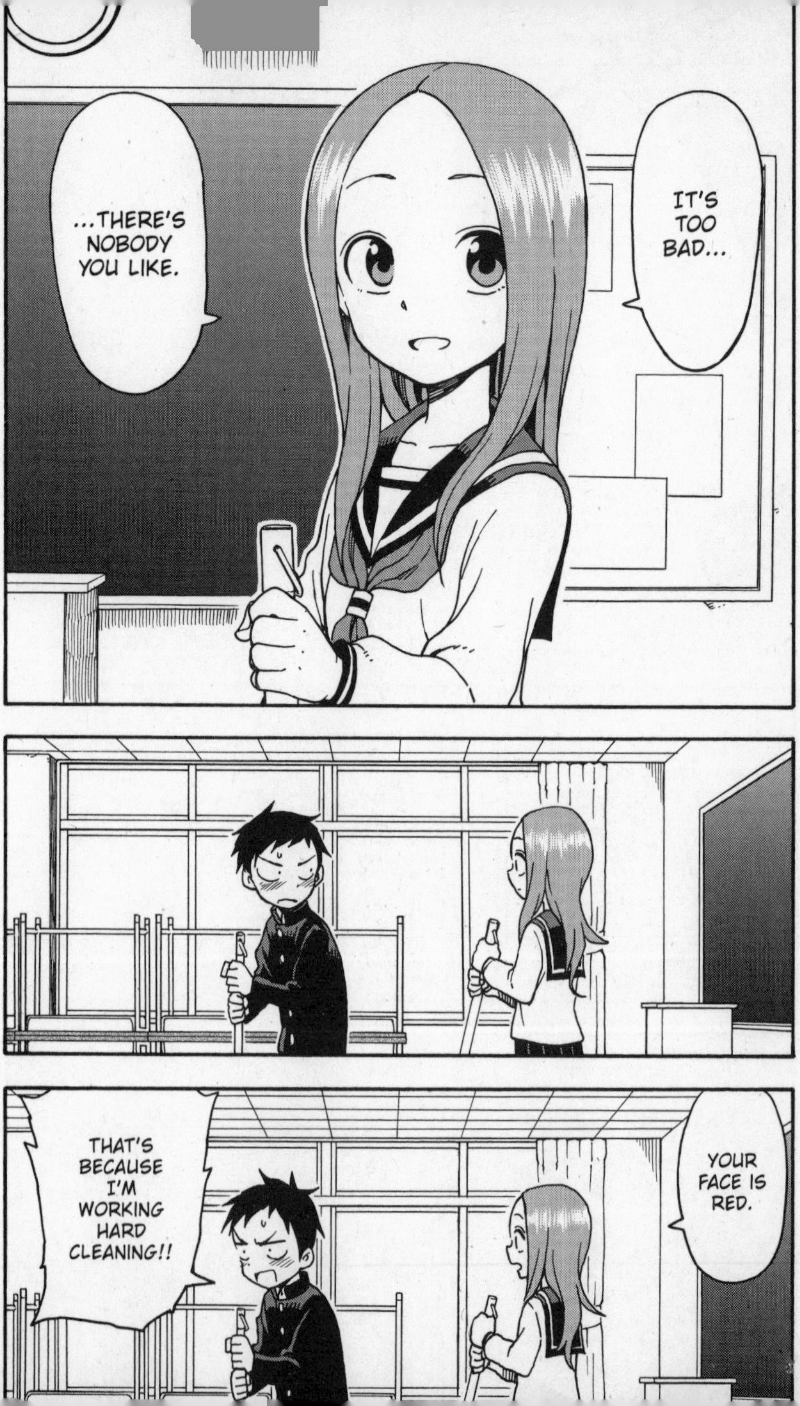
IT'S TOO BAD...
...THERE'S NOBODY YOU LIKE.
YOUR FACE IS RED.
THAT'S BECAUSE I'M WORKING HARD CLEANING!!

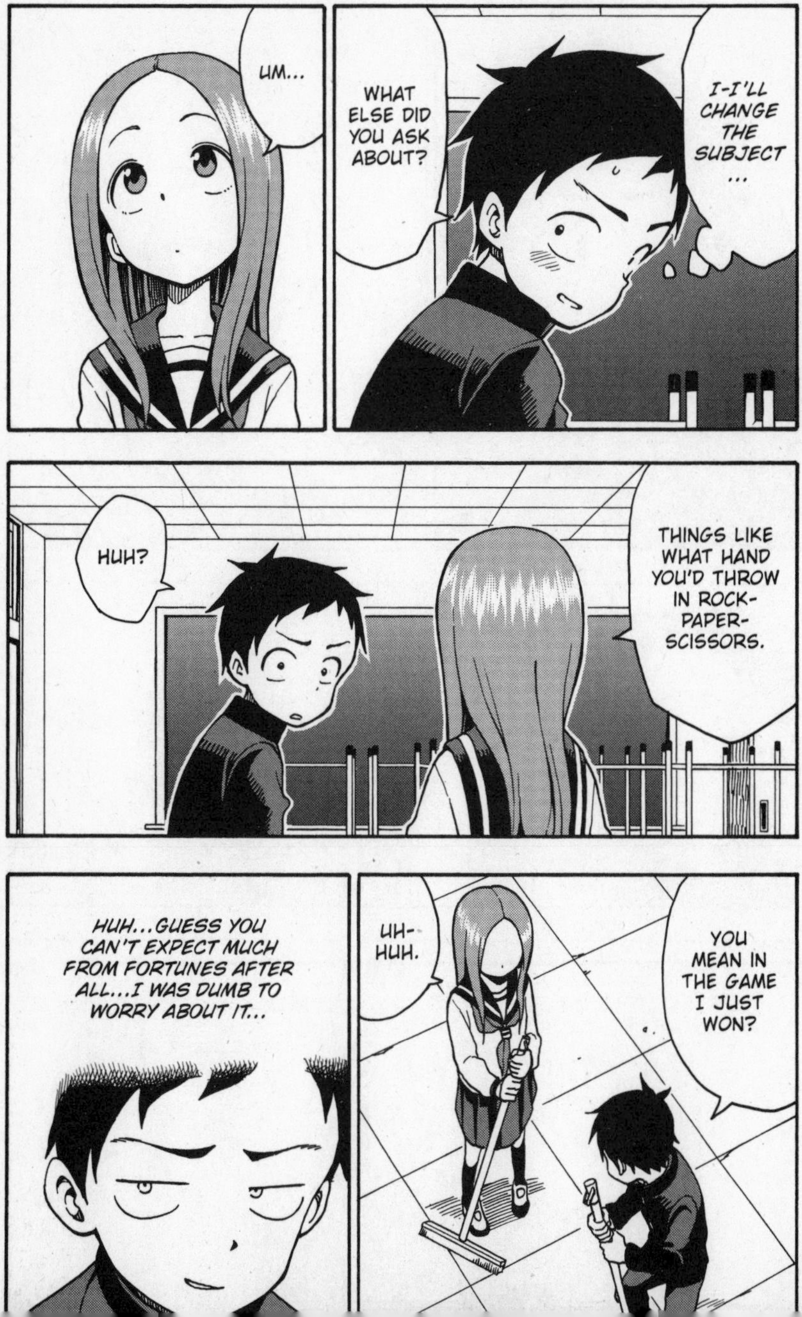
I-I'LL CHANGE THE SUBJECT...
WHAT ELSE DID YOU ASK ABOUT?
UM...
THINGS LIKE WHAT HAND YOU'D THROW IN ROCK-PAPER-SCISSORS.
HUH?
YOU MEAN IN THE GAME I JUST WON?
UH-HUH.
HUH...GUESS YOU CAN'T EXPECT MUCH FROM FORTUNES AFTER ALL...I WAS DUMB TO WORRY ABOUT IT...

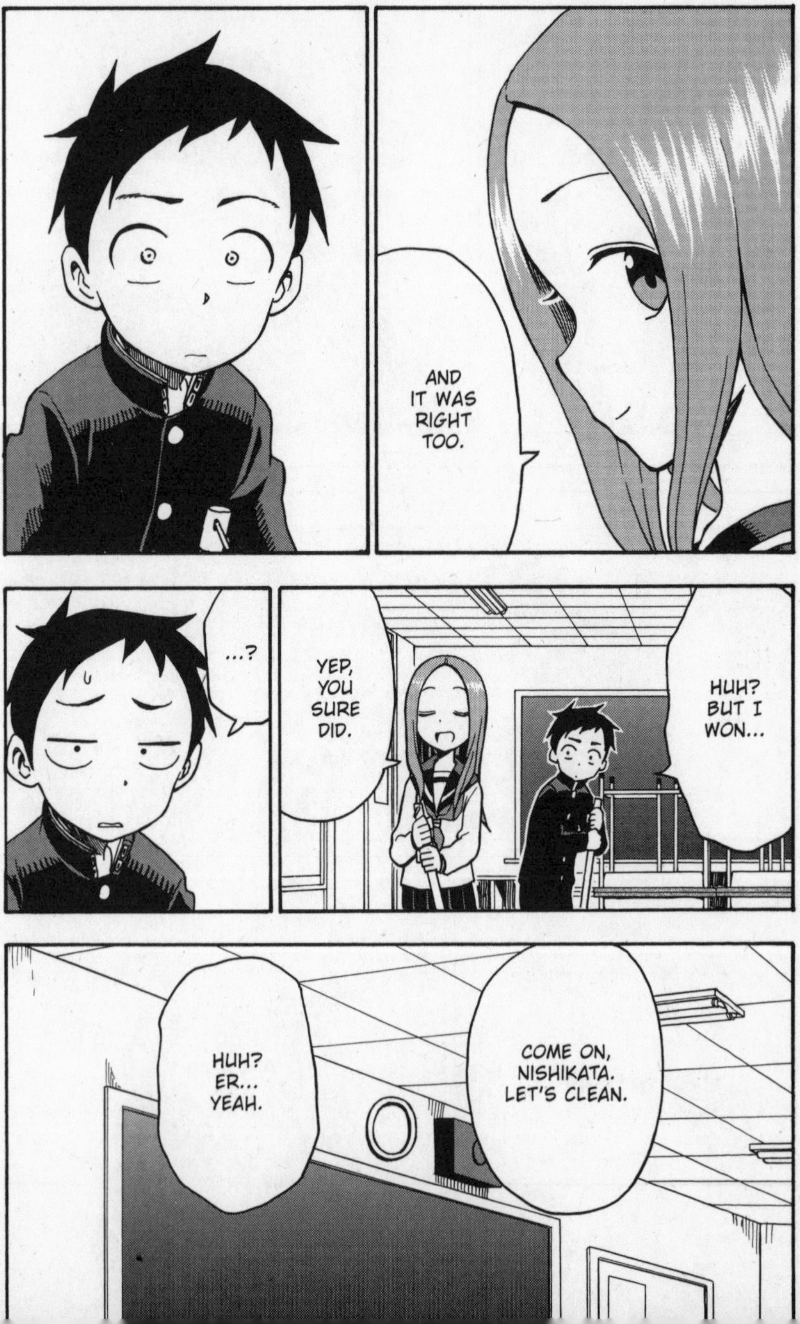
AND IT WAS RIGHT TOO.
HUH? BUT I WON...
YEP, YOU SURE DID.
...?
COME ON, NISHIKATA. LET'S CLEAN.
HUH? ER... YEAH.

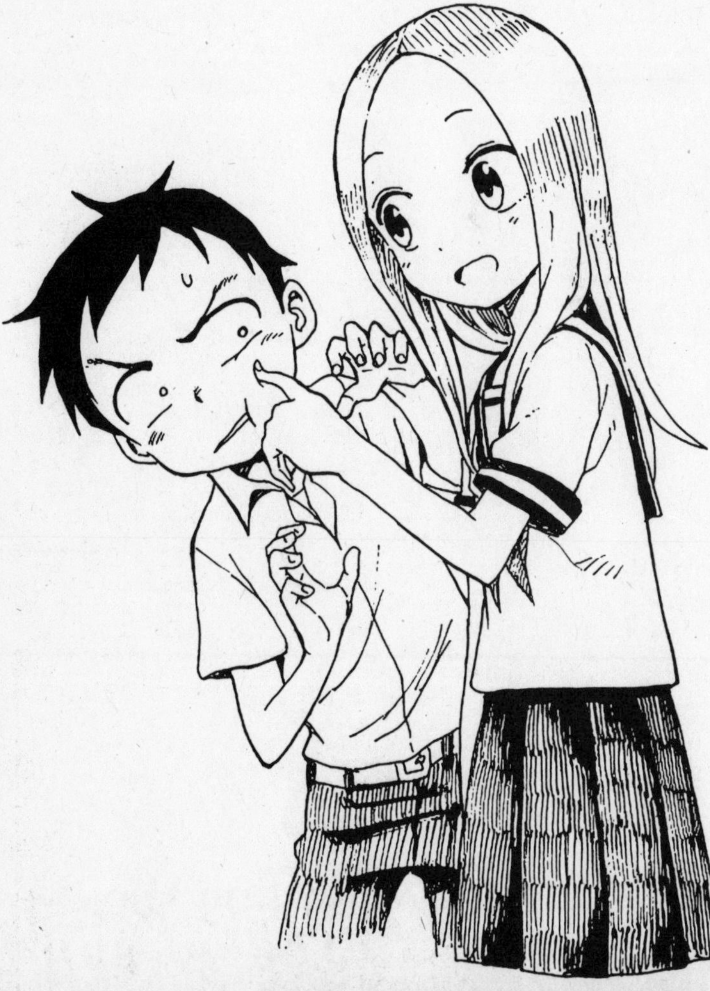

Teasing Master
Takagi-san

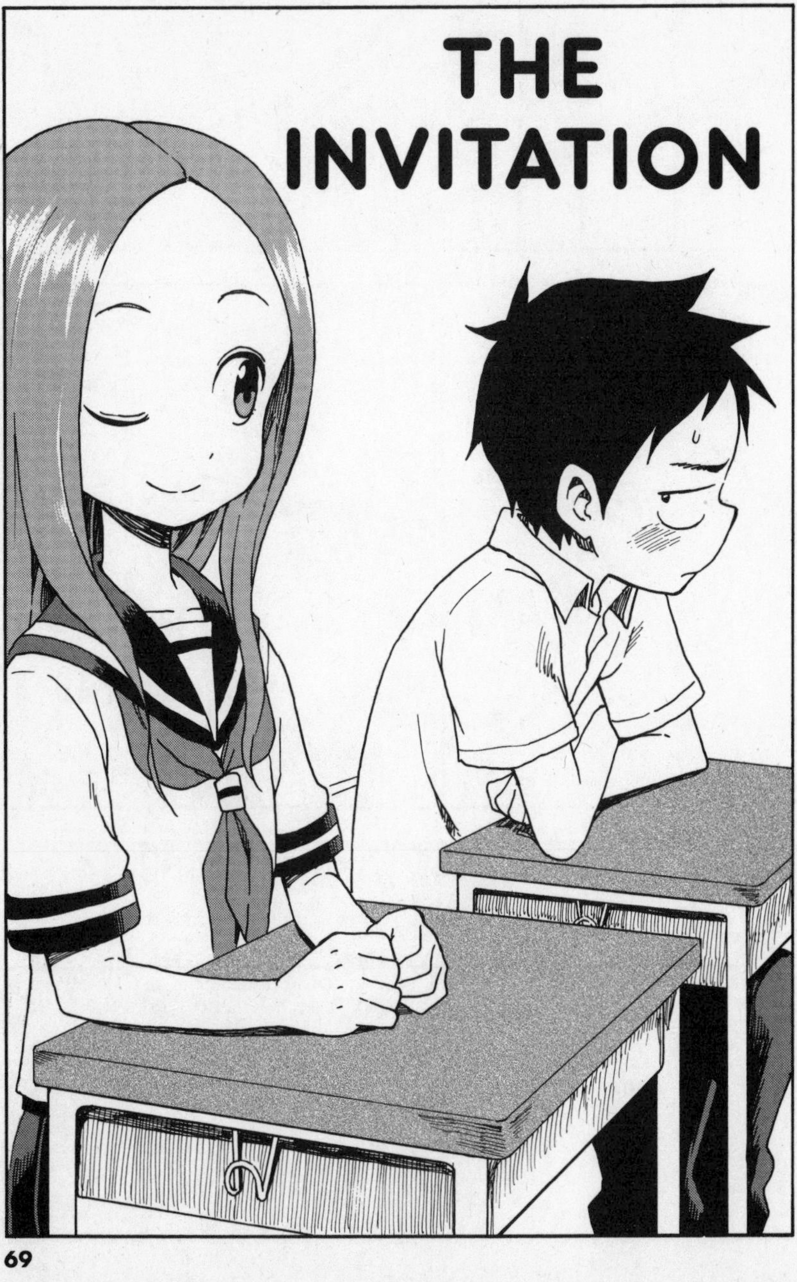
THE INVITATION

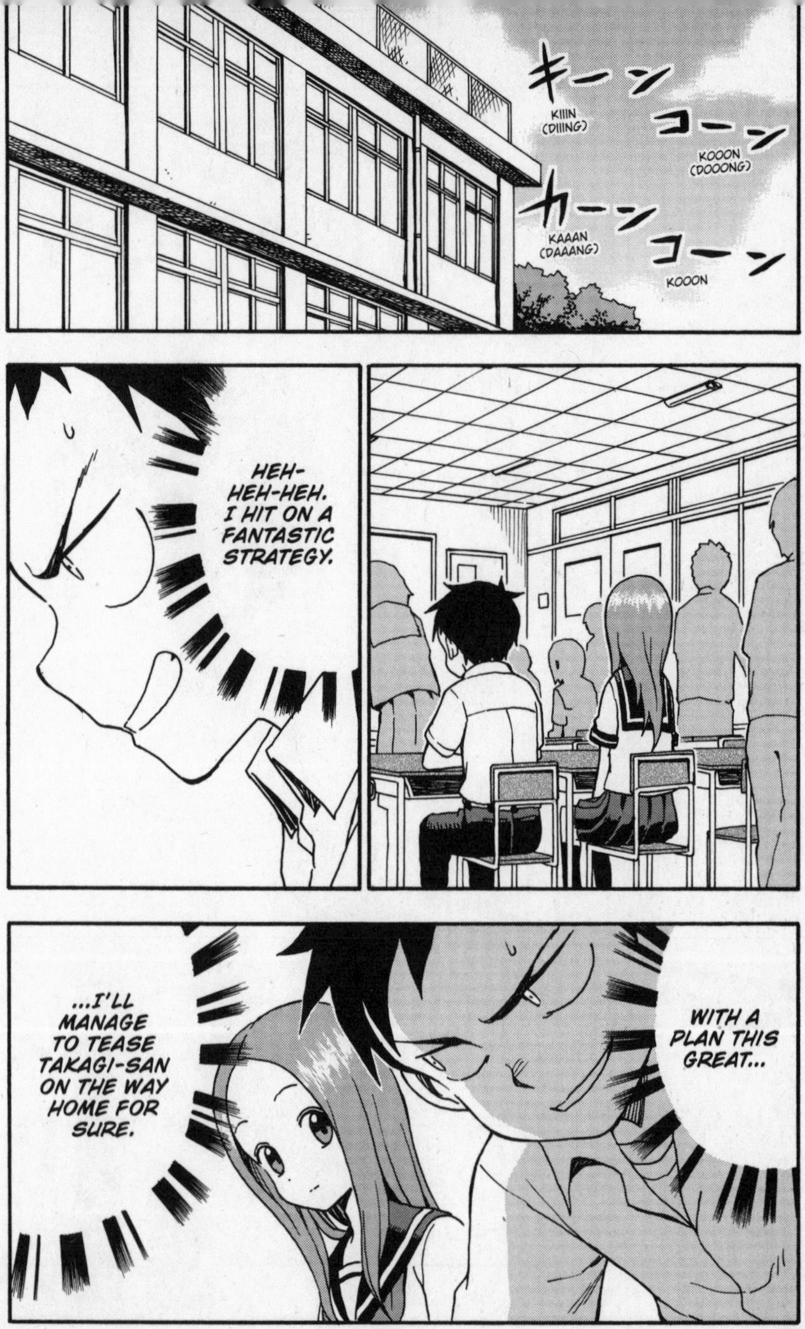
キーン
KIIIN (DIIING)
コーン
KOOON (DOOONG)
カーン
KAAAN (DAAANG)
コーン
KOOON
HEH-HEH-HEH. I HIT ON A FANTASTIC STRATEGY.
WITH A PLAN THIS GREAT...
...I'LL MANAGE TO TEASE TAKAGI-SAN ON THE WAY HOME FOR SURE.

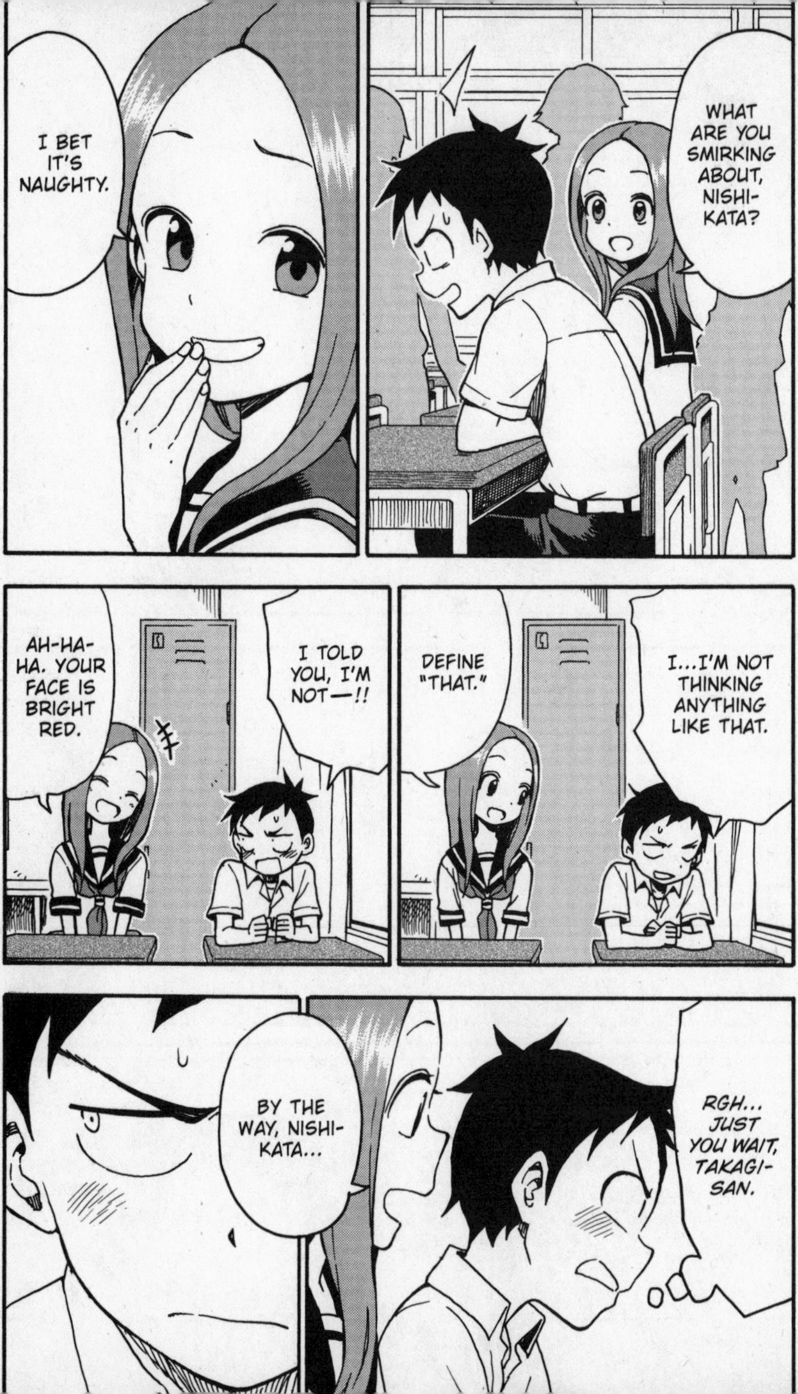
WHAT ARE YOU SMIRKING ABOUT, NISHI-KATA?
I BET IT'S NAUGHTY.
I...I'M NOT THINKING ANYTHING LIKE THAT.
DEFINE "THAT."
I TOLD YOU, I'M NOT—!!
AH-HA-HA. YOUR FACE IS BRIGHT RED.
RGH... JUST YOU WAIT, TAKAGI-SAN.
BY THE WAY, NISHI-KATA...

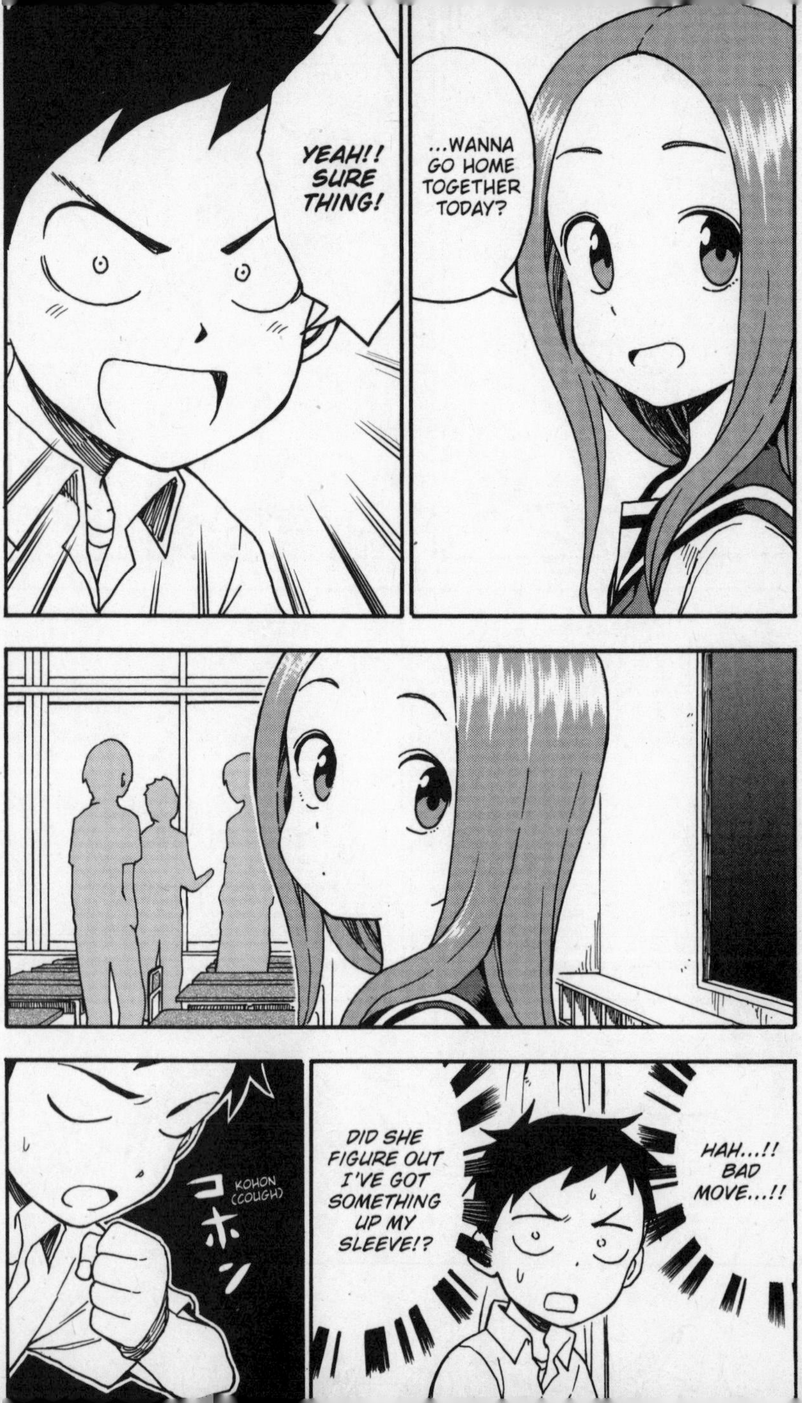
...WANNA GO HOME TOGETHER TODAY?
YEAH!! SURE THING!
HAH...!! BAD MOVE...!!
DID SHE FIGURE OUT I'VE GOT SOMETHING UP MY SLEEVE!?
コホン
KOHON (COUGH)

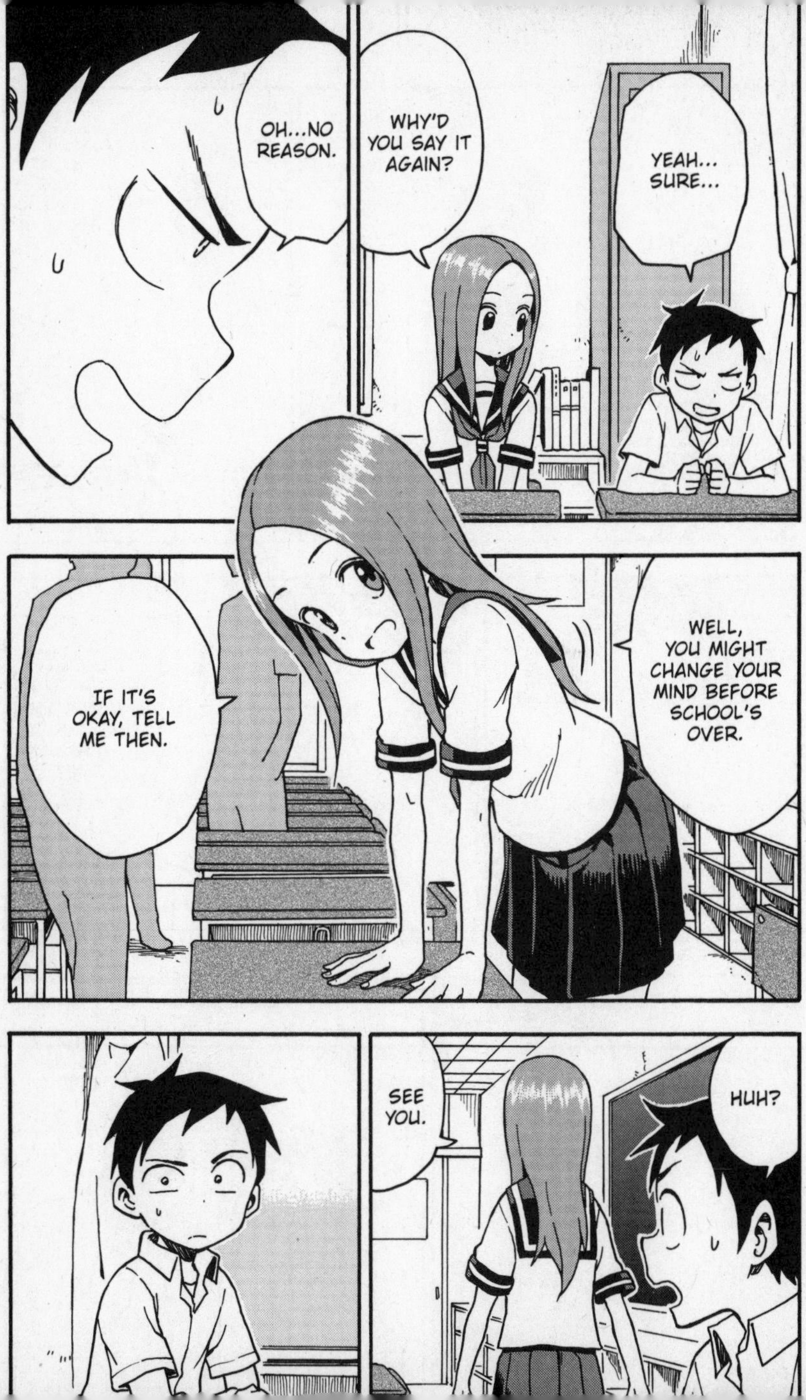
YEAH... SURE...
WHY'D YOU SAY IT AGAIN?
OH...NO REASON.
WELL, YOU MIGHT CHANGE YOUR MIND BEFORE SCHOOL'S OVER.
IF IT'S OKAY, TELL ME THEN.
HUH?
SEE YOU.

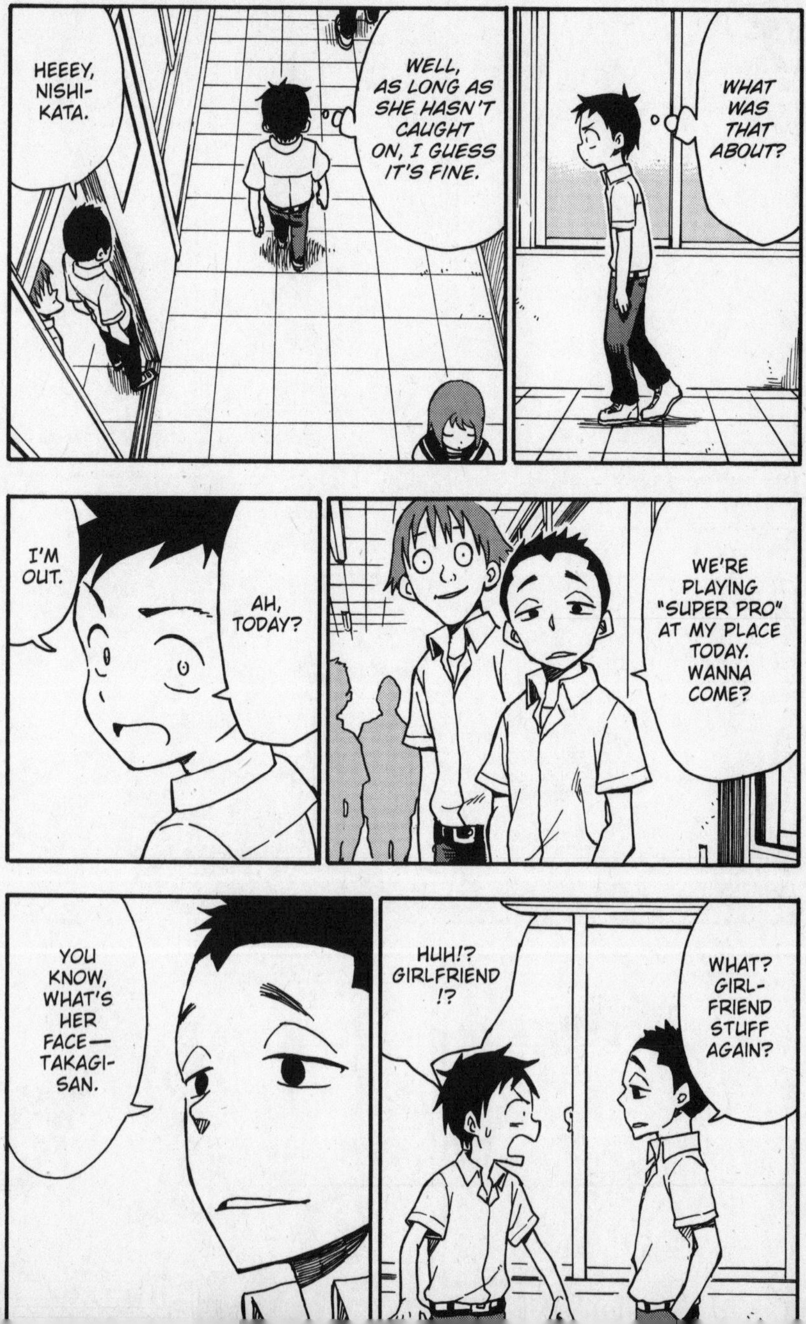
WHAT WAS THAT ABOUT?
WELL, AS LONG AS SHE HASN'T CAUGHT ON, I GUESS IT'S FINE.
HEEEY, NISHI-KATA.
WE'RE PLAYING "SUPER PRO" AT MY PLACE TODAY. WANNA COME?
AH, TODAY?
I'M OUT.
WHAT? GIRL-FRIEND STUFF AGAIN?
HUH!? GIRLFRIEND !?
YOU KNOW, WHAT'S HER FACE—TAKAGI-SAN.

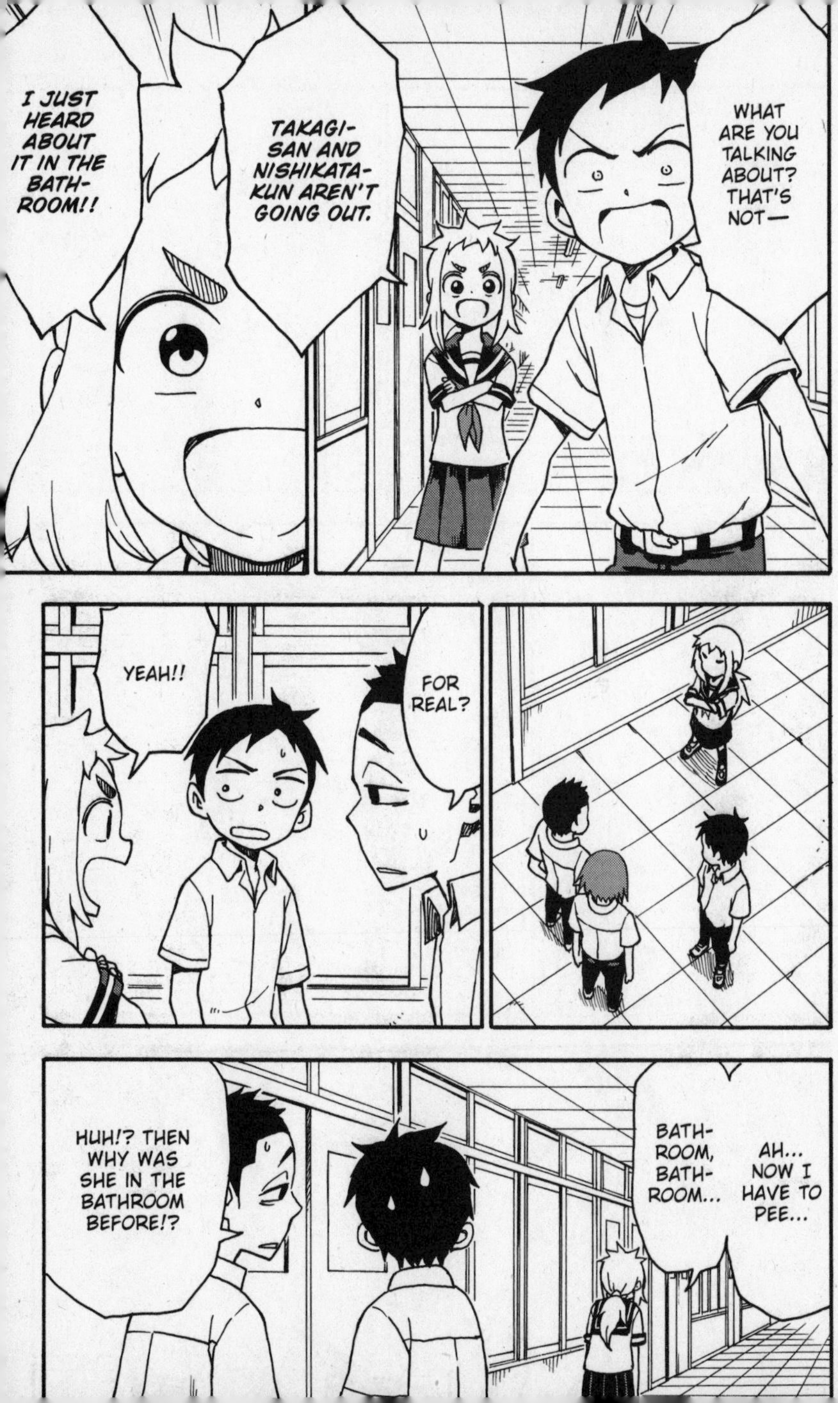
WHAT ARE YOU TALKING ABOUT? THAT'S NOT—
TAKAGI-SAN AND NISHIKATA-KUN AREN'T GOING OUT.
I JUST HEARD ABOUT IT IN THE BATHROOM!!
FOR REAL?
YEAH!!
BATHROOM, BATHROOM... AH... NOW I HAVE TO PEE...
HUH!? THEN WHY WAS SHE IN THE BATHROOM BEFORE!?

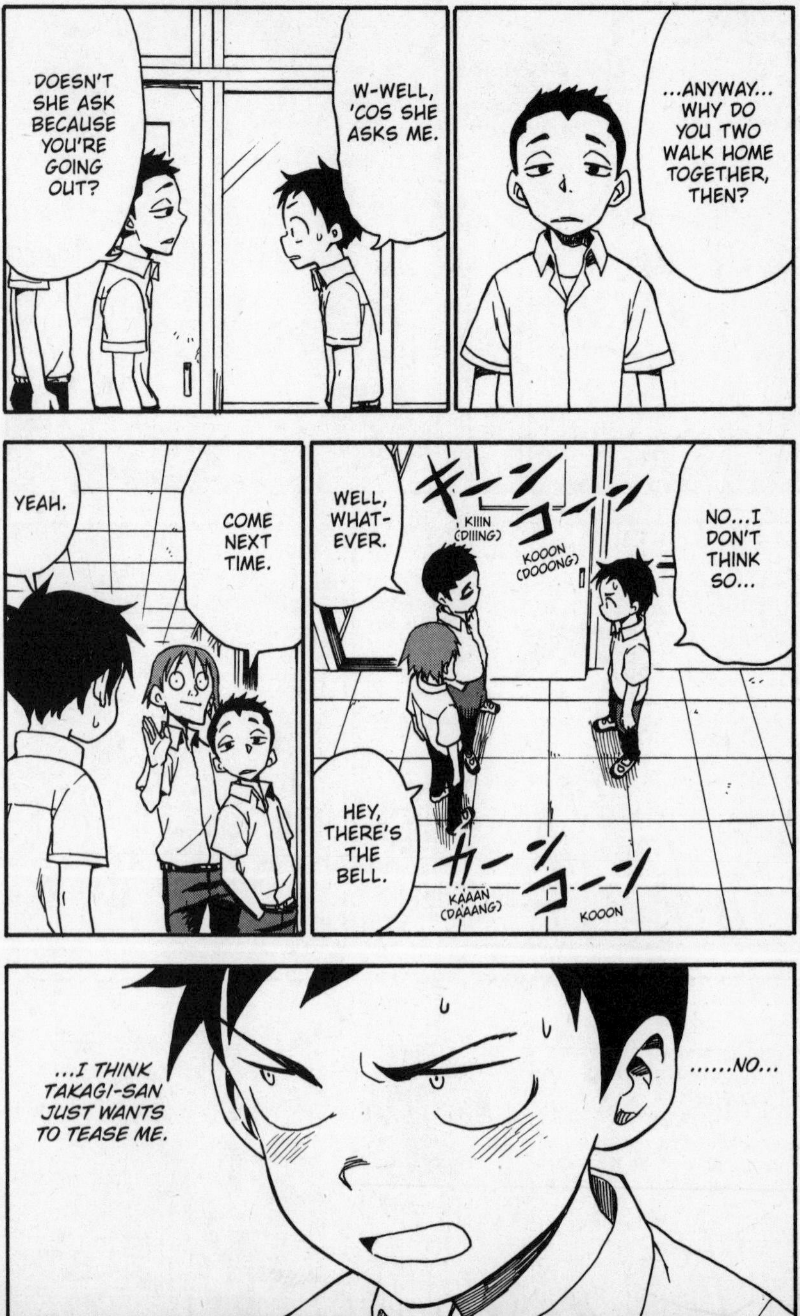
...ANYWAY... WHY DO YOU TWO WALK HOME TOGETHER, THEN?
W-WELL, 'COS SHE ASKS ME.
DOESN'T SHE ASK BECAUSE YOU'RE GOING OUT?
NO...I DON'T THINK SO...
KIIIN (DIIING)
KOOON (DOOONG)
WELL, WHAT-EVER.
HEY, THERE'S THE BELL.
KAAAN (DAAANG)
KOOON
COME NEXT TIME.
YEAH.
......NO...
...I THINK TAKAGI-SAN JUST WANTS TO TEASE ME.

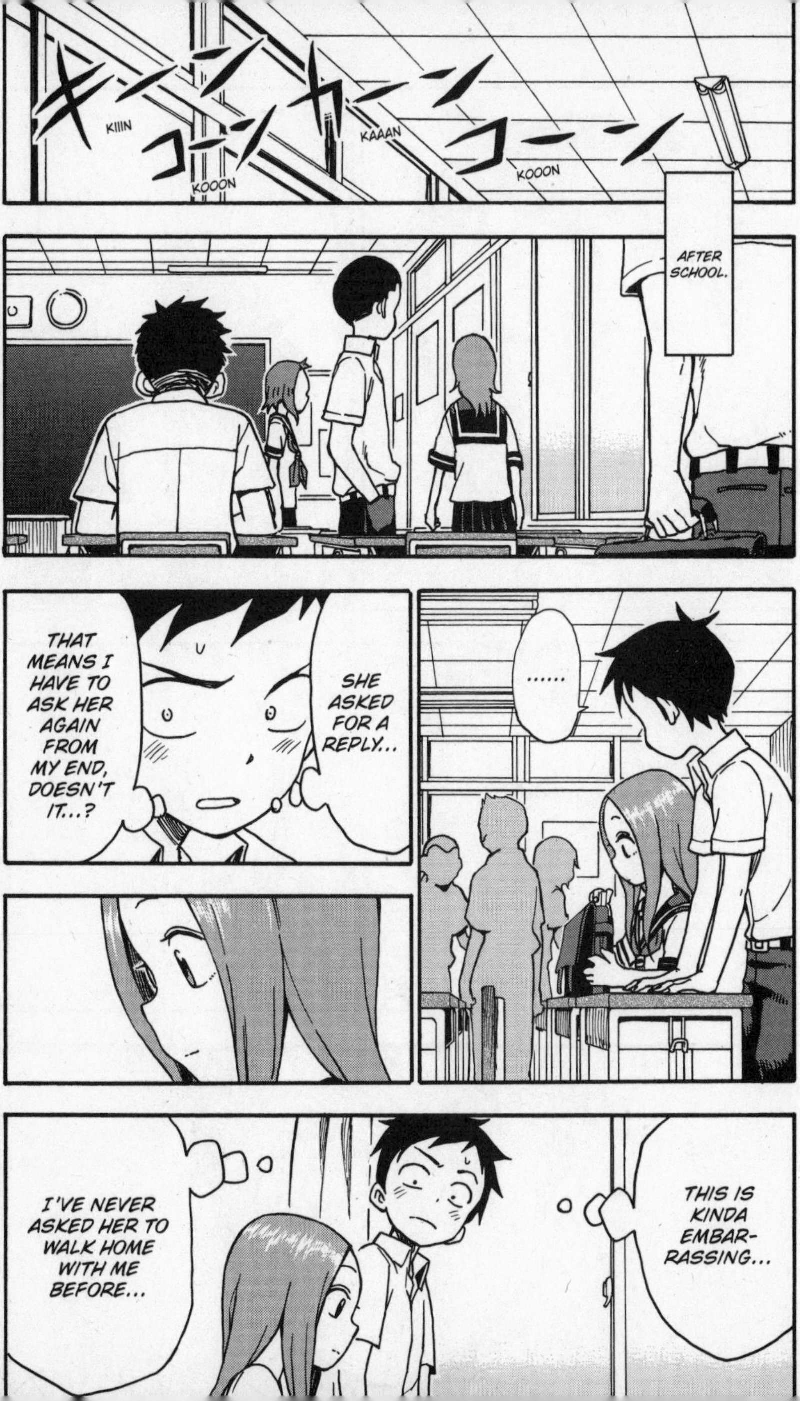
KIIIN
KOOON
KAAAN
KOOON
AFTER SCHOOL.
......
SHE ASKED FOR A REPLY...
THAT MEANS I HAVE TO ASK HER AGAIN FROM MY END, DOESN'T IT...?
THIS IS KINDA EMBAR-RASSING...
I'VE NEVER ASKED HER TO WALK HOME WITH ME BEFORE...

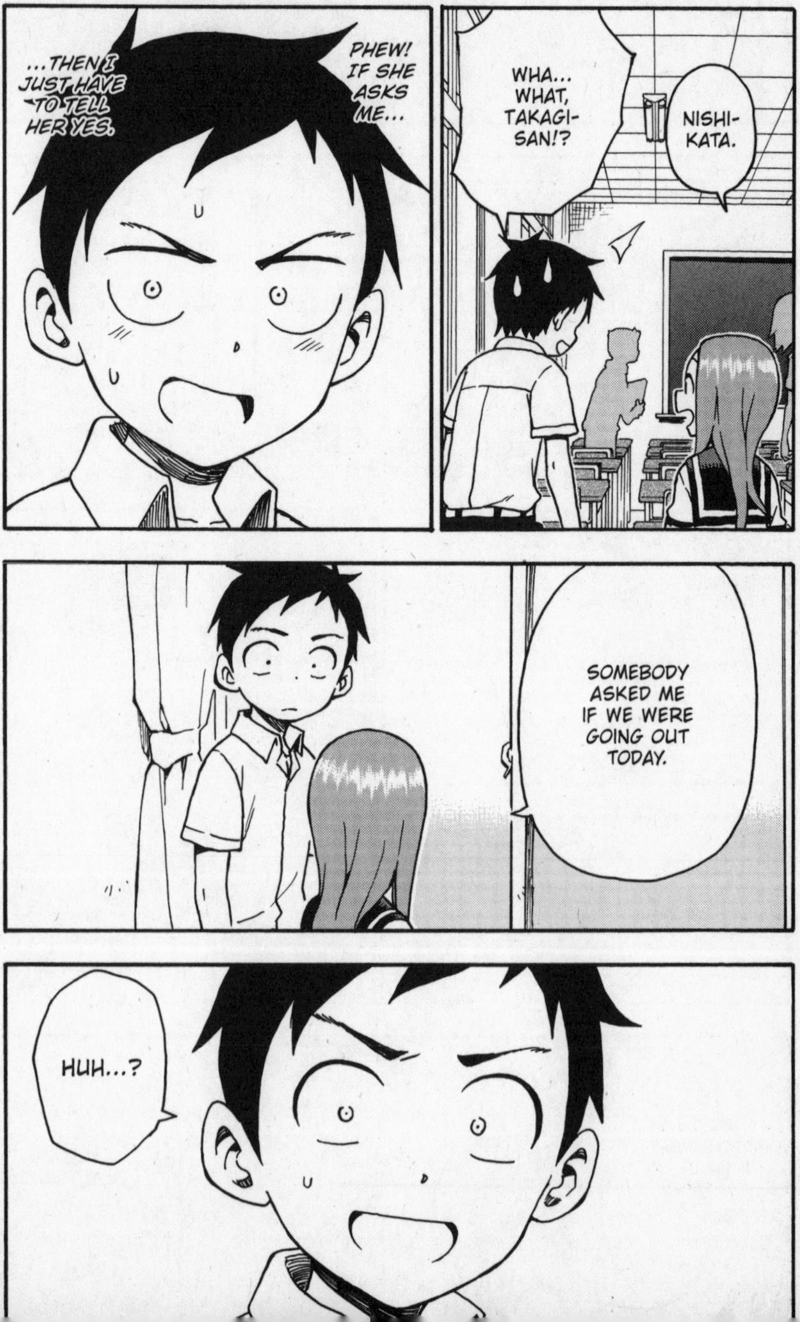
NISHI-KATA.
WHA... WHAT, TAKAGI-SAN!?
PHEW! IF SHE ASKS ME...
...THEN I JUST HAVE TO TELL HER YES.
SOMEBODY ASKED ME IF WE WERE GOING OUT TODAY.
HUH...?

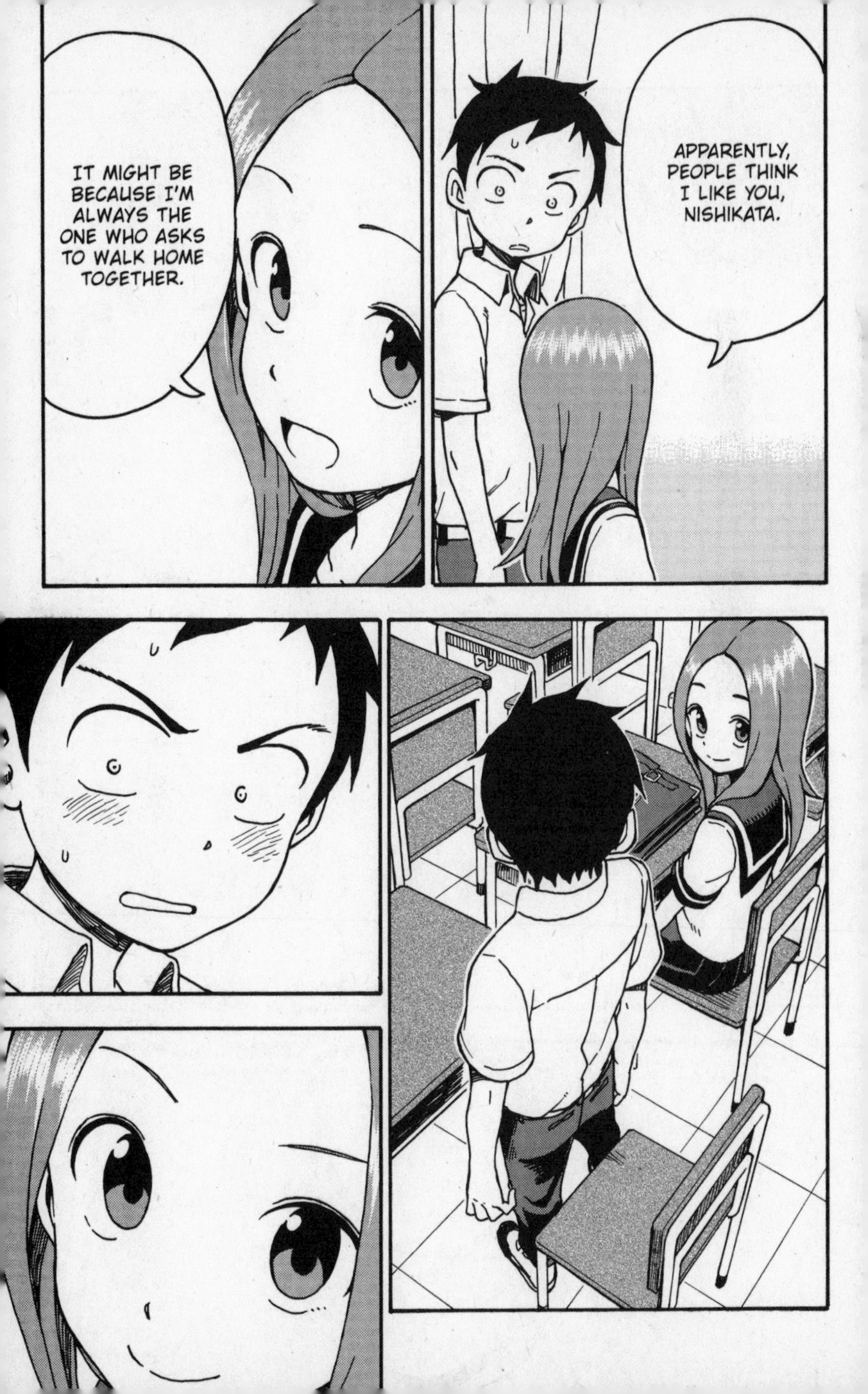
APPARENTLY, PEOPLE THINK I LIKE YOU, NISHIKATA.
IT MIGHT BE BECAUSE I'M ALWAYS THE ONE WHO ASKS TO WALK HOME TOGETHER.

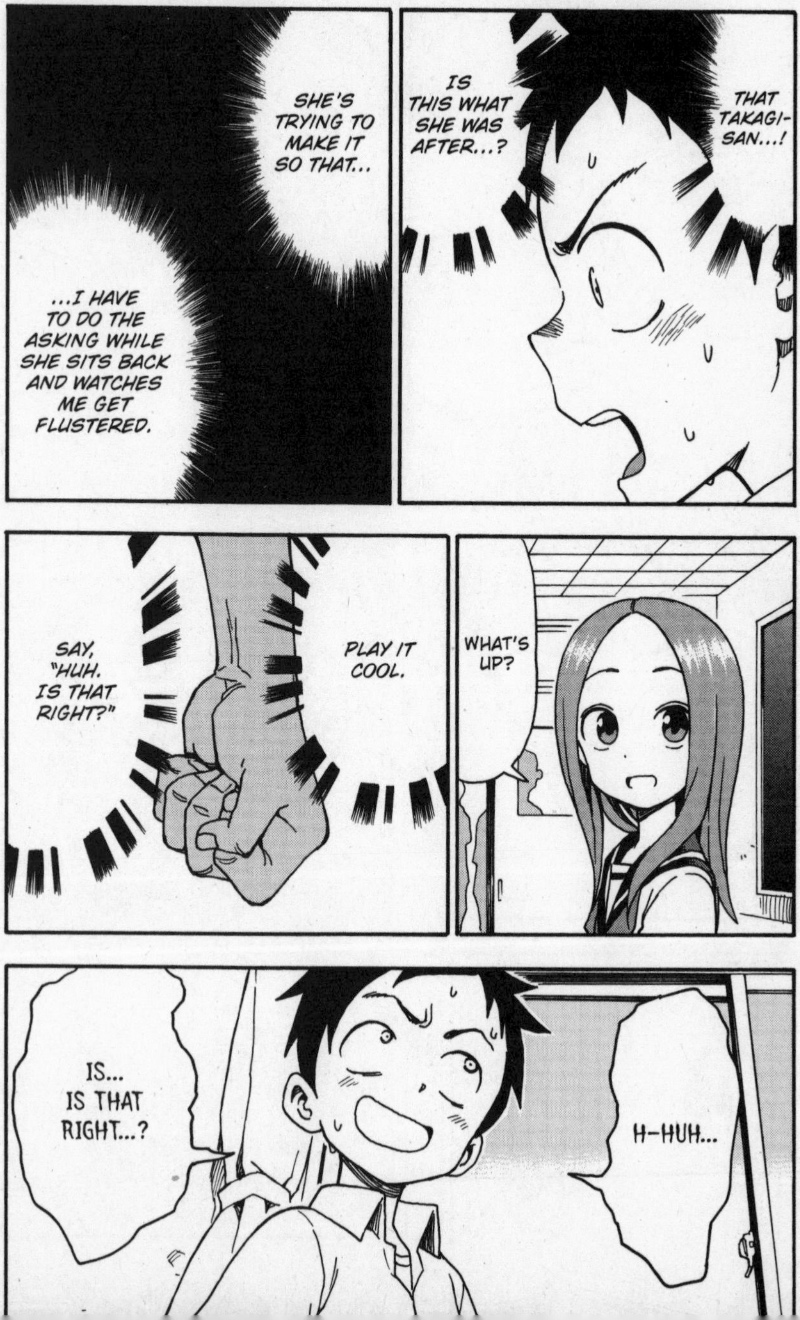
THAT TAKAGI-SAN...!
IS THIS WHAT SHE WAS AFTER...?
SHE'S TRYING TO MAKE IT SO THAT...
...I HAVE TO DO THE ASKING WHILE SHE SITS BACK AND WATCHES ME GET FLUSTERED.
WHAT'S UP?
PLAY IT COOL.
SAY, "HUH. IS THAT RIGHT?"
H-HUH...
IS... IS THAT RIGHT...?

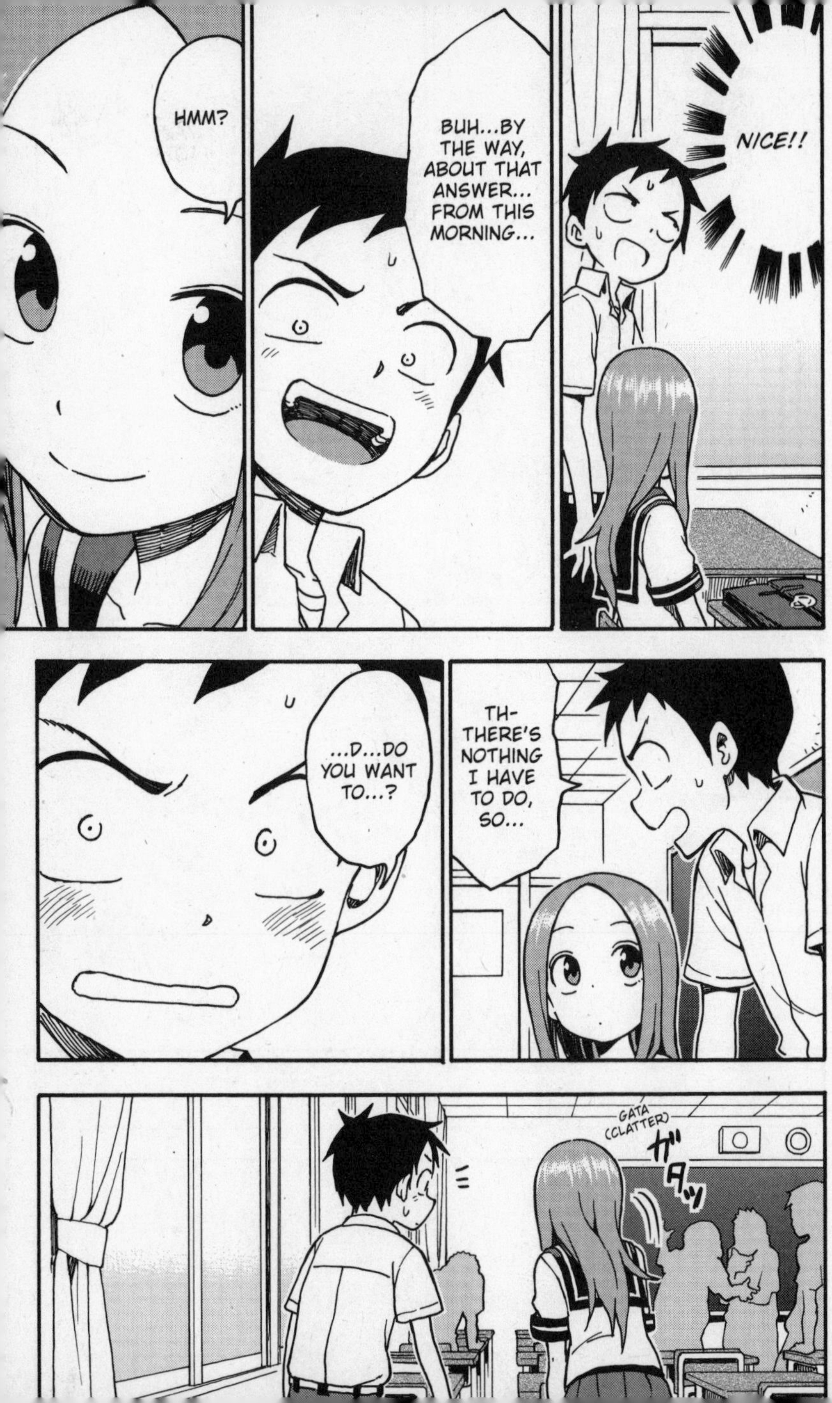
NICE!!
BUH...BY THE WAY, ABOUT THAT ANSWER... FROM THIS MORNING...
HMM?
TH-THERE'S NOTHING I HAVE TO DO, SO...
...D...DO YOU WANT TO...?
GATA (CLATTER)

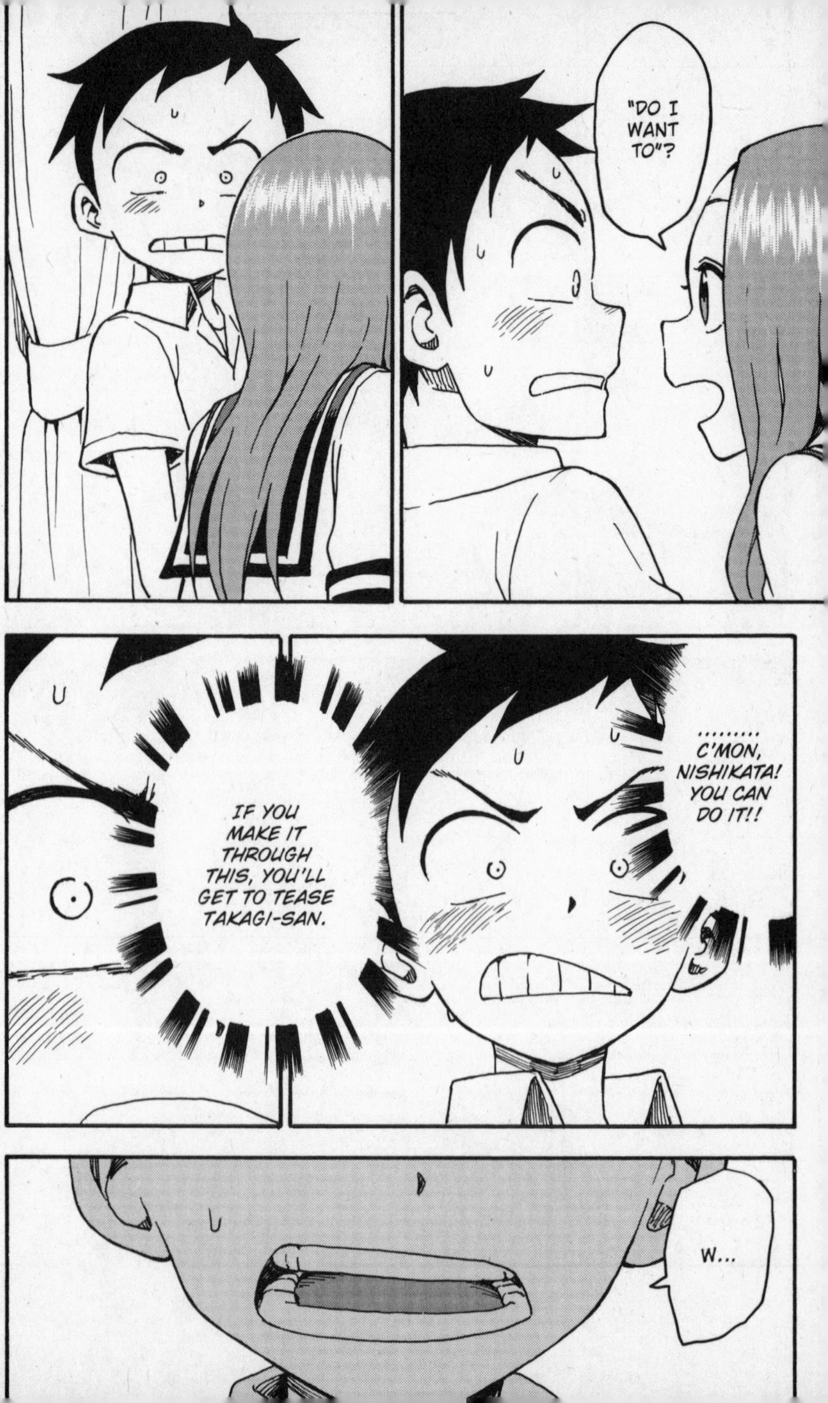
"DO I WANT TO"?
....
C'MON, NISHIKATA! YOU CAN DO IT!!
IF YOU MAKE IT THROUGH THIS, YOU'LL GET TO TEASE TAKAGI-SAN.
W...

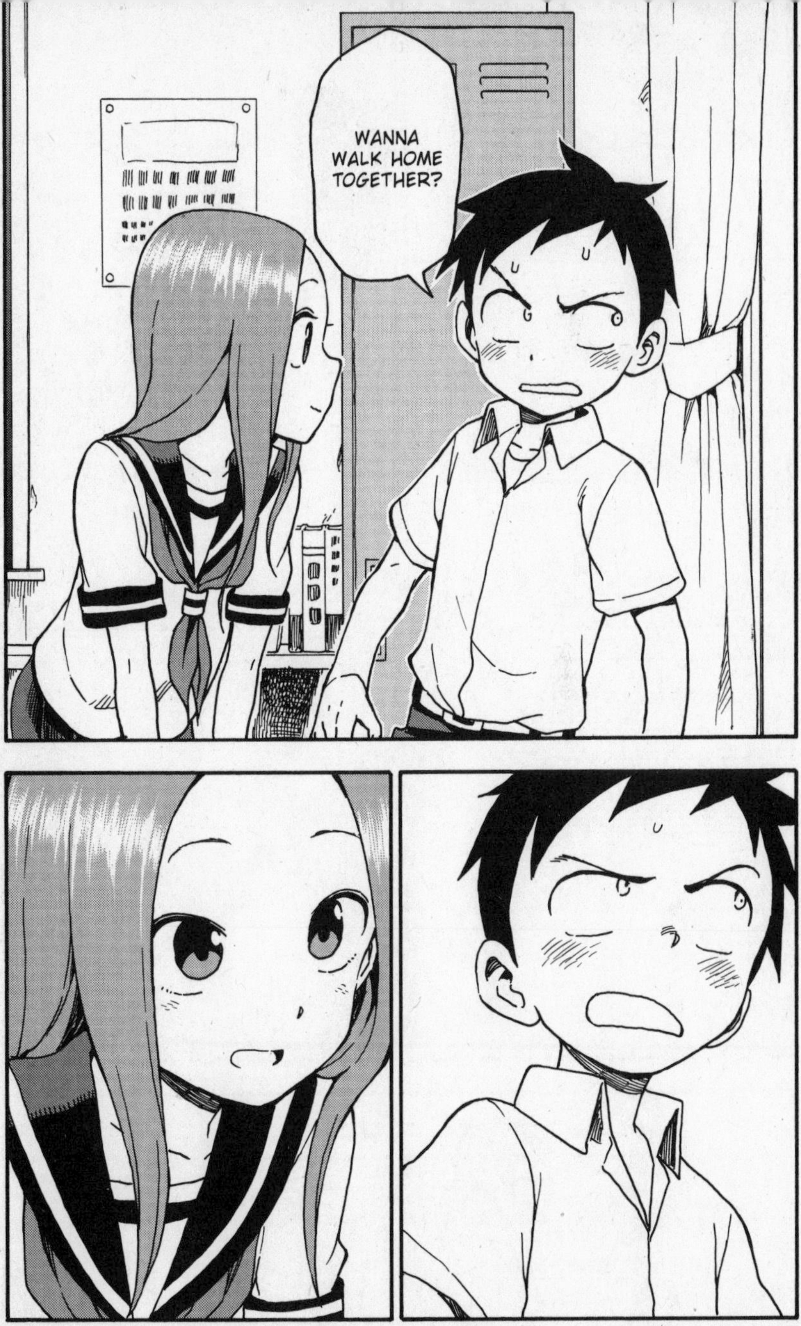
WANNA WALK HOME TOGETHER?

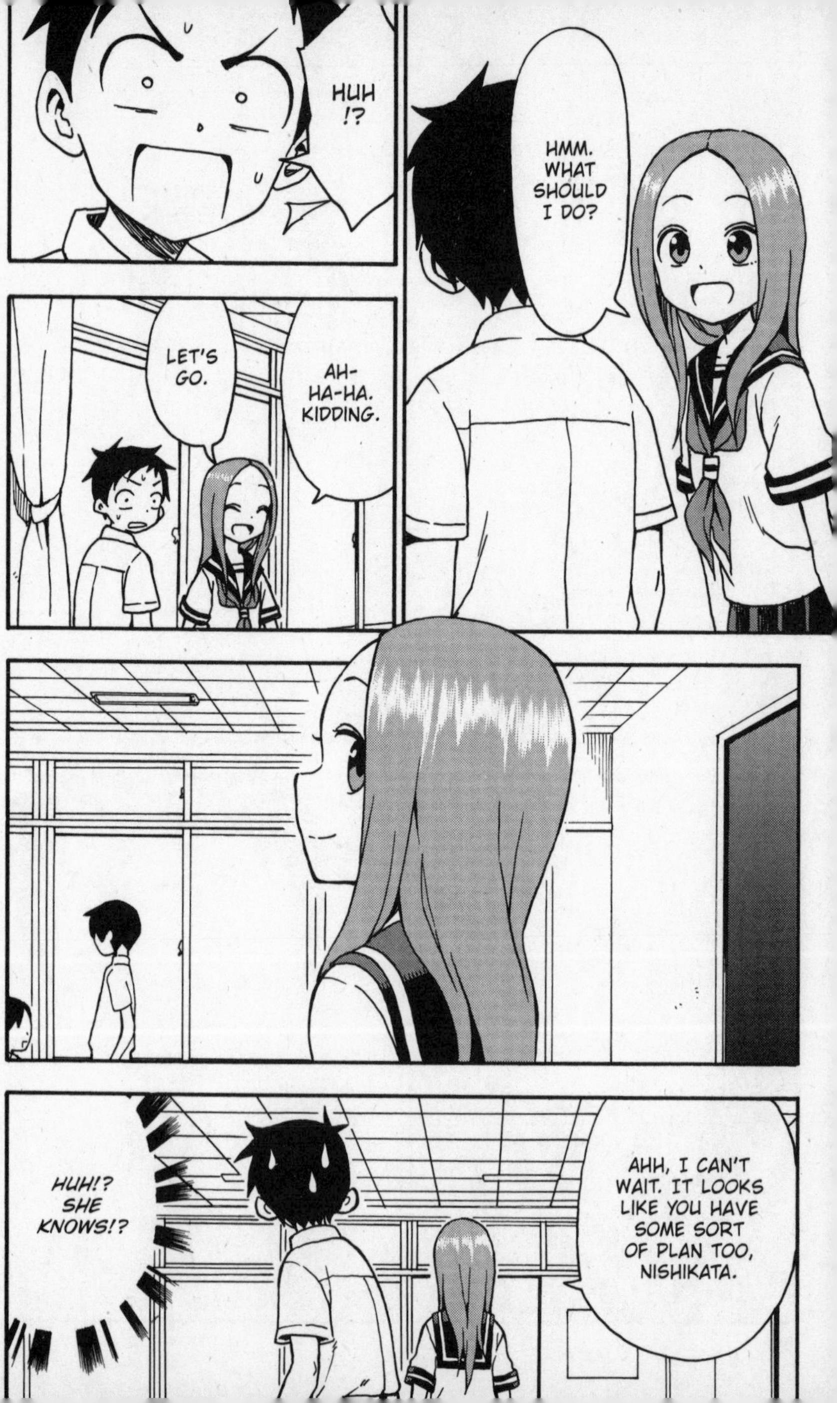
HMM. WHAT SHOULD I DO?
HUH !?
AH-HA-HA. KIDDING.
LET'S GO.
AHH, I CAN'T WAIT. IT LOOKS LIKE YOU HAVE SOME SORT OF PLAN TOO, NISHIKATA.
HUH!? SHE KNOWS!?

POKER

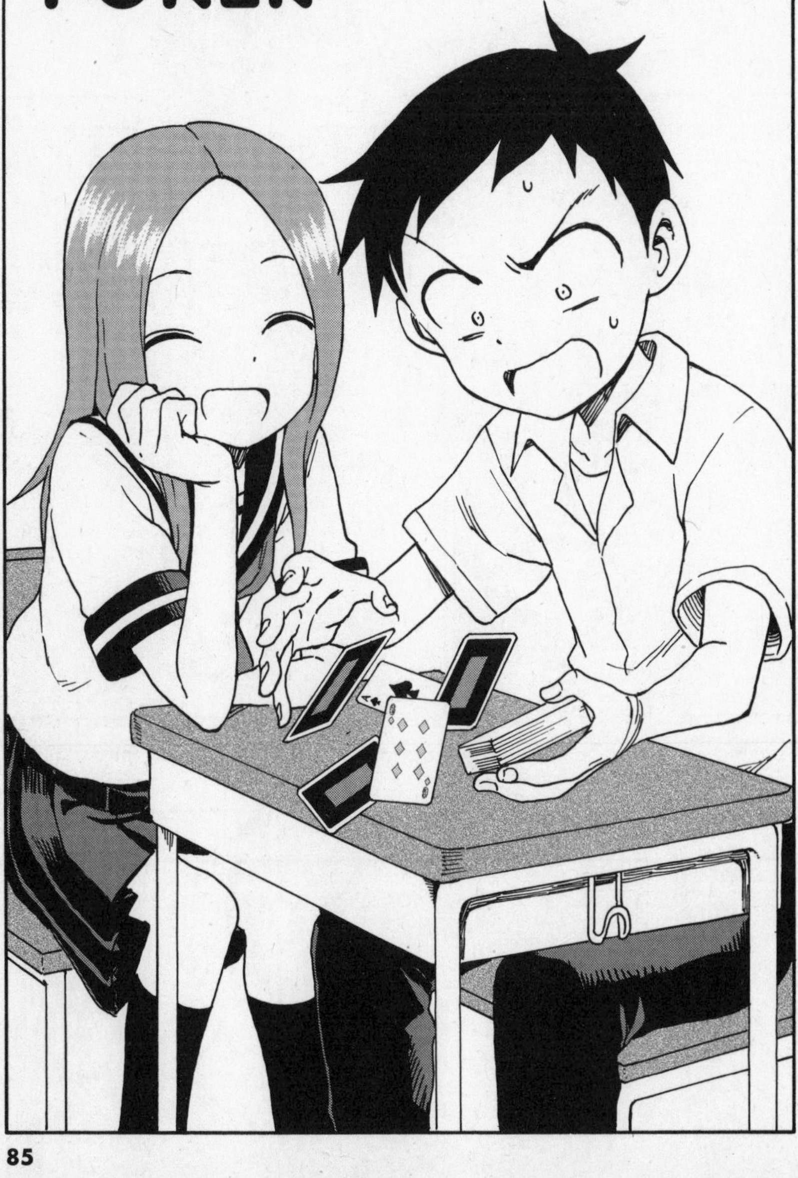

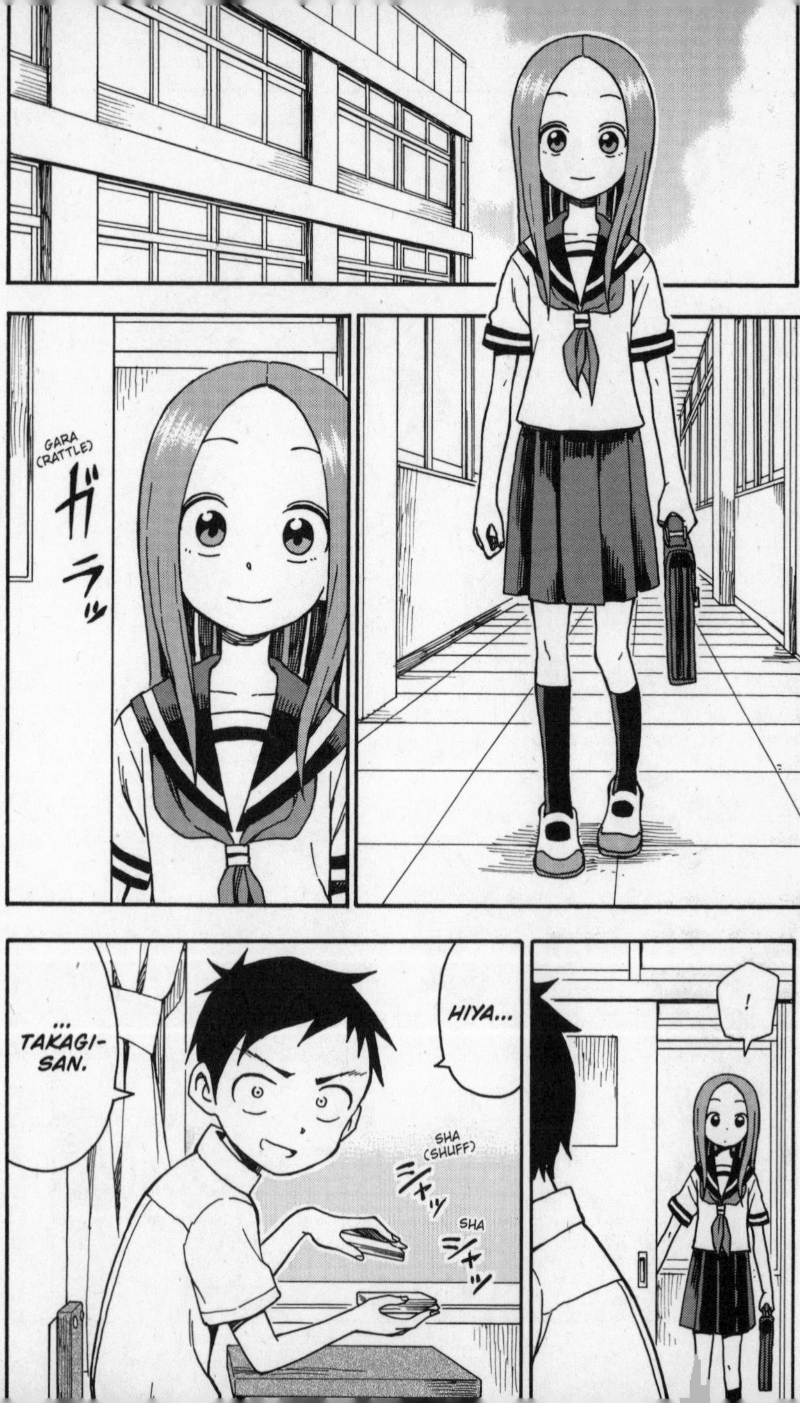
GARA (RATTLE)
!
HIYA...
...TAKAGI-SAN.
SHA (SHUFF)
SHA

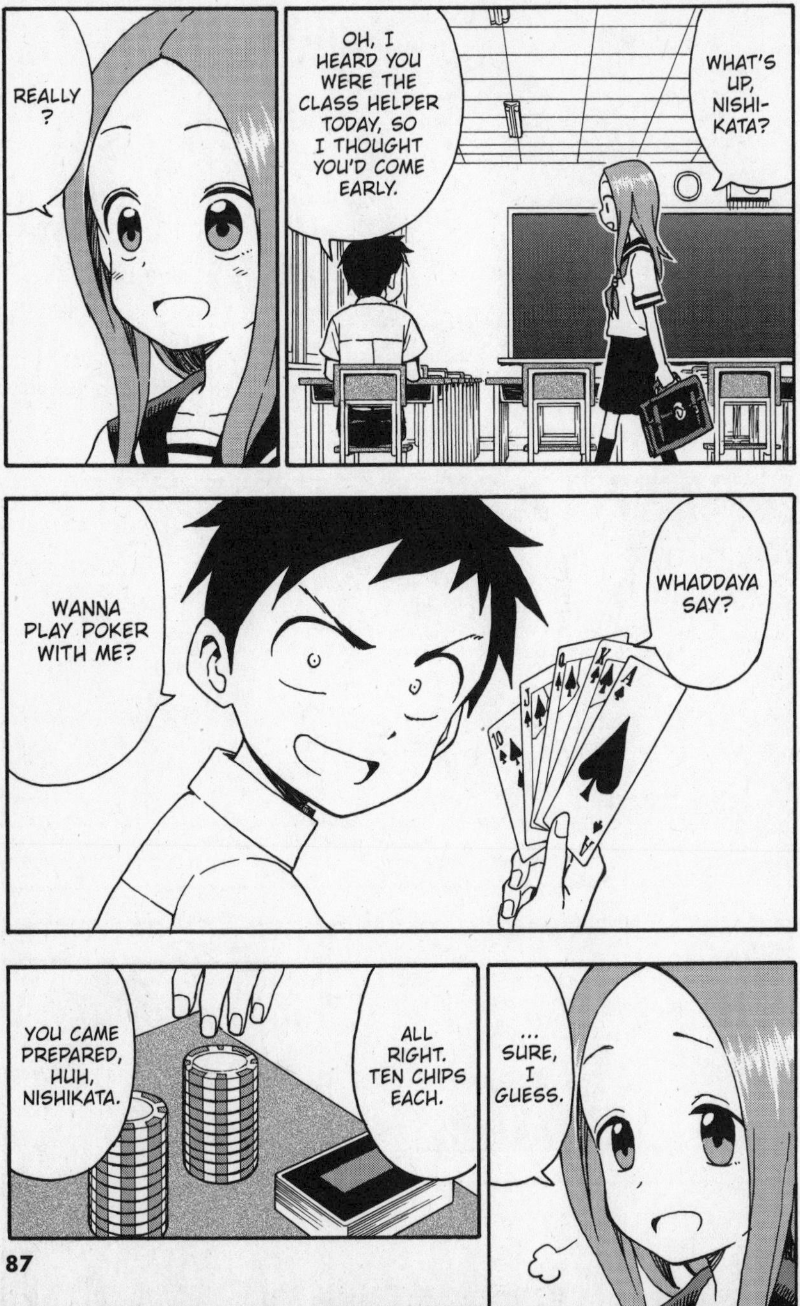
WHAT'S UP, NISHI-KATA?
OH, I HEARD YOU WERE THE CLASS HELPER TODAY, SO I THOUGHT YOU'D COME EARLY.
REALLY?
WHADDAYA SAY?
WANNA PLAY POKER WITH ME?
... SURE, I GUESS.
ALL RIGHT. TEN CHIPS EACH.
YOU CAME PREPARED, HUH, NISHIKATA.

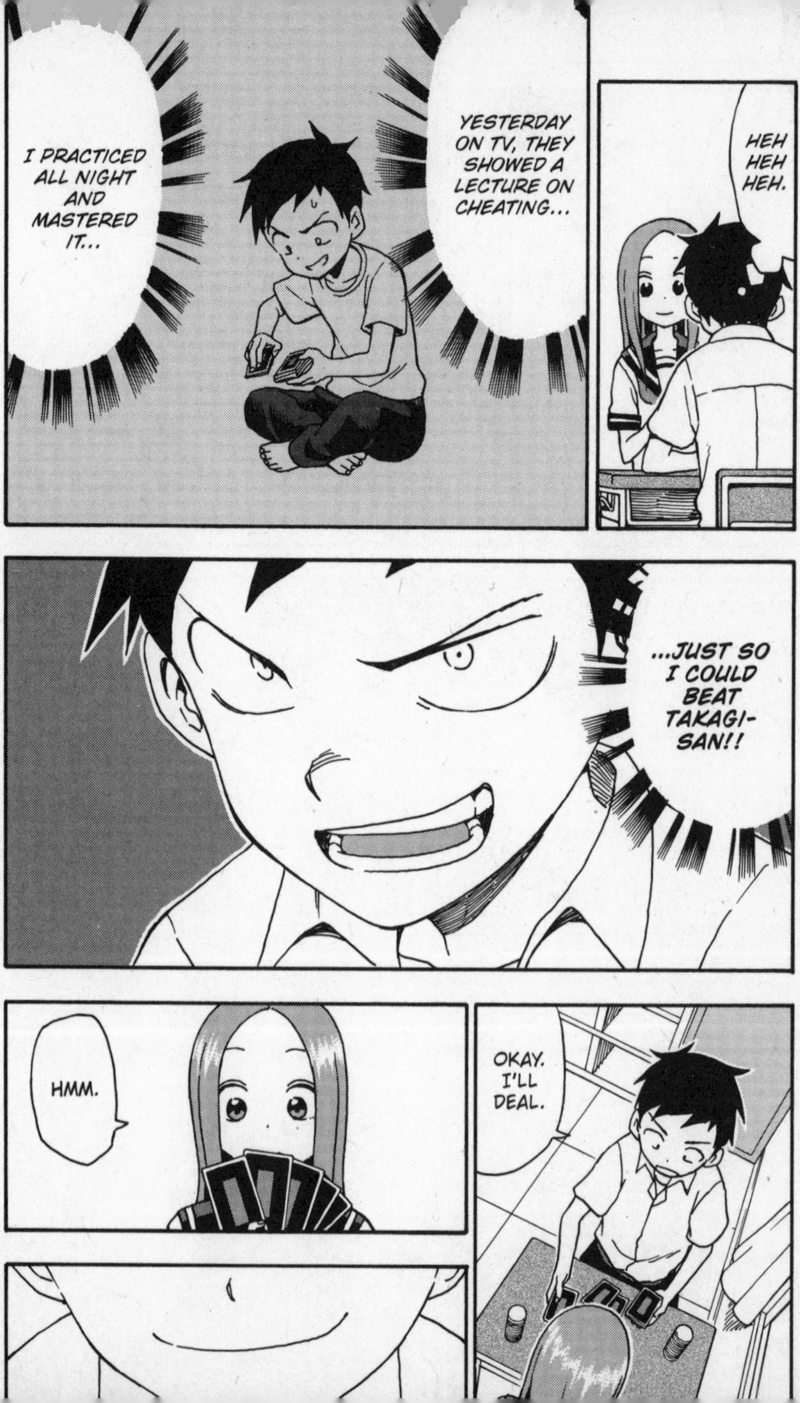
HEH HEH HEH.
YESTERDAY ON TV, THEY SHOWED A LECTURE ON CHEATING...
I PRACTICED ALL NIGHT AND MASTERED IT...
...JUST SO I COULD BEAT TAKAGI-SAN!!
OKAY. I'LL DEAL.
HMM.

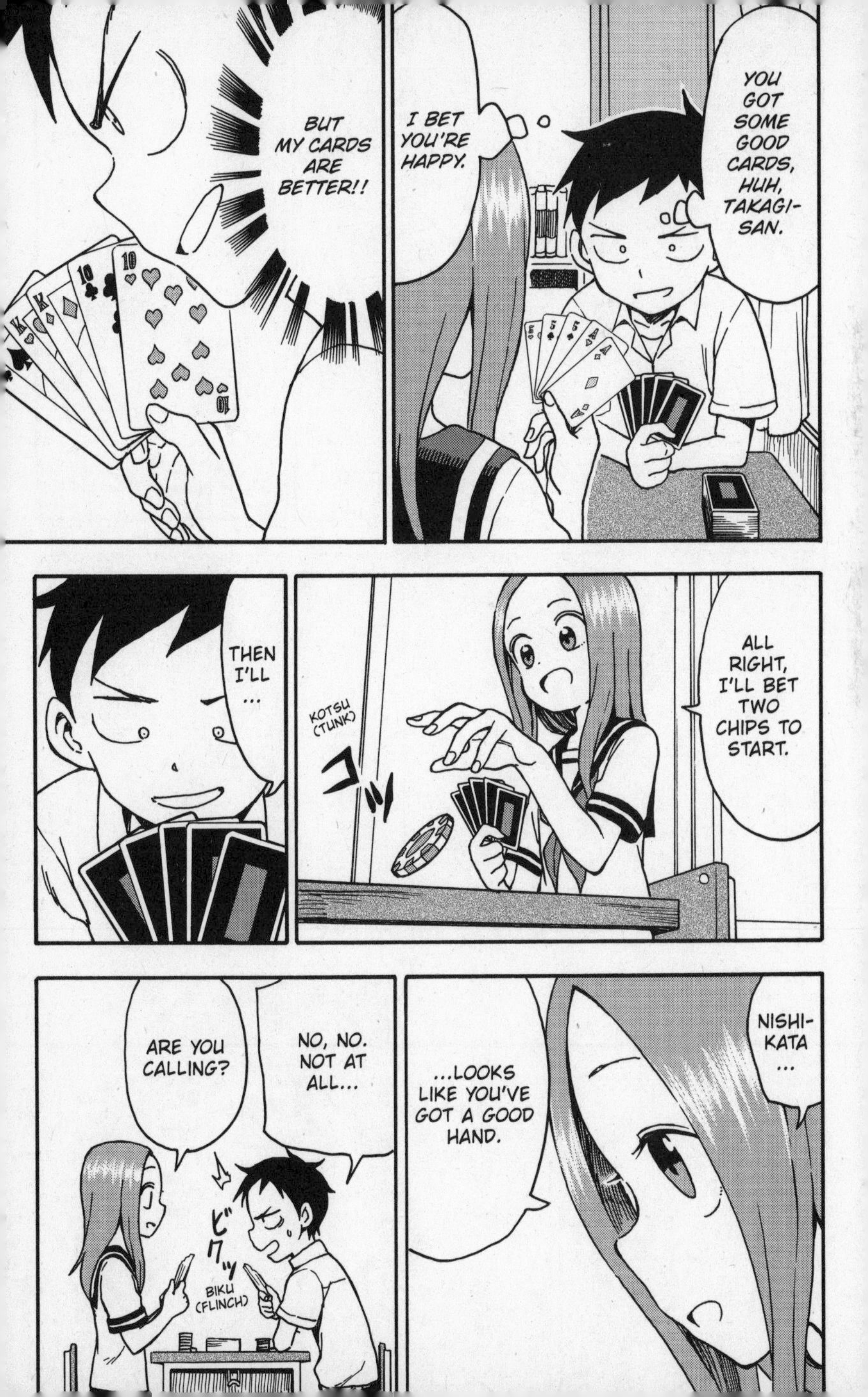
YOU GOT SOME GOOD CARDS, HUH, TAKAGI-SAN.
I BET YOU'RE HAPPY.
BUT MY CARDS ARE BETTER!!
ALL RIGHT, I'LL BET TWO CHIPS TO START.
KOTSU (TUNK)
THEN I'LL ...
NISHI-KATA ...
...LOOKS LIKE YOU'VE GOT A GOOD HAND.
NO, NO. NOT AT ALL...
ARE YOU CALLING?
ビクッ
BIKU (FLINCH)

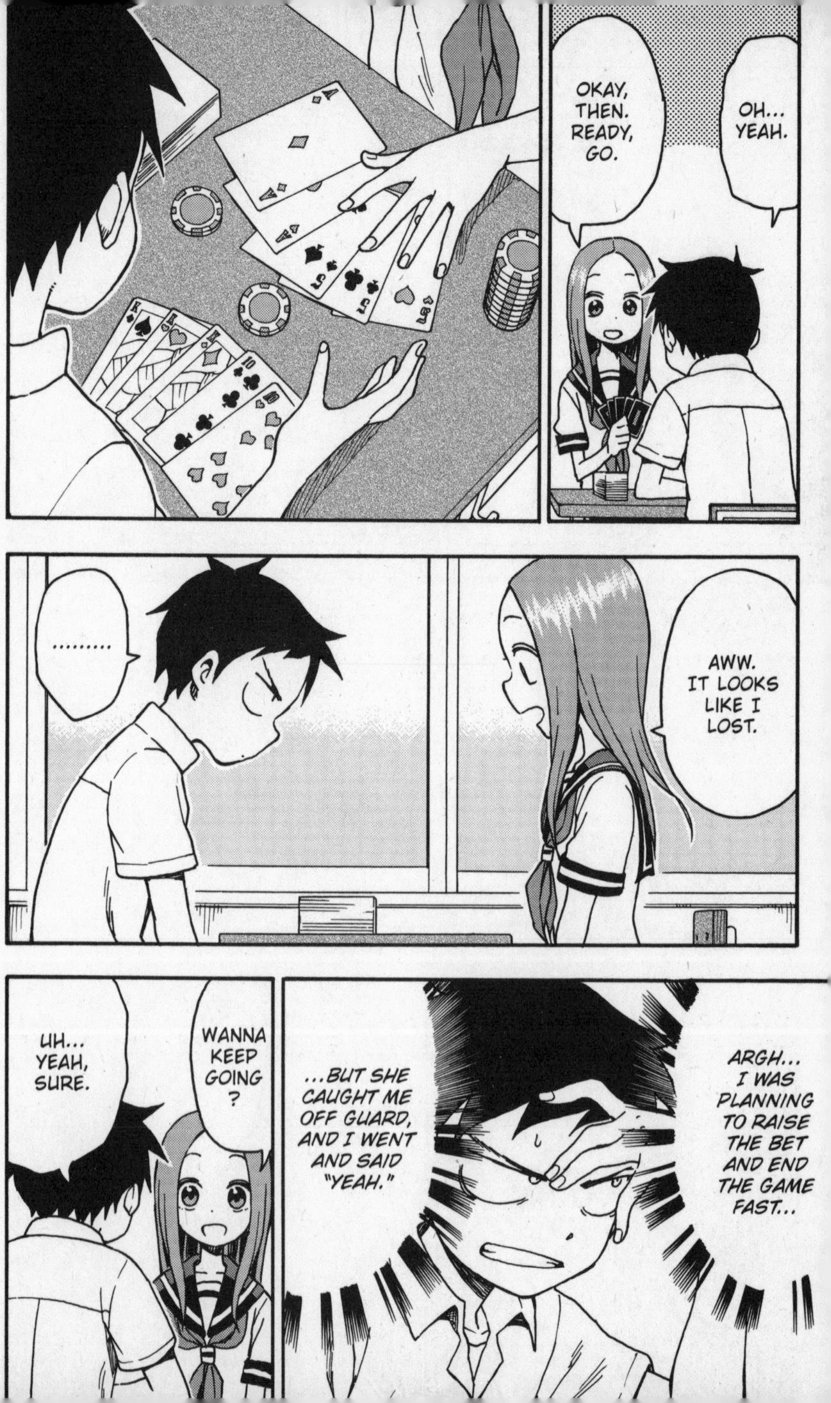
OH... YEAH.
OKAY, THEN. READY, GO.
AWW. IT LOOKS LIKE I LOST.
....
ARGH... I WAS PLANNING TO RAISE THE BET AND END THE GAME FAST...
...BUT SHE CAUGHT ME OFF GUARD, AND I WENT AND SAID "YEAH."
WANNA KEEP GOING?
UH... YEAH, SURE.

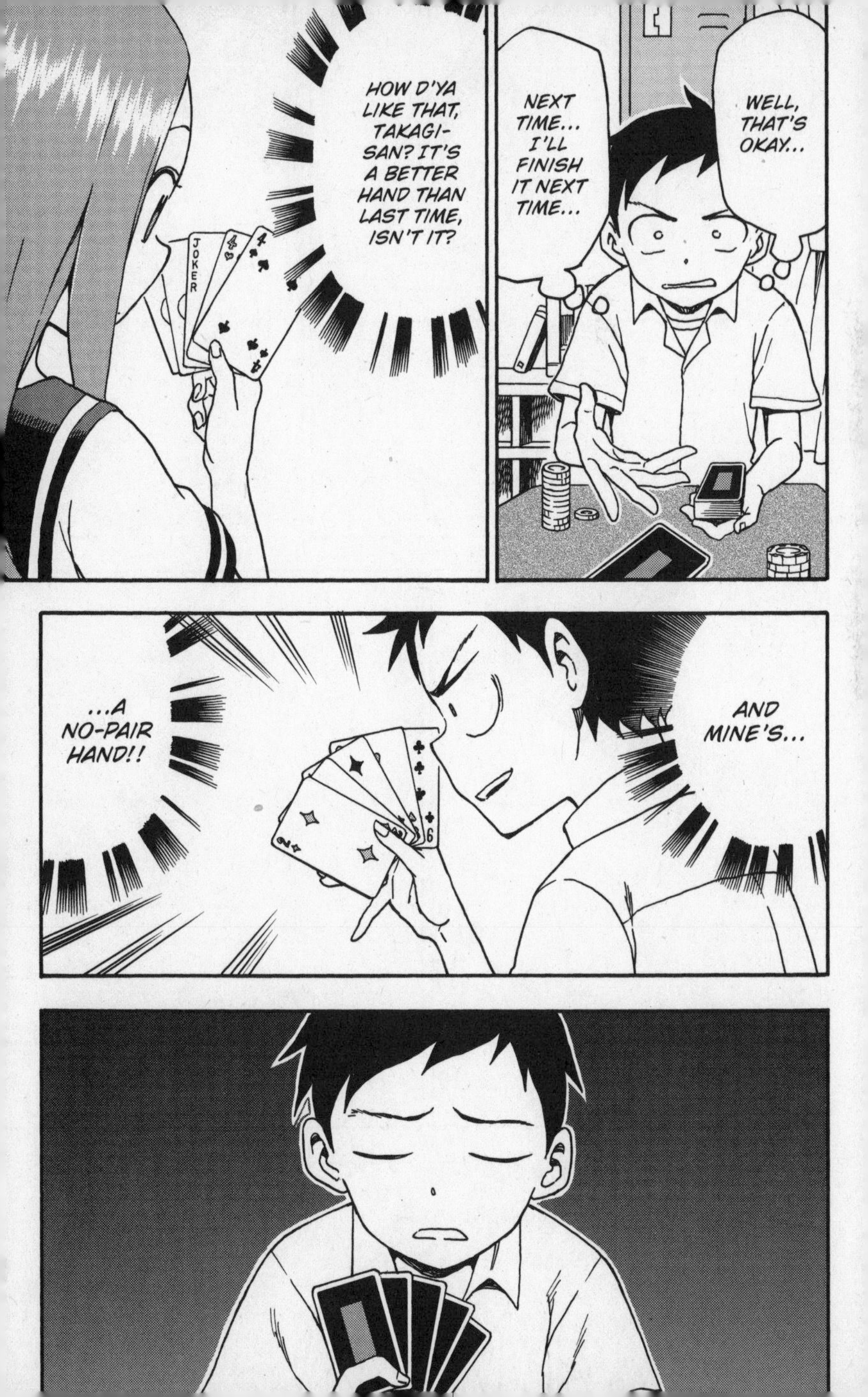
WELL, THAT'S OKAY...
NEXT TIME... I'LL FINISH IT NEXT TIME...
HOW D'YA LIKE THAT, TAKAGI-SAN? IT'S A BETTER HAND THAN LAST TIME, ISN'T IT?
JOKER
AND MINE'S...
...A NO-PAIR HAND!!

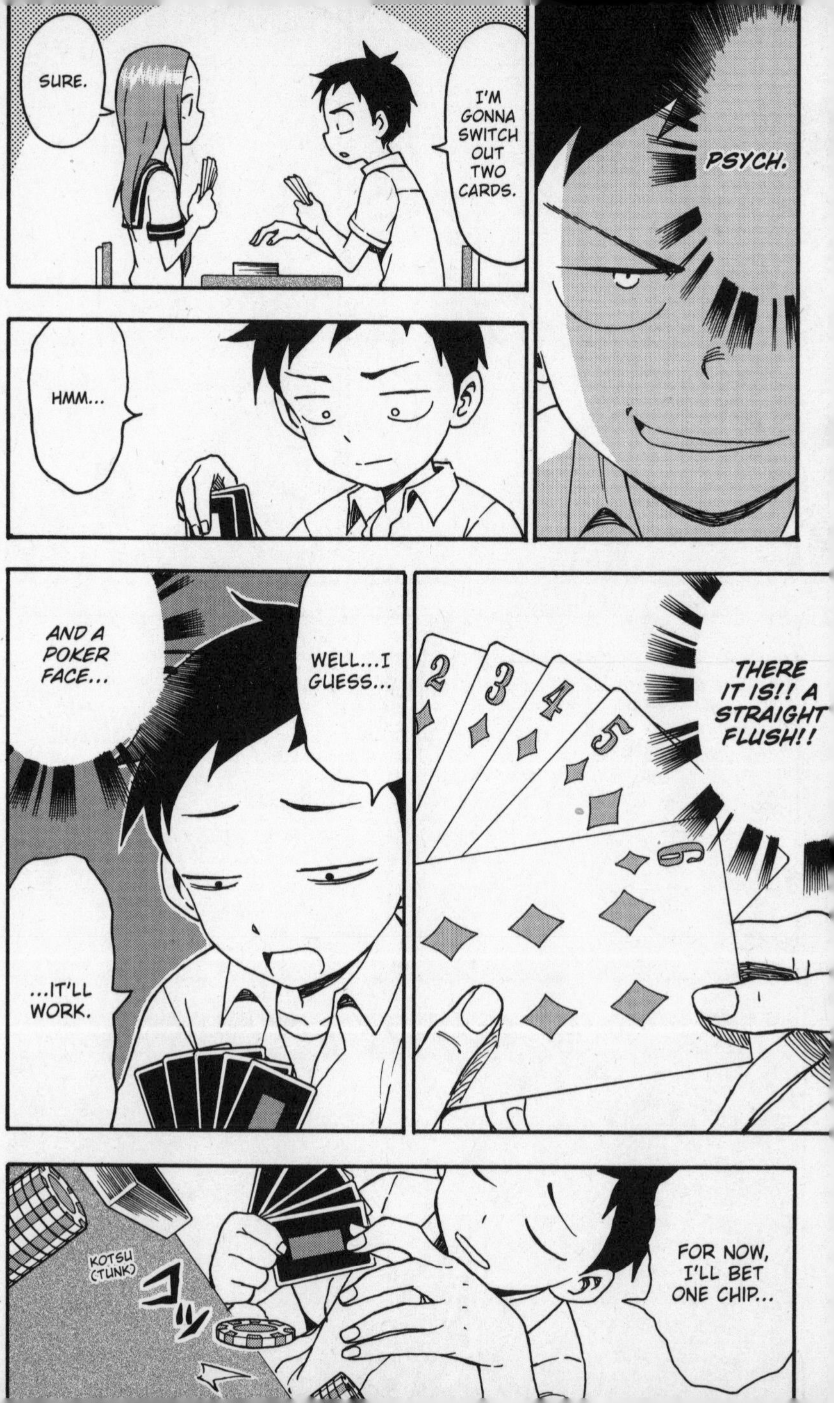
PSYCH.
I'M GONNA SWITCH OUT TWO CARDS.
SURE.
HMM...
THERE IT IS!! A STRAIGHT FLUSH!!
WELL...I GUESS...
AND A POKER FACE...
...IT'LL WORK.
FOR NOW, I'LL BET ONE CHIP...
KOTSU (TUNK)
コツ

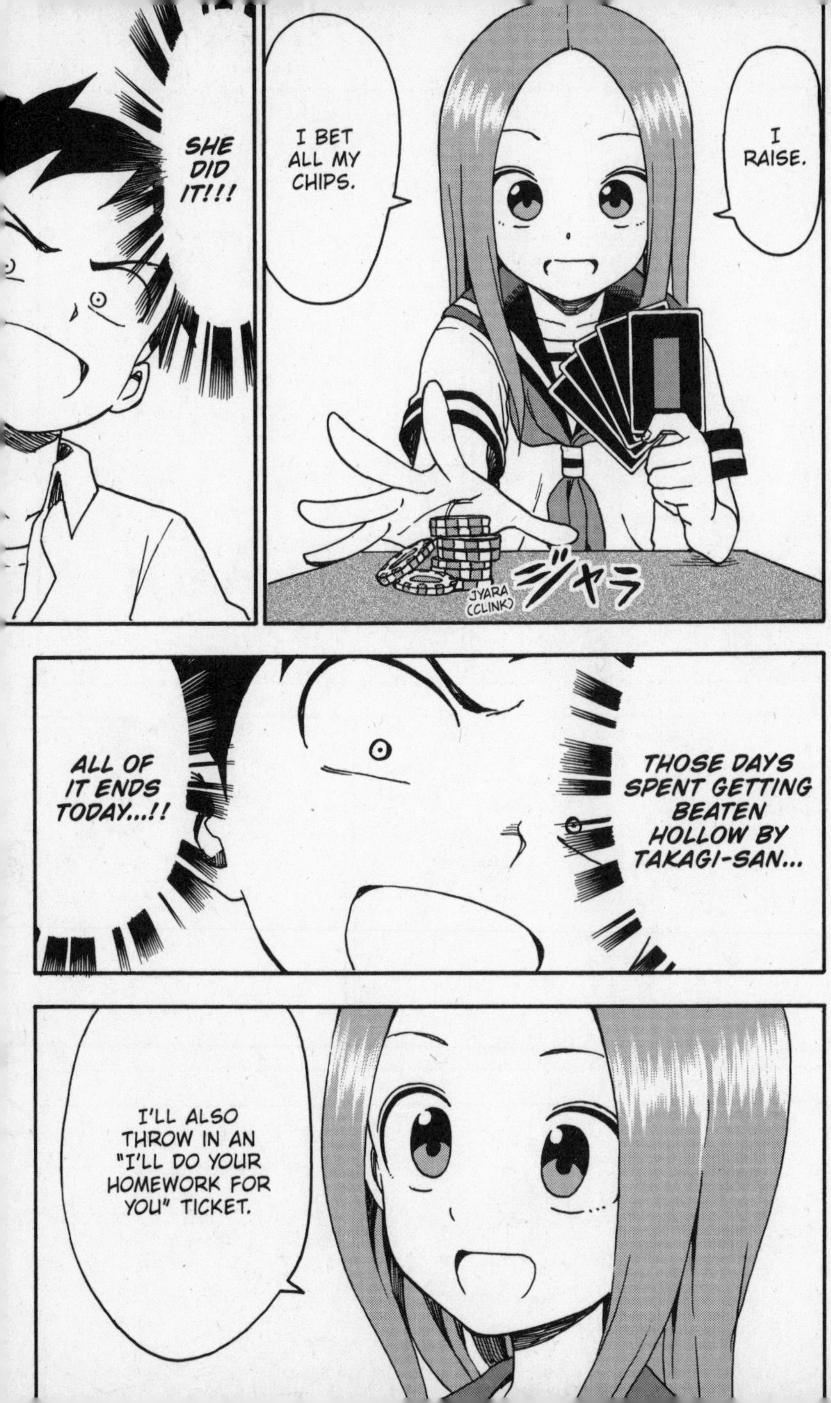
I RAISE.
I BET ALL MY CHIPS.
ジャラ
JYARA (CLINK)
SHE DID IT!!!
THOSE DAYS SPENT GETTING BEATEN HOLLOW BY TAKAGI-SAN...
ALL OF IT ENDS TODAY...!!
I'LL ALSO THROW IN AN "I'LL DO YOUR HOMEWORK FOR YOU" TICKET.

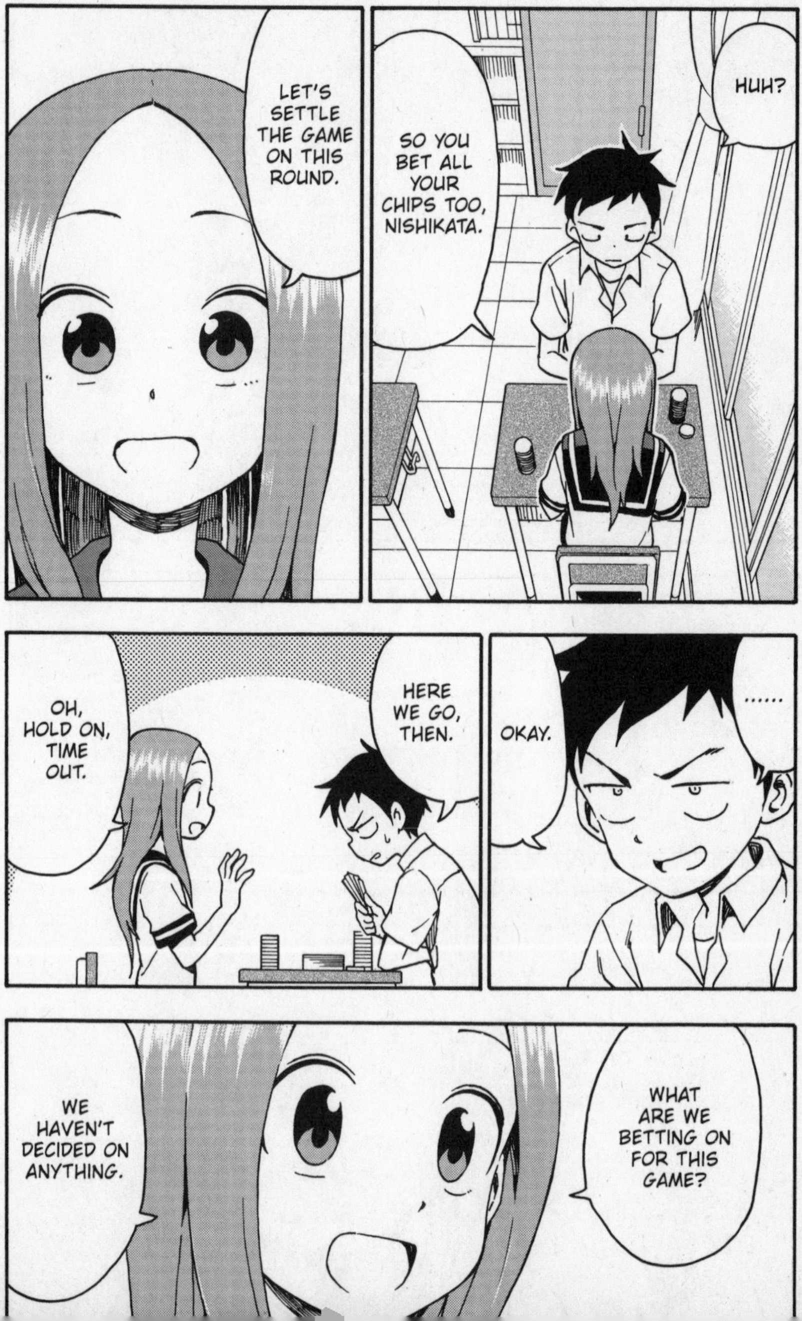
HUH?
SO YOU BET ALL YOUR CHIPS TOO, NISHIKATA.
LET'S SETTLE THE GAME ON THIS ROUND.
......
OKAY.
HERE WE GO, THEN.
OH, HOLD ON, TIME OUT.
WHAT ARE WE BETTING ON FOR THIS GAME?
WE HAVEN'T DECIDED ON ANYTHING.

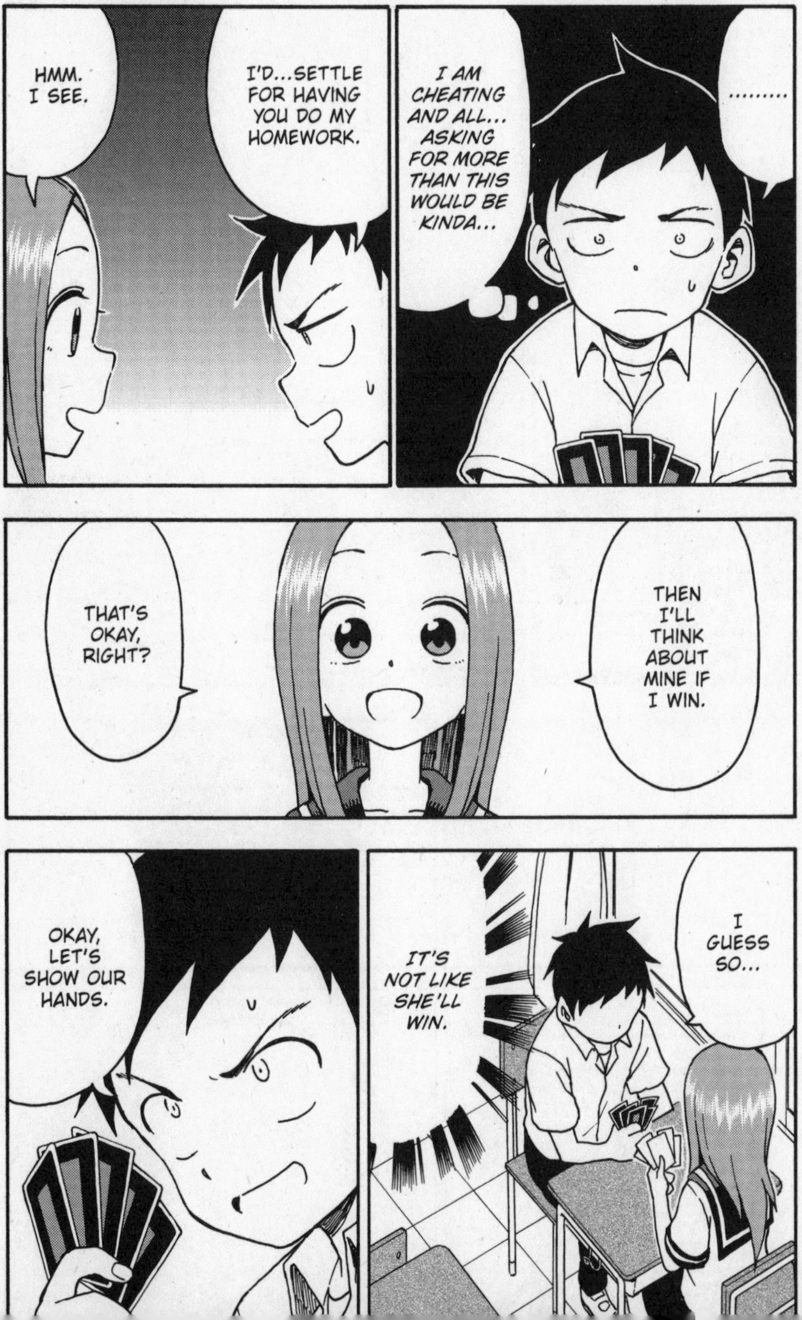
....
I AM CHEATING AND ALL... ASKING FOR MORE THAN THIS WOULD BE KINDA...
I'D...SETTLE FOR HAVING YOU DO MY HOMEWORK.
HMM. I SEE.
THEN I'LL THINK ABOUT MINE IF I WIN.
THAT'S OKAY, RIGHT?
I GUESS SO...
IT'S NOT LIKE SHE'LL WIN.
OKAY, LET'S SHOW OUR HANDS.

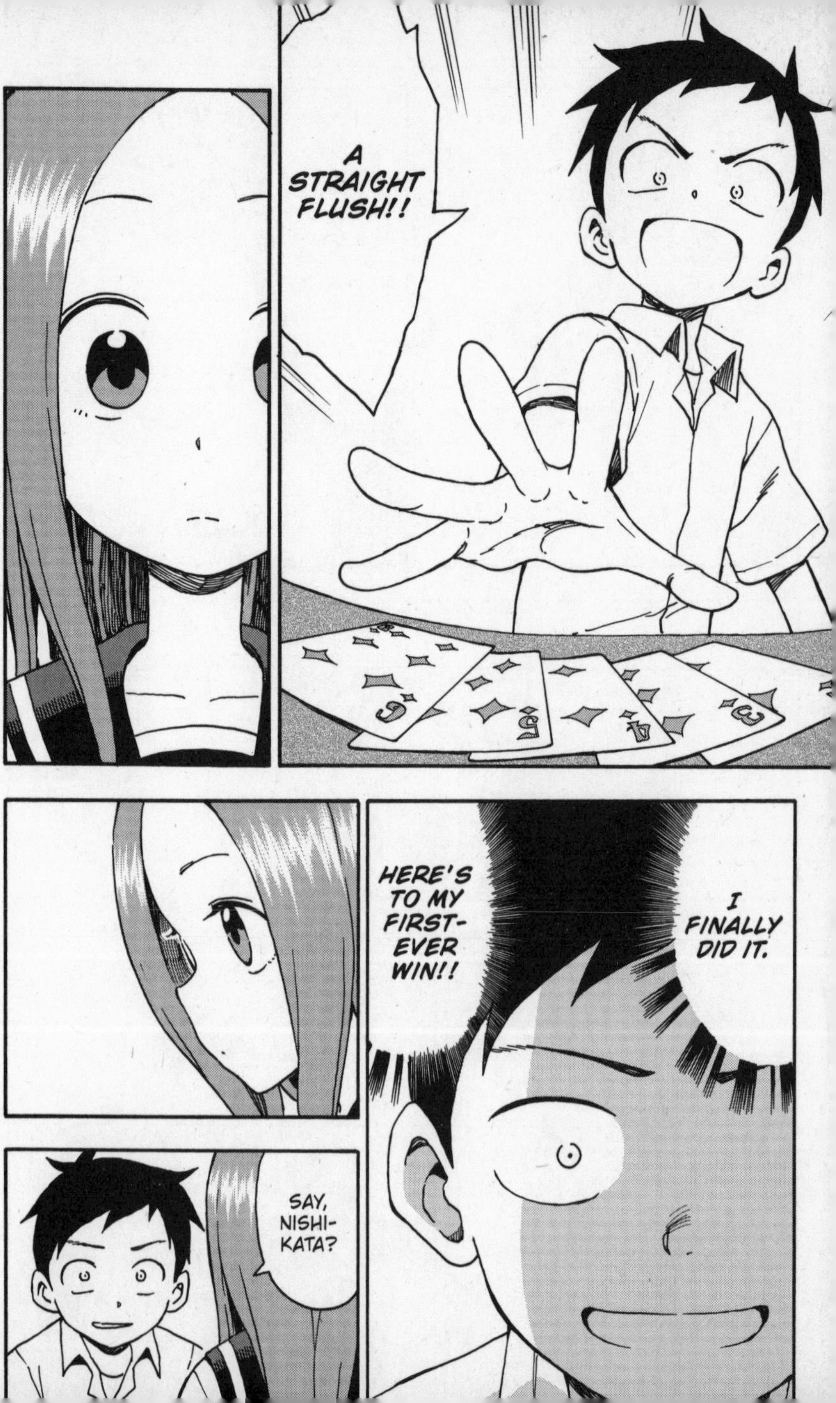
A STRAIGHT FLUSH!!
I FINALLY DID IT.
HERE'S TO MY FIRST-EVER WIN!!
SAY, NISHIKATA?

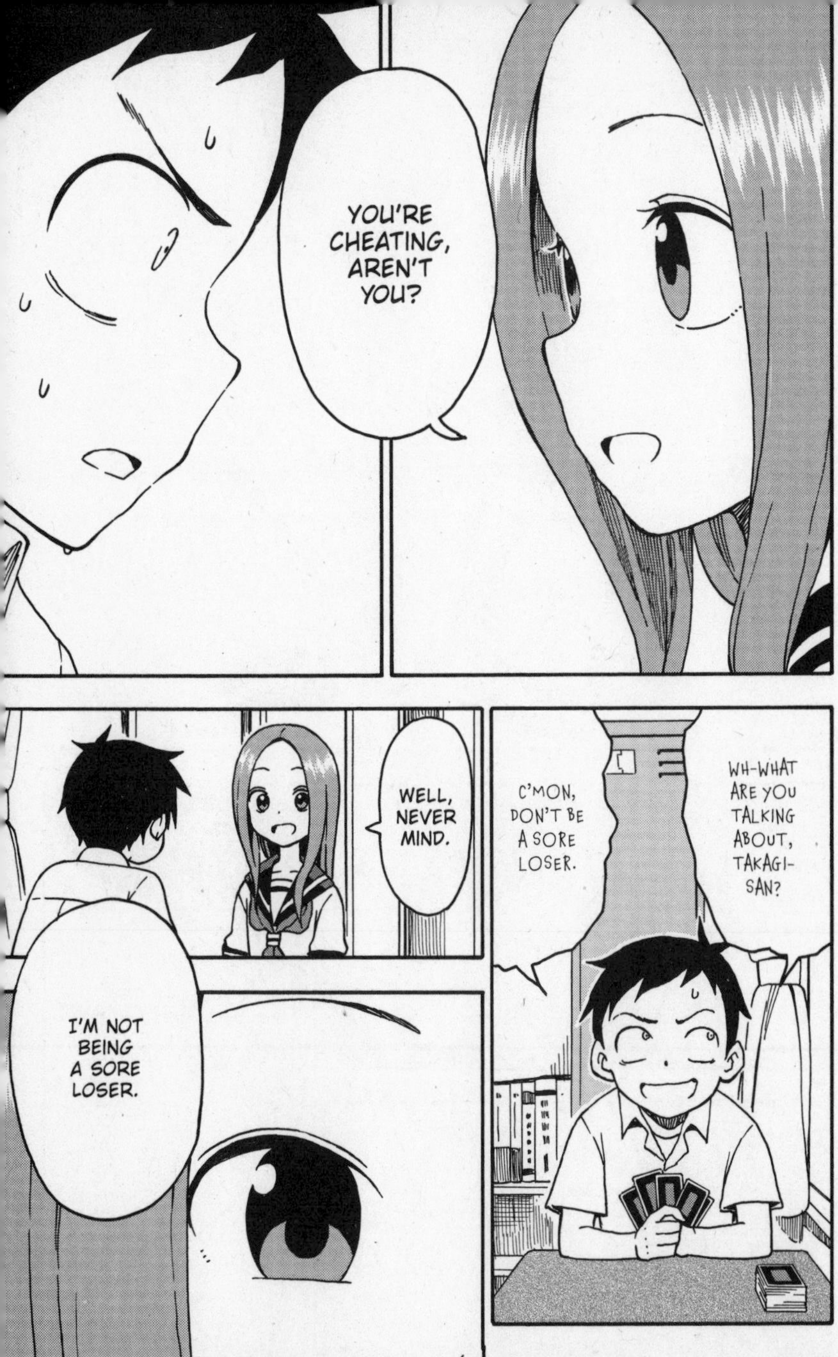
YOU'RE CHEATING, AREN'T YOU?
WH-WHAT ARE YOU TALKING ABOUT, TAKAGI-SAN?
C'MON, DON'T BE A SORE LOSER.
WELL, NEVER MIND.
I'M NOT BEING A SORE LOSER.

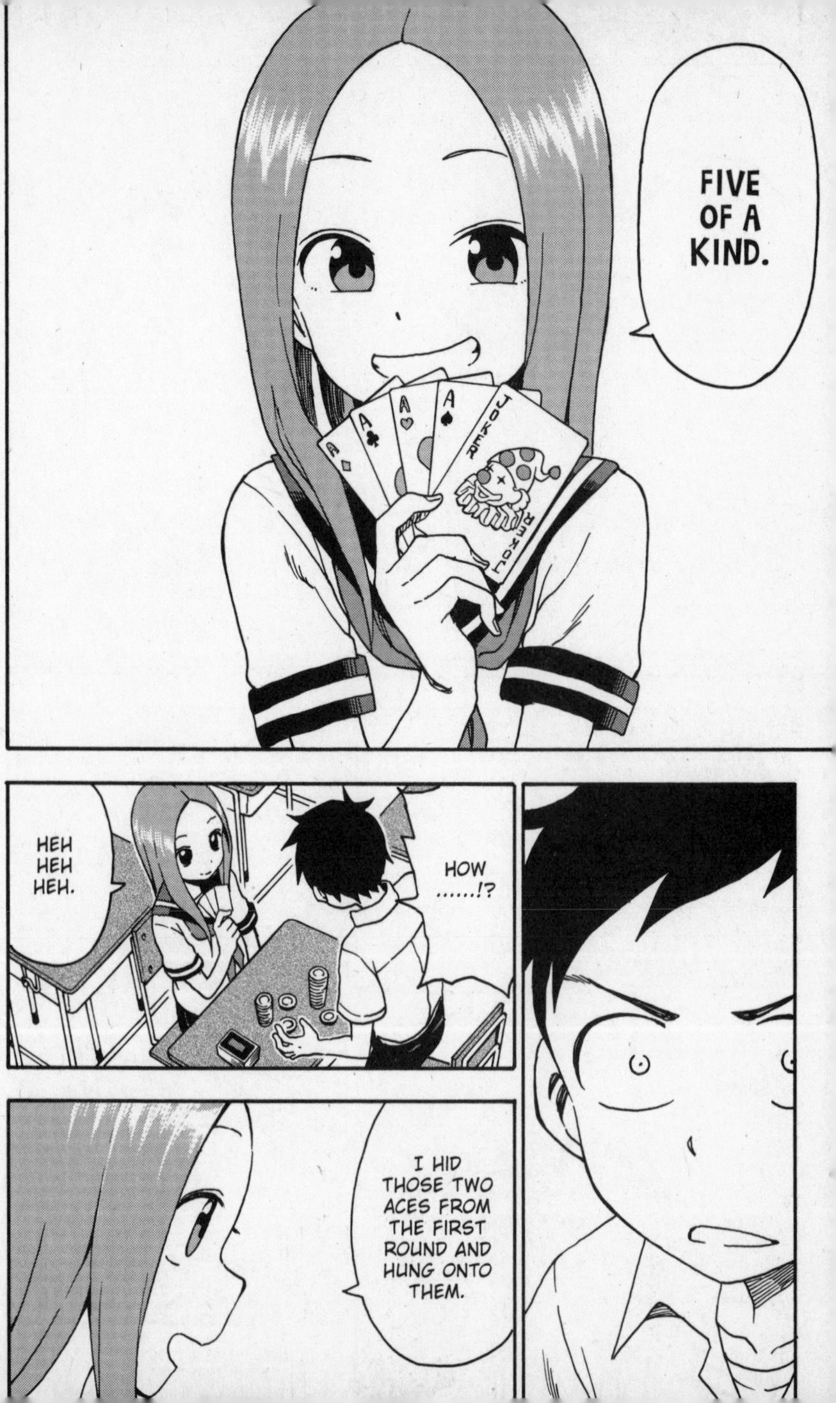
FIVE OF A KIND.
HOW ......!?
HEH HEH HEH.
I HID THOSE TWO ACES FROM THE FIRST ROUND AND HUNG ONTO THEM.

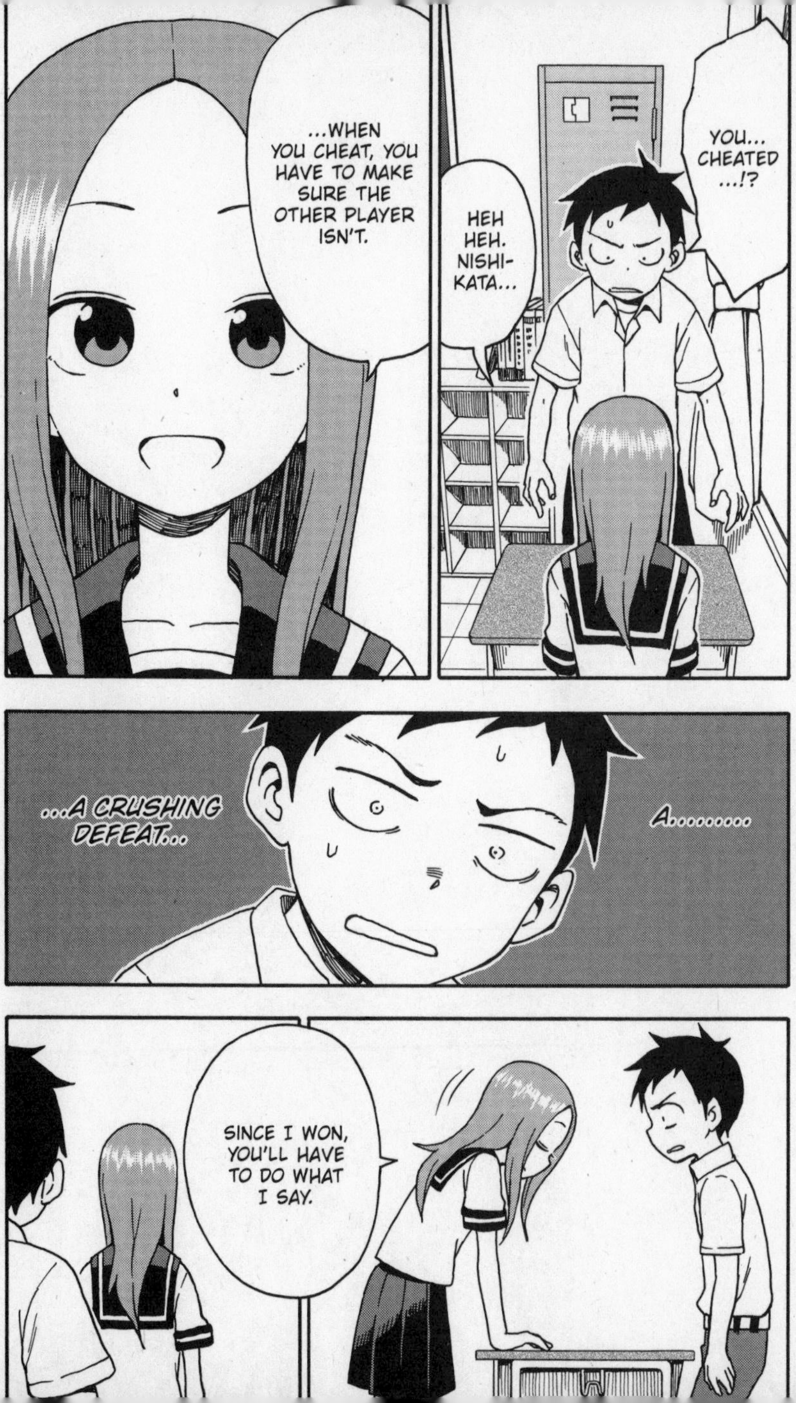
YOU... CHEATED ...!?
HEH HEH. NISHIKATA...
...WHEN YOU CHEAT, YOU HAVE TO MAKE SURE THE OTHER PLAYER ISN'T.
A.........
...A CRUSHING DEFEAT...
SINCE I WON, YOU'LL HAVE TO DO WHAT I SAY.

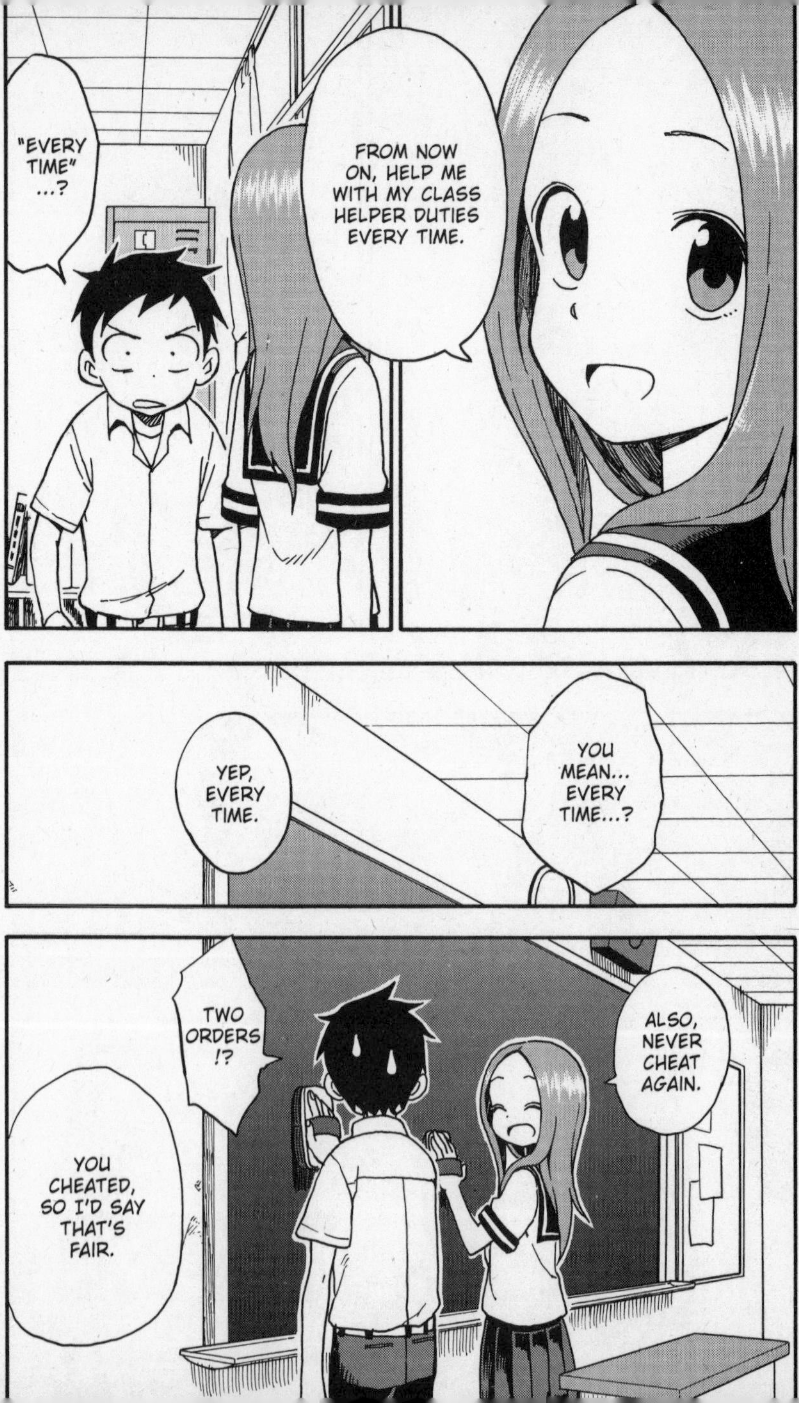
FROM NOW ON, HELP ME WITH MY CLASS HELPER DUTIES EVERY TIME.
"EVERY TIME" ...?
YOU MEAN... EVERY TIME...?
YEP, EVERY TIME.
ALSO, NEVER CHEAT AGAIN.
TWO ORDERS !?
YOU CHEATED, SO I'D SAY THAT'S FAIR.

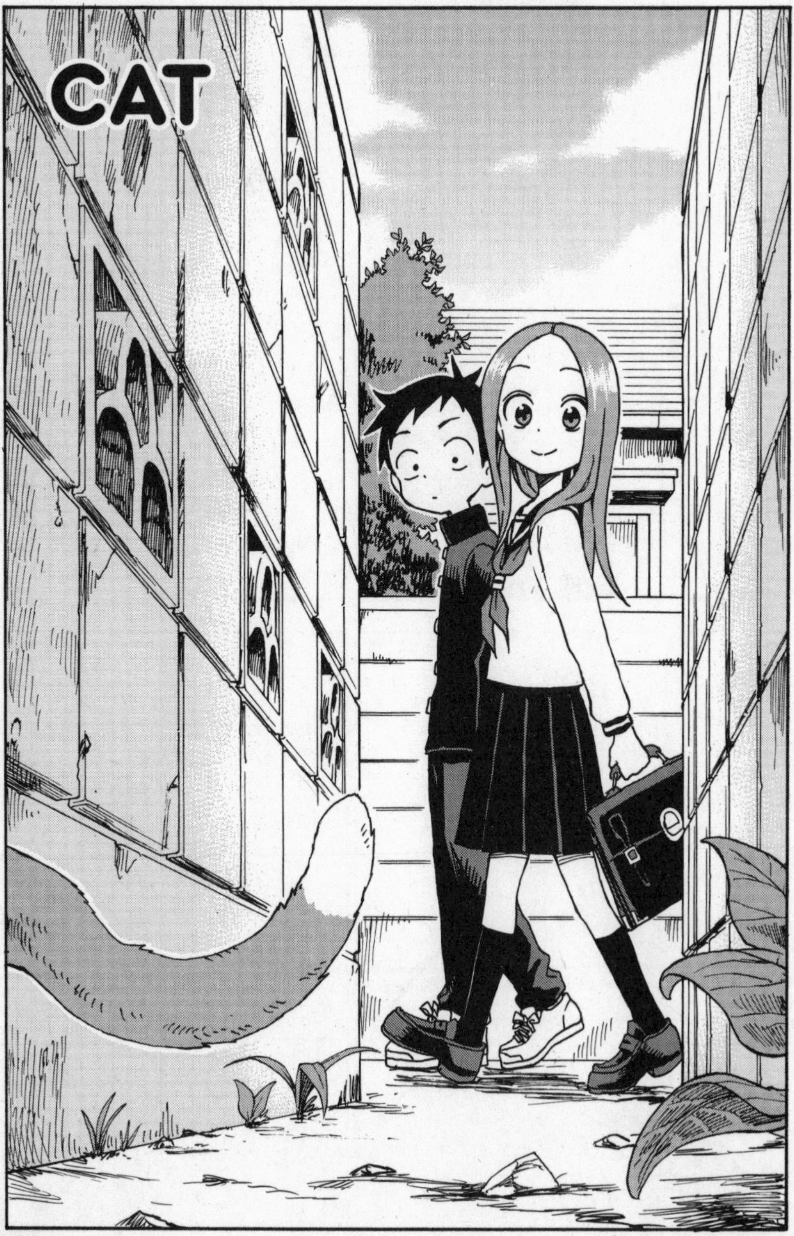
CAT

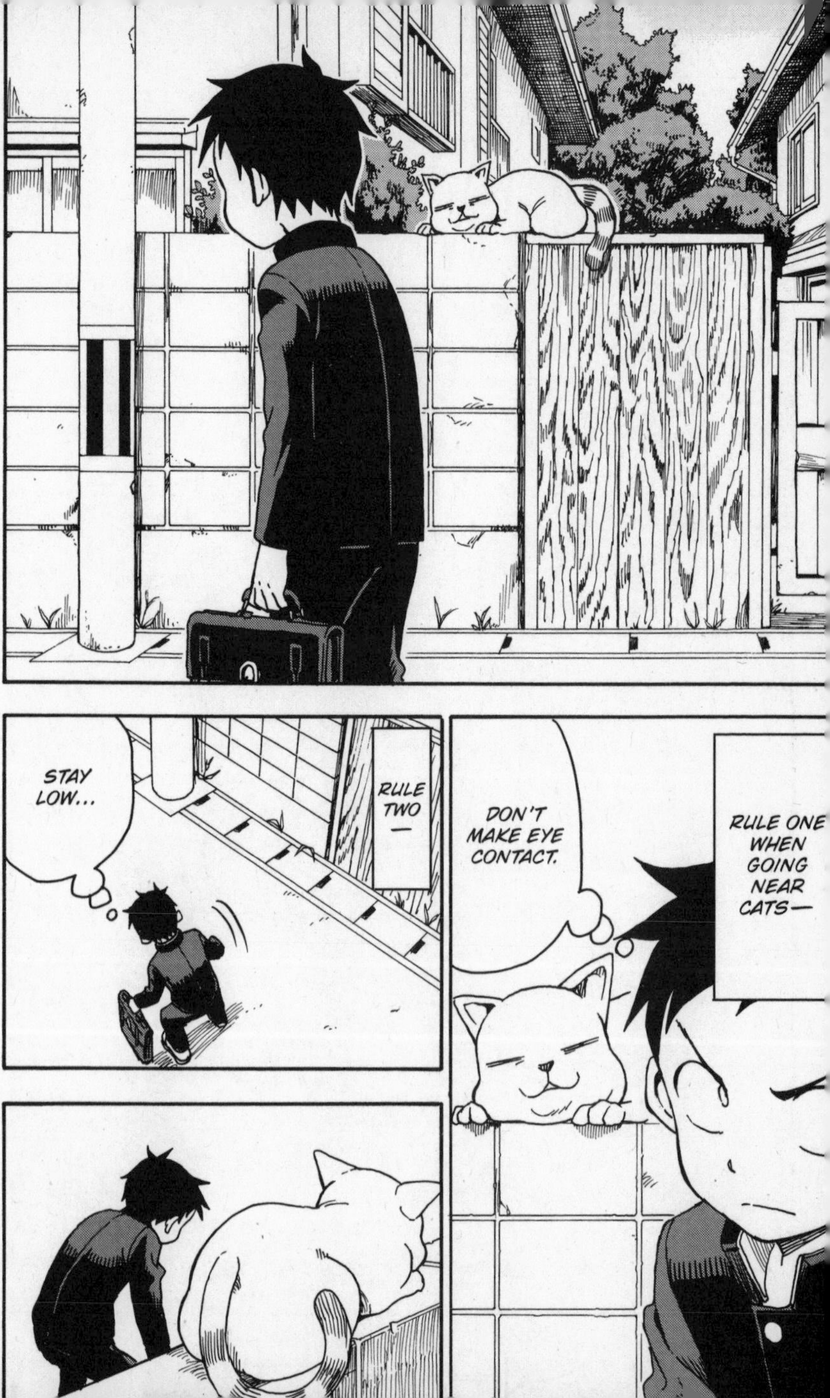
RULE ONE WHEN GOING NEAR CATS—
DON'T MAKE EYE CONTACT.
RULE TWO —
STAY LOW...

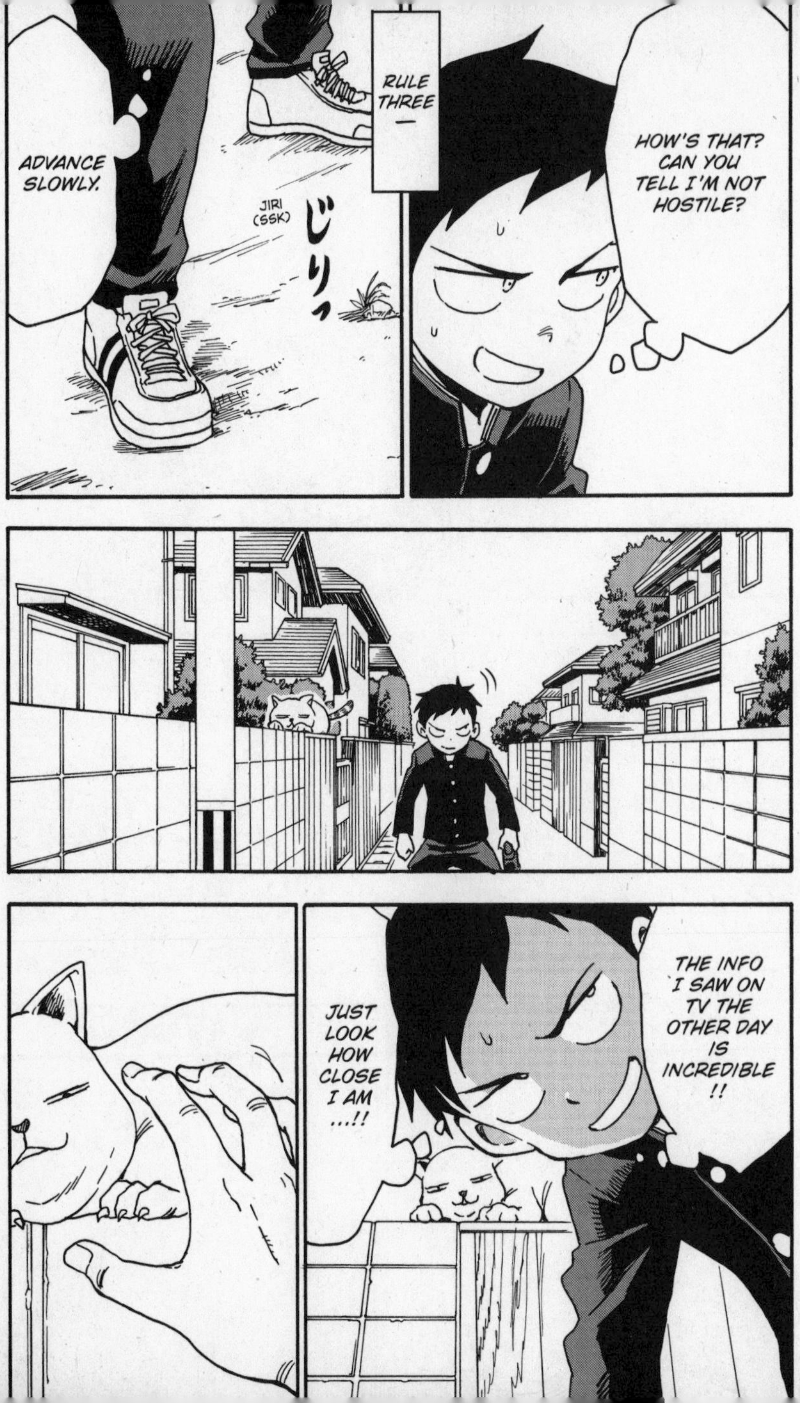
RULE THREE —
HOW'S THAT? CAN YOU TELL I'M NOT HOSTILE?
ADVANCE SLOWLY.
じりっ
JIRI (SSK)
THE INFO I SAW ON TV THE OTHER DAY IS INCREDIBLE !!
JUST LOOK HOW CLOSE I AM ...!!

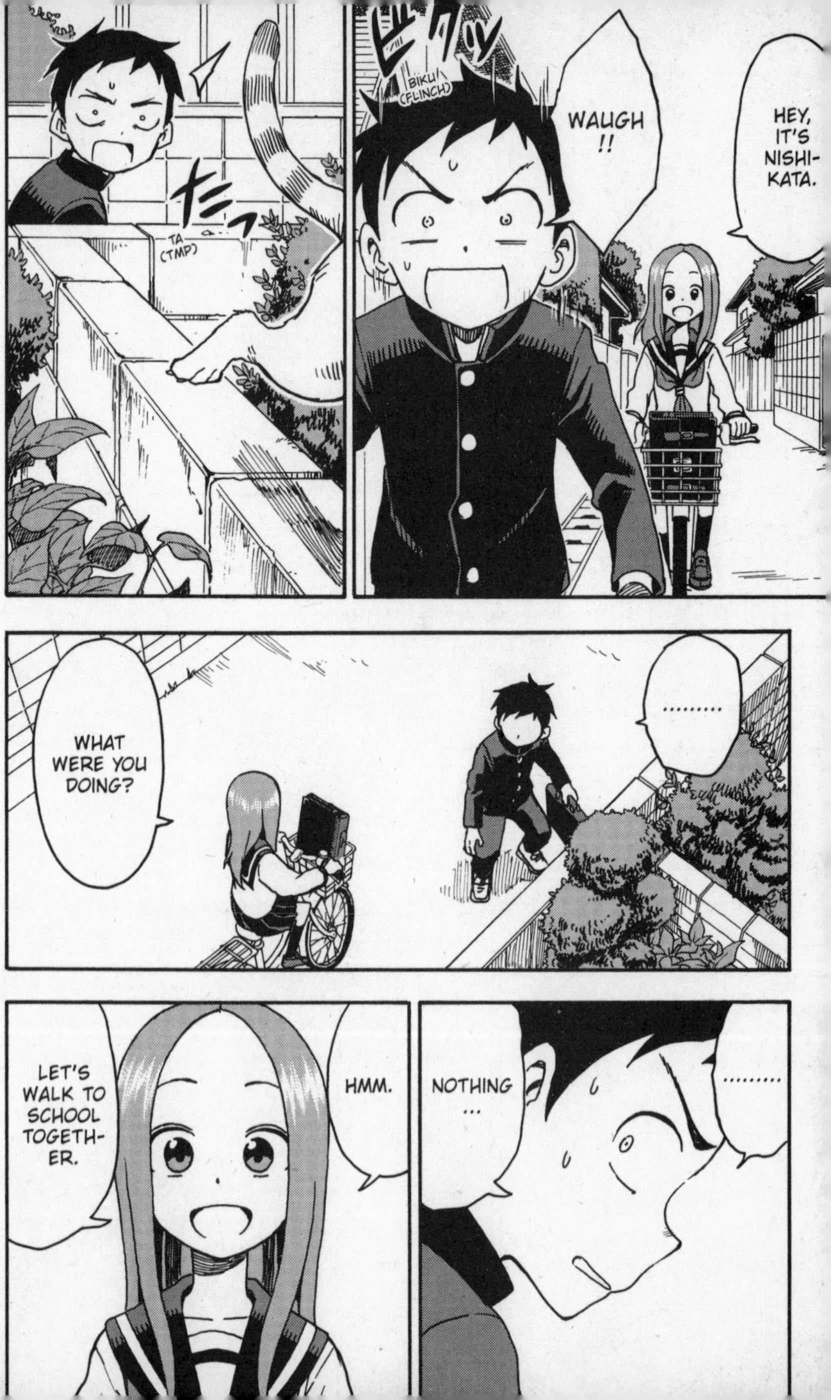
HEY, IT'S NISHI-KATA.
WAUGH !!
BIKU (FLINCH)
TA (TMP)
....
WHAT WERE YOU DOING?
....
NOTHING ...
HMM.
LET'S WALK TO SCHOOL TOGETH-ER.

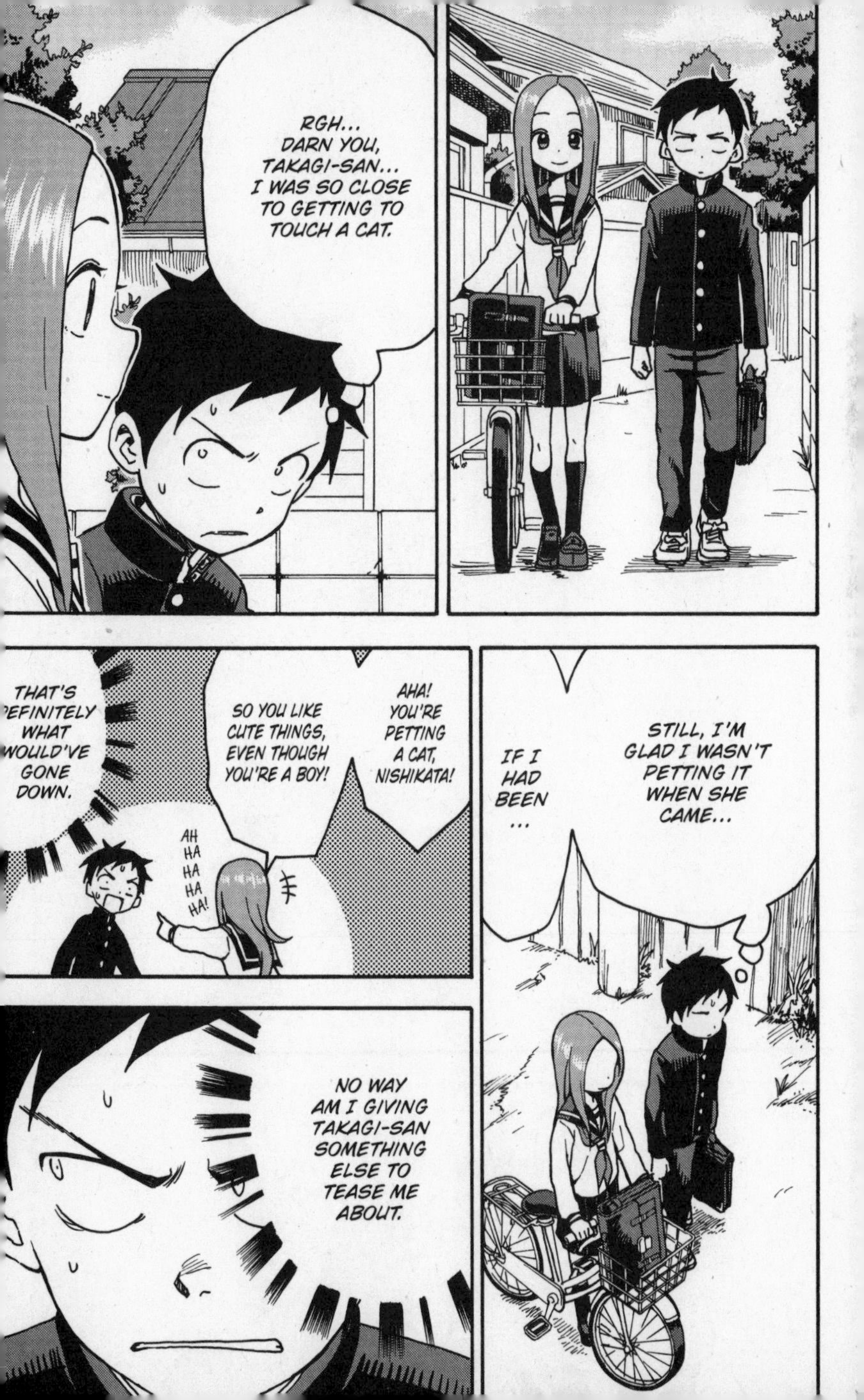
RGH... DARN YOU, TAKAGI-SAN... I WAS SO CLOSE TO GETTING TO TOUCH A CAT.
STILL, I'M GLAD I WASN'T PETTING IT WHEN SHE CAME...
IF I HAD BEEN ...
AHA! YOU'RE PETTING A CAT, NISHIKATA!
SO YOU LIKE CUTE THINGS, EVEN THOUGH YOU'RE A BOY!
AH HA HA HA HA!
THAT'S EFINITELY WHAT WOULD'VE GONE DOWN.
NO WAY AM I GIVING TAKAGI-SAN SOMETHING ELSE TO TEASE ME ABOUT.

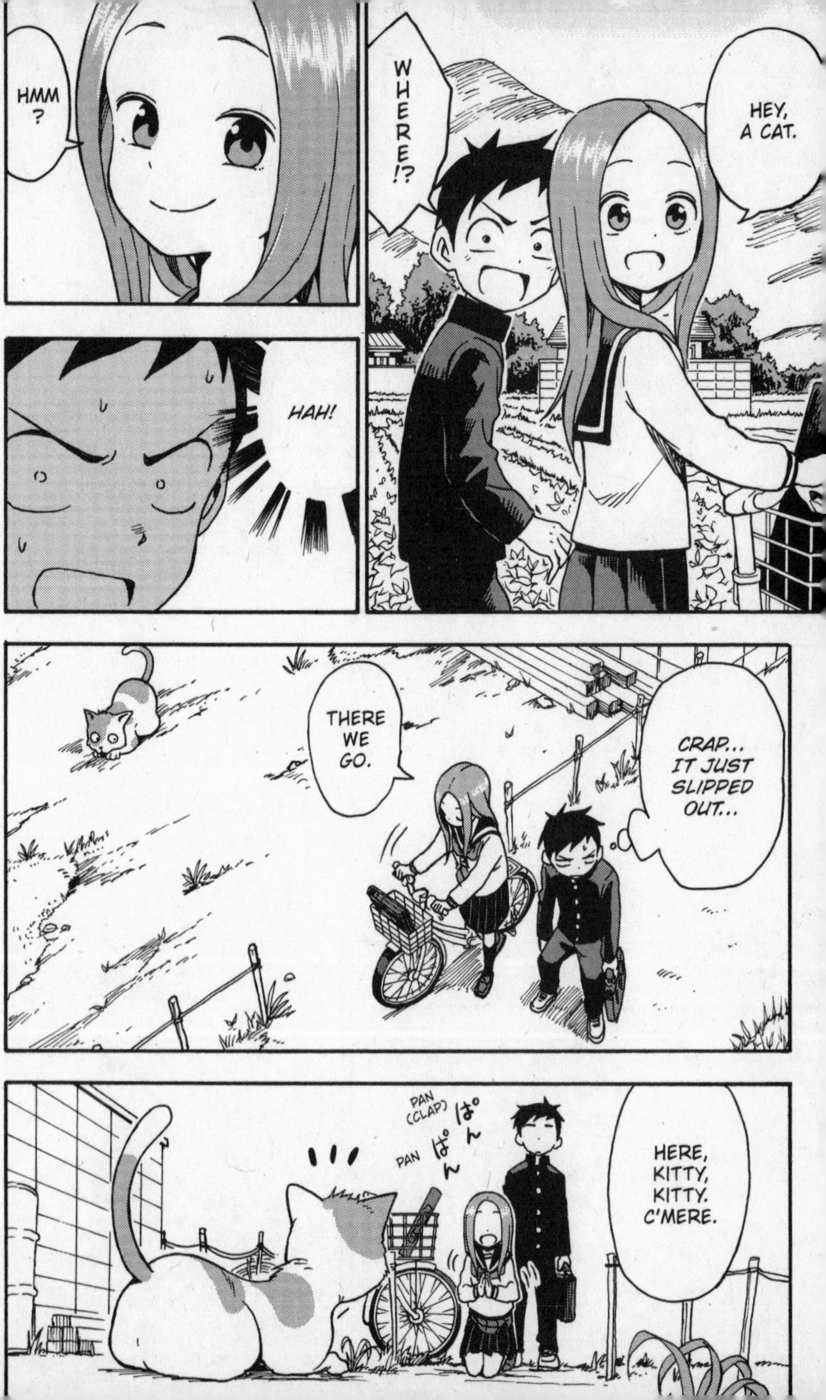
HEY, A CAT.
WHERE!?
HMM?
HAH!
CRAP... IT JUST SLIPPED OUT...
THERE WE GO.
HERE, KITTY, KITTY. C'MERE.
PAN (CLAP) ぱん
PAN ぱん

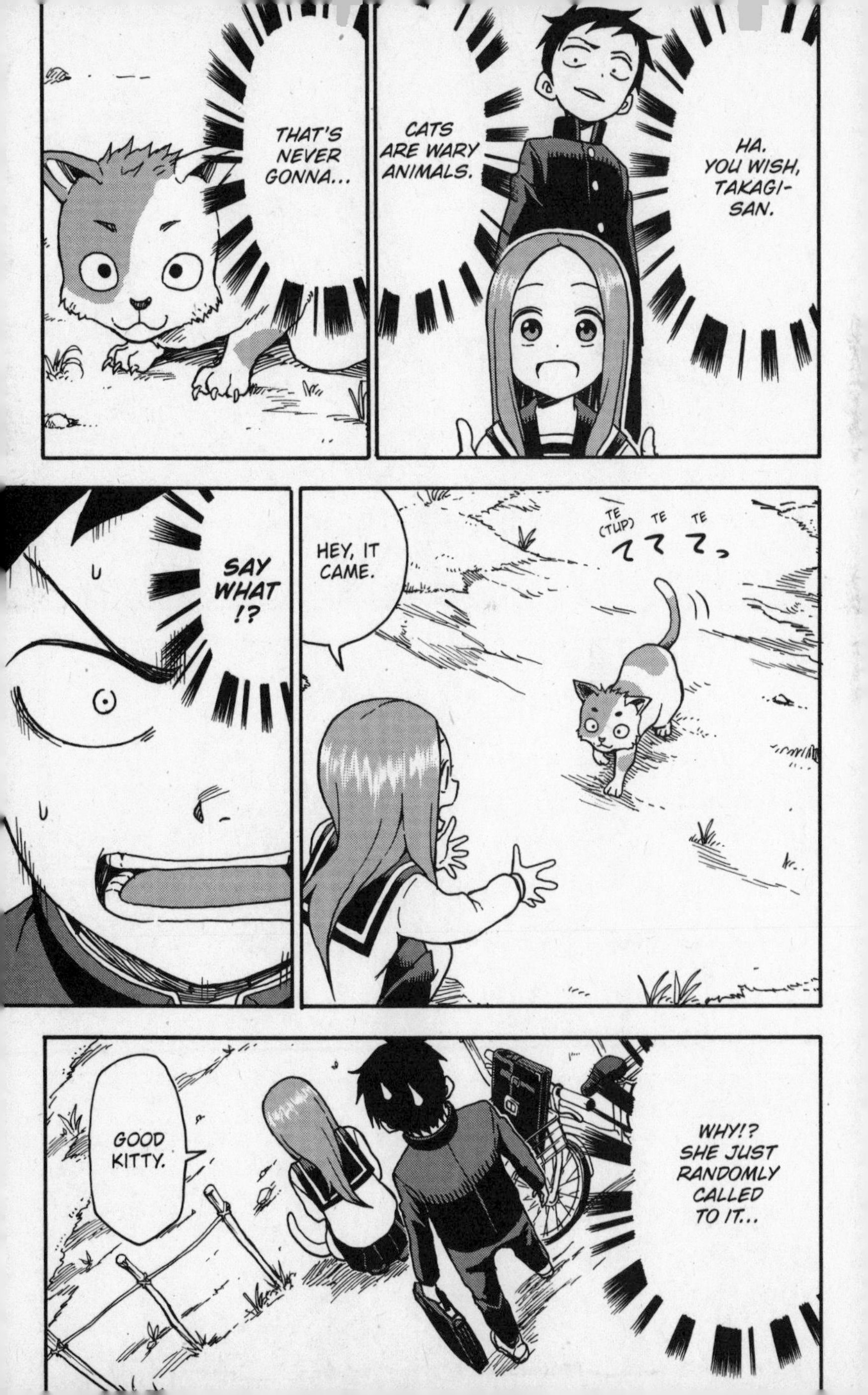
HA. YOU WISH, TAKAGI-SAN.
CATS ARE WARY ANIMALS.
THAT'S NEVER GONNA...
TE (TUP) TE TE
HEY, IT CAME.
SAY WHAT!?
WHY!? SHE JUST RANDOMLY CALLED TO IT...
GOOD KITTY.

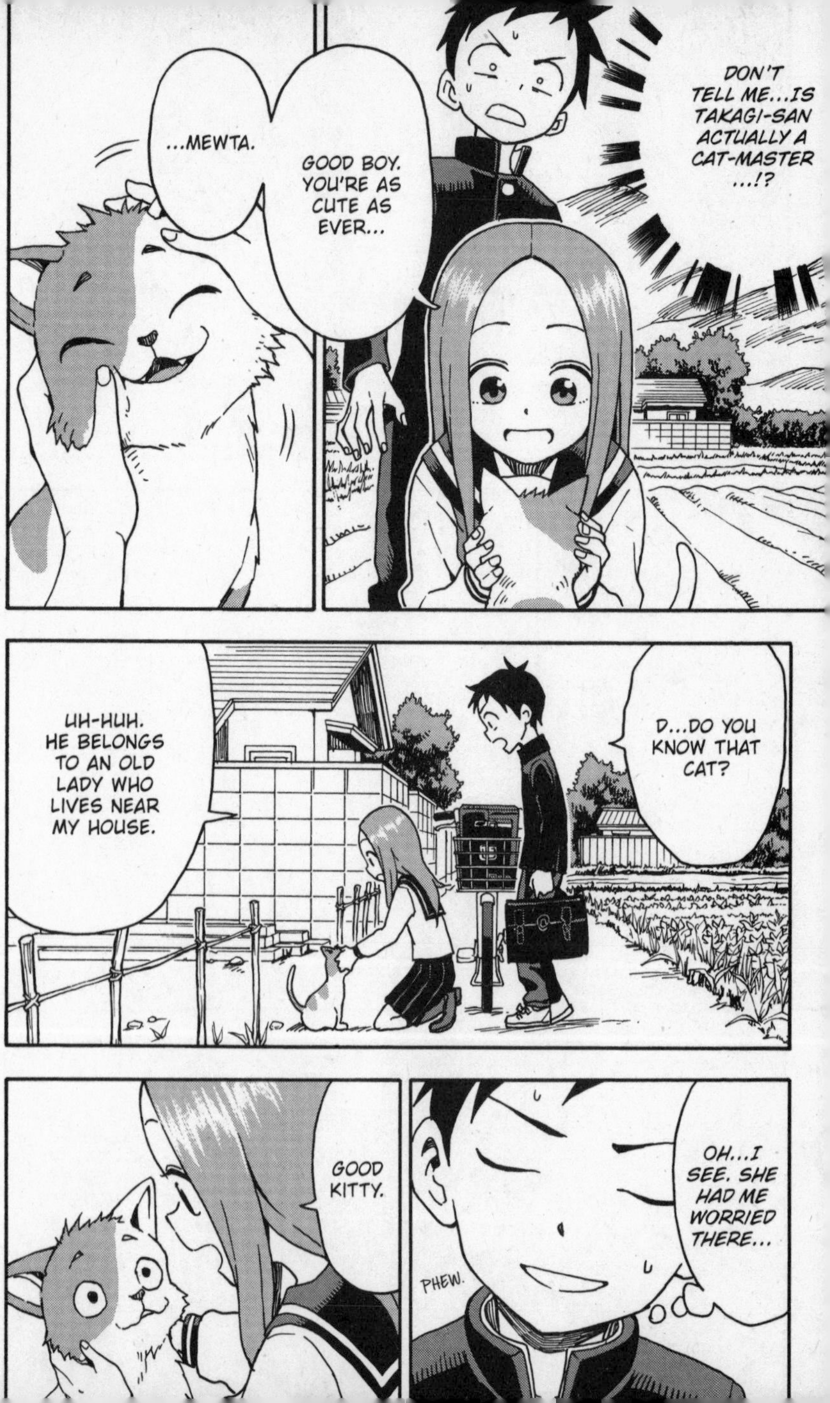
...MEWTA.
GOOD BOY. YOU'RE AS CUTE AS EVER...
DON'T TELL ME...IS TAKAGI-SAN ACTUALLY A CAT-MASTER ...!?
D...DO YOU KNOW THAT CAT?
UH-HUH. HE BELONGS TO AN OLD LADY WHO LIVES NEAR MY HOUSE.
OH...I SEE. SHE HAD ME WORRIED THERE...
PHEW.
GOOD KITTY.

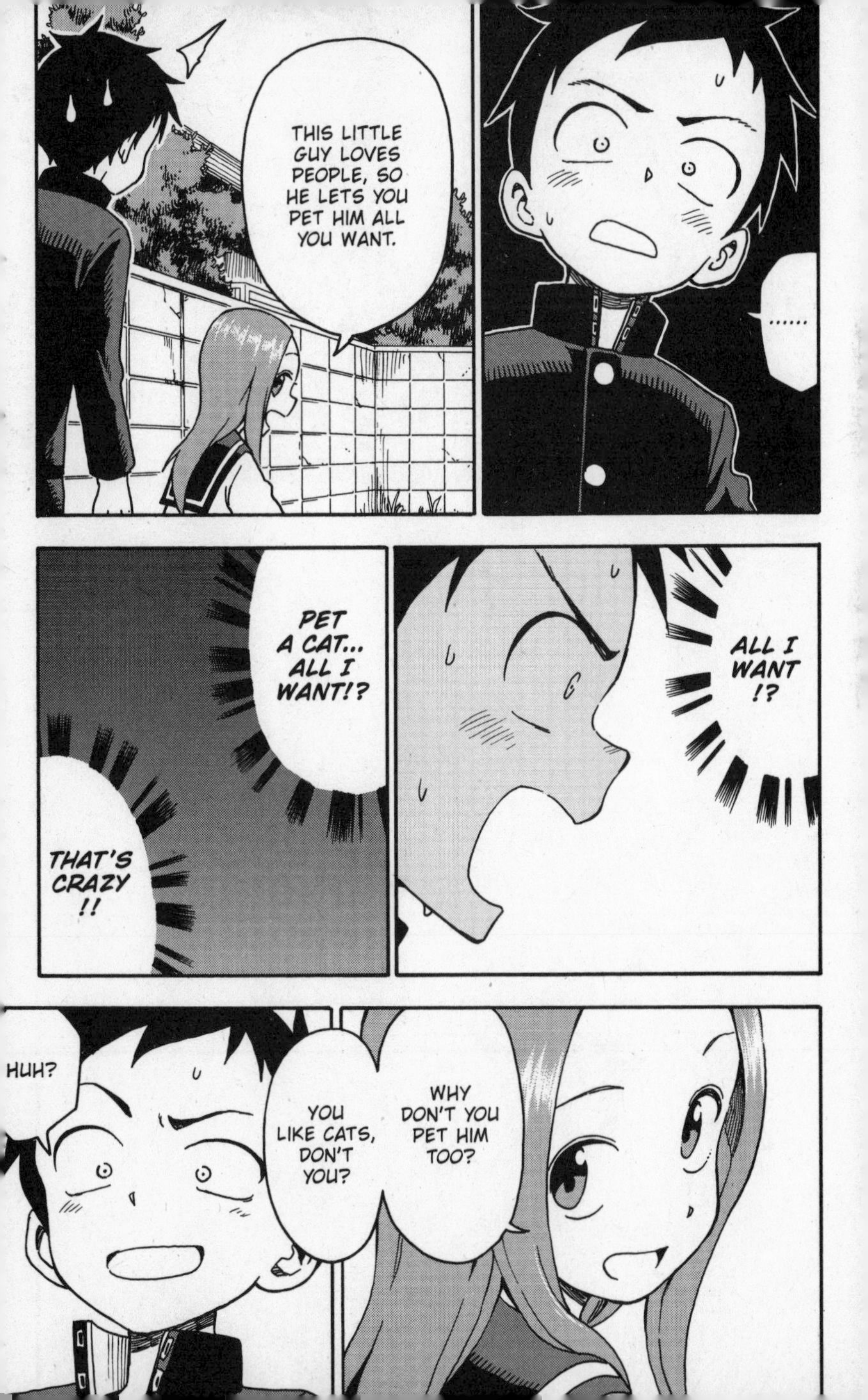
......
THIS LITTLE GUY LOVES PEOPLE, SO HE LETS YOU PET HIM ALL YOU WANT.
ALL I WANT !?
PET A CAT... ALL I WANT!?
THAT'S CRAZY !!
WHY DON'T YOU PET HIM TOO?
YOU LIKE CATS, DON'T YOU?
HUH?

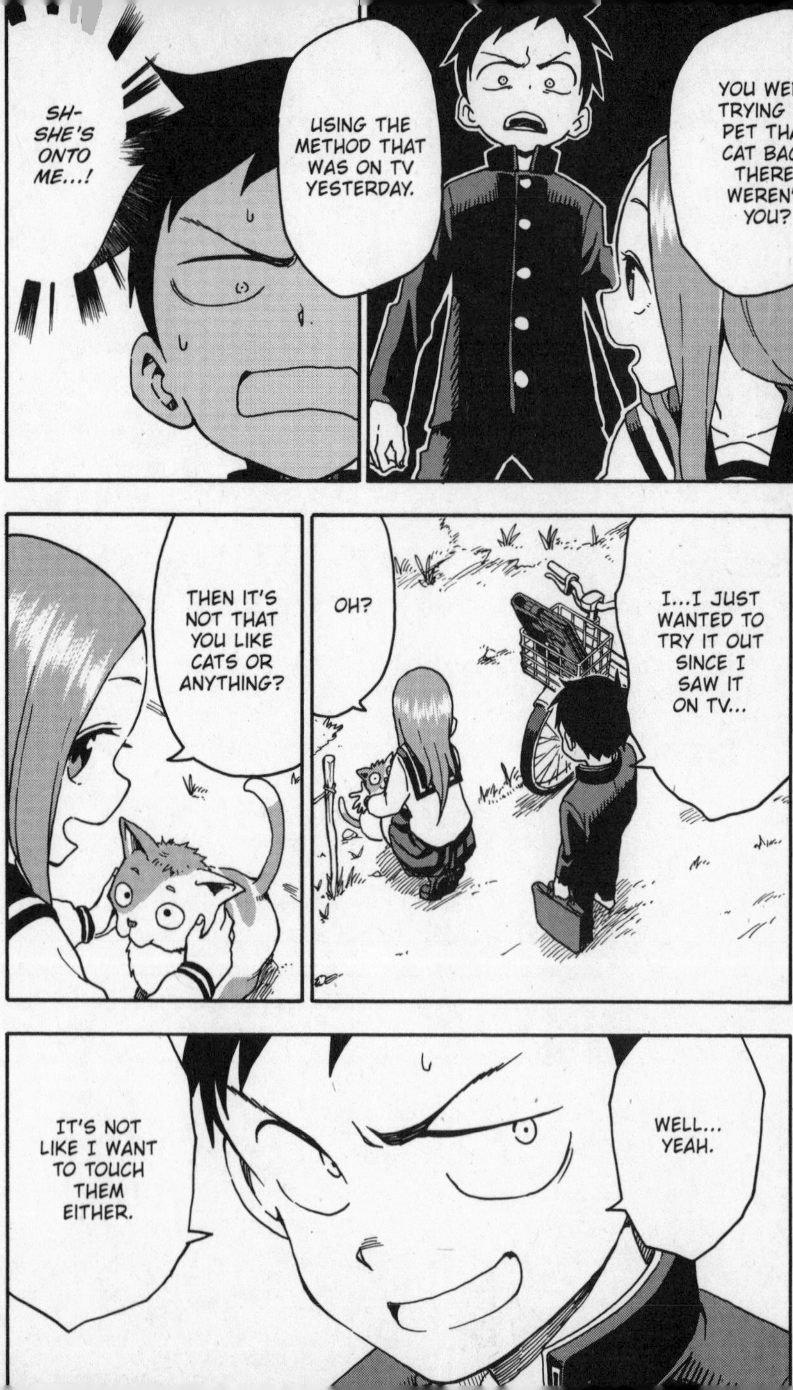
YOU WERE TRYING TO PET THAT CAT BACK THERE, WEREN'T YOU?
USING THE METHOD THAT WAS ON TV YESTERDAY.
SH- SHE'S ONTO ME...!
I...I JUST WANTED TO TRY IT OUT SINCE I SAW IT ON TV...
OH?
THEN IT'S NOT THAT YOU LIKE CATS OR ANYTHING?
WELL... YEAH.
IT'S NOT LIKE I WANT TO TOUCH THEM EITHER.

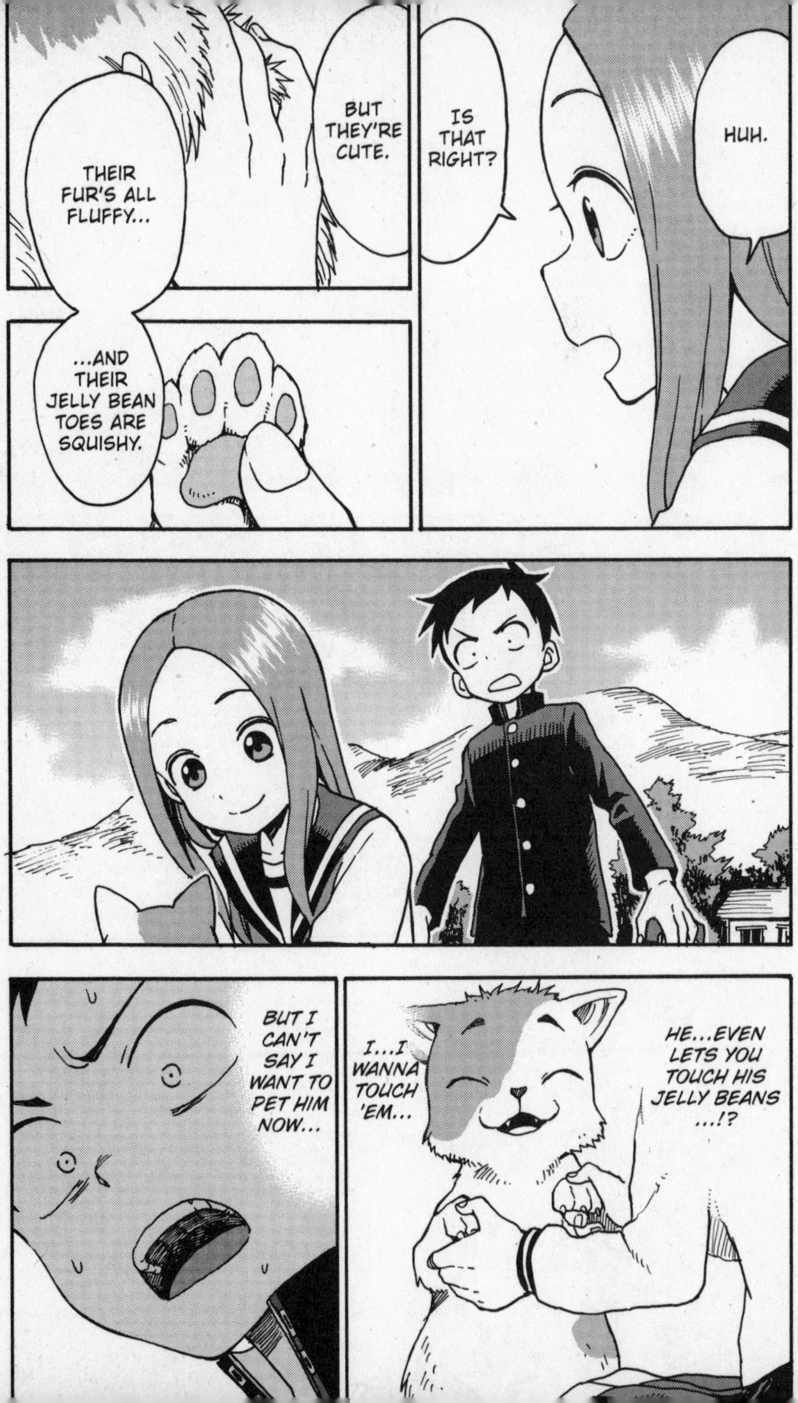
HUH.
IS THAT RIGHT?
BUT THEY'RE CUTE.
THEIR FUR'S ALL FLUFFY...
...AND THEIR JELLY BEAN TOES ARE SQUISHY.
HE...EVEN LETS YOU TOUCH HIS JELLY BEANS ...!?
I...I WANNA TOUCH 'EM...
BUT I CAN'T SAY I WANT TO PET HIM NOW...

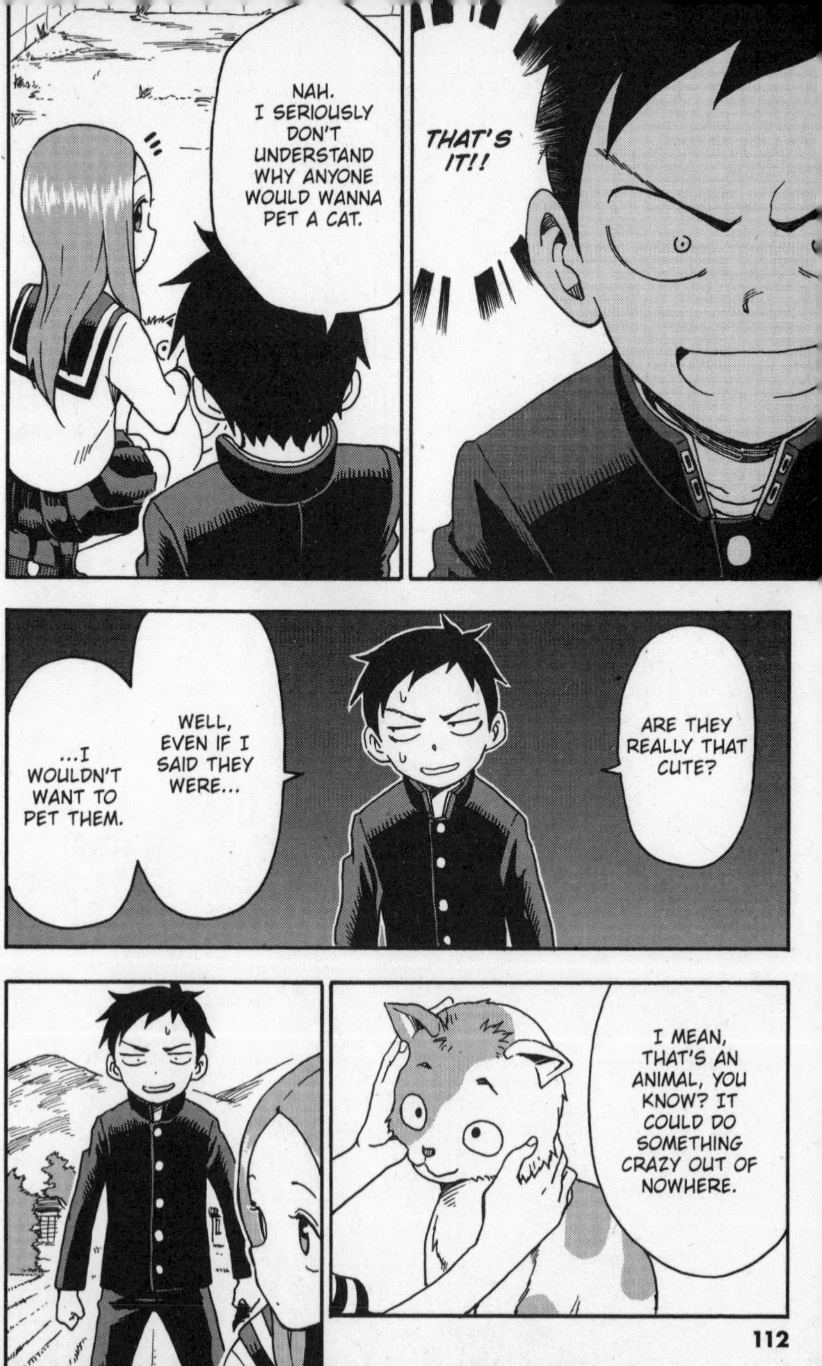
THAT'S IT!!
NAH. I SERIOUSLY DON'T UNDERSTAND WHY ANYONE WOULD WANNA PET A CAT.
ARE THEY REALLY THAT CUTE?
WELL, EVEN IF I SAID THEY WERE...
...I WOULDN'T WANT TO PET THEM.
I MEAN, THAT'S AN ANIMAL, YOU KNOW? IT COULD DO SOMETHING CRAZY OUT OF NOWHERE.

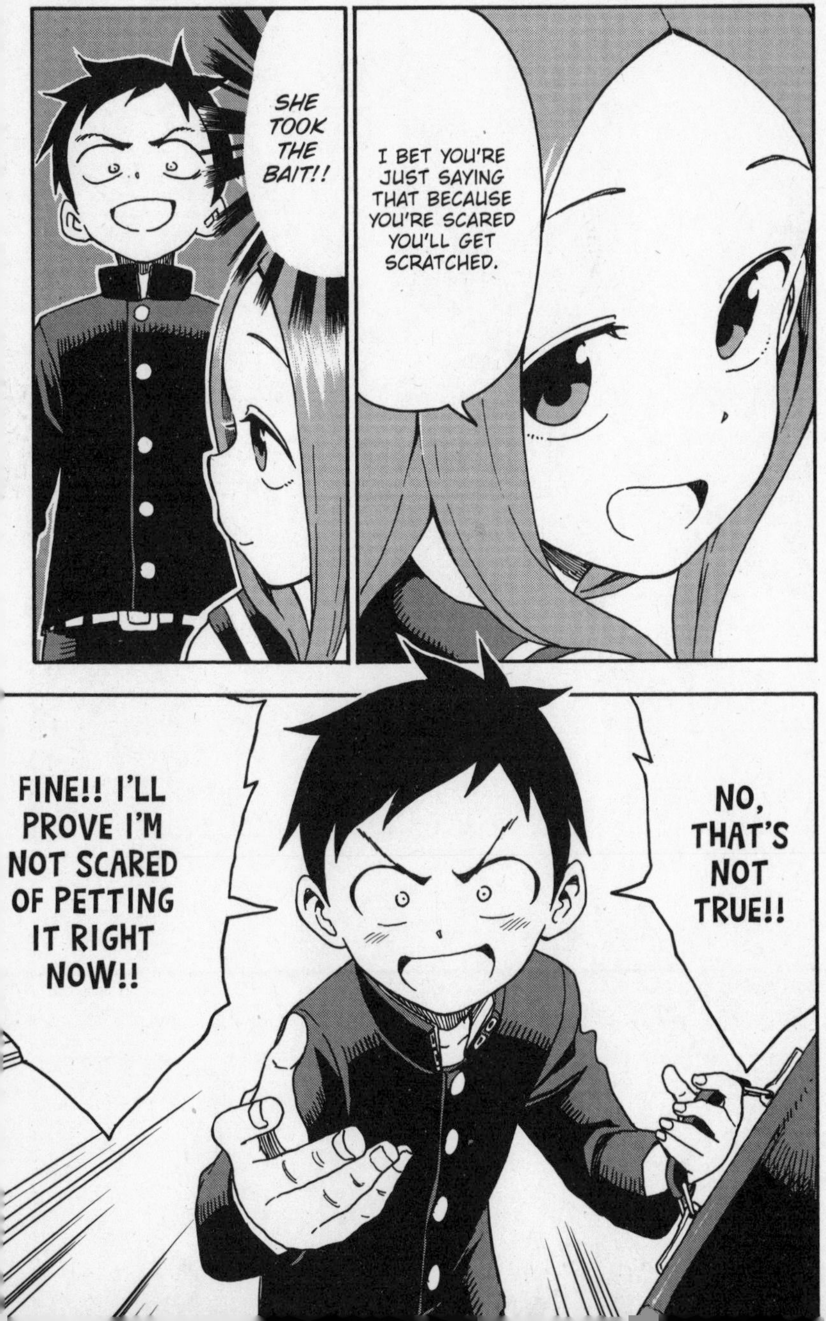
I BET YOU'RE JUST SAYING THAT BECAUSE YOU'RE SCARED YOU'LL GET SCRATCHED.
SHE TOOK THE BAIT!!
NO, THAT'S NOT TRUE!!
FINE!! I'LL PROVE I'M NOT SCARED OF PETTING IT RIGHT NOW!!

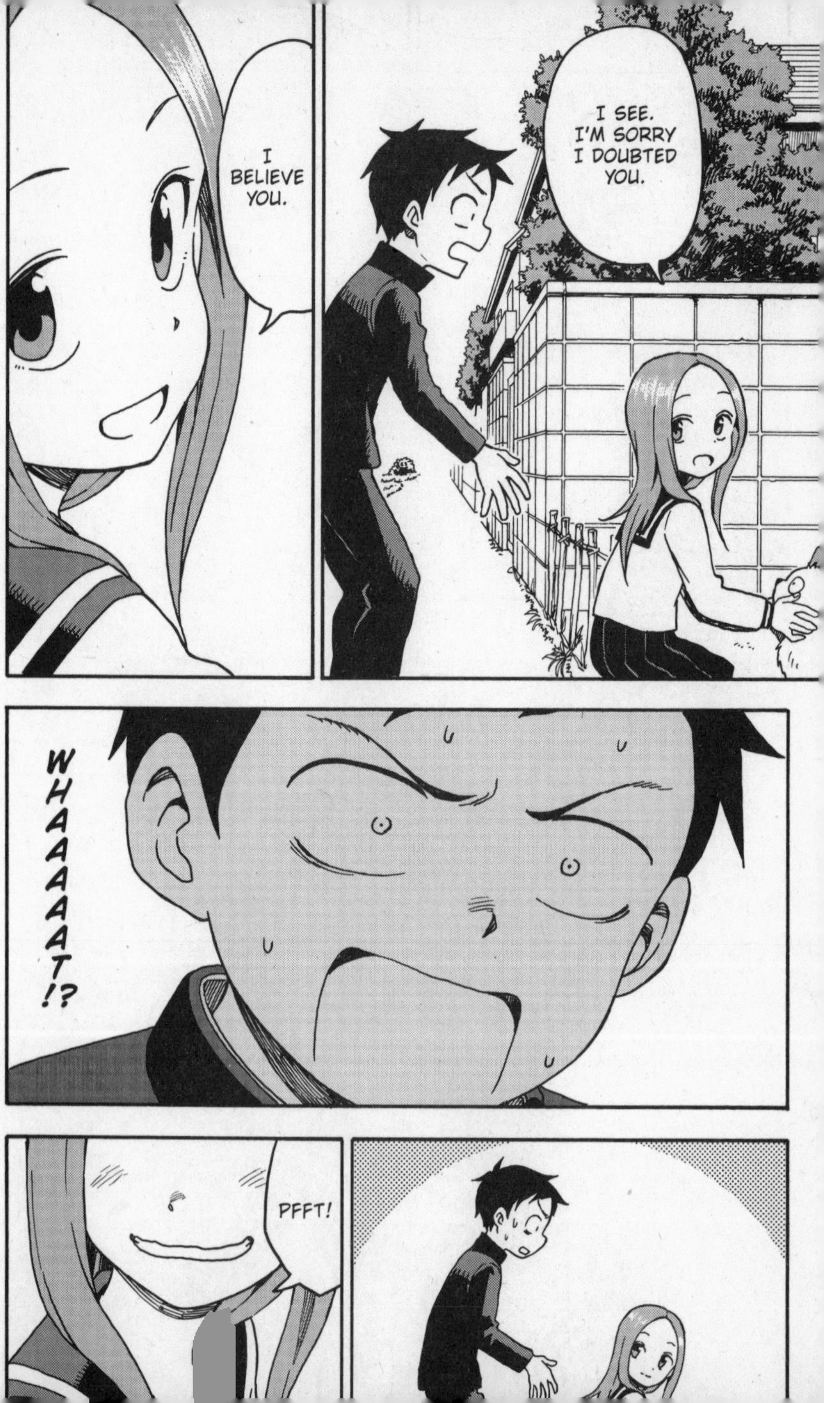
I SEE. I'M SORRY I DOUBTED YOU.
I BELIEVE YOU.
WHAAAAAT!?
PFFT!

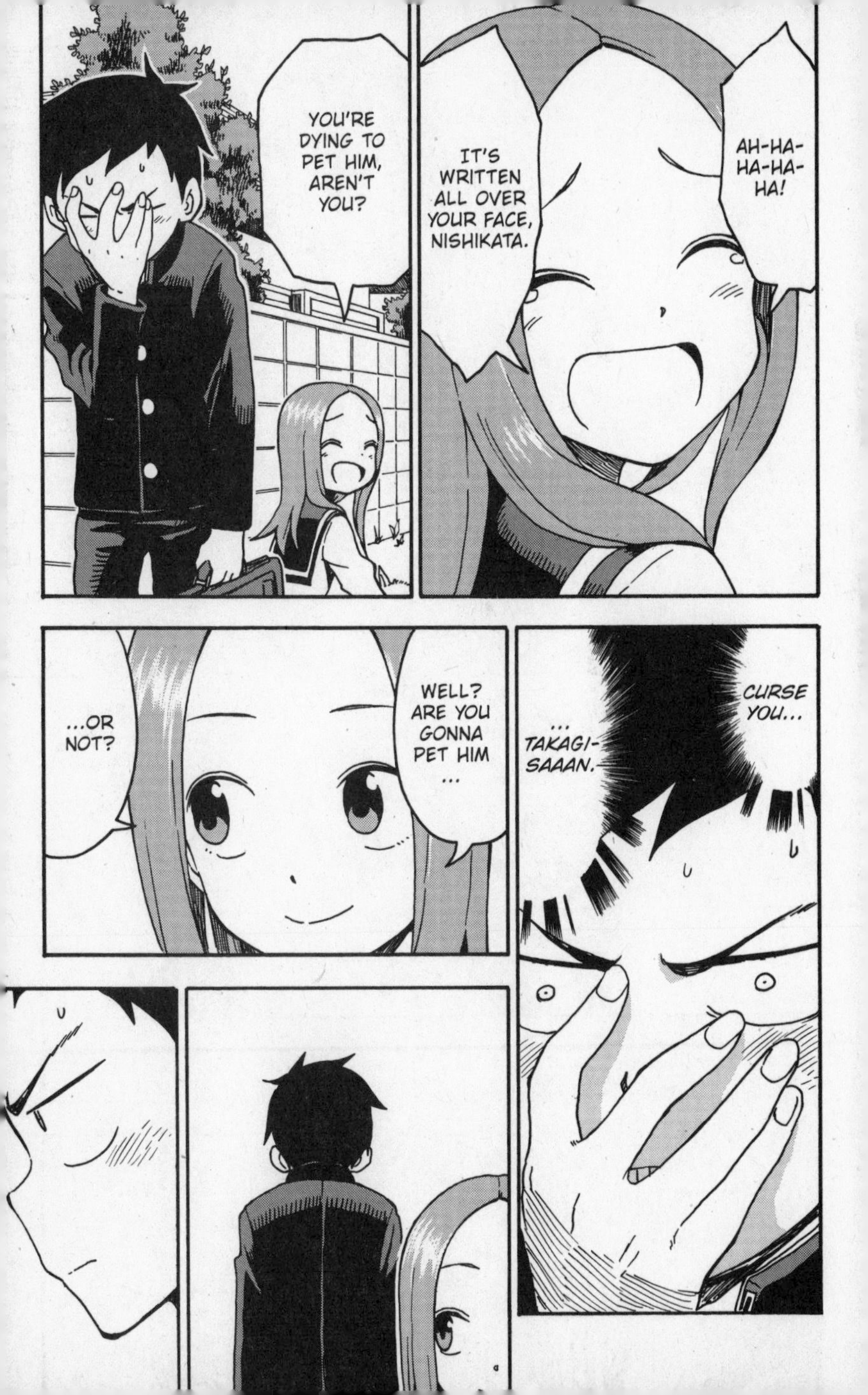
AH-HA-HA-HA-HA!
IT'S WRITTEN ALL OVER YOUR FACE, NISHIKATA.
YOU'RE DYING TO PET HIM, AREN'T YOU?
CURSE YOU...
...TAKAGI-SAAAN.
WELL? ARE YOU GONNA PET HIM...
...OR NOT?

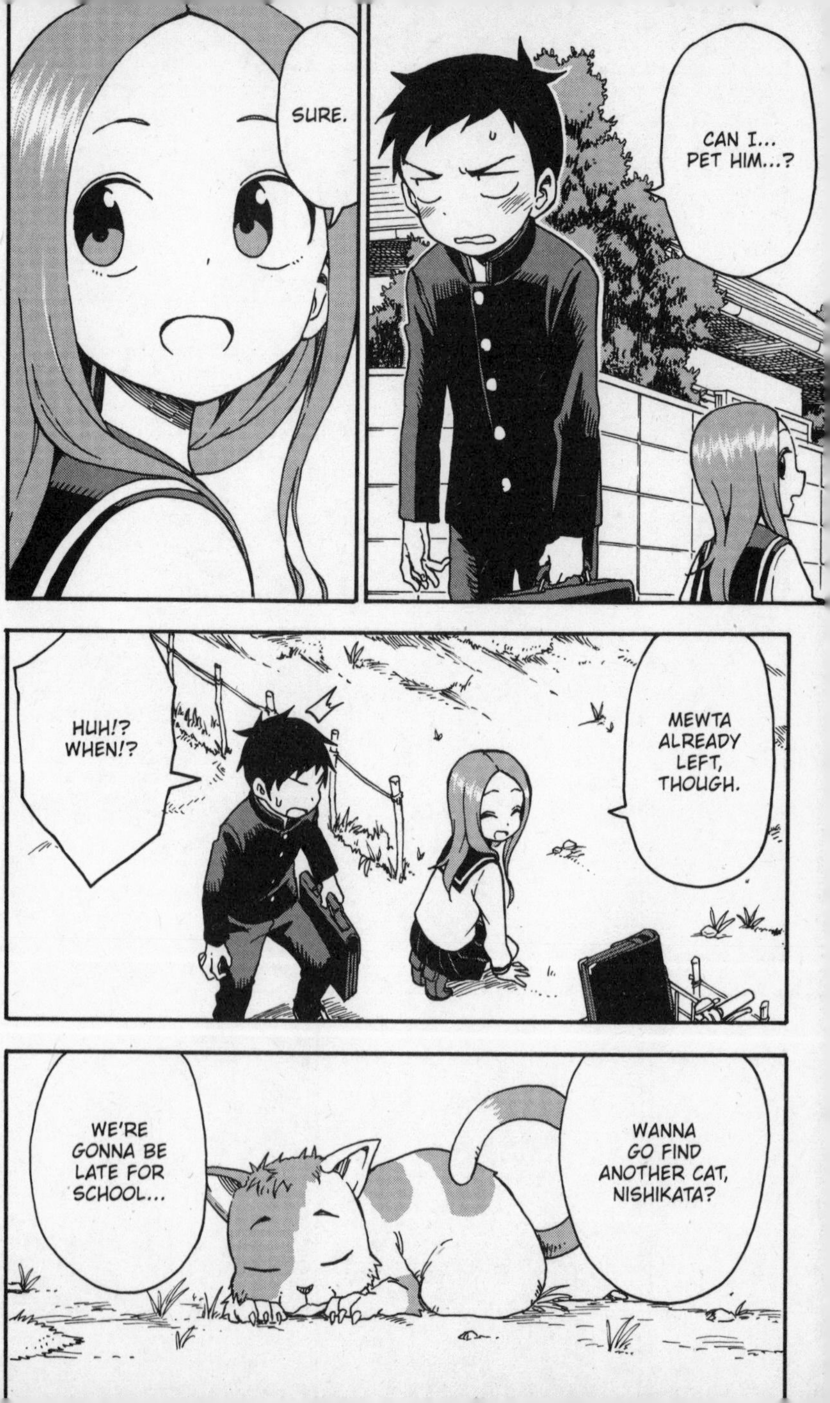
CAN I... PET HIM...?
SURE.
MEWTA ALREADY LEFT, THOUGH.
HUH!? WHEN!?
WANNA GO FIND ANOTHER CAT, NISHIKATA?
WE'RE GONNA BE LATE FOR SCHOOL...

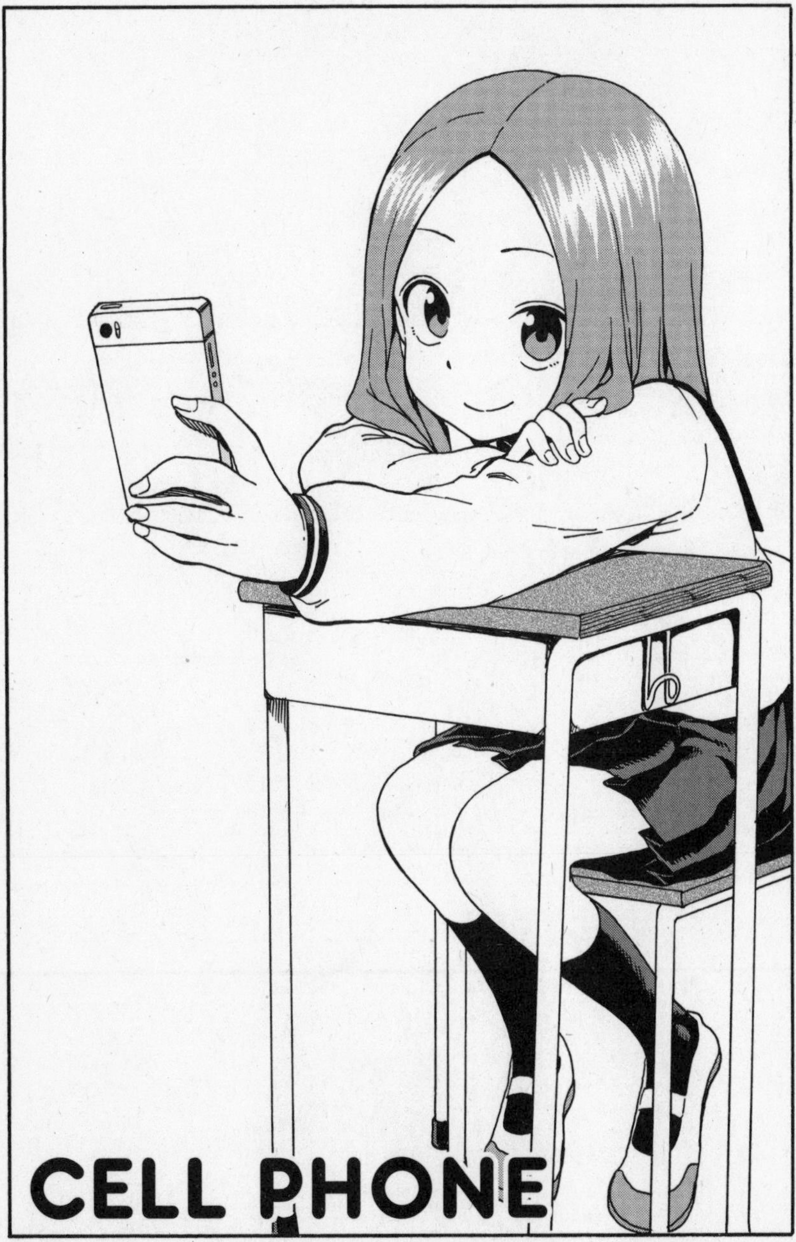
CELL PHONE

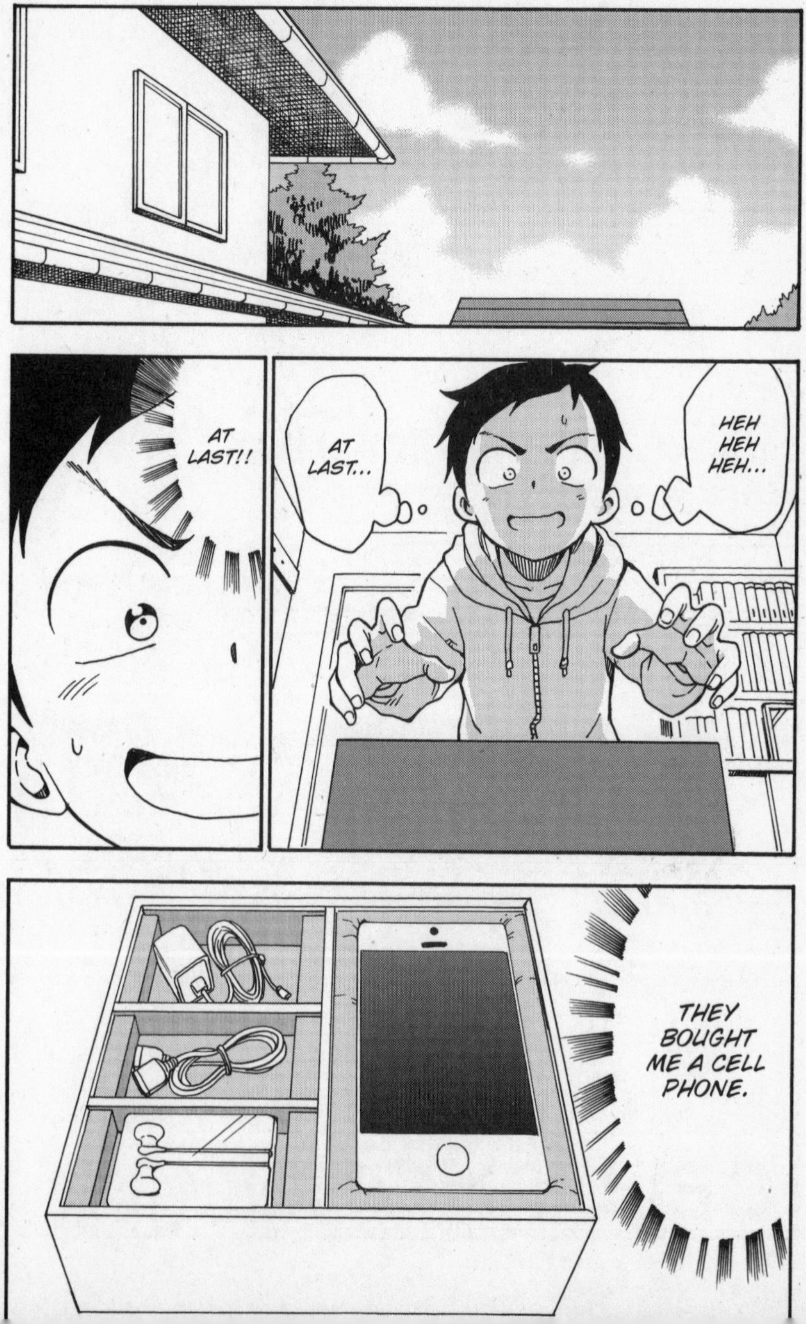
HEH HEH HEH...
AT LAST...
AT LAST!!
THEY BOUGHT ME A CELL PHONE.

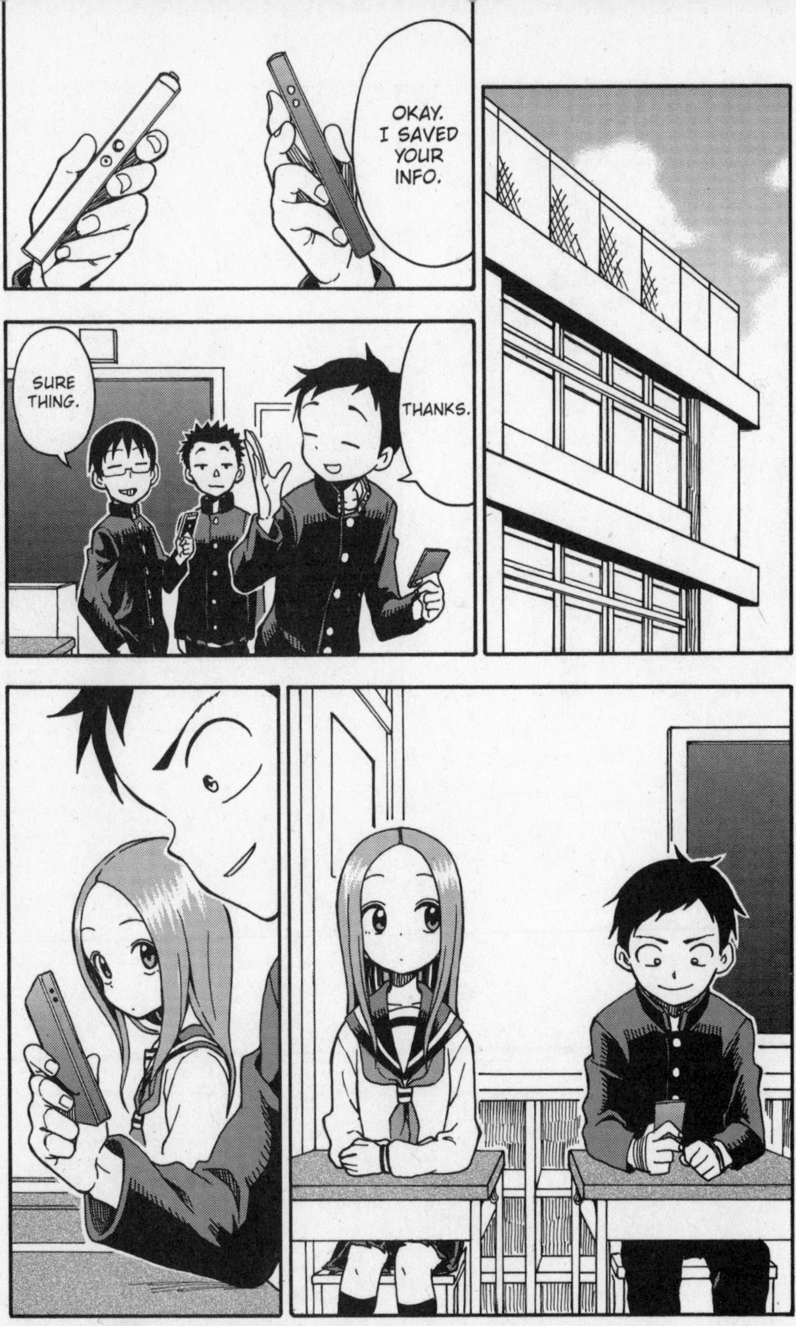
OKAY. I SAVED YOUR INFO.
THANKS.
SURE THING.

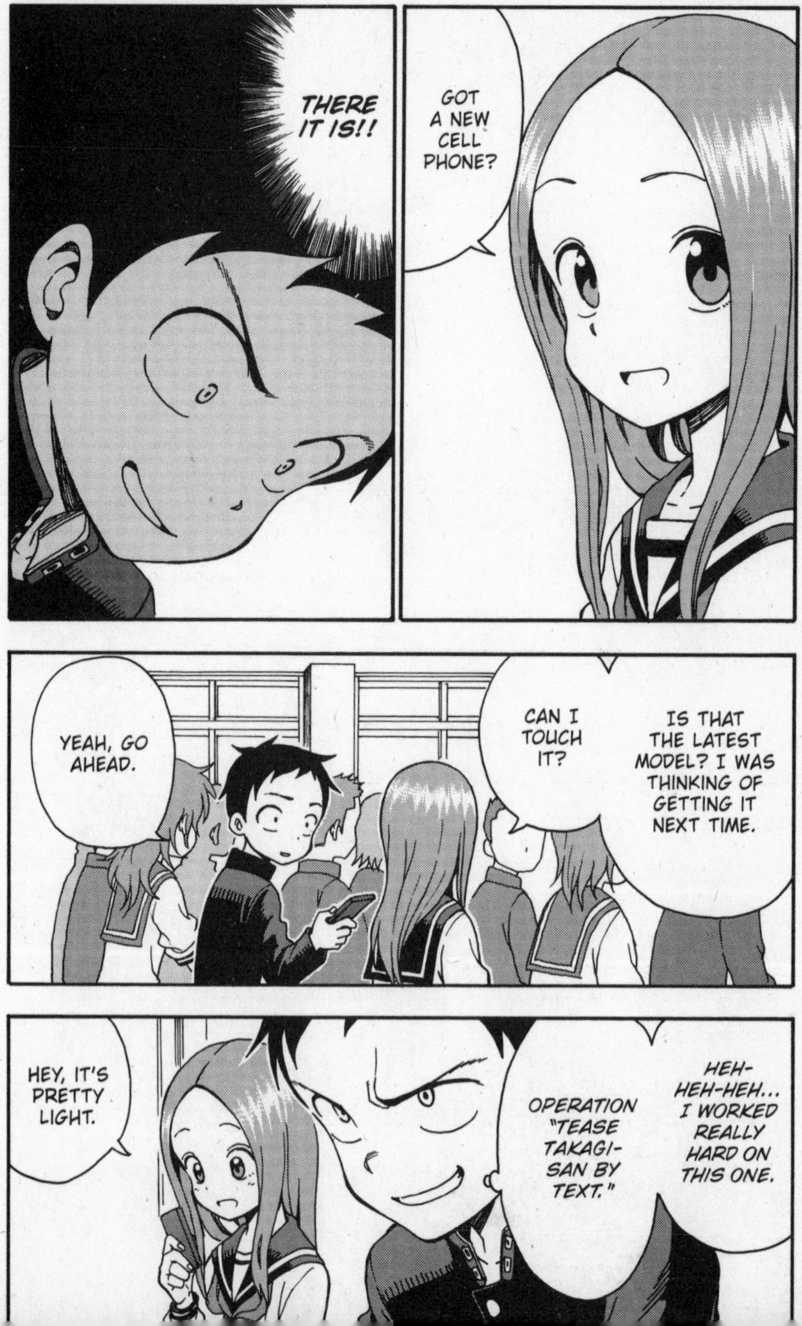
GOT A NEW CELL PHONE?
THERE IT IS!!
IS THAT THE LATEST MODEL? I WAS THINKING OF GETTING IT NEXT TIME.
CAN I TOUCH IT?
YEAH, GO AHEAD.
HEH-HEH-HEH... I WORKED REALLY HARD ON THIS ONE.
OPERATION "TEASE TAKAGI-SAN BY TEXT."
HEY, IT'S PRETTY LIGHT.

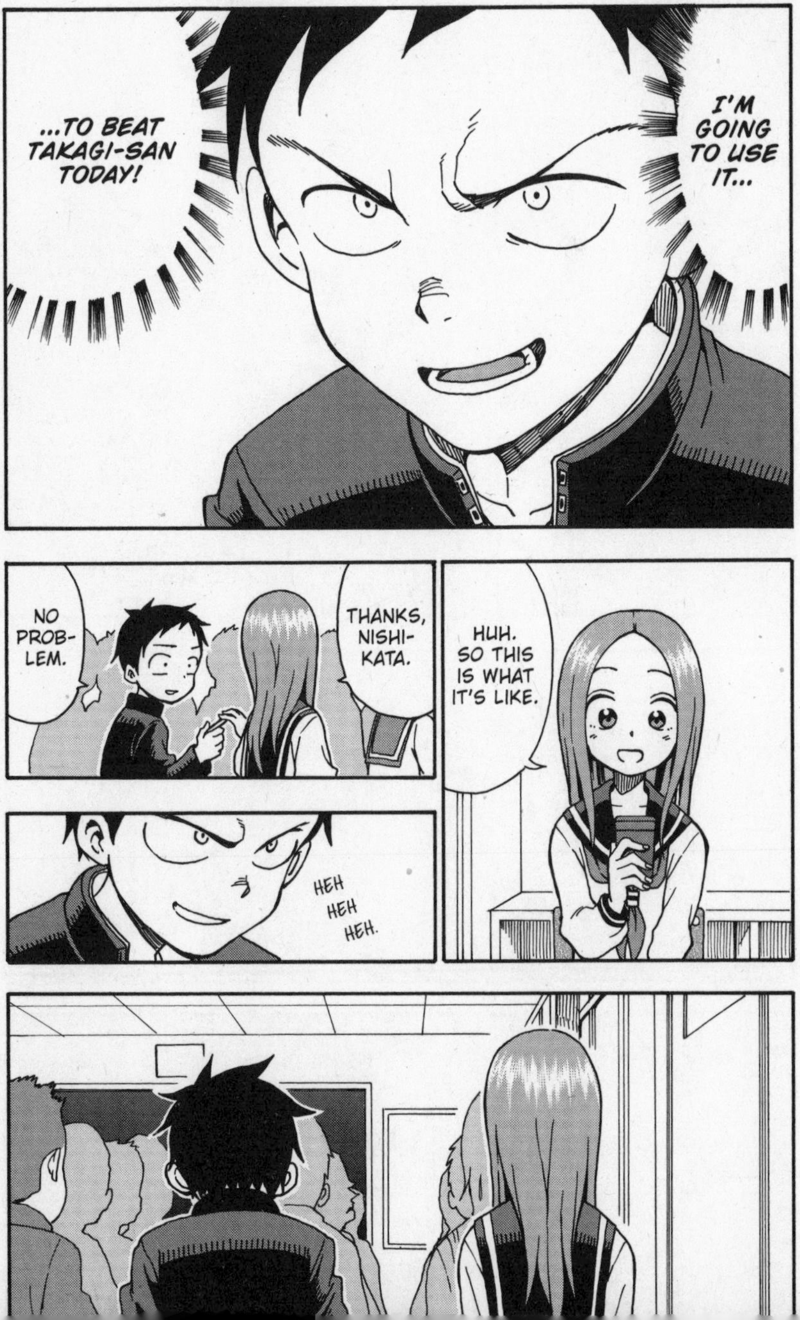
I'M GOING TO USE IT...
...TO BEAT TAKAGI-SAN TODAY!
HUH. SO THIS IS WHAT IT'S LIKE.
THANKS, NISHI-KATA.
NO PROB-LEM.
HEH HEH HEH.

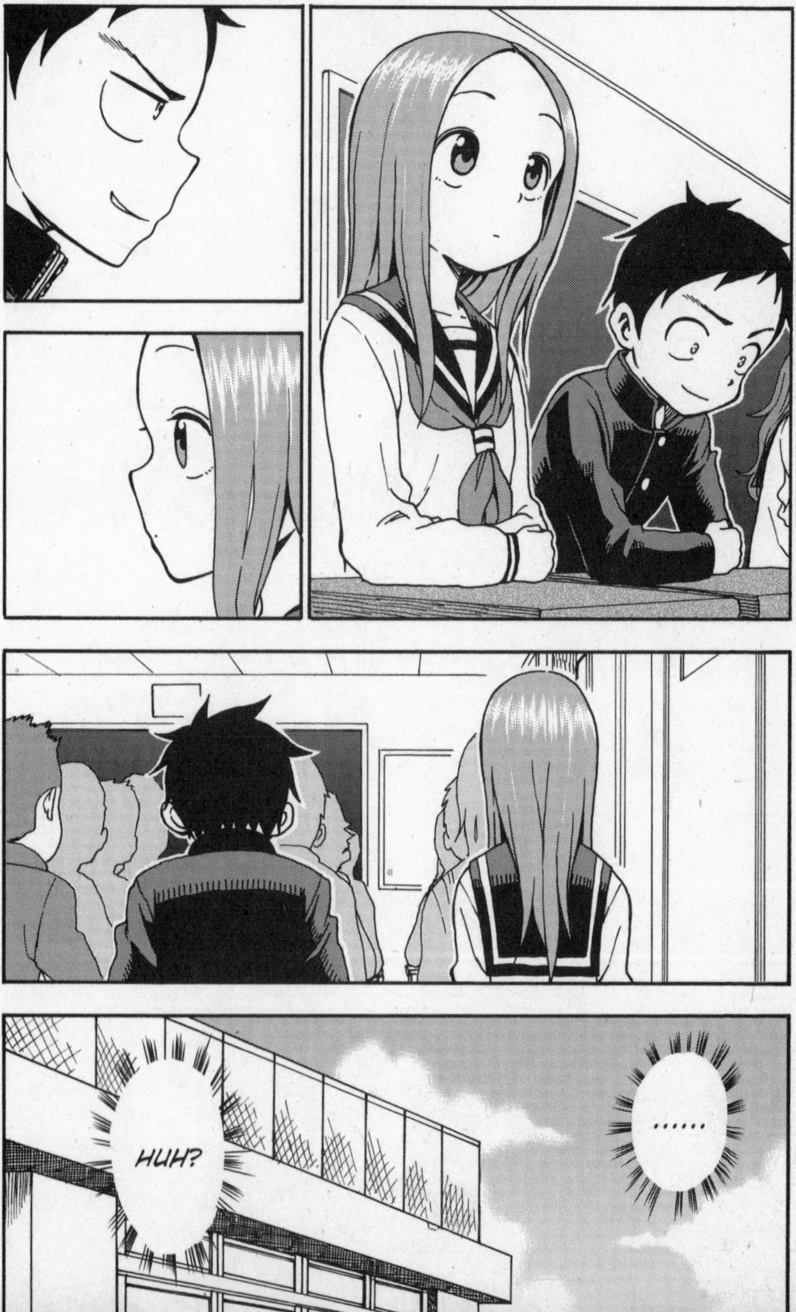
......
HUH?

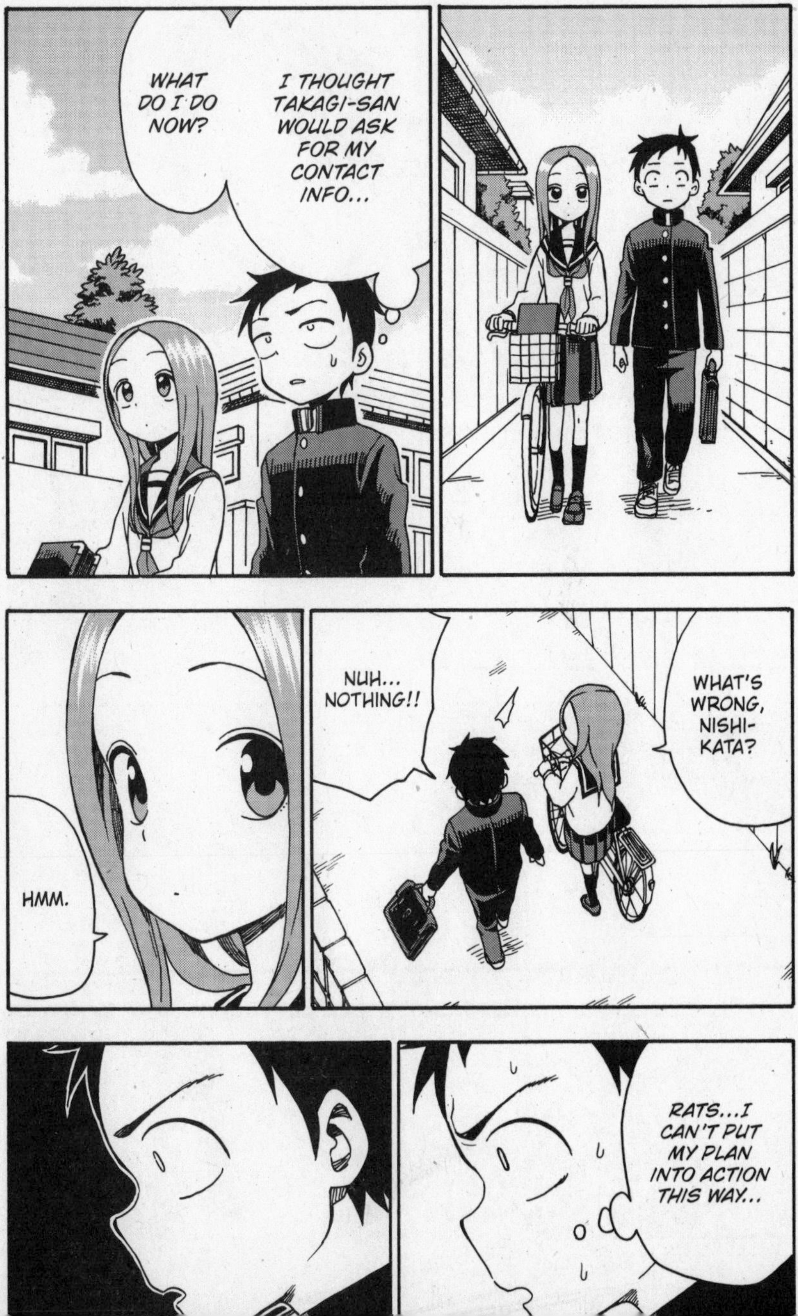
I THOUGHT TAKAGI-SAN WOULD ASK FOR MY CONTACT INFO...
WHAT DO I DO NOW?
WHAT'S WRONG, NISHI-KATA?
NUH... NOTHING!!
HMM.
RATS...I CAN'T PUT MY PLAN INTO ACTION THIS WAY...

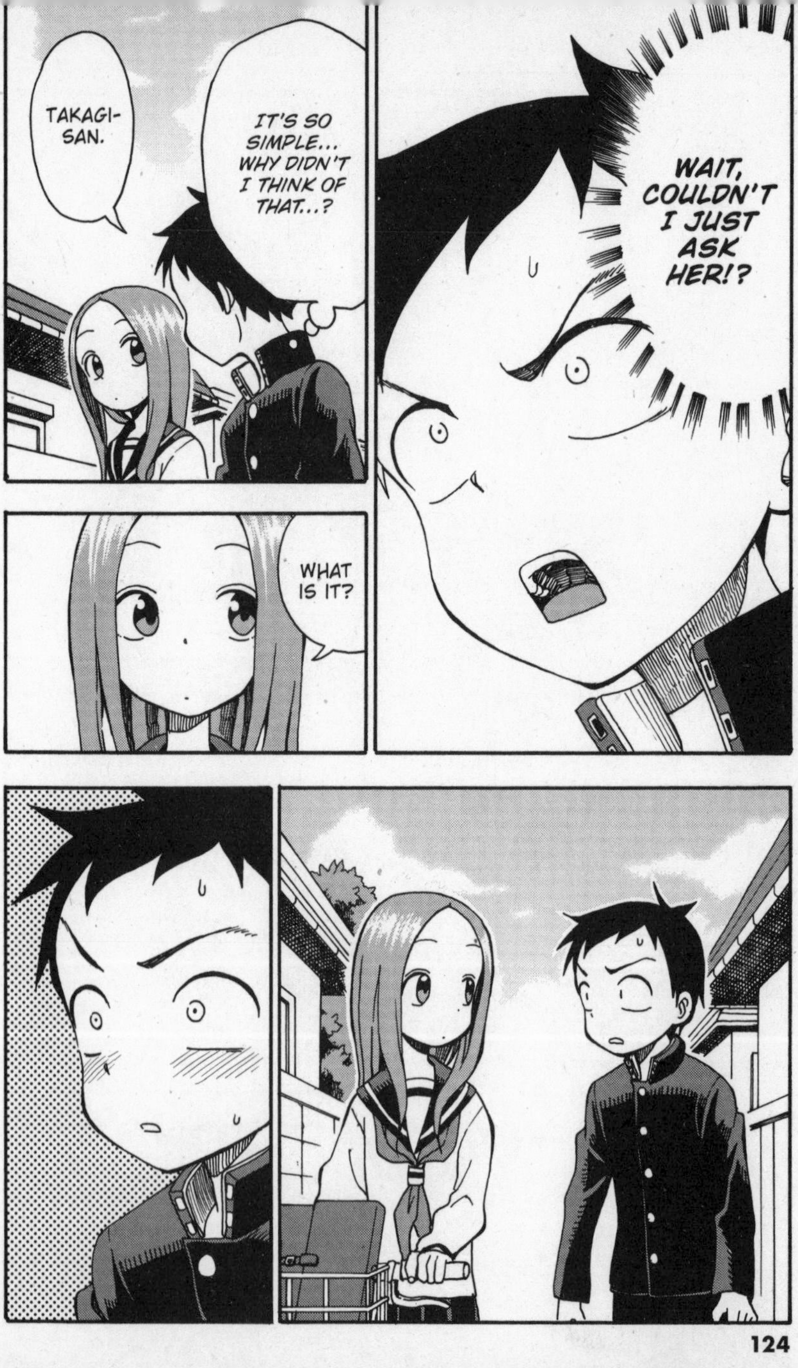
WAIT, COULDN'T I JUST ASK HER!?
IT'S SO SIMPLE... WHY DIDN'T I THINK OF THAT...?
TAKAGI-SAN.
WHAT IS IT?

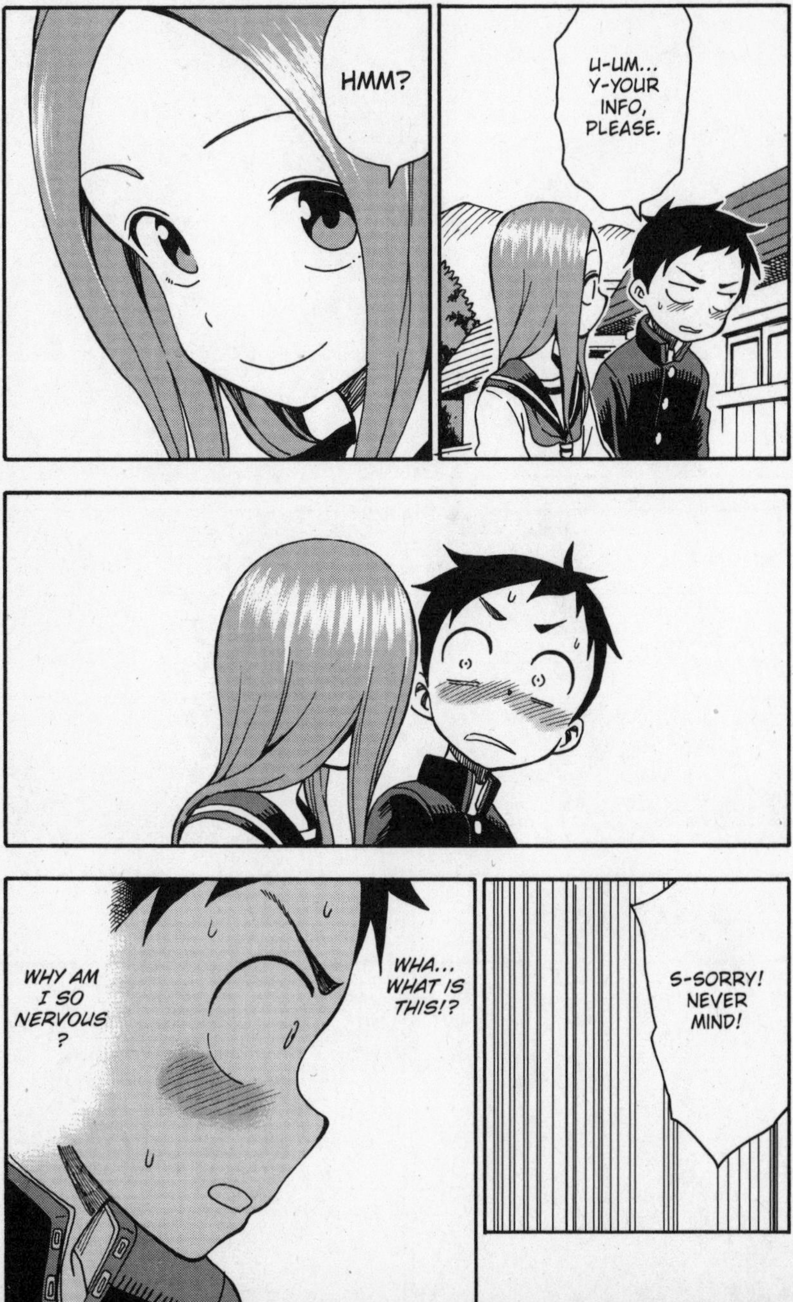
U-UM... Y-YOUR INFO, PLEASE.
HMM?
S-SORRY! NEVER MIND!
WHA... WHAT IS THIS!?
WHY AM I SO NERVOUS?

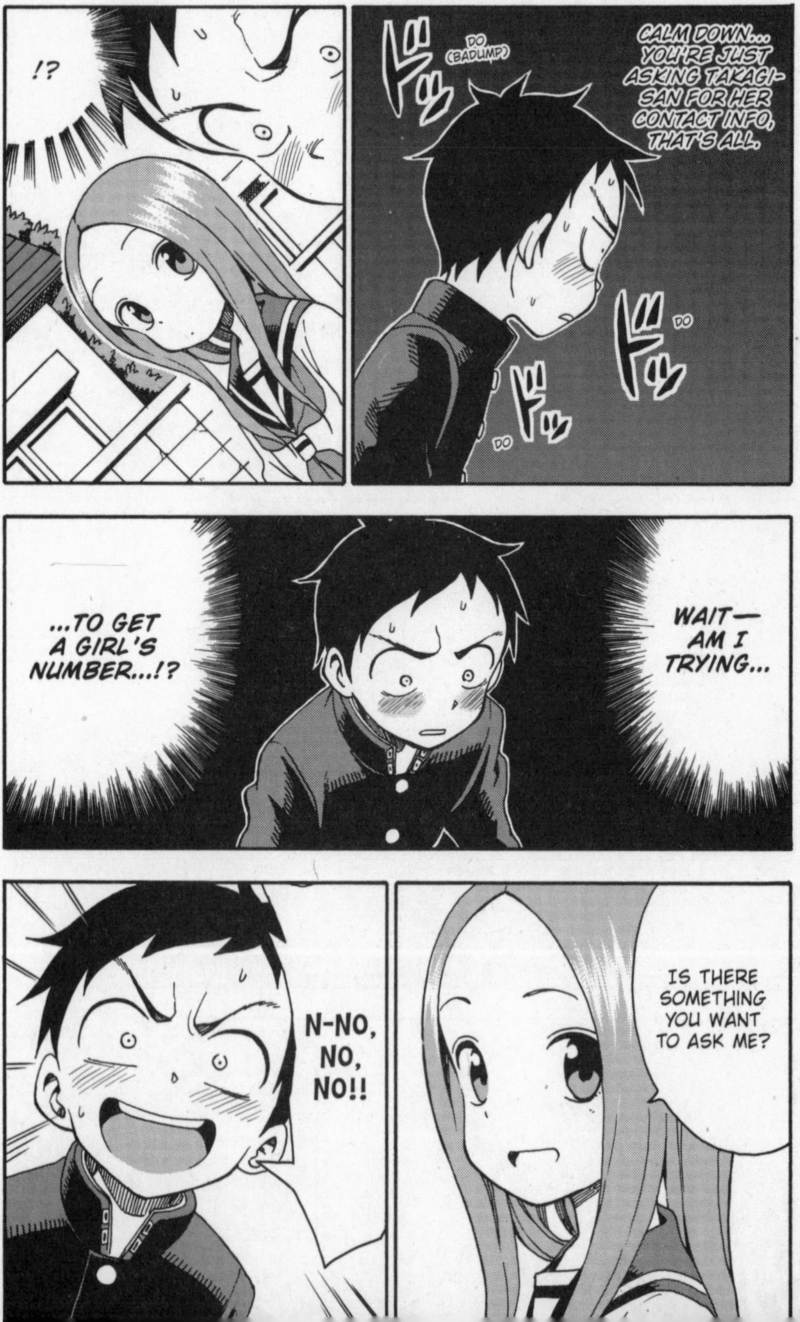
CALM DOWN... YOU'RE JUST ASKING TAKAGI-SAN FOR HER CONTACT INFO, THAT'S ALL.
DO (BADUMP)
DO
DO
!?
WAIT— AM I TRYING...
...TO GET A GIRL'S NUMBER...!?
IS THERE SOMETHING YOU WANT TO ASK ME?
N-NO, NO, NO!!

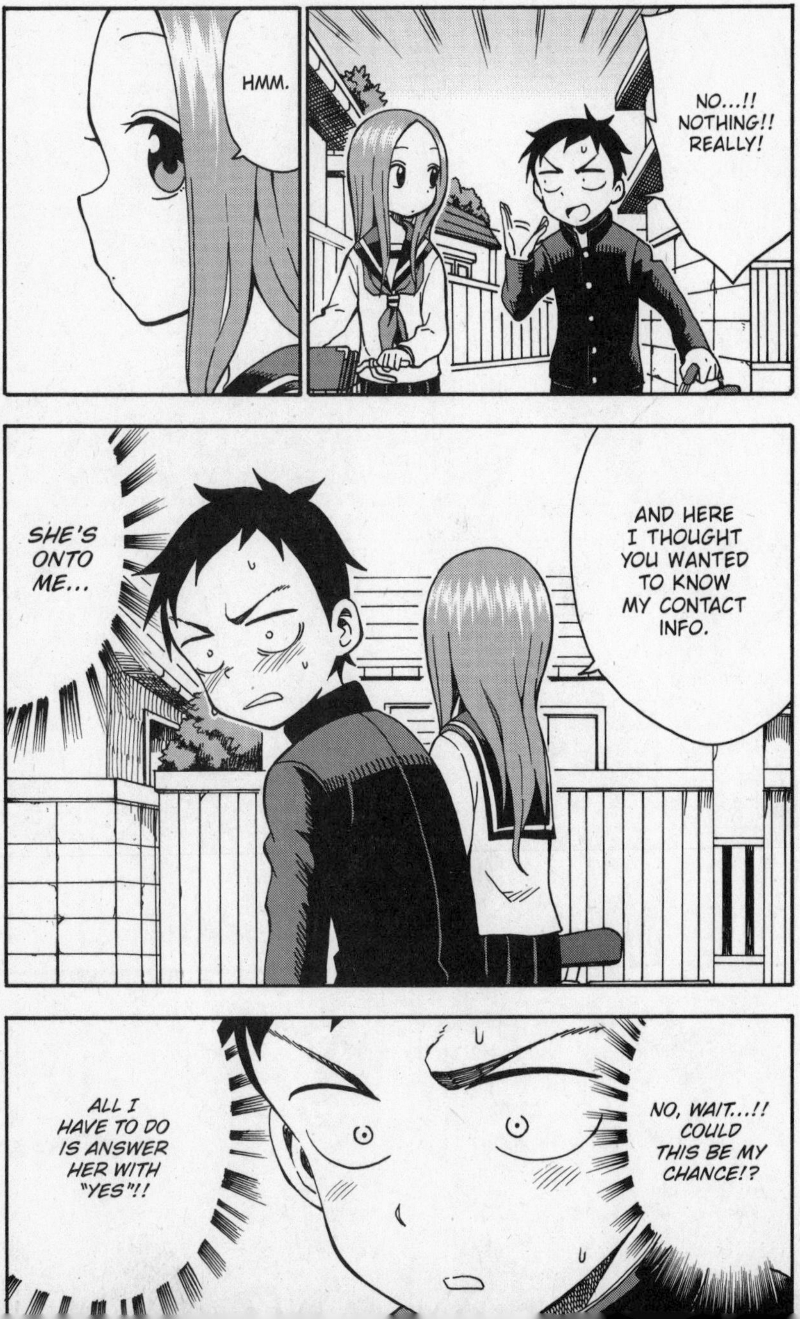
NO...!! NOTHING!! REALLY!
HMM.
AND HERE I THOUGHT YOU WANTED TO KNOW MY CONTACT INFO.
SHE'S ONTO ME...
NO, WAIT...!! COULD THIS BE MY CHANCE!?
ALL I HAVE TO DO IS ANSWER HER WITH "YES"!!

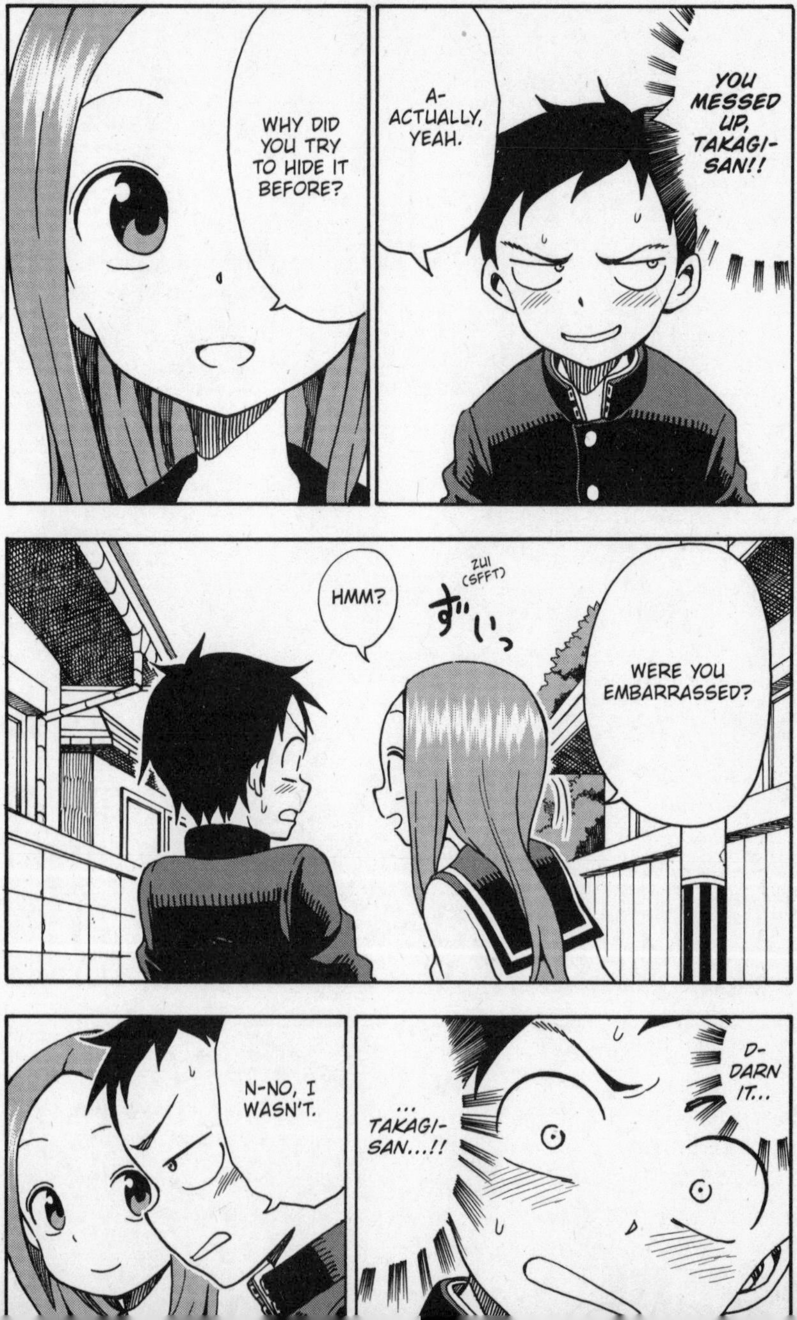
YOU MESSED UP, TAKAGI-SAN!!
A- ACTUALLY, YEAH.
WHY DID YOU TRY TO HIDE IT BEFORE?
WERE YOU EMBARRASSED?
ずいっ
ZUI (SFFT)
HMM?
D- DARN IT...
... TAKAGI-SAN...!!
N-NO, I WASN'T.

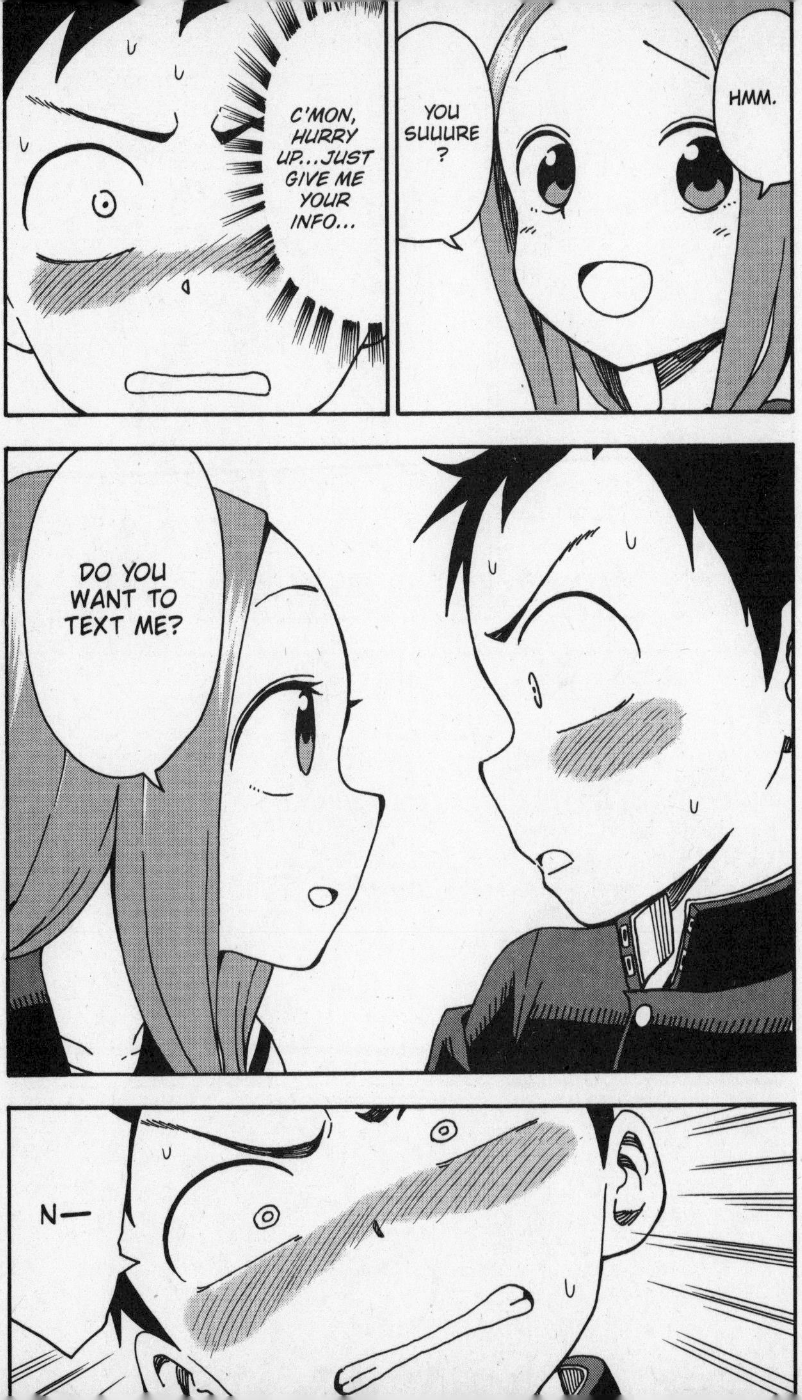
HMM.
YOU SUUURE?
C'MON, HURRY UP...JUST GIVE ME YOUR INFO...
DO YOU WANT TO TEXT ME?
N—

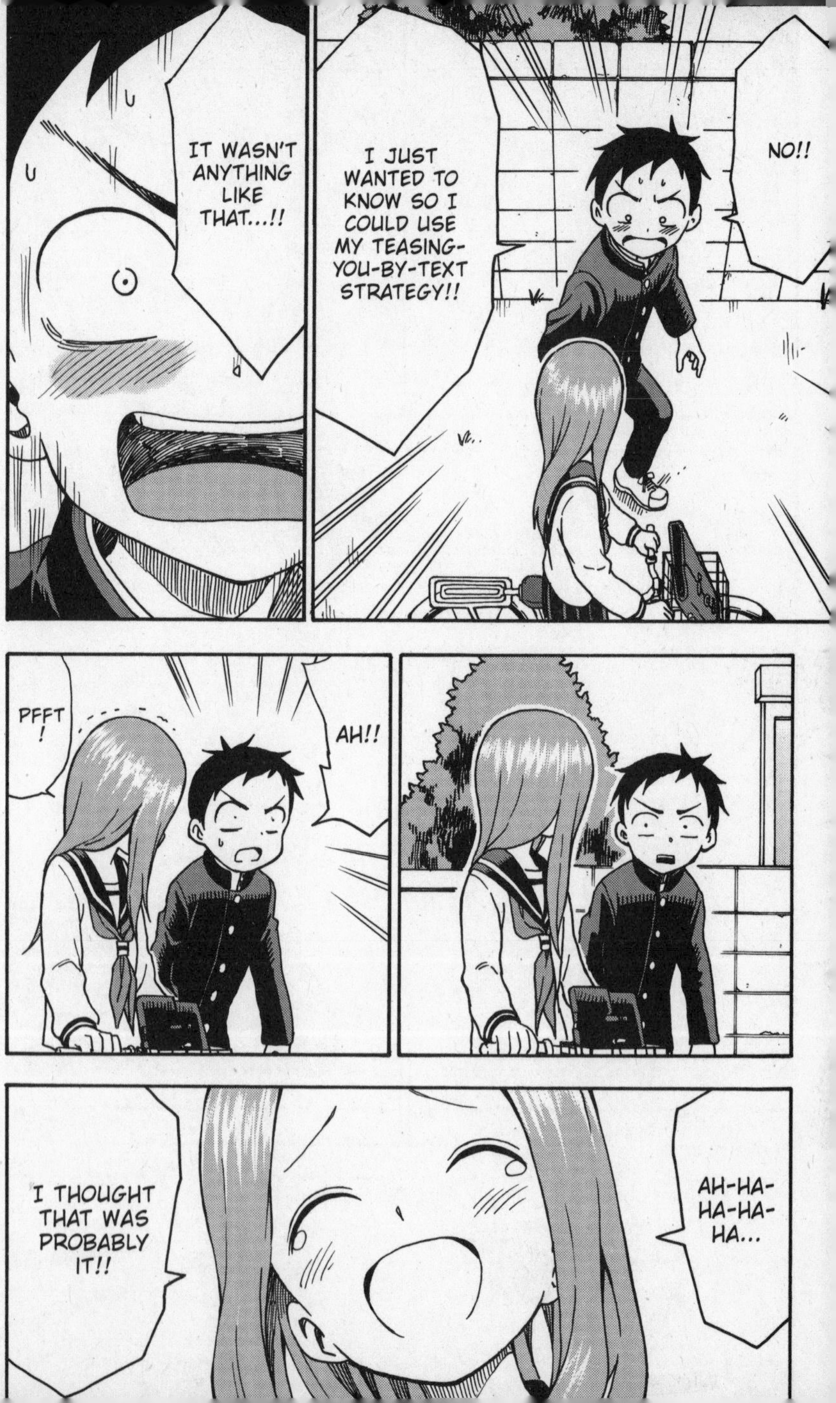
NO!!
I JUST WANTED TO KNOW SO I COULD USE MY TEASING-YOU-BY-TEXT STRATEGY!!
IT WASN'T ANYTHING LIKE THAT...!!
AH!!
PFFT!
AH-HA-HA-HA-HA...
I THOUGHT THAT WAS PROBABLY IT!!

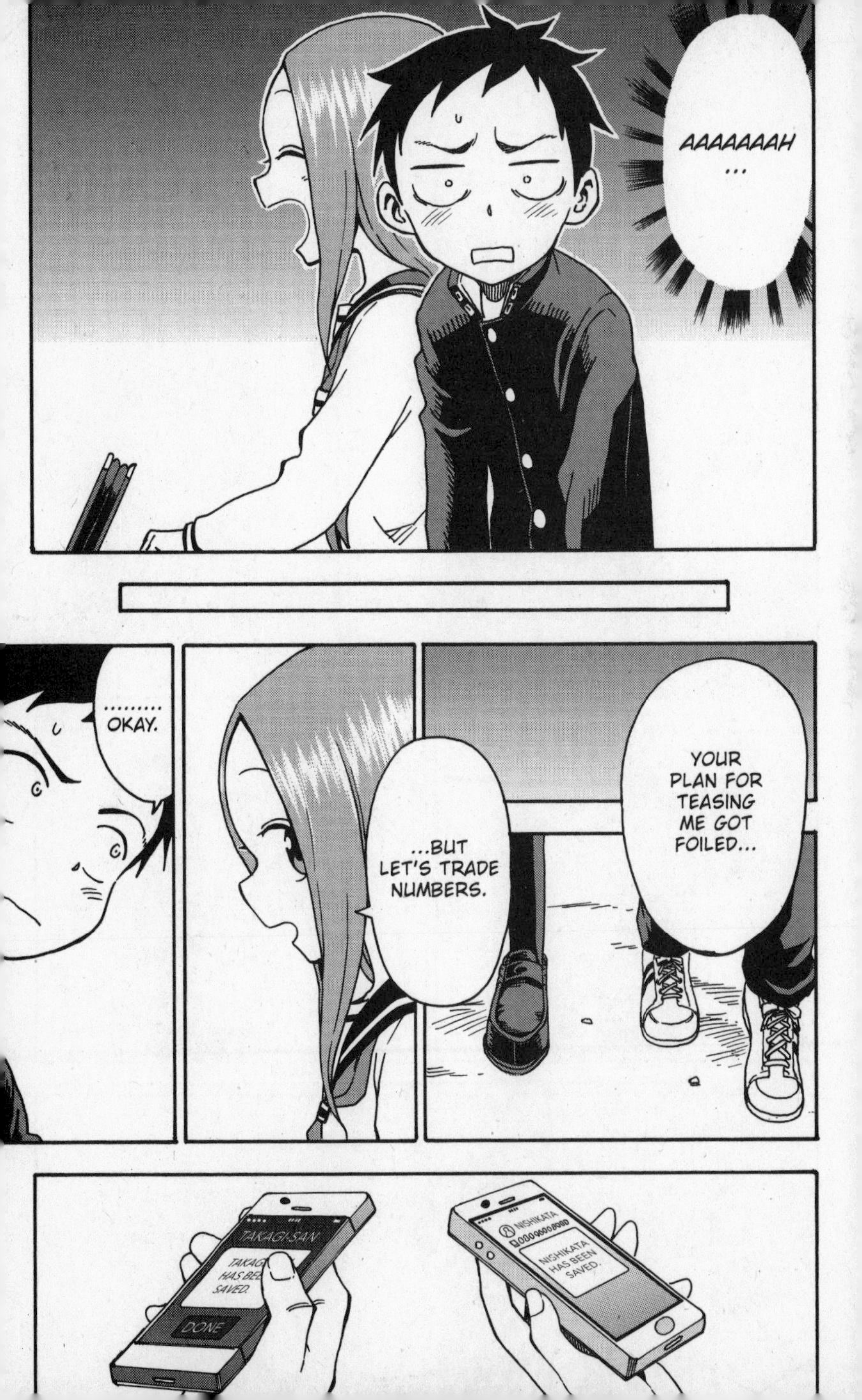
AAAAAAAH
...
YOUR PLAN FOR TEASING ME GOT FOILED...
...BUT LET'S TRADE NUMBERS.
....
OKAY.
TAKAGI-SAN
TAKAGI HAS BEEN SAVED.
DONE
NISHIKATA
NISHIKATA HAS BEEN SAVED.

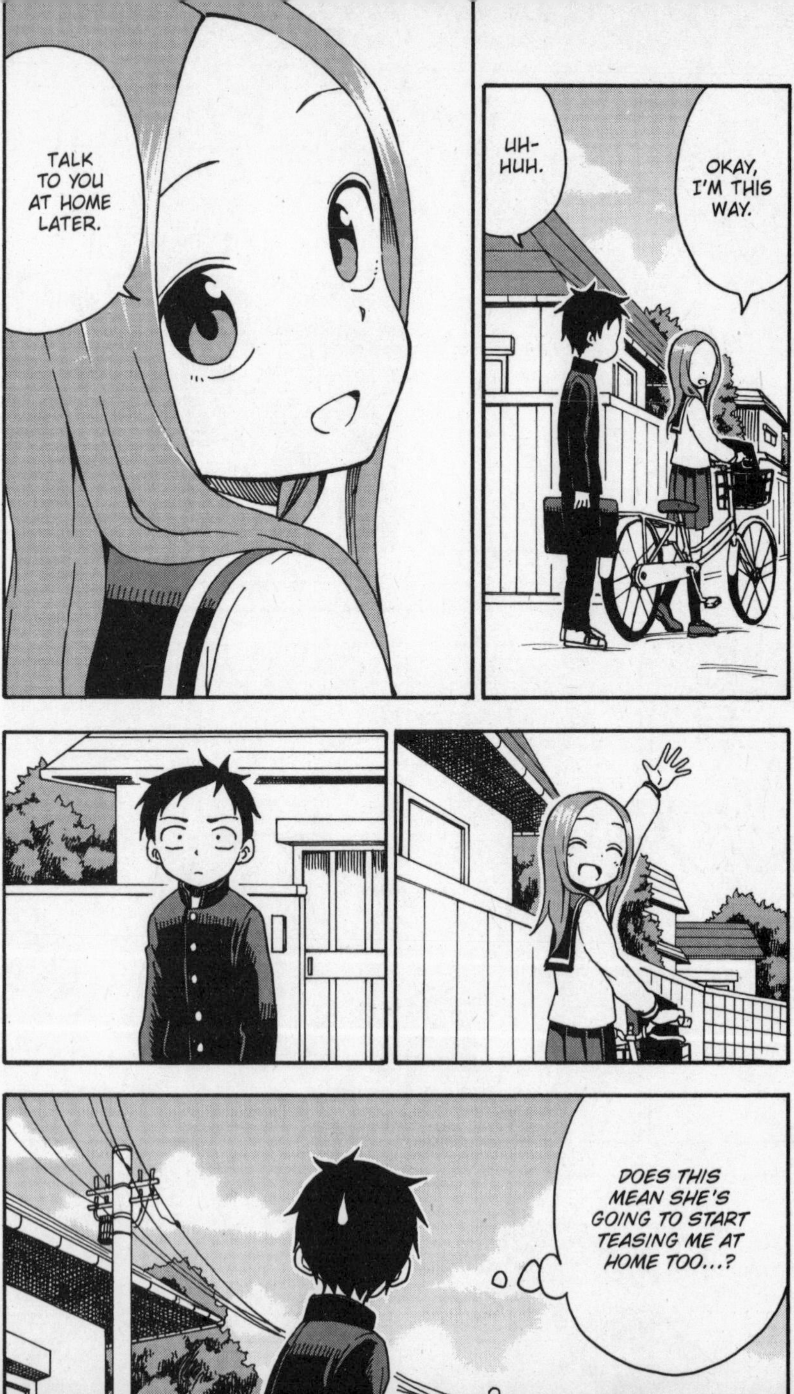
OKAY, I'M THIS WAY.
UH-HUH.
TALK TO YOU AT HOME LATER.
DOES THIS MEAN SHE'S GOING TO START TEASING ME AT HOME TOO...?

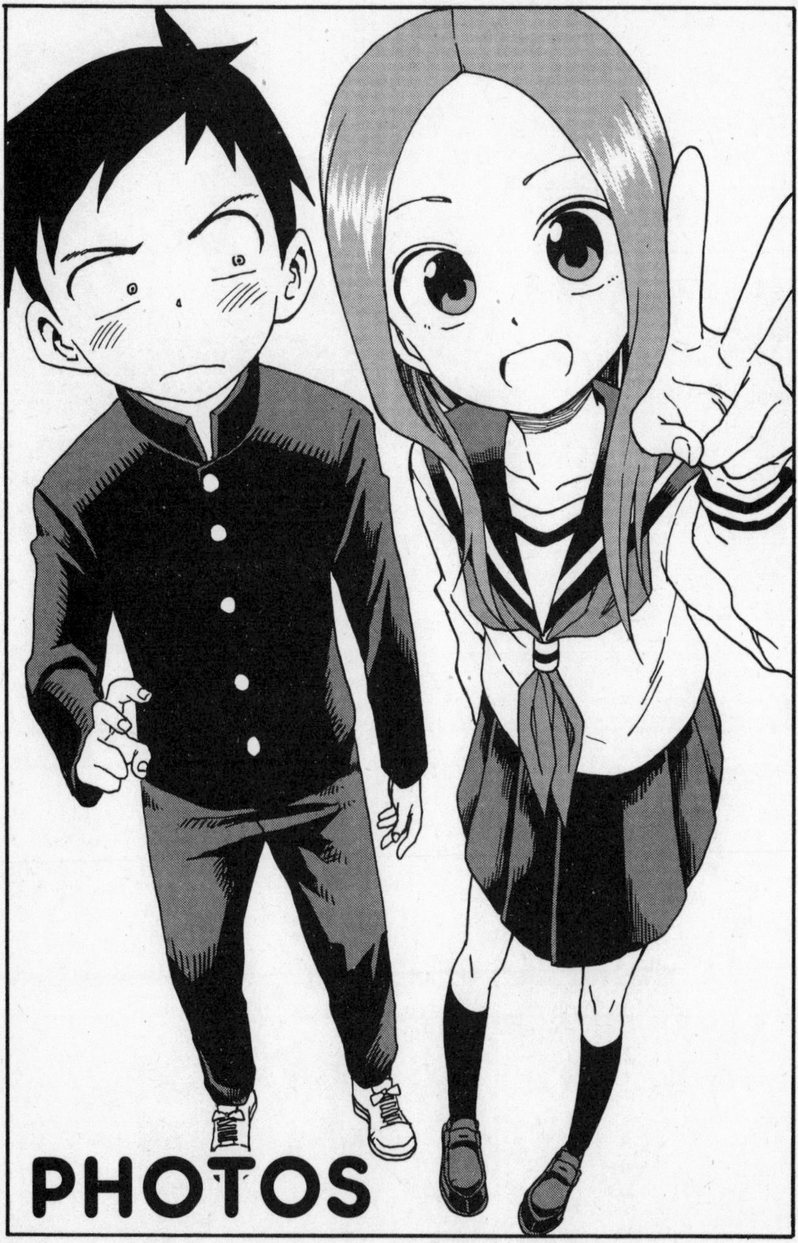
PHOTOS

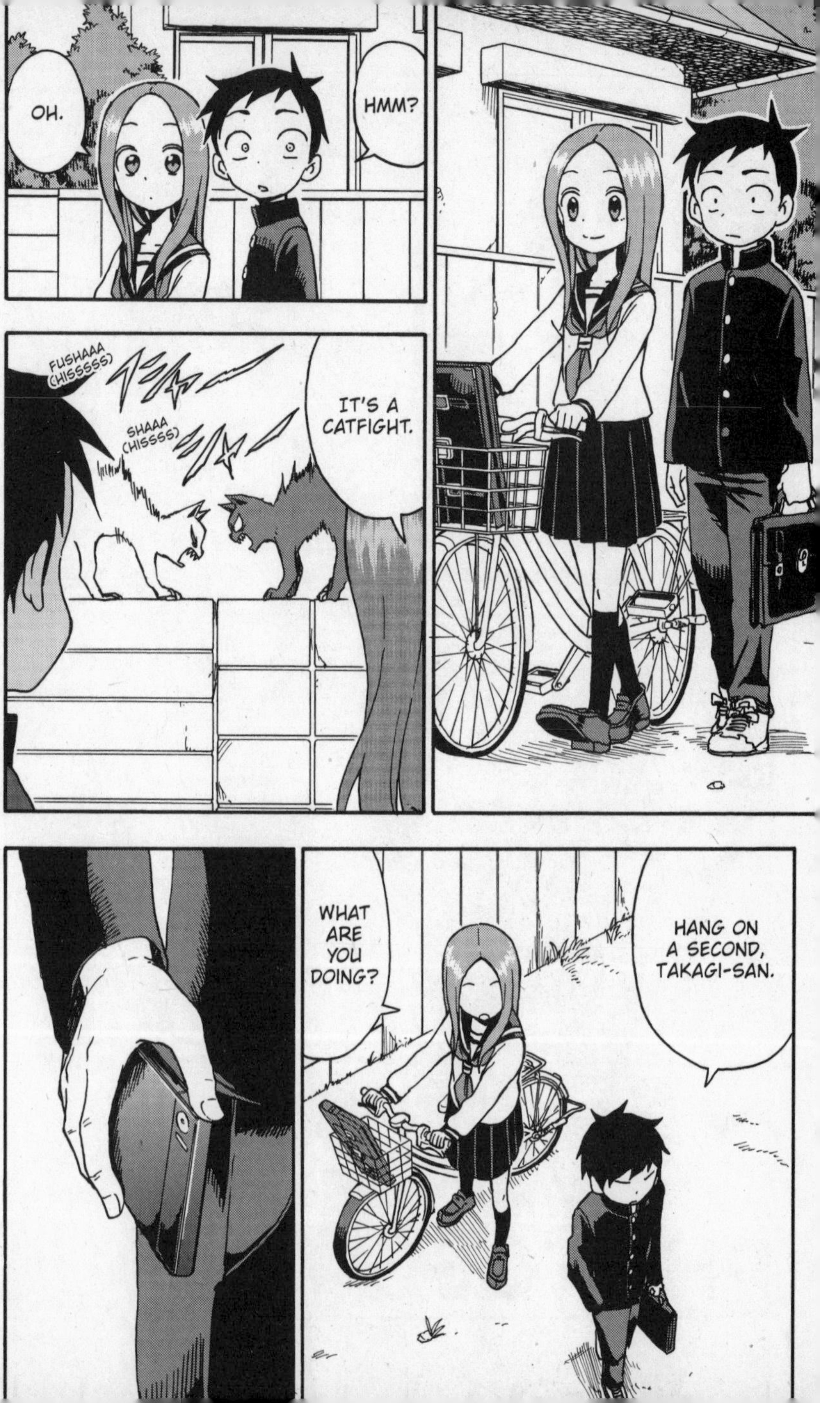
HMM?
OH.
IT'S A CATFIGHT.
FUSHAAA (HISSSSS)
SHAAA (HISSSS)
HANG ON A SECOND, TAKAGI-SAN.
WHAT ARE YOU DOING?

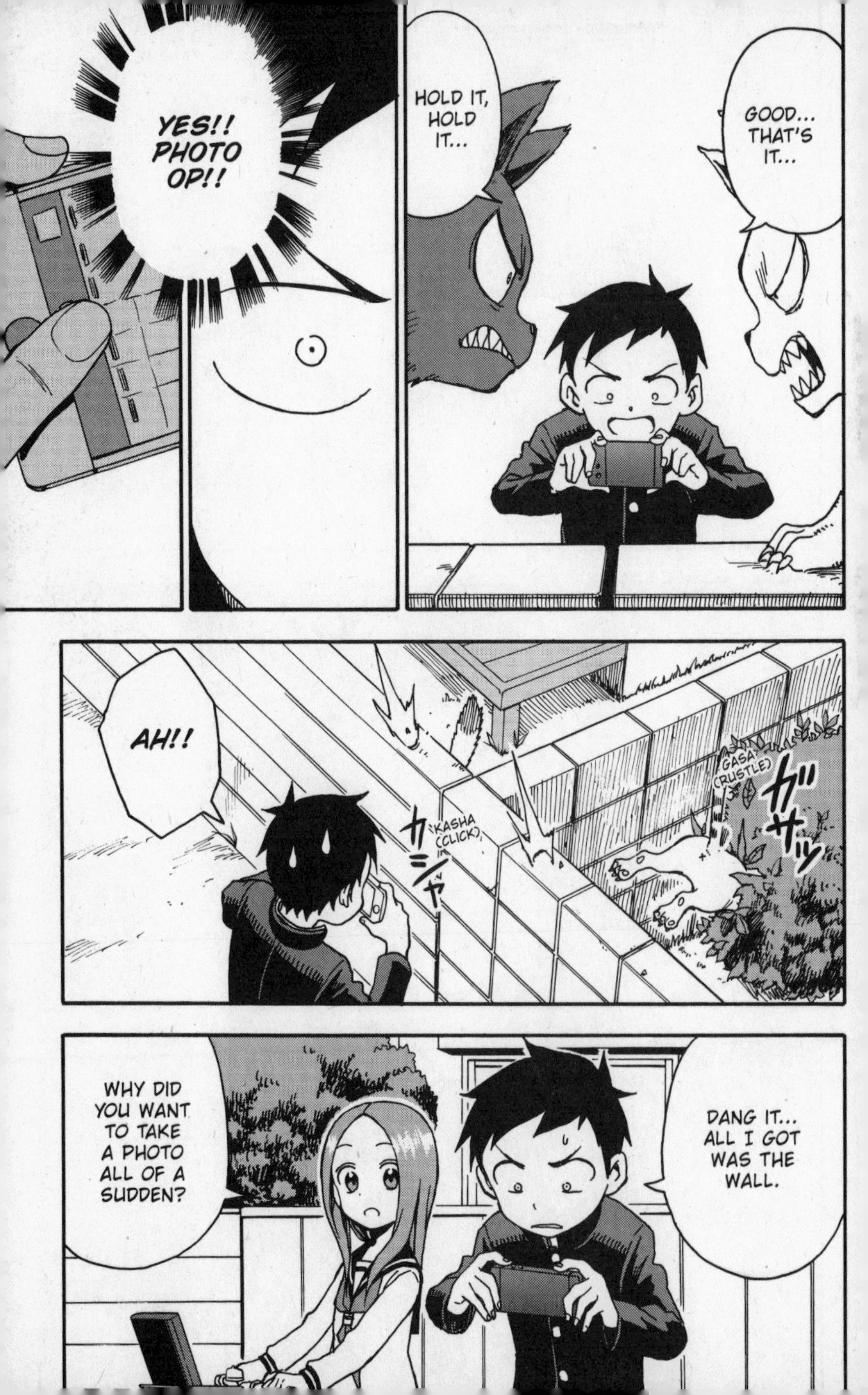
GOOD... THAT'S IT...
HOLD IT, HOLD IT...
YES!! PHOTO OP!!
AH!!
GASA (RUSTLE)
KASHA (CLICK)
DANG IT... ALL I GOT WAS THE WALL.
WHY DID YOU WANT TO TAKE A PHOTO ALL OF A SUDDEN?

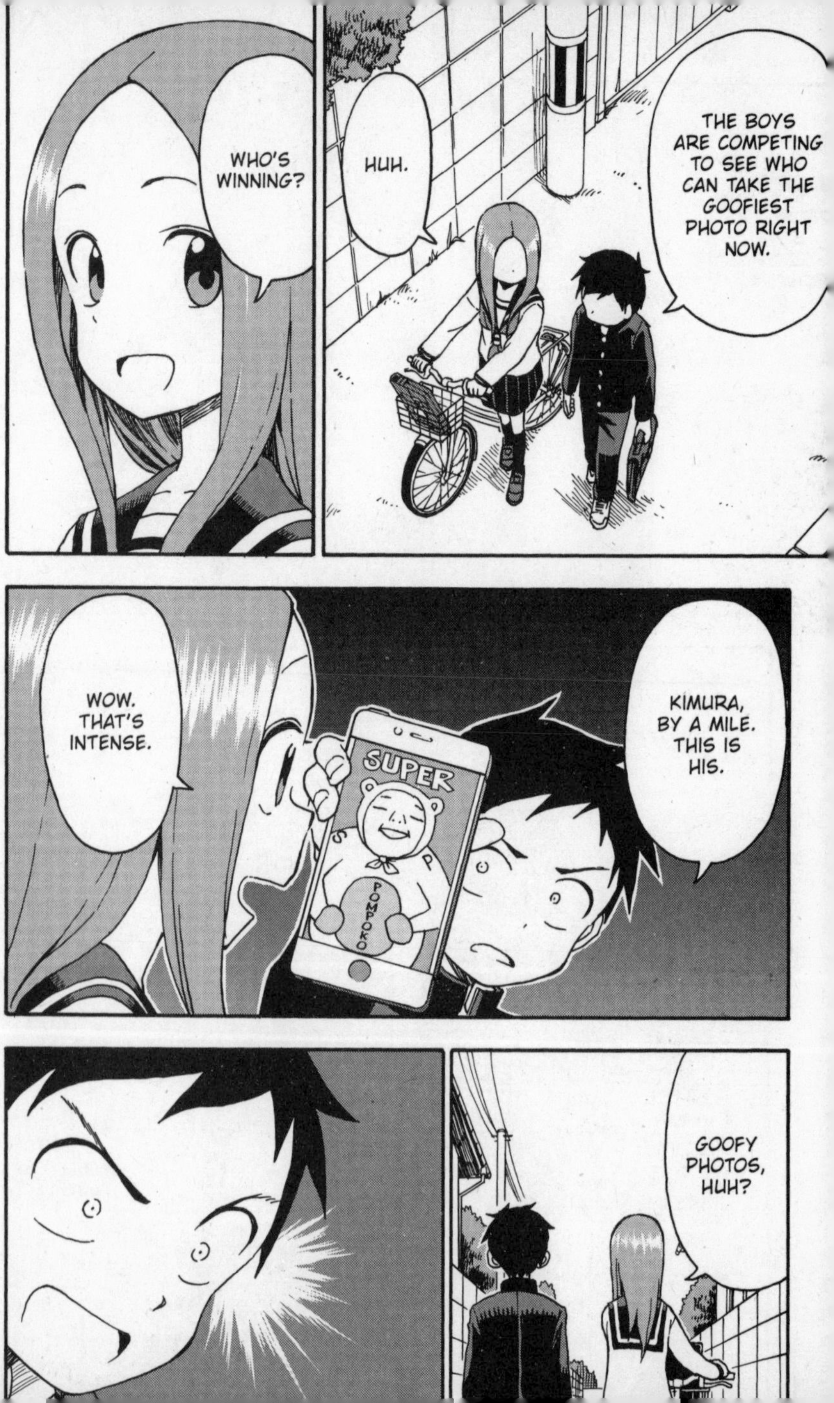
THE BOYS ARE COMPETING TO SEE WHO CAN TAKE THE GOOFIEST PHOTO RIGHT NOW.
HUH.
WHO'S WINNING?
KIMURA, BY A MILE. THIS IS HIS.
SUPER
S P
POMPOKO
WOW. THAT'S INTENSE.
GOOFY PHOTOS, HUH?

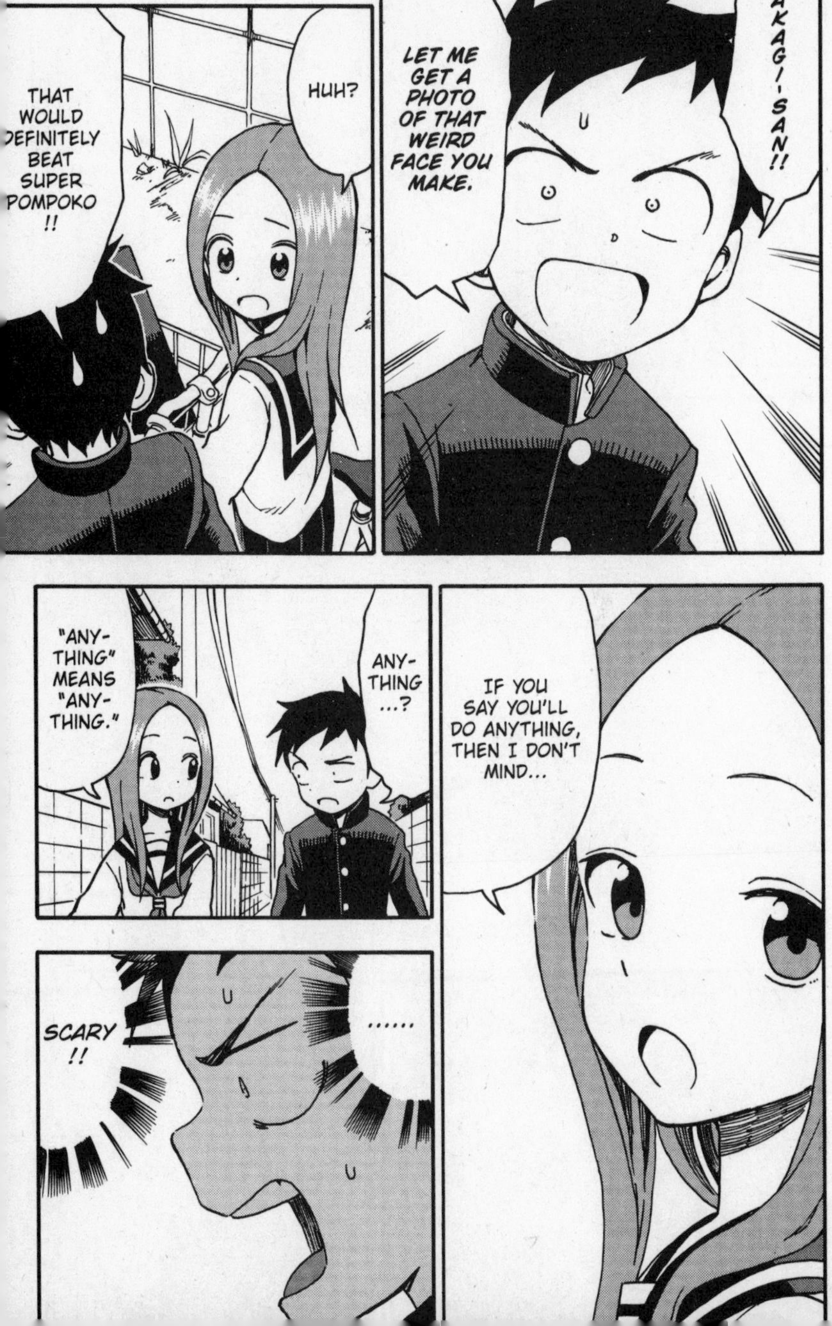
TAKAGI-SAN!!
LET ME GET A PHOTO OF THAT WEIRD FACE YOU MAKE.
HUH?
THAT WOULD DEFINITELY BEAT SUPER POMPOKO!!
IF YOU SAY YOU'LL DO ANYTHING, THEN I DON'T MIND...
ANY-THING...?
"ANY-THING" MEANS "ANY-THING."
......
SCARY!!

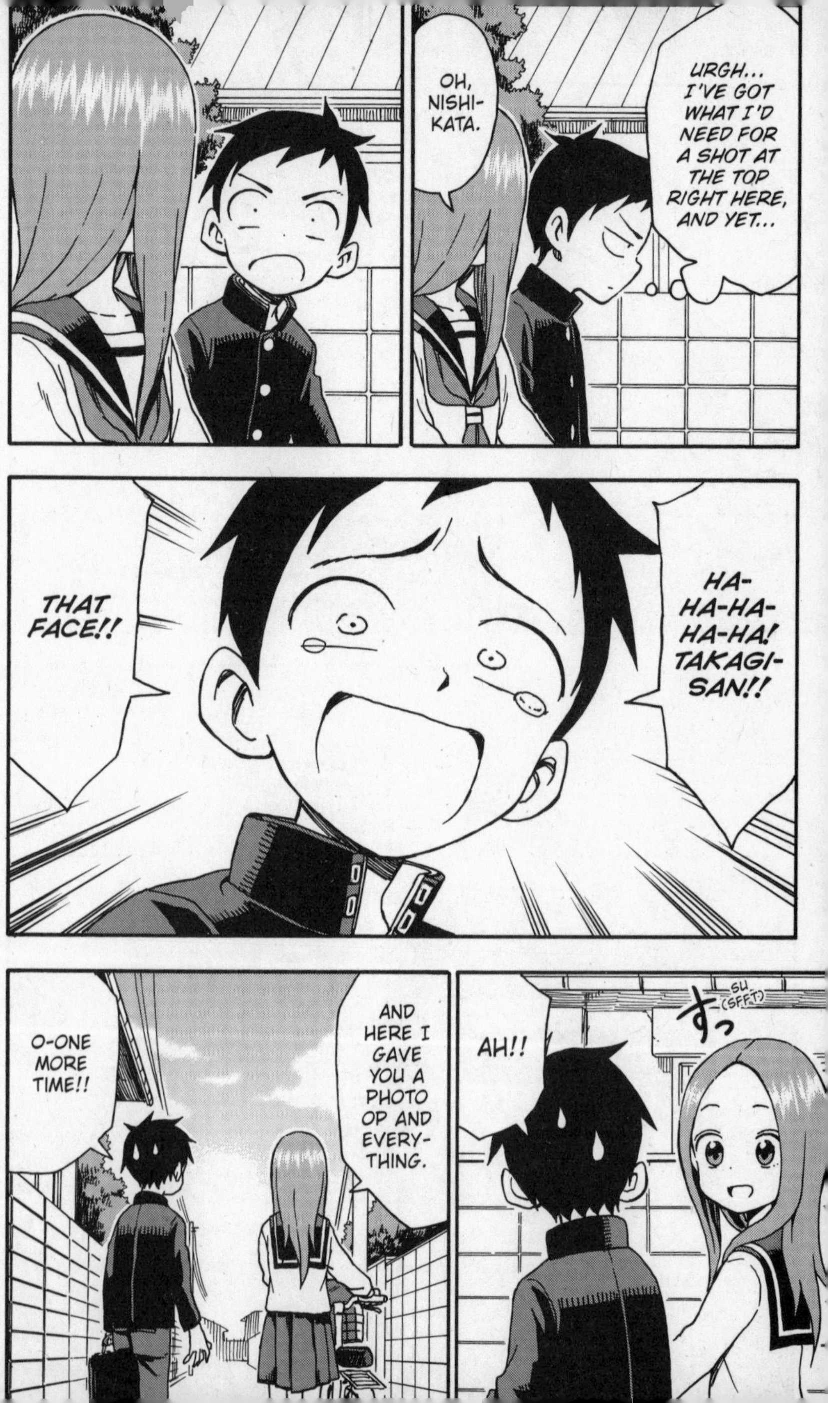
URGH... I'VE GOT WHAT I'D NEED FOR A SHOT AT THE TOP RIGHT HERE, AND YET...
OH, NISHI-KATA.
HA-HA-HA-HA-HA! TAKAGI-SAN!!
THAT FACE!!
すっ
SU (SFFT)
AH!!
AND HERE I GAVE YOU A PHOTO OP AND EVERY-THING.
O-ONE MORE TIME!!

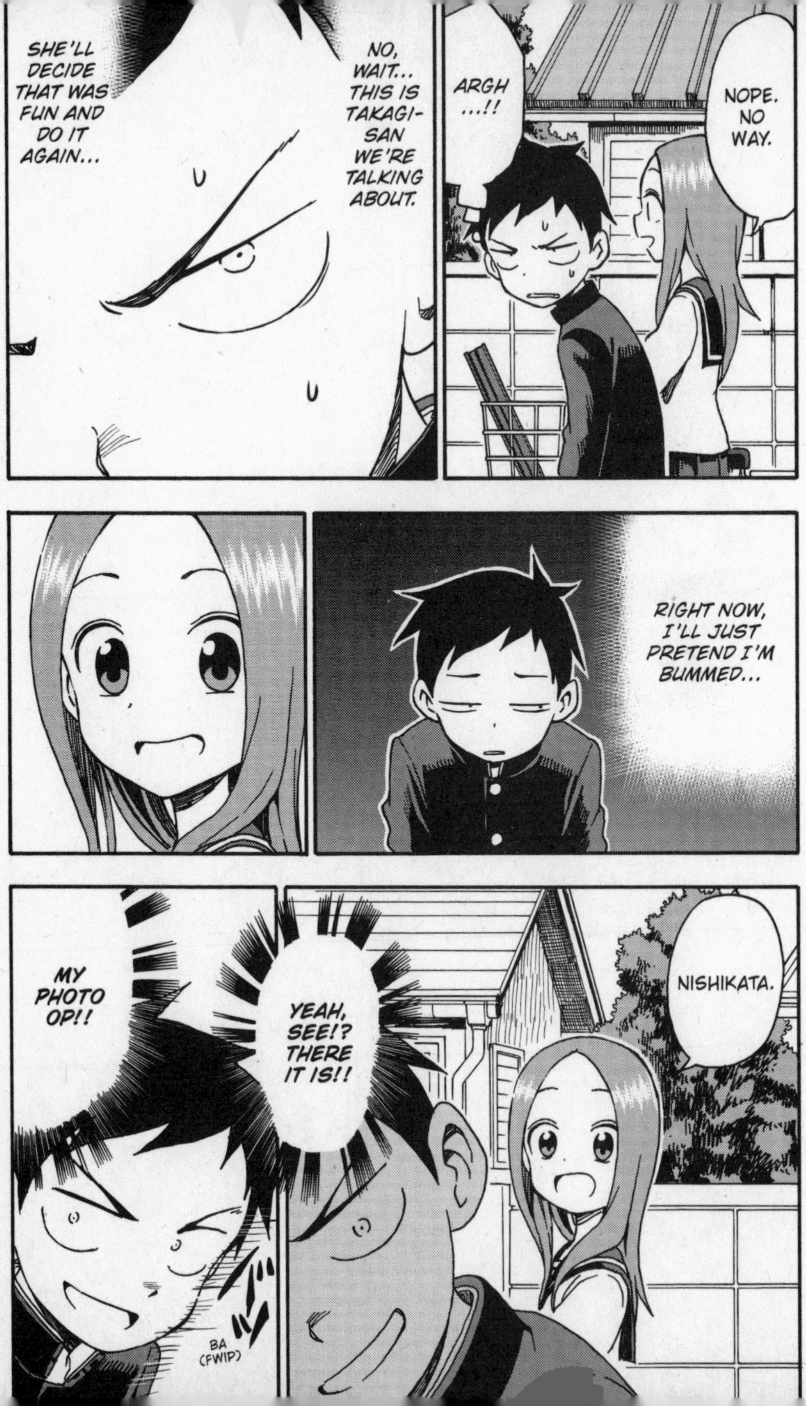
NOPE. NO WAY.
ARGH ...!!
NO, WAIT... THIS IS TAKAGI-SAN WE'RE TALKING ABOUT.
SHE'LL DECIDE THAT WAS FUN AND DO IT AGAIN...
RIGHT NOW, I'LL JUST PRETEND I'M BUMMED...
NISHIKATA.
YEAH, SEE!? THERE IT IS!!
MY PHOTO OP!!
BA (FWIP)

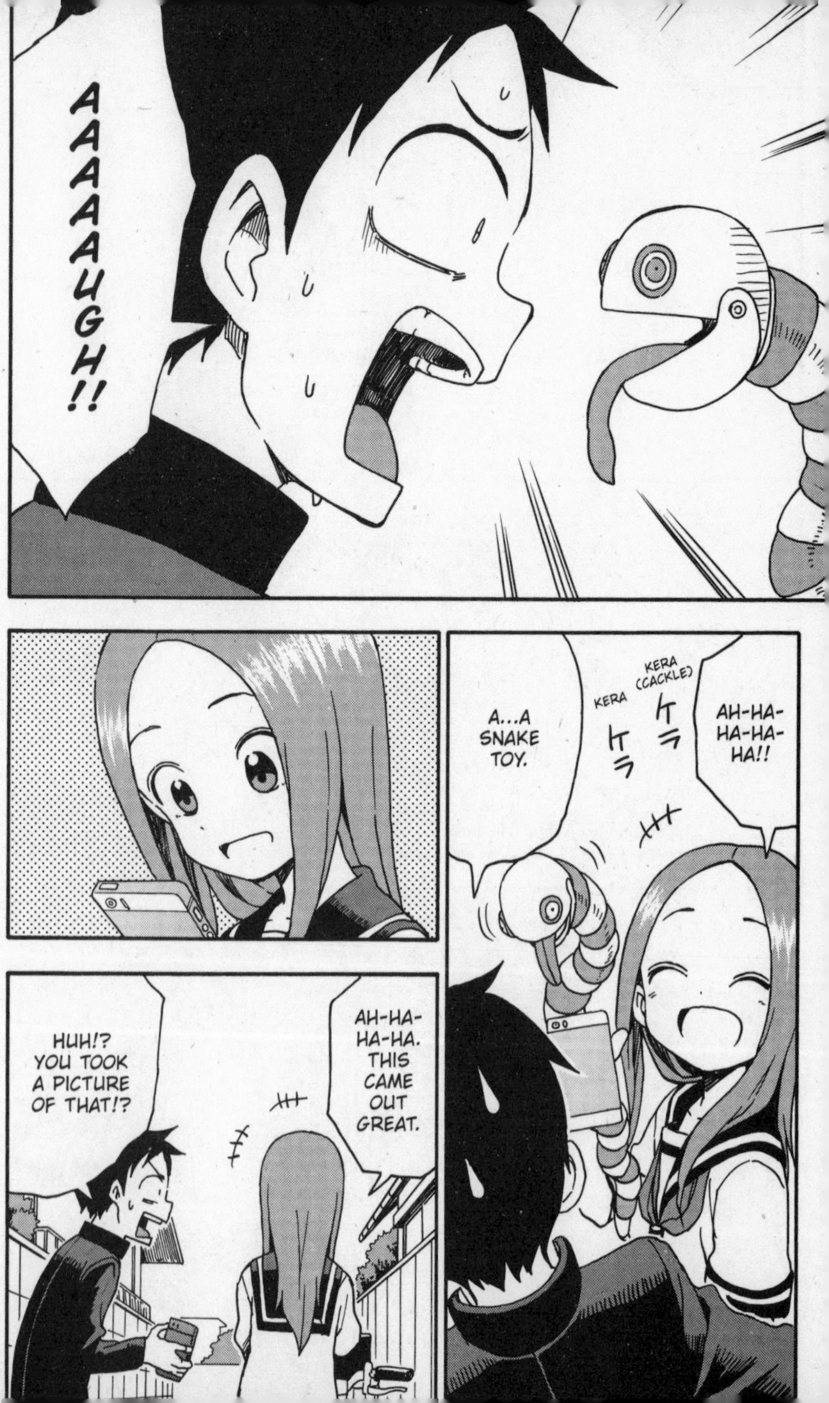
AAAAAAUGH!!
AH-HA-HA-HA-HA!!
KERA (CACKLE)
ケラ
KERA
ケラ
A...A SNAKE TOY.
AH-HA-HA-HA. THIS CAME OUT GREAT.
HUH!? YOU TOOK A PICTURE OF THAT!?

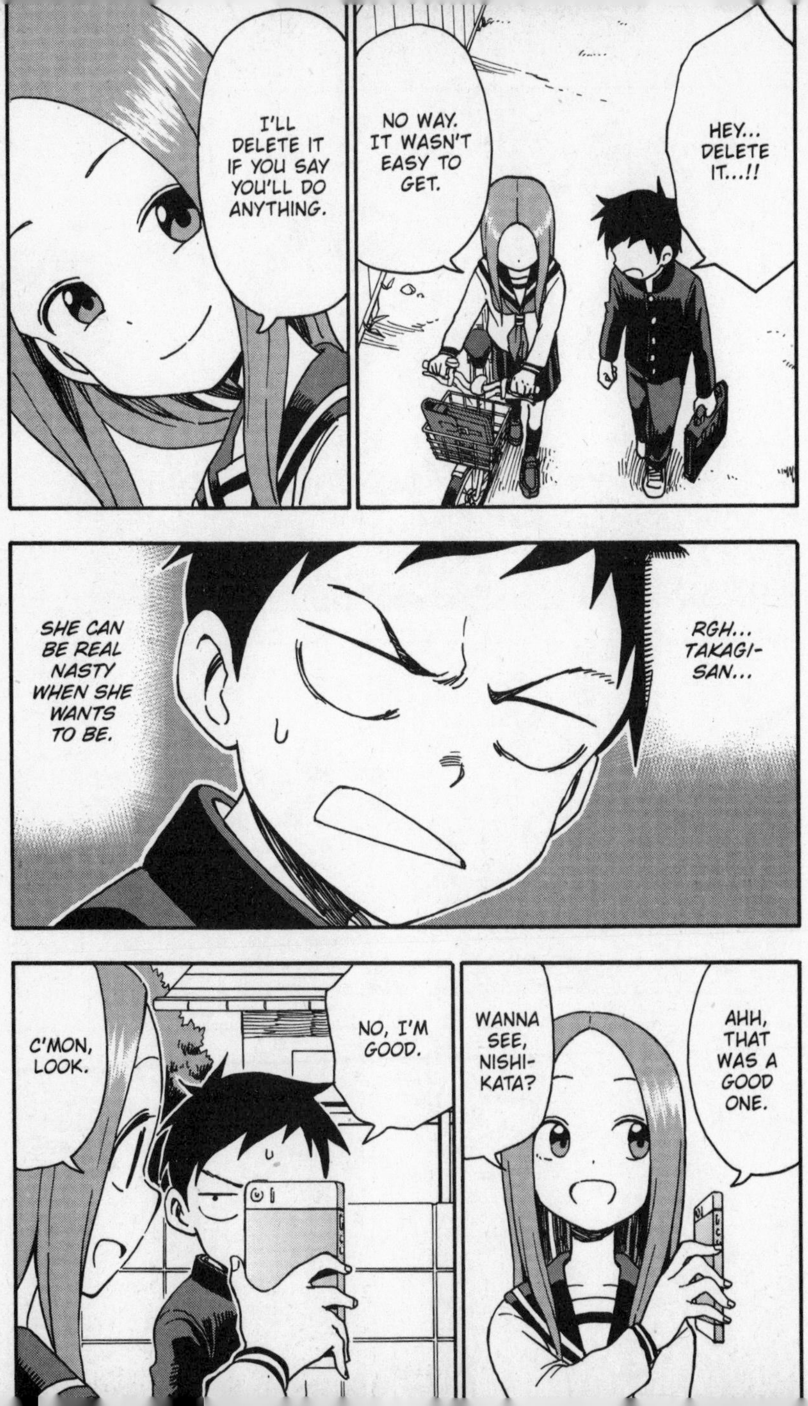
HEY... DELETE IT...!!
NO WAY. IT WASN'T EASY TO GET.
I'LL DELETE IT IF YOU SAY YOU'LL DO ANYTHING.
RGH... TAKAGI-SAN...
SHE CAN BE REAL NASTY WHEN SHE WANTS TO BE.
AHH, THAT WAS A GOOD ONE.
WANNA SEE, NISHI-KATA?
NO, I'M GOOD.
C'MON, LOOK.

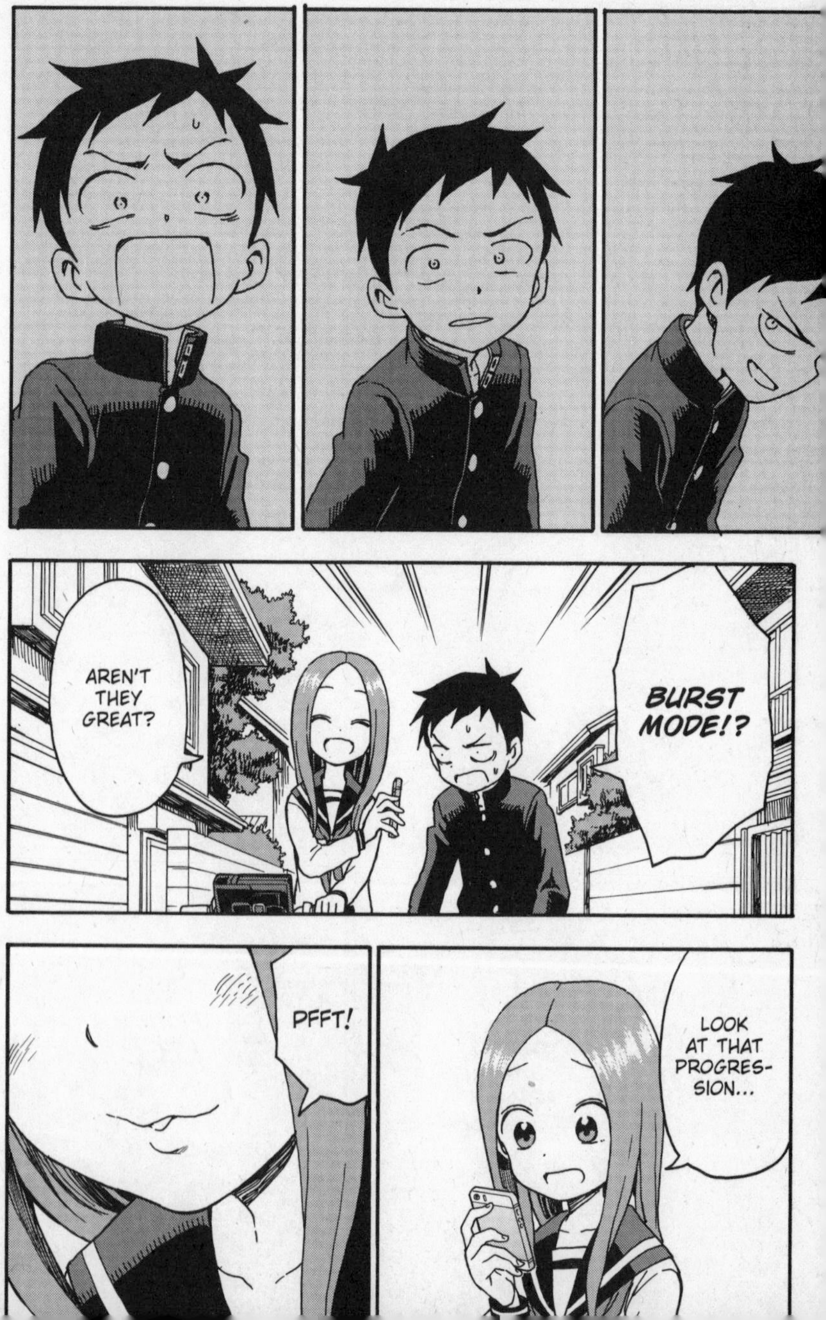
BURST MODE!?
AREN'T THEY GREAT?
LOOK AT THAT PROGRES-SION...
PFFT!

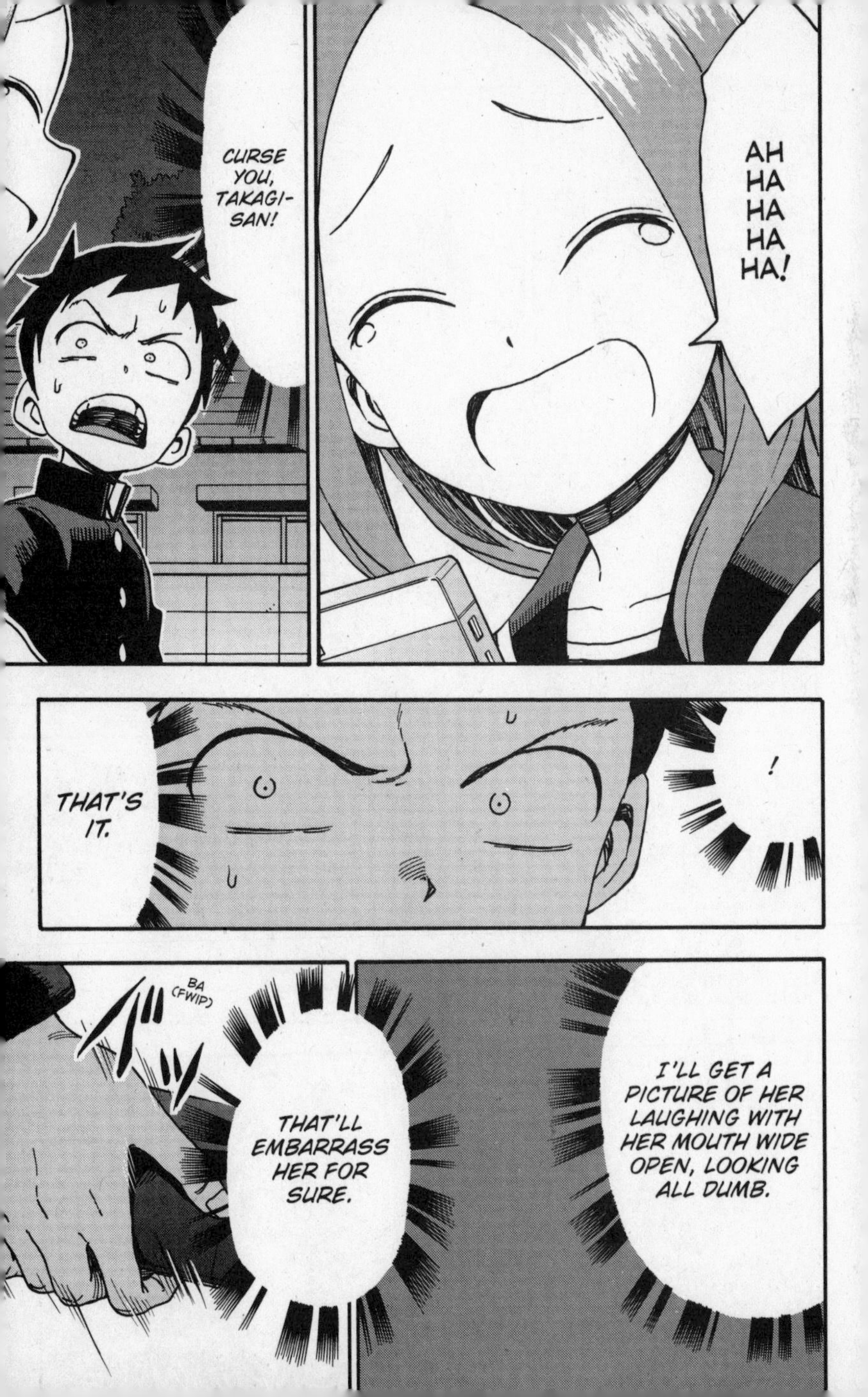
AH HA HA HA HA!
CURSE YOU, TAKAGI-SAN!
!
THAT'S IT.
I'LL GET A PICTURE OF HER LAUGHING WITH HER MOUTH WIDE OPEN, LOOKING ALL DUMB.
THAT'LL EMBARRASS HER FOR SURE.
BA (FWIP)

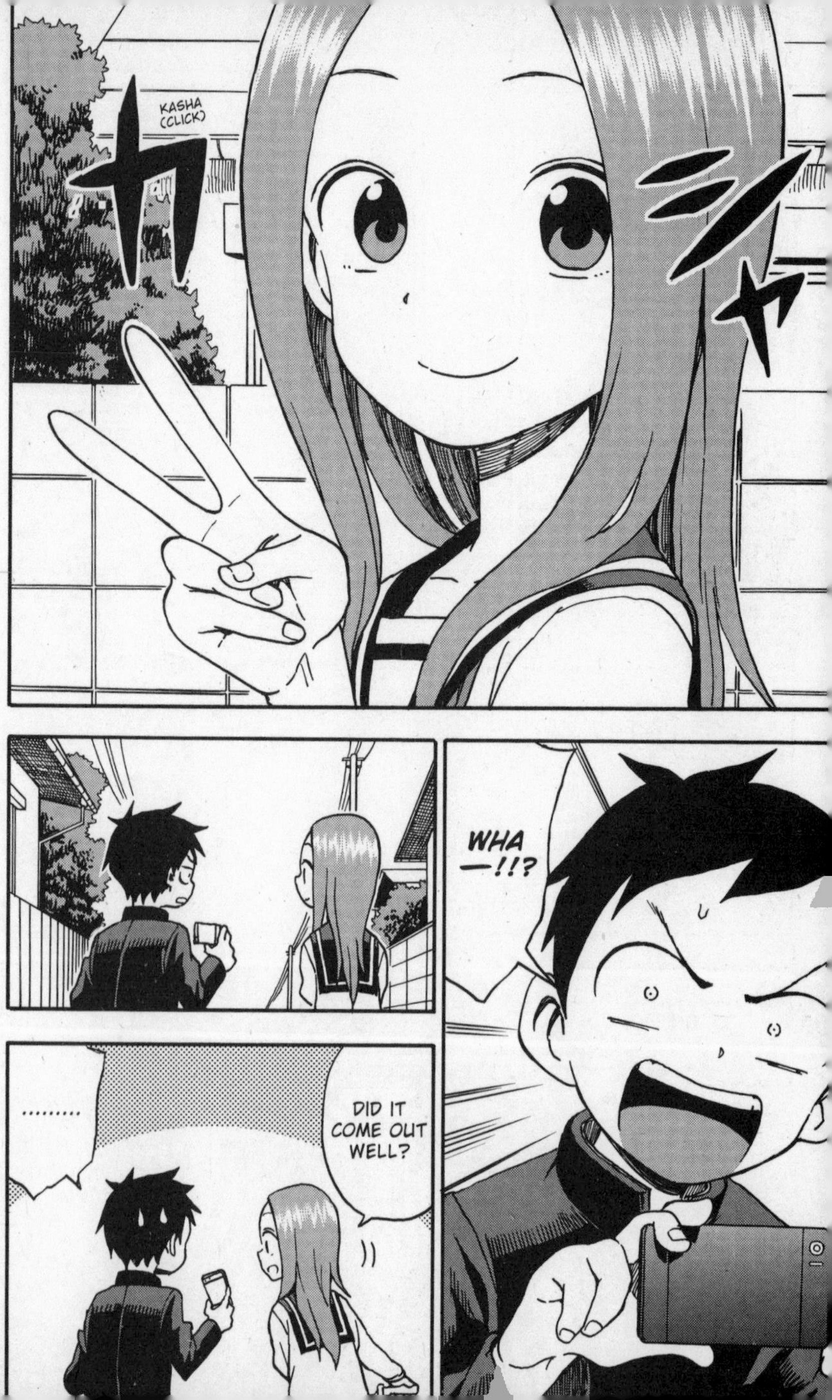
KASHA (CLICK)
WHA—!!?
DID IT COME OUT WELL?
....

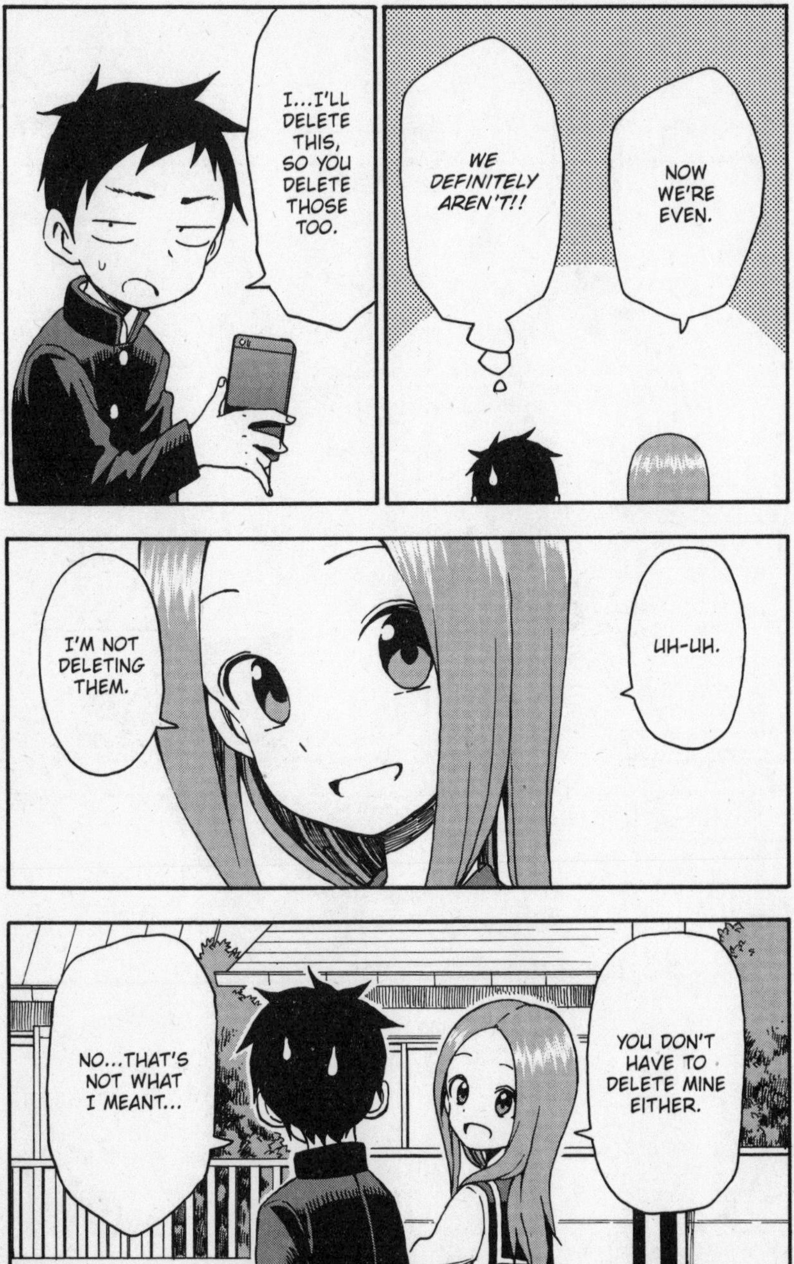
NOW WE'RE EVEN.
WE DEFINITELY AREN'T!!
I...I'LL DELETE THIS, SO YOU DELETE THOSE TOO.
UH-UH.
I'M NOT DELETING THEM.
YOU DON'T HAVE TO DELETE MINE EITHER.
NO...THAT'S NOT WHAT I MEANT...

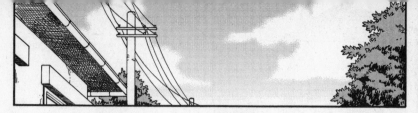

URGH... SHE'S IN A GOOD MOOD.

YEAH.

SEE YOU LATER.

NISHI-KATA...

AND I DIDN'T GET A SINGLE GOOFY PHOTO...

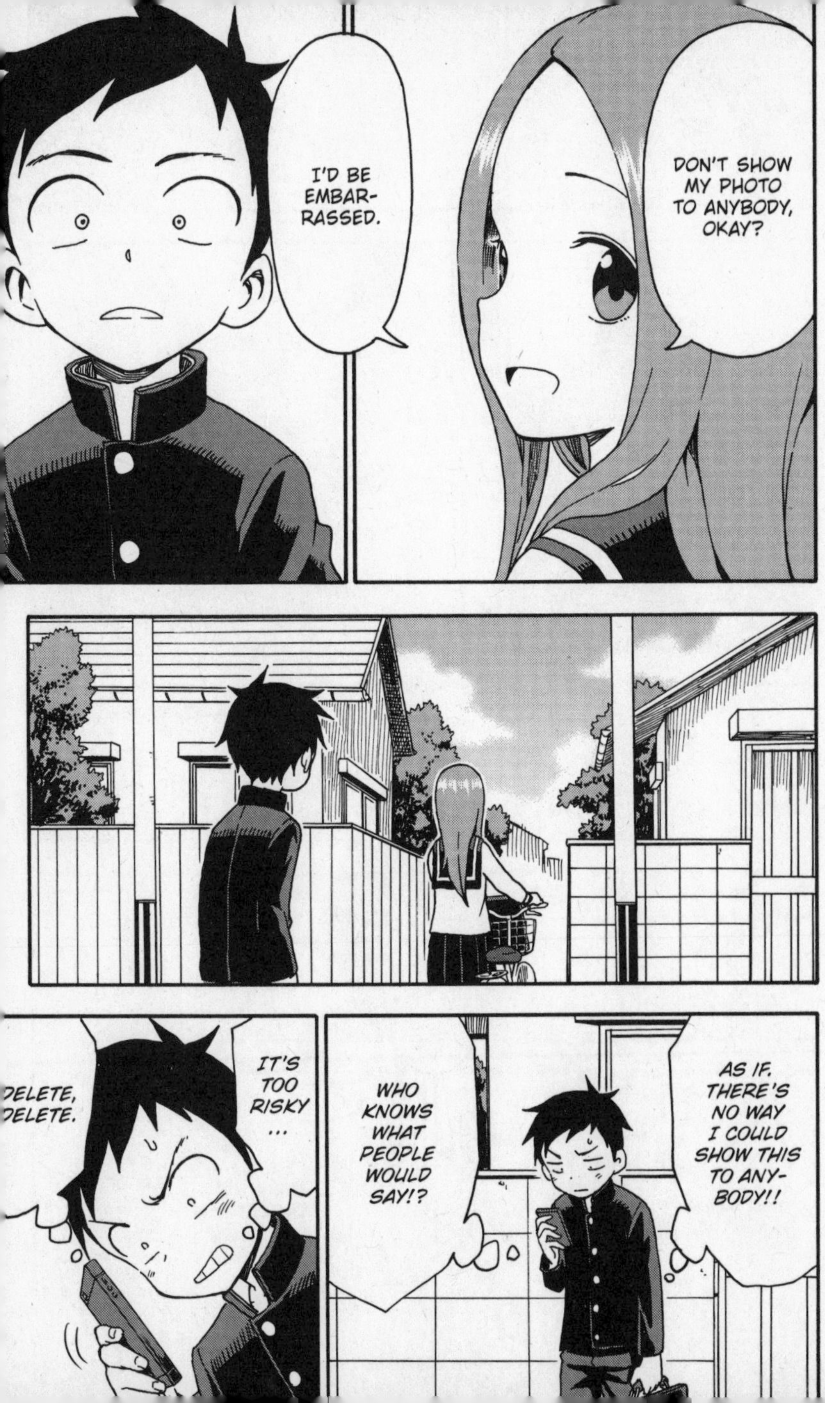
DON'T SHOW MY PHOTO TO ANYBODY, OKAY?
I'D BE EMBAR-RASSED.
AS IF. THERE'S NO WAY I COULD SHOW THIS TO ANY-BODY!!
WHO KNOWS WHAT PEOPLE WOULD SAY!?
IT'S TOO RISKY ...
DELETE, DELETE.

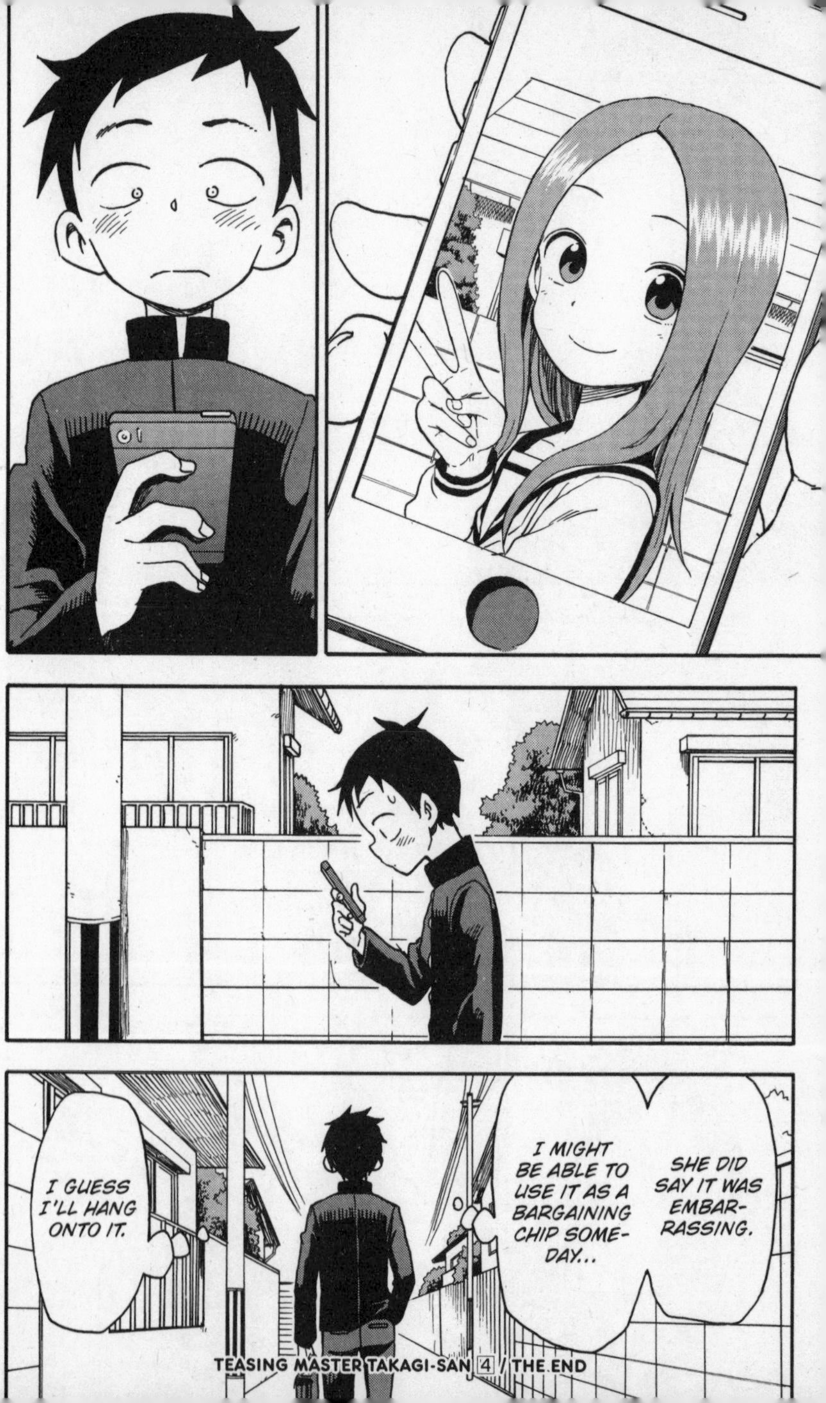
SHE DID SAY IT WAS EMBARRASSING.
I MIGHT BE ABLE TO USE IT AS A BARGAINING CHIP SOMEDAY...
I GUESS I'LL HANG ONTO IT.
TEASING MASTER TAKAGI-SAN 4 / THE END

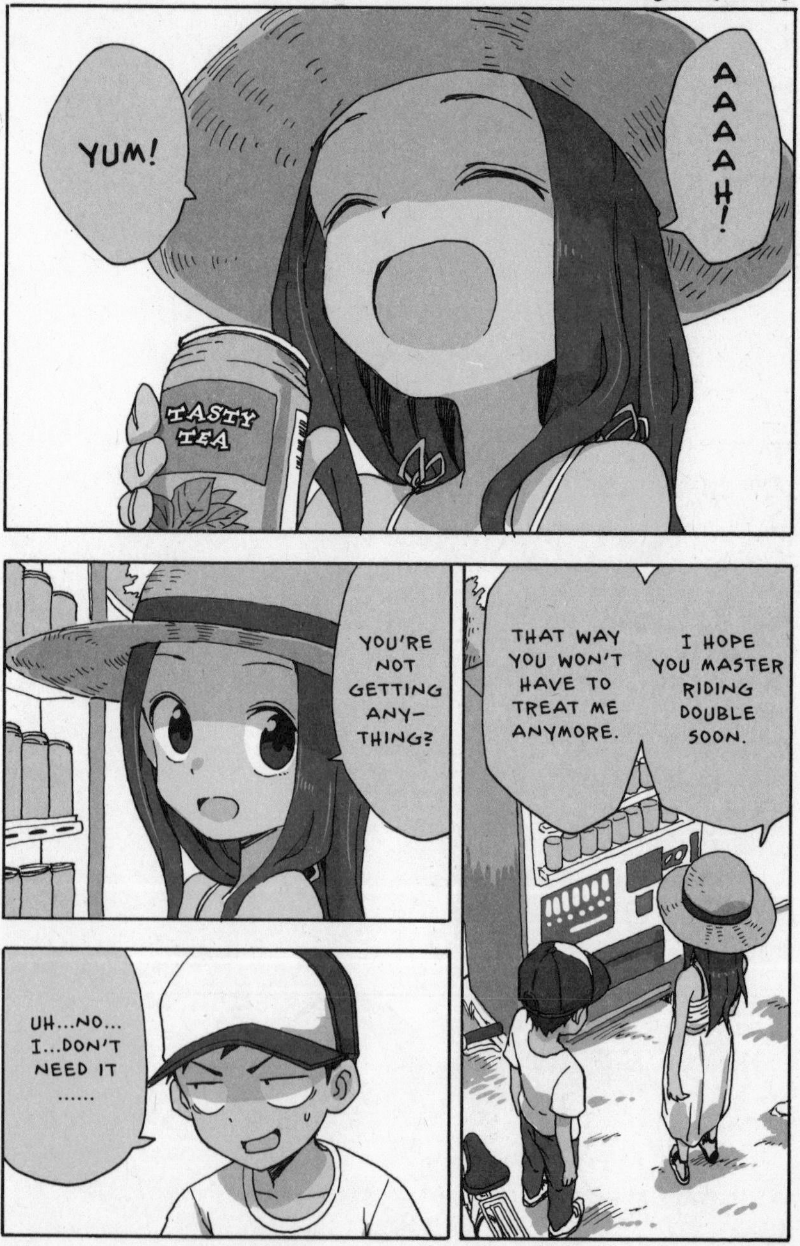
AAAAH!
YUM!
TASTY TEA
I HOPE YOU MASTER RIDING DOUBLE SOON.
THAT WAY YOU WON'T HAVE TO TREAT ME ANYMORE.
YOU'RE NOT GETTING ANY-THING?
UH...NO... I...DON'T NEED IT ......

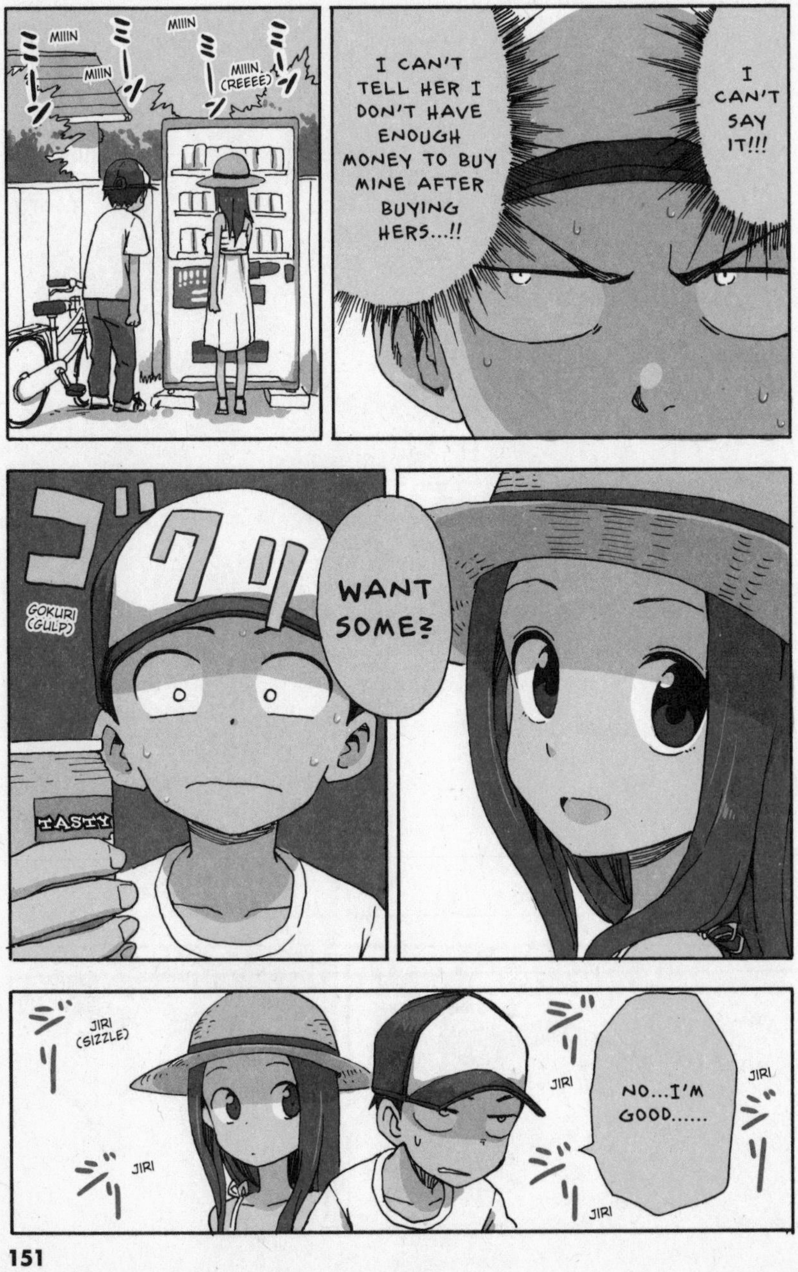
I CAN'T SAY IT!!!
I CAN'T TELL HER I DON'T HAVE ENOUGH MONEY TO BUY MINE AFTER BUYING HERS...!!
MIIIN (CREEEE)
MIIIN
MIIIN
MIIIN
WANT SOME?
ゴクリ
GOKURI (GULP)
TASTY
JIRI
NO...I'M GOOD......
JIRI
JIRI
JIRI
JIRI (SIZZLE)

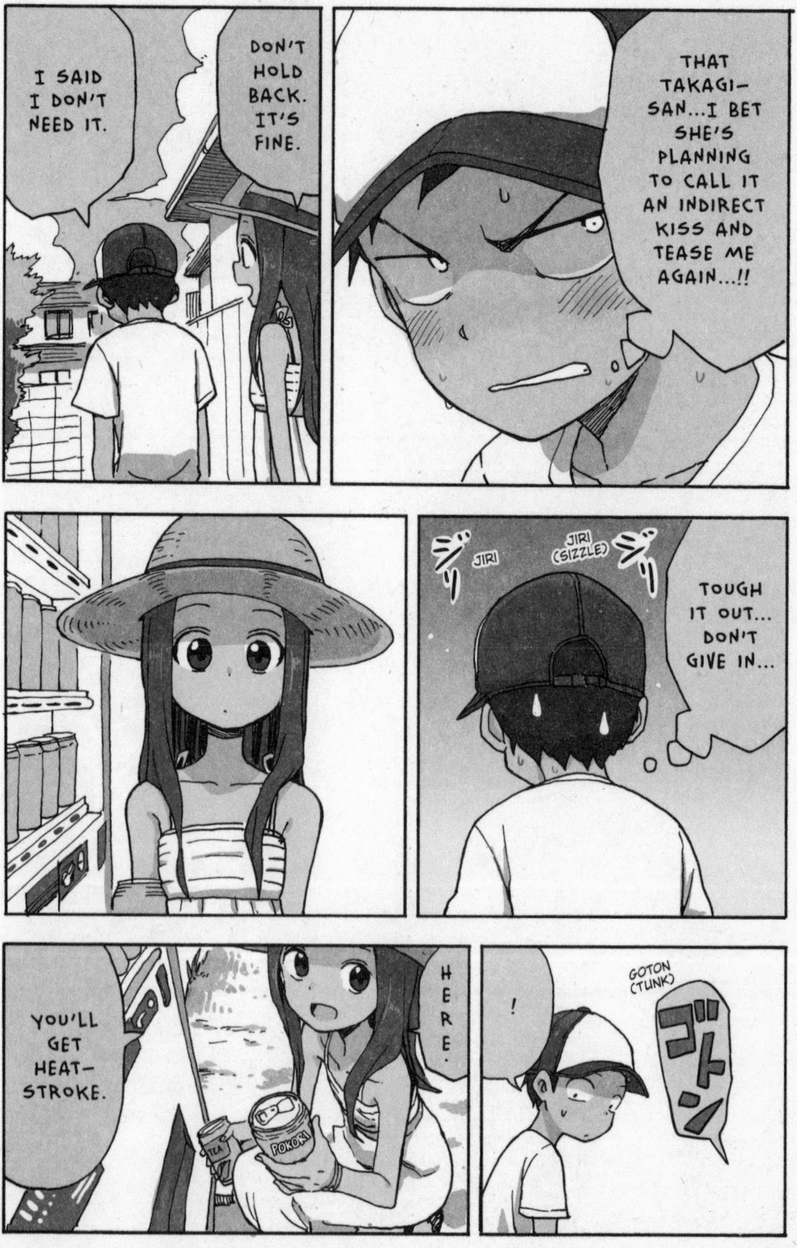
THAT TAKAGI-SAN...I BET SHE'S PLANNING TO CALL IT AN INDIRECT KISS AND TEASE ME AGAIN...!!
DON'T HOLD BACK. IT'S FINE.
I SAID I DON'T NEED IT.
JIRI (SIZZLE)
JIRI
TOUGH IT OUT... DON'T GIVE IN...
GOTON (TUNK)
ゴトン
!
HERE.
YOU'LL GET HEAT-STROKE.
TEA
POKORI

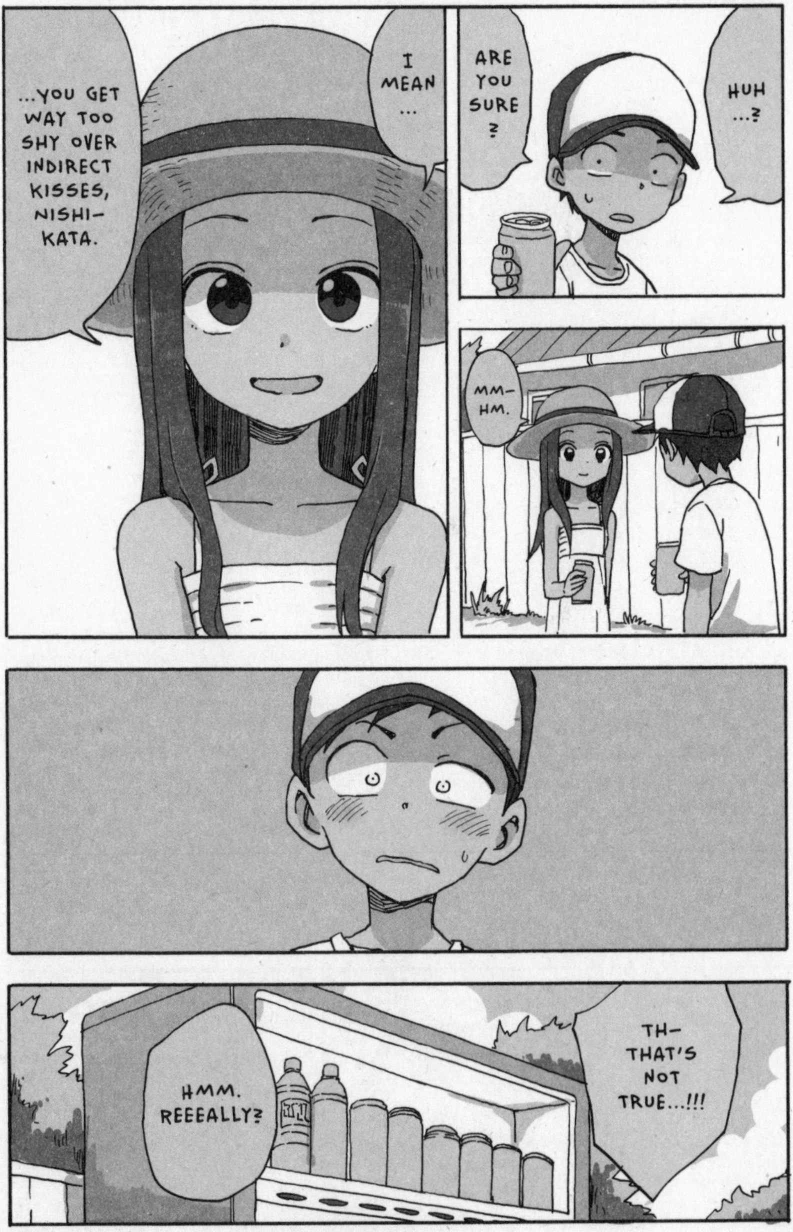
HUH...?
ARE YOU SURE?
MM-HM.
I MEAN...
...YOU GET WAY TOO SHY OVER INDIRECT KISSES, NISHI-KATA.
TH-THAT'S NOT TRUE...!!!
HMM. REEEALLY?

THE END

Translation Notes

COMMON HONORIFICS

no honorific: Indicates familiarity or closeness; if used without permission or reason, addressing someone in this manner would constitute an insult.

-san: The Japanese equivalent of Mr./Mrs./Miss. If a situation calls for politeness, this is the fail-safe honorific.

-kun: Used most often when referring to boys, this indicates affection or familiarity. Occasionally used by older men among their peers, but it may also be used by anyone referring to a person of lower standing.

-chan: An affectionate honorific indicating familiarity used mostly in reference to girls; also used in reference to cute persons or animals of either gender.

-senpai: A suffix used to address upperclassmen or more experienced coworkers.

-sensei: A respectful term for teachers, artists, or high-level professionals.

Page 5
The "line-a-day journal" is a very common homework assignment for elementary and middle school students over summer vacation. Students are supposed to write short, one- or two-sentence entries about what they did each day and then turn the journal in at the end of vacation.

Page 33
Japanese students learn to read and write *kanji*, or Chinese characters, as a part of their curriculum. This is done by rote memorization and writing out each character over and over. Therefore, copying Takagi's *kanji* homework saves Nishikata absolutely no work whatsoever.

Page 50
The key to the 21 game is getting your opponent to say "seventeen," and making sure you're the one who says the numbers that are multiples of four. Since players can only say a maximum of three numbers, Nishikata did have a shot at winning that first round, but he blew it on the first turn.

Page 91
A no-pair hand is the lowest-ranking poker hand you can get.

Page 136
Super Pompoko is the mascot for Nishinari Ward in the city of Osaka, Japan. The character's head resembles a potato while the rest of its body looks like a mix between a cat and a superhero.

Author's Note

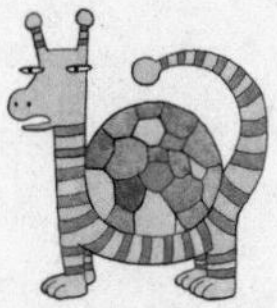

WE'RE ALREADY ON VOLUME 4, BUT THE STORY'S STILL SWINGING BACK AND FORTH BETWEEN SPRING AND FALL. I'D LIKE TO DRAW WINTER TOO ONE OF THESE DAYS.

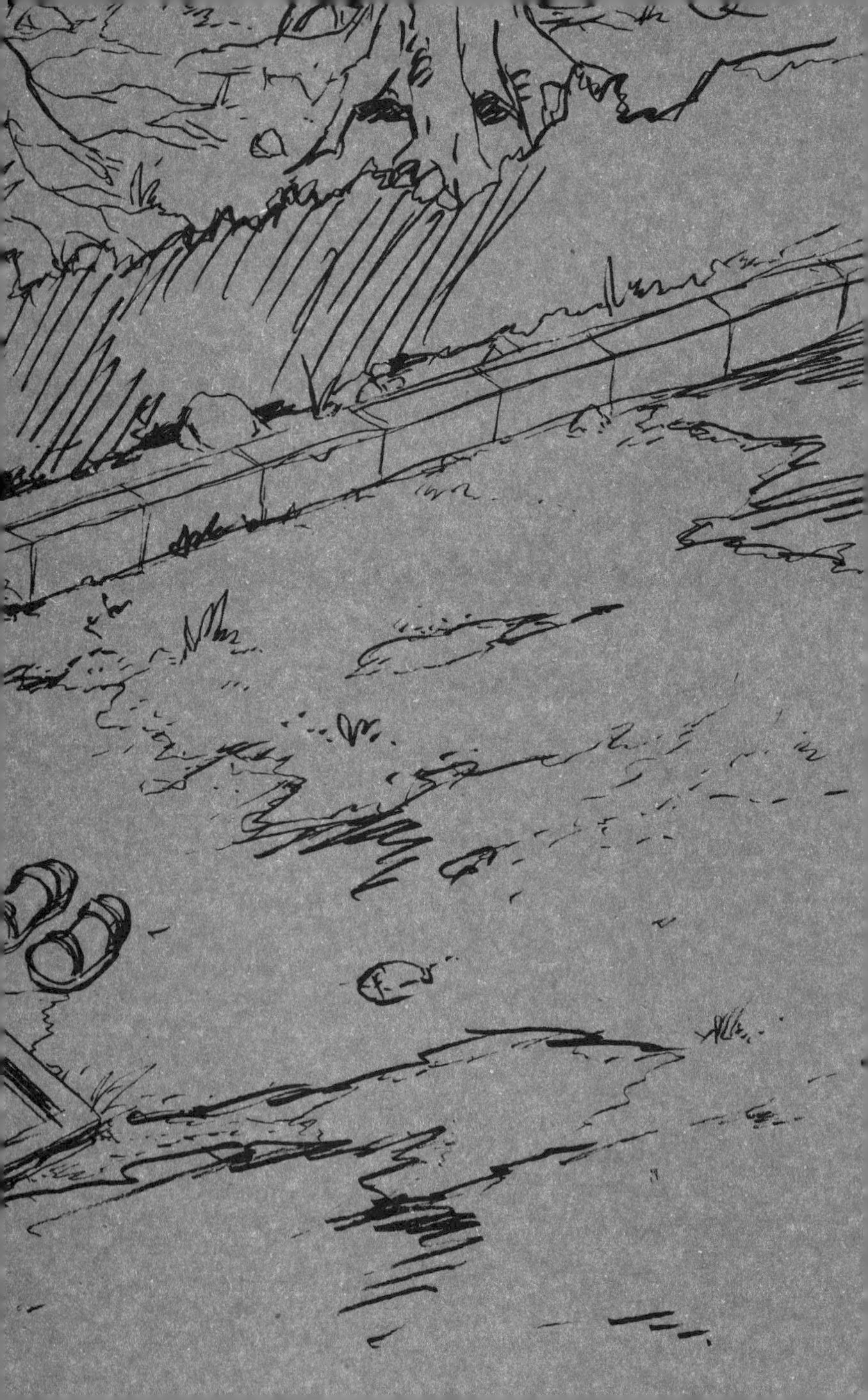

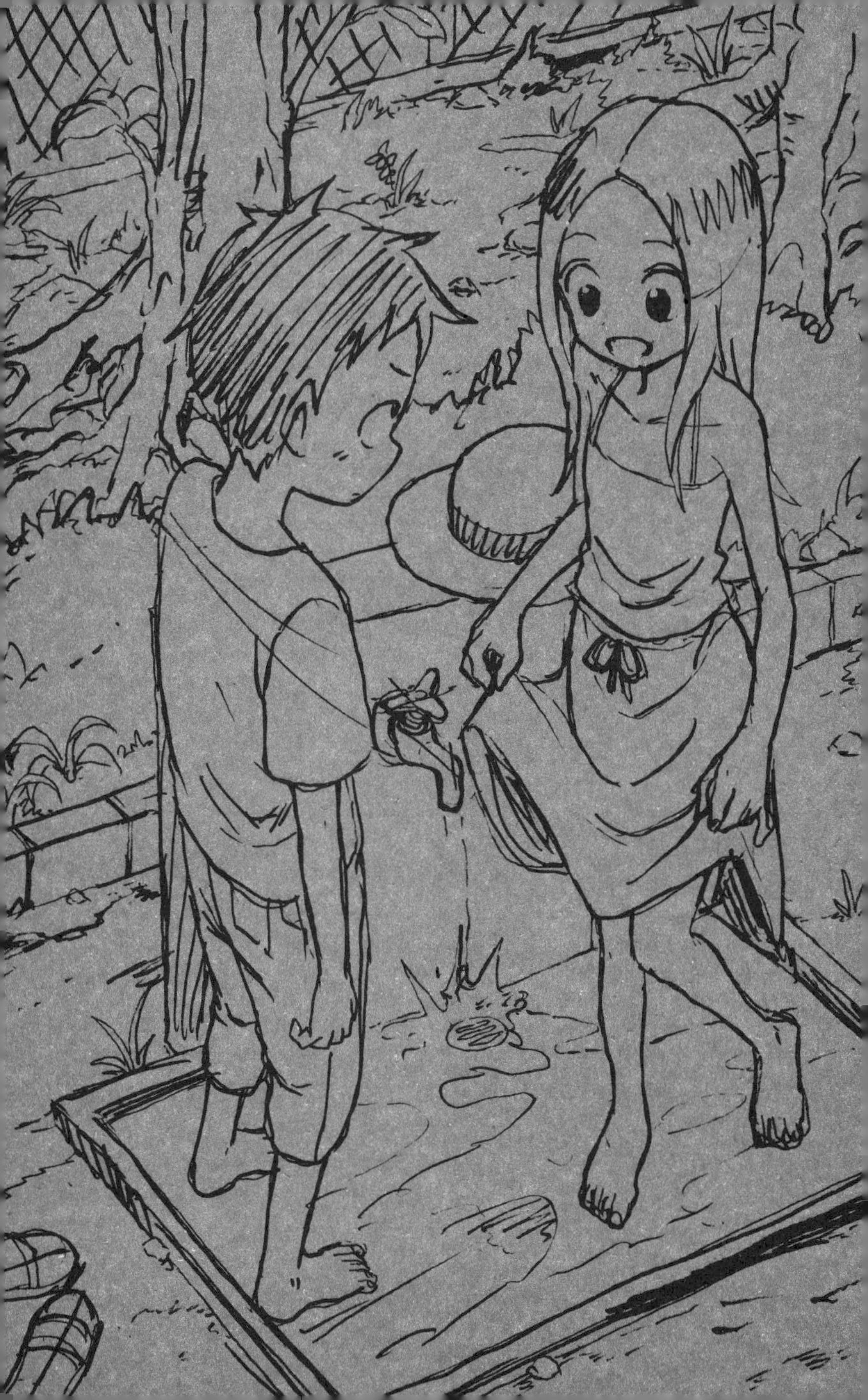

A Loner's Worst Nightmare: Human Interaction!

MY YOUTH ROMANTIC COMEDY iS WRØNG, AS I EXPECTED

Hachiman Hikigaya is a cynic. He believes "youth" is a crock—a sucker's game, an illusion woven from failure and hypocrisy. But when he turns in an essay for a school assignment espousing this view, he's sentenced to work in the Service Club, an organization dedicated to helping students with problems! Worse, the only other member of the club is the haughty Yukino Yukinoshita, a girl with beauty, brains, and the personality of a garbage fire. How will Hachiman the Cynic cope with a job that requires—*gasp!*—social skills?

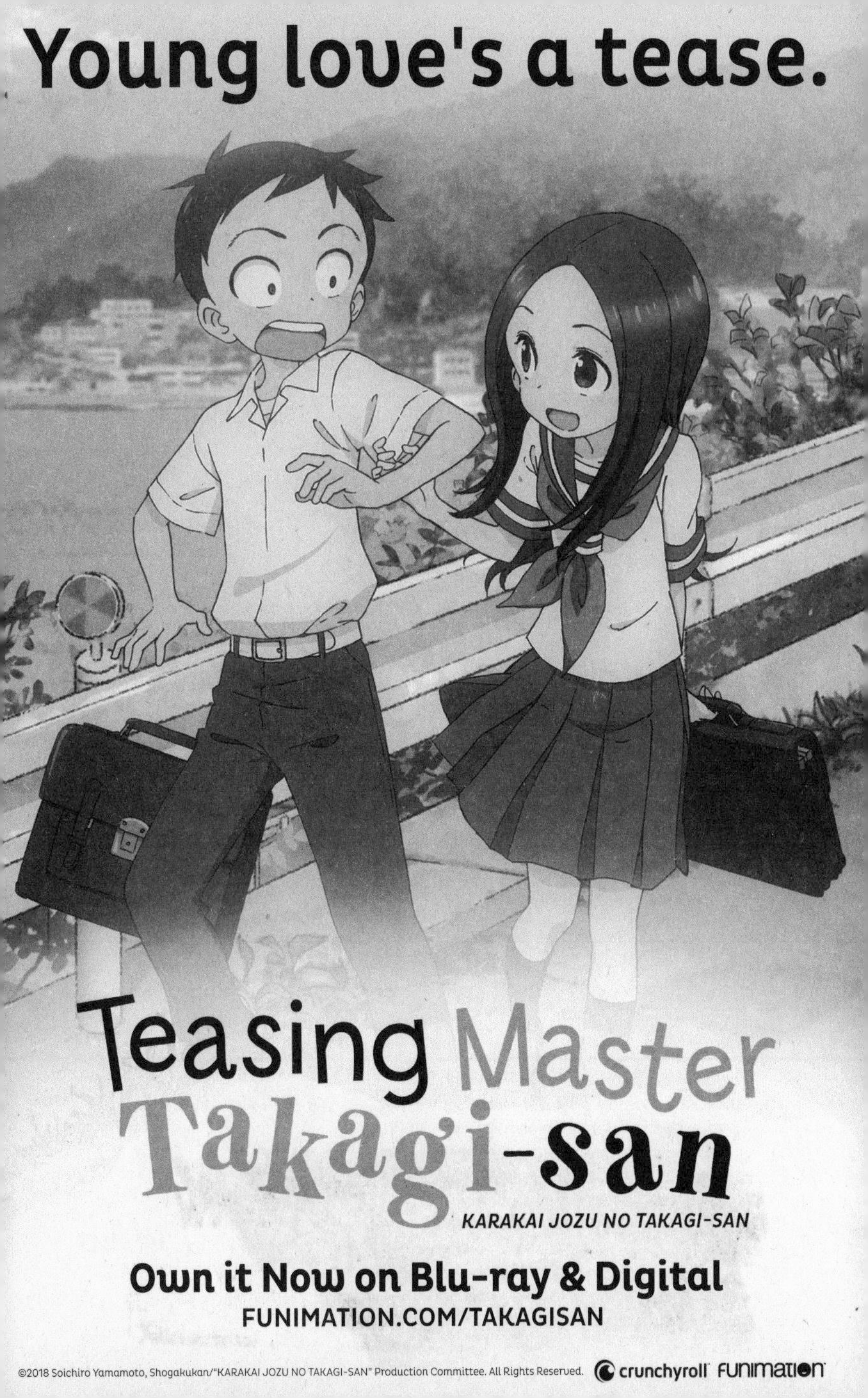
Young love's a tease.
Teasing Master Takagi-san
KARAKAI JOZU NO TAKAGI-SAN
Own it Now on Blu-ray & Digital
FUNIMATION.COM/TAKAGISAN
©2018 Soichiro Yamamoto, Shogakukan/"KARAKAI JOZU NO TAKAGI-SAN" Production Committee. All Rights Reserved.
crunchyroll
FUNIMATION

JUL 19 ◀

Teasing Master
Takagi-san ④

Soichiro Yamamoto

TRANSLATION: Taylor Engel ♦ LETTERING: Takeshi Kamura

KARAKAI JOZU NO TAKAGI-SAN Vol. 4
by Soichiro YAMAMOTO
© 2014 Soichiro YAMAMOTO
All rights reserved.
Original Japanese edition published by SHOGAKUKAN.
English translation rights in the United States of America, Canada, the United Kingdom, Ireland, Australia and New Zealand arranged with SHOGAKUKAN through Tuttle-Mori Agency, Inc.

English translation © 2019 by Yen Press, LLC

Yen Press
1290 Avenue of the Americas
New York, NY 10104

Visit us at yenpress.com

facebook.com/yenpress   yenpress.tumblr.com
twitter.com/yenpress   instagram.com/yenpress

First Yen Press Edition: April 2019

Yen Press is an imprint of Yen Press, LLC.
The Yen Press name and logo are trademarks of Yen Press, LLC.